T0379118

THE
MIDDLEMAN

Also by Mike Papantonio

Novels

Suspicious Activity—A Legal Thriller (2024; with Christopher Paulos)
Inhuman Trafficking—A Legal Thriller (2021; with Alan Russell)
Law and Addiction—A Legal Thriller (2019)
Law and Vengeance—A Legal Thriller (2017)
Law and Disorder—A Legal Thriller (2016)

Nonfiction

Closing Arguments—The Last Battle (2003; with Fred Levin)
Resurrecting AESOP—Fables Lawyers Should Remember (2000)
Clarence Darrow, the Journeyman—Lessons for the Modern Lawyer (1997)
In Search of Atticus Finch—A Motivational Book for Lawyers (1996)

THE MIDDLEMAN

A LEGAL THRILLER

MIKE PAPANTONIO

Arcade Publishing • New York

Copyright © 2025 by Mike Papantonio

All rights reserved. No part of this book may be reproduced in any manner without the express written consent of the publisher, except in the case of brief excerpts in critical reviews or articles. All inquiries should be addressed to Arcade Publishing, 307 West 36th Street, 11th Floor, New York, NY 10018.

Arcade Publishing books may be purchased in bulk at special discounts for sales promotion, corporate gifts, fund-raising, or educational purposes. Special editions can also be created to specifications. For details, contact the Special Sales Department, Arcade Publishing, 307 West 36th Street, 11th Floor, New York, NY 10018 or arcade@skyhorsepublishing.com.

Arcade Publishing® is a registered trademark of Skyhorse Publishing, Inc.®, a Delaware corporation.

Visit our website at www.arcadepub.com.

Please follow our publisher Tony Lyons on Instagram @tonylyonsisuncertain.

10 9 8 7 6 5 4 3 2 1

Library of Congress Cataloging-in-Publication Data is available on file.

Cover design by Erin Seaward-Hiatt
Cover image from Getty Images

Print ISBN: 978-1-64821-105-8
Ebook ISBN: 978-1-64821-106-5

Printed in the United States of America

ACKNOWLEDGMENTS

The author wishes to thank the following individuals for their help in the preparation of this novel: Raymond Benson, Cynthia Manson, and my colleagues at Levin-Papantonio Law Firm.

This is a work of fiction but it is inspired by true events.

June 2024

Now

She recognized the pungent odor of blood.

It was the first thing to which Amy's senses reacted when she opened her eyes. Everything else was a blur—her vision, certainly, and also her ability to think straight. Her mouth was dry, and it hurt to swallow. The room was spinning, and she was nauseated.

The smell, though, *that* she immediately knew. Amy Redmond had worked as an assistant to a hospital administrator during her college years. Her uncle had wanted her to have experience in the medical profession before joining the family business. She had spent many nights helping to oversee a Chicago ER, and there was no better place to become familiar with blood.

Eventually, she managed to rise from the bed, stride unsteadily over an undulating floor, and stumble into the bathroom, where she was violently sick.

After the visit to the toilet, Amy reentered the suite and surveyed the horror show in front of her. She was obviously still in the Drake Hotel. She had attended the EirePharma marketing event earlier that night in the Camellia Room, and she had purposefully avoided drinking much of the well-stocked liquor that her company had provided to the guests. But although she had tried, Amy couldn't avoid the celebratory champagne. She remembered talking to the various investors and to her attorney, Paul Baker.

Trembling, she sat in a chair by the dresser, now dressed in one of the hotel's terrycloth robes she'd found in the bathroom. Prior to that she had been completely naked, lying in the bed with . . . with . . .

Amy began hyperventilating, aware that she was going into shock. But then her upper body slumped over the top of the dresser. All of her senses went blank.

Pounding . . . knocking . . .

"Amy? Amy, are you in there? Open up!"

The door. Someone was at the door.

Her eyes opened and she managed to raise herself into a sitting position. She forced herself to concentrate. To try to stay calm. Breathe.

What the hell happened?

A man was lying in a pool of blood on the king-sized bed. A knife protruded from his chest.

Her knife.

The one with the pink, gem-encrusted handle that she carried in her purse for protection whenever she had to be in the mean streets of Chicago.

Amy didn't remember a damned thing.

I was drugged . . . I was drugged . . .

That had to be it.

But how the hell did she end up in bed with *him*? And why had he been *stabbed*?

It didn't make sense.

Or . . . did it?

"Amy! Open the door!"

More pounding.

"Oh, God," she whispered.

The police would clearly consider Amy the top suspect in the victim's death.

Not death . . . murder!

"Oh, no, please, no . . . what have I done?" she whispered to the corpse in the bed.

PART ONE
FEBRUARY–MAY 2024

1

Four Months Earlier: February 2024

Nick "Deke" Deketomis sighed as he gazed out the window of his office and wondered when the rain would end. While winter in Spanish Trace, Florida, was usually always moderately warm—a perfect destination for snowbirds from the north—for some reason, the rain had been relentless for three days. He was dying to take the *Jurisprudence* out into the Gulf. The yacht had been docked too long. Deke and his pal, Robin, were itching to spend a couple of days spearfishing.

Accepting that "it is what it is," he turned away from the gray late-morning skies outside and focused on the piles of paperwork on his desk. That was something that never ended, too. The bureaucracy associated with law work was enough to drive most attorneys out of the business. Luckily, the Bergman-Deketomis firm had a diligent and professional staff that could take care of much of the tedious labor.

At least the stacks of paper were a reminder that the law firm was doing well. Deke and his partners had experienced some major successes in the past few years. The busting of a human trafficking ring by the Feds and Deke's firm holding accountable hotel chains in the United States, and the recent case taking down a New York bank for allowing illegal wire transfers to overseas terrorist groups had given Bergman-Deketomis more publicity than Deke had ever expected. The workload was pouring in fast and furious, so much so that they were turning down more cases than he would have liked. Many would have created the kind of high-intensity adventures on which the lawyers in his firm thrived. But there were only so many hours in a day, so many employees in the firm, and so many years left of his life. Deke was approaching the big 6-0 milestone in June, and the dreaded "R-word"—*retirement*—loomed somewhere in the near future.

But not yet. Deke would probably work until he was in his seventies if his health held up. So far, thankfully, he was in pretty good shape.

The intercom buzzed, startling him out of his thoughts. He pushed the button. "Yes, Diana?"

"Deke, I hope I didn't disturb your wallowing in the pool of melancholy."

Deke laughed. The office administrator who doubled as his assistant, Diana Fernandez, could read him like a book.

"I wasn't wallowing, Diana."

"Yes, you were. You get all dreamy when it rains. I know these things."

"I suppose you do. What's up?"

"You have an unannounced visitor. Matt Redmond. He says he's a friend of yours from 'yesteryear.'"

Deke blinked. "Matt Redmond?"

"That's what he said."

"Holy cow, send him back!"

Deke leaned back in his chair in disbelief. He hadn't heard from his old law school pal in years, maybe decades. For a good portion of their time at the Cumberland School of Law in Alabama, Deke and Matt Redmond had been inseparable, very near blood brothers. The guy had come from a wealthy family that was in the medical industry. Was it pharmaceuticals? Insurance? Deke couldn't recall. Matt was also a lawyer who had spent part of his career until recently with a silk stocking firm, but his famous temper—which was legendary even back at Cumberland—put him at odds with the powers that be. Had he been fired? Blackballed in the corporate defense business? Again, Deke couldn't remember, even though it was within the last year or so.

He stood, went around his desk to the office door, and looked into the hallway. Diana was leading Matt Redmond in his direction. The guy had a huge smile on his face, one that said, "Ha, ha, surprise, surprise!" The funny thing was that Deke might not have recognized him. Matt had put on weight since college, maybe a hundred pounds. The red hair had faded to whitish pink. The skin pallor and lightly crimson nose indicated what Deke recognized as an alcohol problem.

"Hey, Deke! Surprise, surprise!"

"I knew you were going to say those very words. My God, Matt, it's good to see you!"

The two men embraced and slapped each other on the backs.

Diana, grinning, said, "I'll leave you two to it."

"Thanks, Diana. Geez, Matt, how are you? What are you *doing* here?"

"I'm fine, Deke. I happened to be in Pensacola and I thought, 'You know, my old—and *older*—buddy from Professor Sennett's class is not too far away in Spanish Trace. Maybe I should pop in and give him a shock.'"

"That's right, you're a couple of years younger than me. I'd forgotten that. Anyway, I'm glad you did surprise me. Come into my office, let's catch up."

The two men went into the comfy sitting area of Deke's office and sat down. "Timing is perfect. You can join me for lunch," Deke said.

"Why do you think I showed up around eleven? But listen, I'm buying."

"Probably not, but you can try."

Matt held up a finger and wiggled it. "No, no, this will be . . . well, this will be a business lunch. There's something that I'd actually like to talk to you about."

Deke raised his eyebrows. "Okay, you got my attention."

"In due time, Deke. Over lunch. First tell me about yourself. I know you're the big TV star lawyer who gets to be a talking head on news programs, and I'm well aware of the many successes you and your firm have had recently. Kudos, my friend, kudos."

"Thank you, Matt. Yes, we've been fortunate. There's a lot of wild luck that goes into it, too, as you know."

"Or in my case, bad luck."

Deke pursed his lips. "What happened, Matt?"

"What did you hear?"

"Only that you and your former employer parted ways. I don't know why."

"Ha! Well, I'm relieved to hear that they kept it quiet, like they promised. Deke, I assaulted a senior partner at the firm. Punched him and rearranged his nose just a tad. I'm not going to justify my actions because I know it was clearly crazy and wrong, but I'll let you in on a secret."

"What's that?"

"The guy deserved it. He was an A-1 asshole. He had insulted the Redmond family, saying we were greedy bastards for allowing the price of insulin to go up so much, among other drugs. Never mind that *we* didn't raise the prices. Never mind that I have nothing to do with EirePharma. Anyway, he went too far, and I punched him. I'd also had a couple of bourbons. Maybe three or four, I can't remember."

"Hm."

Matt threw up his hands. "What can I tell you? My temper got the best of me. We worked it out, though. They basically told me if I resigned then he wouldn't press charges. So I left. And you know what? Over the last year I couldn't have been happier. The truth is I didn't enjoy being a lawyer. I think there's too much of my Uncle Andy's blood in me. You remember my Uncle Andy?"

Deke did. "The rock star."

"Yeah. The black sheep of the Redmond family. Now maybe I'm the second black sheep of the clan. Anyway, I don't know if you heard. Uncle Andy died recently."

"What? No, I hadn't heard that."

"It was in all the music and entertainment news."

"I don't pay much attention to that, Matt. I'm sorry to hear it. You have my condolences. I remember you were close to him."

"I worshipped the guy, Deke. He was my idol. If I'd had any musical ability at all, I would have followed in his footsteps. Andy Redmond was the leader of the Red Drops, for Chrissake! He was a big deal back in the day."

"I remember us going to see him perform in Gainesville when we were at college. It was great! We went backstage, and I met him. That was a fantastic night."

Matt laughed. "It was. But, you know, that was the mid-eighties. It wasn't the original Red Drops then. It was just Andy and some hired guns pretending to be the Red Drops. More like Andy Redmond and a cover band. By then Andy was just playing in small venues—clubs, college campuses like where we saw him, bowling alleys, and such. He was sort of a has-been then. His real heyday was the late sixties and the seventies."

Deke shrugged. "I just recall really loving his music. What was that hit song about the fever?"

"That was 'Face Fever!'" Matt began to sing a bit of the chorus, moving his upper body as if he were dancing. "*Show me that face fever, baby, you know you got it bad, baby, face fever, baby, yeah . . . !*" Both men laughed and Matt added, "I remember you made a comment about all the groupies around him!"

Deke smiled and nodded his head. "Yeah, that stands out in my mind, for sure. Your uncle, umm, had his hands full. Again, I'm sorry to hear that. You lost a dear friend, and the music business lost an icon."

"Thanks. I'll tell you more over lunch, because what I have to say also concerns him."

"Okay. So, what are you doing now that you're not practicing law, Matt?"

"Nothing. A big fat nothing. I retired early." He shrugged. "I'm a Redmond, you know. I have . . . well, I have a nest egg. You knew that."

"I understand. No judgment from me. Where's home now?"

"I live in Chicago. I have two ex-wives and two children from the first one. A boy and a girl, both in their twenties. I've been divorced since 2012. So I'm what you call an 'eligible divorcee,' although my age and weight might put some qualifiers on the eligibility part."

"Don't you have a sister?" Deke asked.

"Yes. Good memory, Deke. Candace lives in France with her family." He shrugged again. "We talk every now and then, but we're not really close. She has nothing to do with the Redmond family business. Neither do I, for that matter. What about you, Deke? You still married?"

"I am. Teri and I celebrated our thirty-ninth anniversary a few months ago. We have two great kids—also a boy and a girl—both grown. Our daughter, Cara, is a lawyer who's been working with the firm several years now. Our son Andrew is a chef at a Michelin star restaurant in Miami with job offers all over the world. It's all good, Matt, all good." He looked at his watch. "Hey, why don't we grab a couple of umbrellas and run across the street for that lunch? I'm dying to hear what you have to tell me."

Matt slapped the arms of his chair. "Let's do it."

Ten minutes later they were at a table in a secluded corner of Colliers Fish House. It was always reserved for Deke. The law firm often entertained clients at the popular restaurant, and it didn't hurt that the catches of the day had been swimming in the Gulf of Mexico earlier in the morning. The food was always superb.

Matt insisted that they eat before he started his story. They continued to catch up on events in their lives over the past few decades as they chowed down. Deke noticed, though, that Matt seemed nervous. The man kept looking over his shoulder, and he checked his cell phone for messages six times. He also drank two vodka martinis in the space of a half hour while Deke had stuck to water throughout the meal. When the dirty dishes were taken away and the waiter offered dessert menus, Matt actually said, "Maybe another martini."

Deke quickly ordered coffee for himself, and then Matt got the message. "Yeah, scratch the martini," he said to the waiter. "Bring me a cup of coffee, too. Black."

When the waiter left, Deke asked, "Matt, what's wrong? There's something bothering you. I can tell."

Matt looked at Deke for several seconds before replying. "Bad guys are watching me, Deke. Very dangerous bad guys."

"Bad guys?" Deke cocked his head. "Tell me more, Matt. It's okay, nobody can hear us. My table here is isolated from the rest of the restaurant by design."

Matt sat back and appeared to relax a bit. "All right. So . . . just to refresh your memory, the Redmond family business is a company called EirePharma. Nice Irish name, huh?"

Deke smiled. "I remember now."

"EirePharma is now one of the biggest PBMs in the country. You know what that is?"

"I do. It stands for pharmacy benefit manager. As I understand it, a PBM is the go-between that connects drug manufacturers to medical insurance companies, retail pharmacies, and consumers."

"That's correct. My father, Terrence Redmond, ran EirePharma until he passed away. Then my Uncle Charles took over the company. He's now deceased, too, and I'll tell you that story in a minute. Anyway, my Uncle Andy never wanted to be in the family business. In fact, he was a high school dropout—fitting for a future rock star. He was famous for a while until the Red Drops broke up in the late seventies and Uncle Andy tried to go solo. It didn't work out, and he sank deeper into drugs and alcohol. He remained in that hippie culture lifestyle for the rest of his life. Uncle Andy died last year of myocardial infarction due to diabetes mellitus, which is what the medical examiner said, but we all know it was caused by decades of drug addiction and alcohol abuse. And I have to say that I believe the high cost of insulin was a big, big factor here."

Deke shook his head.

Matt waved his hand. "It was bound to happen sooner or later. So, enter my cousin, Amy Redmond. Did you ever meet Amy?"

"I don't think so, no."

"Amy is Uncle Andy's daughter. Uncle Andy got a groupie pregnant in the early eighties. They had a kid, and this was Amy."

"So Amy is, what, fifteen years younger than you?" Deke asked.

"About that. Fourteen. She's forty-four. So, Amy's mother died in an accident a year or so after she was born and my Uncle Andy couldn't handle taking care of her. My grandparents took her in as an infant, but then Uncle Charles and his wife Mary stepped up and legally adopted her themselves when she was four because they never had, or couldn't have, children of their own. But this was all good for Amy, who grew up in a nice home and is now in the family business, and in fact she's now the president of EirePharma. She's smart, beautiful, driven, and an incredible businessperson."

"That's terrific."

"Yeah. Anyway, Amy came to me not long ago with a remarkable story. She had become closer to her father, my Uncle Andy, after he had moved back to Illinois about twenty years ago when he was pushing sixty. I started seeing him every now and then, too. He lived in one of the outlying northern suburbs of Chicago in a dilapidated, old house. His only income was royalties from his music—which after a few decades wasn't much—and once he turned sixty-five, Social Security. Then he got to be in his seventies, in poor health, and he had a lot of trouble paying for insulin. Medicare covers it in Illinois and, in fact, our governor signed a bill that kicks in next year that caps a thirty-day supply at $35 for most insured people and there are discount plans for uninsured folks."

Deke interrupted him. "That might work, but we're finding that insurance companies and pharmacy benefit managers have ways of working around laws like that. But do go on."

"You're right," Matt said, "but anyway, with Medicare, Uncle Andy really should have been able to afford it, but I think he didn't keep up his monthly premiums. I imagine he was spending his money on shit like heroin instead. I don't know. Deke, I'm sure you're aware that insulin manufacturers have raised the cost of the drug. A lot. It's ridiculous how expensive it is, and if your insurance doesn't cover much of the cost, or if you don't *have* insurance, the cost of insulin could bankrupt a diabetic."

"I know," Deke said. "As a matter of fact, my firm has been looking into some of these class action lawsuits that are going after insulin manufacturers, as well as the PBMs that work with them."

"Have you taken on any of those cases?"

"Not yet. We're still evaluating if they're winnable, and we think they are."

"Well. Anyway, all this background on my Uncle Andy leads us to the real crux of the matter. I hate to say it, but EirePharma is conspiring with at least one drug manufacturer to keep the costs of insulin extremely high, and EirePharma is receiving kickback money while doing it. Amy came to me and told me this. She's going through . . . I don't know, she's in a difficult situation. She's the only Redmond still at EirePharma and she tells me that the company is doing potentially illegal things. She's not sure what to do about it."

"Like what kinds of things?"

"Better for Amy to explain it to you. I'd like you to talk to her."

"What happened to your Uncle Charles?" Deke asked.

"Oh," Matt rolled his eyes. "I lost both uncles within a few months of each other. *Uncle Charles* jumped off a high-rise in Chicago eleven months ago. He allegedly killed himself."

"My God! Why? Did he have issues with depression?"

"Well, he *did* jump off a building! The police said it was straight up suicide, but Amy isn't sure, and neither am I. You'd think someone would have to be pretty depressed to do that, but my Aunt Mary, his widow, says 'no.' It's a big frikkin' mystery. Amy and I . . . Well, we think he may have been murdered."

"Murdered?"

Matt nodded slowly. "Now we get to the very dangerous bad guys I mentioned earlier. Around the time that Uncle Charles did the swan dive, EirePharma was taken over by an entrepreneur named Connor Devlin. Have you ever heard of him?"

"I don't think so."

"Very flashy guy, very wealthy. He's in his fifties, very handsome. Looks like a movie star. An unscrupulous businessman with incredibly strong ties in Ireland. I don't know how he did it, but he got Uncle Charles to sell his shares of EirePharma to him. The sale actually occurred after Charles made that leap off the building. Amy works for Devlin, who's now the CEO. And it's Devlin who's running a long string of unethical and, from what I can see, illegal hustles with the insulin manufacturers. As I hear more about what is going on, I would go as far as saying it sounds like the equivalent of the Irish mob moving into the insulin sales business. Amy says she needs to do something about it but her hands are tied, obviously. She's one of the damned *faces* of the company! Deke, I think this guy Devlin is a highly educated deep-pockets criminal. He runs the business like a mobster disguised as a Harvard-educated MBA. There are a lot of shady things about him. Maybe other murders. And I think the goons he surrounds himself with, who are dressed up in Brooks Brothers suits, do the dirty work for him. Big muscular henchmen who are 'assistants' in name but are really bodyguards and musclemen. I think they're watching me. In fact, I know they are; I've caught one or two of them sitting outside of or driving by my house. Amy believes that Devlin knows she came to me with this information. She's freaking out now, because they're watching her, too."

"Damn, Matt. None of that sounds good."

Matt sighed. "There's something else that complicates the matter."

"What's that?"

"Amy is engaged to Connor Devlin. They've been in a relationship for a year. For months I think she was completely bamboozled by the romance, but now she's starting to wise up. Deke, I think this man Devlin has been gaslighting my cousin. He's been using his charm and good looks and wealth to fool a woman who, after a divorce some years ago, might have been, and I don't know because I'm speculating and don't want to make her out to be a cliché, but maybe she was starved for affection at the time. Or he simply showered her with sudden wealth, fame, and good times, and she fell for it. They became a couple in the Chicago society pages, and for a while that was a high for her that she'd never experienced. But now she's finally seeing the light. She continues to live with Devlin in order to spy on the guy. Deke, she's trying to gather evidence against him, and, frankly, I believe she's in danger."

"I see."

"Deke, I'm here to ask if you and your law firm would sue the hell out of Connor Devlin and get to the bottom of what happened to my Uncle Charles. And, you know, what happened to my Uncle Andy is also a consequence! This insulin thing is a big problem in our country, and it's guys like Devlin who are making it happen. It's not just the disgusting overpricing of insulin I'm talking about that needs your attention, but we need to expose Devlin's criminal activities and at the same time save Amy."

Deke said nothing, obviously mulling over what Matt had told him. He finally chuckled slightly. "Matt, this reunion of ours, decades in the making, has unloaded much more onto my plate than I could have ever thought. My first take on what you are telling me is that we can look at several civil case angles surrounding the insulin pricing issues. Most of the time in the big pharma cases we handle we uncover blatant criminal conduct that is virtually ignored by both regulators and the Department of Justice. You worked in the corporate defense business long enough to have seen that firsthand, I'm sure. Nevertheless, our most logical way in to shine a light on this guy Devlin is to file, probably, an antitrust case and peel back Devlin's disguise with insanely aggressive discovery and hit-and-run court hearings. But at some point the feds will have to get involved, and that is not something we can predictably count on. They have no guts where it comes to white-collar crime, even when the case is handed to them on a plate."

"Deke, I will admit my ask is not exactly a simple one. First protect Amy, uncover the truth about this bastard, and if you can get my family's pharma business back intact, that would be an extraordinary result."

Deke was silent for a few seconds. He looked out the window near their table and saw that the rain was still coming down. Could the rain be a message? Could this be a "rainmaker" case or an ugly and deadly supercell thunderstorm?

"Matt, we'd need a lot more information than what you've told me here. I have some top-notch investigators. One of my associates, Michael Carey, is a former military guy who now practices law with me, and he'd be perfect for something like this. I can't promise anything, but why don't we do some preliminary work, do a little investigating, come to Chicago and talk to your cousin Amy, and see what all the edges of this case look like? I don't like to take on anything that I don't think I can possibly win, especially when a dear friend is asking. I would never want to disappoint you."

"I understand, Deke. I know this won't be a cakewalk. All I'm asking is that you take your best shot, nothing more." He held out his palm.

"Let's go back to the office and draw up an agreement," Deke said as he reached over and clasped his friend's hand.

2

The corporate headquarters of EirePharma in Deerfield, Illinois, sat on a thirty-acre campus that consisted of a two-story, airy, modern building of 650,000 square feet, a parking lot with spaces for eight hundred vehicles, and an expansive manicured lawn with a small pond. A hangar attached to the structure stored a platform dolly holding a Sikorsky S-76 twin-engine corporate helicopter. The dolly acted as a mobile flatbed trailer, from which the chopper can take off or land. Approximately 160 employees occupied the offices within the headquarters, and there was room for 160 more. A cafeteria and private art gallery took up a quarter of the place. Architectural critics praised the site's design as one of the most eye-friendly and functional business properties in the Chicago area.

While it was raining in Spanish Trace, Florida, Chicagoland was blanketed with snow and more was on the way. In Deerfield, a northwest suburb about thirty miles from the Windy City, snowplows were working overtime and salt trucks were right behind them. The sun had broken through the clouds, though, and Amy Redmond stood at the wide picture window of her office on the second floor of EirePharma to allow the midday rays to bathe her face. Her red shoulder-length hair visibly reflected in the glass, but her pale skin disappeared against the frosty tableau outside. Despite her current anxiety, she appreciated the aching beauty of the ice-covered pond and undisturbed snow on the field surrounding the headquarters; it all sparkled in the sunshine, reminding her of sledding on a hill behind her uncle and aunt's home in Highland Park when she was a child.

That thought was a prompt that she needed to visit her Aunt Mary. She had unintentionally allowed too many weeks to lapse since the last time she'd seen the woman who was essentially her mother. Aunt Mary was all alone in that big house, except for the caretaker who helped her out.

Her Uncle Charles, too, for all intents and purposes, had been her father. His mysterious death had been devastating to them all. Suicide, the police said. But was it? She didn't know what to believe, but she did know that she missed him terribly. These feelings, though, didn't preclude her affection for her biological father—Andy Redmond.

She had lost them both less than a year apart. First Uncle Charles, and then her father.

Amy turned away from the window and went back to her desk. There was so much work to do, but she had recently lost the motivation to do it. She picked up her cell phone to check for a message from her cousin, Matt, but there was nothing yet. She now regretted saying anything to him. Matt had gone to Florida to talk to some lawyer he knew. At first, Amy thought it was a good idea. Now, not so much.

The truth was that she was frightened. An hour earlier, she had received a text from Connor saying that he wanted to see her immediately upon his return from his trip out west. What about? Perhaps it was nothing. Maybe she was worrying for no reason.

Actually, though, she had plenty of cause to be concerned.

The desk phone buzzed. It was her secretary, Madeline.

Amy pressed the speaker button. "Yes?"

"Amy, the reporter from the *Tribune* is here. I've put her in the conference room on your floor."

"I'll be right there. See that she gets coffee or whatever she wants."

Damn, she thought. *The last thing I want to do is an interview for the business section of the* Chicago Tribune.

But Amy Redmond was a consummate professional. She went to the full-length mirror on the wall next to the door to her private bathroom and checked her suit and makeup. Yes, she looked like a million bucks, as Connor liked to say, even though she didn't feel that way. Never mind, she was ready.

Before leaving the office, she glanced up at the portrait of Reginald Redmond that hung over the couch in the sitting area. Her grandfather.

She wondered what the patriarch and founder of EirePharma would think of how his company was being managed today.

* * *

The woman from the *Tribune* appeared to be younger than Amy had expected. She introduced herself as Martha Bishop. Amy shook her hand and switched on the charm and charisma for which she was known. Uncle Charles had called it her "happy face."

"Welcome to EirePharma! I can't believe you drove out in this weather," she said. "Did you have any trouble?"

"Oh, I drive in all sorts of nonsense outside," the reporter answered. "The roads are pretty clear now. You know Chicago. They're pretty good at plowing that stuff away quickly. It's not snowing now, but I think we're getting more tonight. No worries." They sat and began. "Ms. Redmond, I—"

"Call me Amy, please."

"All right. Amy, I think my assistant told you that we're profiling you, along with nine other women, as examples of successful business-women in Chicago."

"I was flattered and honored to be chosen."

"We were pleased that you accepted our proposal. My, this is such a gorgeous building!"

"You already got a tour, right?"

"I did. I'm very impressed by the art in your gallery. There are some real treasures there. A Picasso, a Klimt, and even a Warhol. Who was the curator?"

"That would have been my Uncle Terrence. He had a love of fine art."

"I see. Well, let's begin with some basics. You're a successful woman in your forties. I don't mean to be personal, but it's relevant, I think, for the article. You were married once, I believe?"

Amy rolled her eyes. "Yes. He was someone I'd met in college. It lasted four years. The divorce was in 2010. Since then, well, you know.

There were some dates." She laughed and added, "The less said about them, the better. No, I enjoy being single. It goes better with being a workaholic."

"But you're in a serious relationship now, if I'm not mistaken? Engaged, even?" Amy merely smiled and shrugged a little. Bishop chuckled and said, "Okay, we'll get to him in a bit. You were born in Chicago?"

"Uhm, no, I was born in California. In fact, it's not exactly clear *where* I was born. My father and mother were on the road somewhere."

"Oh, pardon me, of course. The rock star. Andy Redmond. My condolences to you. It's just been a few months, hasn't it?"

"Yes. We're all pretty torn up about it. About *all* of it. His death, and my Uncle Charles's death just a few months before that."

"That was such a tragedy. I'm so sorry."

"Thank you."

"You would say that your Uncle Charles, though, was more like a father to you growing up, is that correct?"

"Oh, yes. Uncle Charles and Aunt Mary were my *parents*. I never knew my real mother. Louise Spindler—that was her name—died in a car accident the year after I was born. I lived with my grandparents until my grandfather died, and then Uncle Charles and Aunt Mary took me off my grieving grandmother's hands and officially adopted me. I was four."

"Did you ever become close to your father?"

"Andy? Yes, I did. He moved back to Illinois when I was in grad school and we slowly got to know each other. I never really thought of him as 'Dad.' He was always 'Andy' to me."

"He was big stuff back in the day."

"I guess he was."

"I would bet that your birth drove a wedge further in Andy's relationship with his parents? Did they disapprove of the situation in which it occurred? You know, rock star and a groupie, unmarried . . ."

Amy blinked and interrupted her. "It's ancient history and irrelevant."

Bishop made a slight nod to acknowledge that she should move on. "Your grandfather, Reginald Redmond, started EirePharma in the 1940s?"

"That's correct. It was 1947. It was a simple pharmacy in Chicago, but over the next ten years it grew into a chain of pharmacies across the state and into Wisconsin, Minnesota, Iowa, and Indiana. He was an astute, charismatic businessman who already had one foot in the future. I'm sorry I didn't really know him. He passed when I was three."

"Your family is fascinating," Bishop said. "Your grandfather had three sons—"

"Terrence, Andy, and Charles. Terrence was already a seven-year-old when EirePharma first began, and Andy was an infant. My grandfather divorced and remarried in 1951, and, boom, Charles joined the family in 1952."

"We know that Andy Redmond didn't enter the family business, but your two uncles did."

"Yes. Uncle Terrence got into the business in the 1960s, and Charles did so in the 70s. After my grandfather's death in 1983, Terrence became the CEO. He and Uncle Charles took the company to greater heights by expanding the retail chain."

"Just to clarify, your grandmother is gone?"

"Yes, my grandmother died in 2001 at the age of ninety-one. My step-grandmother died in 2018. My Aunt Julia—Terrence's wife—died of COVID in 2020. My only living relatives are my Aunt Mary and my two cousins, Matt and Candace, who are Terrence and Julia's children."

"Are your cousins in the family business?" Bishop asked.

"No. Matt is . . . he studied law." Amy didn't want to say that Matt had given up practicing as a lawyer. "Candace married a wonderful French man, and she and her family live in Nice. I don't have any contact with her, but Matt and I are fairly close."

Bishop wrote on her notepad and then took a breath. "I'm sorry to bring up the tragedy of what happened to your Uncle Charles, but I do think it's important to our story."

"I understand. Yes, it was heartbreaking." *God, can this please end?*

"How did Charles become CEO of EirePharma?"

"My Uncle Terrence died of a heart attack in 2011. Charles immediately ascended to the throne." She allowed herself to chuckle at that, as did Bishop. "That's when we sold off all the retail pharmacies."

"For a great deal of money."

"Yes, there is that."

"Charles completely reinvented EirePharma."

"He did. We became a pharmacy benefit manager. With our experience in running retail pharmacies, we knew the ins and outs of how the medical industry works. As a PBM, EirePharma is now worth two billion dollars."

"And now you're the president. Did you always want to get into the family business?"

"Indeed. I imagine my uncle influenced my views on this as I was growing up, but I think I knew what I wanted to do by the time I graduated from high school. I went to Northwestern University, where I received a Bachelor of Science degree in Health Science. While I was in school, I also worked as an assistant to the administrator of the emergency room at NorthShore Evanston Hospital."

"I'll bet that was some intense experience."

"Oh, it was. I was in the trenches, you might say. I then went to Cornell University and received my master's in health administration. I immediately returned to Chicago and went to work for EirePharma in a starting position—my uncle didn't give me special treatment! But I worked my way up to become one of the vice presidents, and that was, what, has it already been six years ago? And now I'm president."

Bishop nodded and made more notes. *Okay, that's enough*, Amy thought. *Let's end it there.* But the reporter then brought up the topic Amy was dreading.

"That brings me to Connor Devlin, who is now CEO of your company. How did he manage to obtain control of EirePharma? Did you have no interest in being CEO?"

"Um, well, I—"

"And in light of the recently dismissed class action lawsuit last December, tell me more about EirePharma's approach to pricing insulin. Am I right to say that your CEO, Mr. Devlin, is committed to raising the price so high that it will bankrupt many consumers who depend on the drug?"

Bishop's tone and attitude had changed abruptly and dramatically. Suddenly, the interview had become a hit piece.

"We are well aware of the issues surrounding the pricing of insulin all over the country," Amy managed to answer. "And we're working to create equitable solutions."

"What can you say about your biological father's death? Was that anything to do with the cost of insulin?"

How the hell did she know Andy was a diabetic?

"Amy," the woman continued, "the 'serious relationship' I referred to earlier . . . That's with Connor Devlin, is it not? The CEO of EirePharma? The CEO and the president in a romantic relationship? The society pages are full of your photographs together at various events in the city. You're engaged to be married, are you not?"

Bishop nodded at the quite visible large diamond ring. Amy involuntarily placed her right hand over it. She wanted to snap at the woman and tell her to get the hell out of the building.

Luckily, though, Madeline stuck her head in the conference room door. "Excuse me, pardon my interruption. Amy, you wanted me to tell you when Mr. Devlin's helicopter arrived. They just set down on the helipad."

Amy said, "Thank you, Madeline. I'm sorry, Martha, but I have to see Connor—Mr. Devlin—about something. Please forgive me. Do you mind if we take a half-hour break?"

Bishop's attitude smoothly switched back to smiles and charm. "Not at all, I'll be able to catch up on messages and emails. I'm impressed you have a helipad!"

"Mr. Devlin has a private jet in a hangar at O'Hare. He uses that to zoom around the country and to Europe. He then takes a helicopter from O'Hare to get here."

"That's one way to beat the traffic. Go on, don't worry about me."

"Thank you. I won't be long." With that, Amy got up and went out of the room.

As she walked down the chicly decorated hall of offices, Amy's heart began to pound. She needed an excuse not to continue the interview. More worrying, though, was what did Connor want to see her about? Could it be about Matt? Did Connor know she'd been talking about him to Matt? Did Connor know Matt was talking to a lawyer?

Of course he would know. Connor manages to find out everything.

Outside the CEO's office, Devlin's executive secretary said, "Amy, he just walked in. He's waiting for you."

"Thanks, Charlotte."

Amy steeled herself, opened the door, and prepared to greet the man for whom she worked.

And with whom she shared a bed.

3

"Amy, dear, come in!"

Connor Devlin stood by the vintage mahogany desk that was the size of a pool table. He had his cell phone to his ear, but he beckoned her in with the other hand, and then he turned away to look out his broad picture window while he talked.

"Yeah, I agree," he said with his subtle Irish accent. After a few drinks, that brogue could become much heavier. "Uh huh. Well, the man's a fool. No, no, I'm not going to do business with him. He's nothing. Forget it." He listened for a few seconds as Amy closed the door behind her and stepped into the largest office in the building. "Right. Just do what you have to do." He ended the call and turned back to her.

Even after all this time, Amy could still be struck by the man's commanding presence. He oozed charisma and energy, rendering him extremely attractive to anyone—male or female—who came in close contact with him. At six-foot-seven-inches tall, broad-shouldered, and ridiculously fit, he might have been a former linebacker. For a man in his mid-fifties, he had a youthful face accented by clear blue eyes. His prematurely solid white hair matched the virgin snow outside, and its tasteful length reminded just about everyone who met him of Marlon Brando's characterization of Superman's father. In fact, some of his closest friends called him "Jor-El" to get his goat, and Devlin usually feigned annoyance at the nickname; internally, though, Amy knew that he liked it.

"How was your trip, Connor?" she asked, putting on a big smile.

"Amy, dear. Come here." He held out his arms and she moved toward him. Devlin stepped forward and took her in his strong arms. The embrace was genuine and warm. He kissed her strongly on the mouth and then said, "I missed you."

"Connor, you were only gone four days."

"I can still miss you! Did you miss me?"

"Of course!"

He kissed her forehead and then released her. "The trip was good. I need a drink, though." He walked over to the well-stocked bar in the sitting area of the office, retrieved a glass from the cabinet, plopped in three ice cubes from the fridge's dispenser, and poured two inches of Absolut Elyx vodka into it. "Want one?"

"No, thanks," Amy said with a slight laugh. "I haven't had lunch yet, and I'm actually in the middle of an interview with the *Chicago Tribune*."

"You are?"

"It's that piece I told you about that they wanted to do on successful women in Chicago."

"Oh, right! Well, you are indeed a successful woman. They picked a good subject for their article. I like that you're keeping up the good face of the company." He cocked his head at her. "Are you all right?"

"Sure. Just a bit tired, and I need to get back to that interview. I'm not sure I like the interviewer, though."

He cocked his head at her. "Asking tough questions? Maybe about me?"

"Yes."

"Just tell her you don't comment on your personal life. Keep it focused on all the good things we're doing here and how I've taken the company from the lowest profits it's ever had to the highest. And, as president, you're part of that success. Got it?"

"I can do that." She exhaled and shifted gears. "Tell me about your trip."

"Oh, it was fine. Those people I saw in Los Angeles will be caught in the EirePharma web within the month."

"This was that rival PBM in Santa Monica?"

"Yes. All that bad press they got over the last several weeks really did a number on them. My spin doctors did a good job, no question about it. Their shareholders are jumping ship like drowning rats. The board has no choice but to sell the company. And guess who's swooping in with the best—and only—offer! Isn't that a big break?"

Amy's smile faltered a little but she reminded herself to stay perky.

Spin doctors . . . bad press . . .

She made a mental note to jot down his words when she got back to her office. Something more to add to the material she was gathering.

"You sure know how to do these things, don't you, Connor?"

"Oh, yeah! Pretty soon, the company will be another EirePharma outpost, and then they'll turn around and start making money. Their outdated business plans just need a little tweaking."

"That's great, Connor."

"Everything all right on the home front?"

She gave a little shrug. "As far as I can tell. We haven't burned down the building or anything."

He emitted a boisterous guffaw and then sipped his vodka.

Amy cleared her throat. "You texted that you wanted to see me when you got back?"

"I did? Oh, right, I did. I just wanted to see you! I missed you, like I said."

She felt an immense amount of relief. "Oh! I thought it was . . ."

"Thought it was what?"

"I, uh, I thought you had something important to discuss. About your trip. Or whatever."

"Nah, just wanted to see my number one girl!"

Amy played along. "Well, I hope there's not a number two or three!"

That elicited another guffaw. "You always could make me laugh, Amy. There haven't been many women in my life that could."

She gave him a smile and then turned toward the window and the whiteness outside. Her past year dating Connor Devlin had been full of roller coaster ups and downs, to say the least. She had been caught in a sweeping Irish romance, unbelieving that such an eligible bachelor had eyes only for her. But like the weather slowly eating away at stone, the cracks were showing, especially in light of Amy's recent discoveries.

Amy went to a mirror that was affixed to the wall near the door. She set her purse on the small table beneath it, opened it, and rummaged through the contents. "Kissing you messed up my lipstick, I need to reapply it. Where is it . . ." She pulled out, among other things, a knife with a pink handle that was encrusted with white gems.

"Ha! I see you're still carrying your back-alley weapon of death!" he said with a laugh.

"You know I have it in my purse all the time."

"Oh, I know. For 'protection.'"

"Ah, here it is." She removed the lipstick and applied it as she peered into the mirror.

"Say," Devlin said, "I've been thinking. Have you noticed how Deamhan's been acting lately?"

Deamhan was Devlin's German shepherd that resided at their home in Kenilworth. The dog's name was the Celtic word for "demon," and it was pronounced "De-amhan."

She finished with her makeup and threw the items she had removed back into her purse. Amy turned back around to him. "No, how is he acting?"

"He thinks you and I are going away on a vacation. Back to Ireland! He already misses us!"

Amy laughed. "He does? How do you know that?"

He winked at her. "I just do."

"Maybe he just wants more treats."

Devlin pointed a finger at her. "And *you* need to stop giving so many to him! I decide when to reward him."

Amy allowed herself a wry laugh. "If you showed him a little more love he might not be such a scary dog. Anyway, we have no plans to return to Ireland."

He let the barb about his dog go, and then he shrugged. "What do you say? Would you fancy a trip back to the Emerald Isle? I know you love it there. It's time for another trip to the castle, don't you think?"

Amy moved toward the bar, took a glass, and filled it with water from the sink. Her mouth had suddenly become dry. She took a swallow and then said, "Well, Connor, you know my Aunt Mary has been ill. I feel like I need to be nearby at all times. I don't have much family left. After everything that's happened—"

"Amy, dear, it's been months," he interrupted. "I know how you and your aunt feel, and I'm sorry your uncle is gone. But look how the company is thriving. I'm taking it into the stratosphere! And you're riding that rocket ship with me. Surely that helps ease some of the pain? Some of the heartache? I really think your uncle's spirit is up there sending his blessings down on you and the company."

What an insensitive shit, she thought. "Of course, Connor."

"Well, think about it. Ireland is beautiful in the springtime."

"We'll have to see, Connor. I must get back to the interview now."

Devlin's face abruptly lost its exuberance. His expression became something as icy as the drink he held. Amy had noted that this often happened when the man was displeased.

"All right, Amy. Better go, then. I'll see you later."

She turned and headed to the door.

"Amy?"

She stopped and turned back to him. "Yes, Connor?"

"How's your cousin, Matt?"

There it was. She felt the chill from his eyes in her spine.

"Matt? Why do you ask?"

Devlin shrugged. "Just wondering. You were talking about family."

Amy forced a smile and gave a little shrug. "As far as I know, he's okay."

"You haven't spoken to him recently?"

Oh, dear God . . .

"Not for a few weeks," she lied. "Why, should we invite him over for dinner?"

Devlin stared at her for a beat. Then he answered, "If you like, Amy, dear. If you like. Go on. You can't keep the *Chicago Tribune* waiting."

"I'll see you at home later," she said, and then she was out the door in a flash.

4

March 2024

Flying in or out of Chicago's O'Hare Airport was always iffy in March. The weather was unpredictable. It was almost guaranteed to be cold, but whether or not a blizzard would be shutting things down was a gamble. Luckily, while there was still dirty snow and ice covering the landscape, there were no inclement storms on the day that the flight from Pensacola carrying Deke and Michael Carey landed in Illinois.

After Matt Redmond's visit to the Bergman-Deketomis law offices, Deke had called his team together to discuss the situation that his friend had painted. At the moment, they didn't have much to go on except for Matt's words. Deke set Sarah Mercer, the firm's chief trial paralegal, on the task of looking into EirePharma's history and studying the pharmacy benefit manager industry. One of the firm's more mercurial but thorough lawyers, Gina Romano, volunteered to dig into the life of Connor Devlin to see what turned up. It was agreed, though, that the firm could not move forward without first informally interviewing Amy Redmond and hearing her story. Deke had not promised Matt anything, only that the team was willing to gather some preliminary information to see if there was a case.

Matt had suggested that they meet for lunch not too far from EirePharma's Deerfield headquarters, so that Amy could slip away from work and not be gone too long, but also at a place that would be off Devlin's radar. Matt settled on a small, strip mall eatery in Buffalo

Grove that specialized in Greek dishes. Nothing fancy, just good food, and the place had a room containing legal video gaming machines that no one seemed to use. It was a joint Devlin and his minions would likely never set foot in, and the man would expect the same from Amy.

"Don't get me wrong," Matt had said, "they have the best gyros in town!"

Deke and Michael rented a car at the airport and, following Matt's directions, Michael drove north on I-294/94 for twenty minutes toward Wisconsin until they reached the Deerfield exit. They passed EirePharma heading west.

"There it is," Deke said.

"It's a nice-looking building," Michael commented. "It's probably prettier after winter."

They arrived at the restaurant ten minutes later. Matt was inside waiting for them. Deke introduced him to Michael, they all shook hands, and the trio sat at a table to wait for Amy.

"If I didn't know better," Matt said, "I wouldn't think you guys were lawyers at all. You look more like a pro wrestler and his manager who earlier in life was also a pro wrestler!"

Deke and Michael both laughed at that. Michael replied, "Actually, you nailed it. That's exactly what we are. This lawyer thing is all an act."

Deke and Michael made a great team despite the differences in age and temperament. Deke, a veteran of many courtroom battles, had the looks of a television-ready spokesman and still cut a striking figure at six-foot-one. His love of the outdoors showed on his sun-beaten face, but he appeared to be much younger than his fifty-nine years. He'd been raised in foster care by eight different families, so his sympathy for and desire to help came from deep within. His friends respected that he was both inwardly and outwardly a very spiritual person.

Michael, on the other hand, was twenty years younger than Deke and a couple of inches shorter, but he exhibited the bulk of a bodybuilder. He shared with Deke a less-than-happy childhood—he hadn't known his father, and he'd lost his mother at the age of seventeen. His Iraq War Air Force experience as a pararescueman, though, forged his outlook on life. It had also hardened edges on him that were not apparent to most people. There was no question that he was the most athletic and toughest individual in the law firm, but he was remarkably sensitive toward what he perceived to be unjust. Clients called him one of the kindest men they knew—until he came across a threat to his or his loved ones' safety. The truth was that Michael Carey could be a killing machine if the occasion called for it. The military had spent millions teaching him how to survive.

"I appreciate you flying up here to meet," Matt said.

"It's the only way we can get a handle on your story," Deke offered. "I like to interview folks in person."

"Deke has a sixth sense when it comes to individuals and if they tell the truth or not," Michael added. "I'm going to figure out a way to patent the Deketomis Lie Detector someday and make a million bucks."

"I assure you," Matt said, "Amy will not be lying to you."

"I didn't mean to imply that she might. Sorry."

"No apologies necessary, I understand," Matt said. "I was once a lawyer, too. Apologies, though, for bringing you to a strip mall diner, but I dated a woman out here once and this was a favorite spot. The food is—oh, here's Amy now."

They looked up to see the diminutive frame of Matt's cousin walk through the door. At five-foot-four, Amy Redmond made up for her lack of physical stature in natural beauty. The flaming red hair flowed gracefully on her head. She wore a Burberry trench coat that, when removed, revealed a white, tailored Chanel double-breasted suit with pants. She wore sensible black block heels that worked for short distances in the colder temperatures outdoors.

Matt and Amy embraced with quick kisses on the cheeks, and then he said, "Gentlemen, this is my cousin, Amy Redmond." He introduced the two men, who stood and shook her hand.

"Call me Deke."

"Call me Michael."

Amy grinned. "I guess you can call me Amy, then!" Her piercing green eyes sparkled.

Matt asked, "Gyros good for everyone? I'll order. Why don't you go on in to the other room? No one's in there. Don't mind the video gaming machines, unless you want to lose some money."

27

"I don't want a gyro," Amy said. She was eyeing the menu displayed over the counter. "I just want a Greek salad with grilled chicken."

"Coming up."

Deke, Michael, and Amy moved to the other room and sat away from the machines that looked like Vegas-style slot machines.

"These things are legal?" Michael asked Amy.

"Yeah, video gaming is legal in restaurants and such in Illinois. Has been for a few years. Illinois also has some riverboat casinos. They have to be on water to be legal, if that makes any sense to you."

"I knew that about Illinois, and no, it doesn't make sense. Whatever."

As they sat, Amy said, "I've asked my attorney to join us. He should be here soon."

Matt rejoined them after placing the order. "Paul's coming, right?"

"Yes." She nervously glanced out the window at the parking lot.

"You okay?" Matt asked. "No one followed you?"

"No, I don't think so. Look, here's Paul."

A medium-built, slender man in his sixties entered the back room. Deke and Michael stood as Amy said, "Gentlemen, this is Paul Baker, the Redmond family attorney who's been with us as long as I can remember." She introduced Deke and Michael to him.

"Very happy to meet you," Baker said. "Mr. Deketomis, I greatly admire all the work you've been doing for social justice. Your reputation precedes you."

"Thank you. I just look at it as being honest with the profession we're in," Deke responded.

The food was ready very quickly, including the added order for Baker, and Matt brought everything to the table. They spoke of Chicago, the Cubs, the Bulls, and the Bears, and Deke mentioned that the Art Institute was one of his favorite museums in the country. The small talk continued until they finished their food, which Michael declared was "fantastic."

Deke had noticed, though, that Amy continued to appear on edge. She had sat at the table so that she could always see out the window. She often glanced over Deke's shoulder to see who drove up and parked a vehicle, and she especially checked out anyone who came through the front door of the restaurant. Matt had behaved the same way in Florida. It was plain as day that the two cousins were indeed fearful about *something*.

"Amy," Matt said, "you want to tell Deke and Michael some of the things you've told me?"

Amy took a sip of water and then began. "Sure, but I want to make it clear up front. It's one reason why I asked Paul to join us today. I will never testify in court. I can't be named in any lawsuit. I can't be a witness. I can't be *anything*. I can just tell you about some things off the record."

Deke and Michael exchanged glances, and then Deke said, "Amy, we're not in a court of law. This is not a deposition. It's an informal fact-finding meeting. That said, if what Matt has told us is true, then we will need solid evidence of wrongdoing on the part of this man, Devlin. And if your company is running an illegal price-fixing scam causing the price of insulin to go up in the interest of profit at the detriment of the public, then you would have to decide which side of the line you're on. But I don't want to get ahead of myself here. We're nowhere near that point yet. We're here to listen to you. This could end up being something we can't get involved in. We could feel that it's not strong enough to litigate, or there could be any number of obstacles. I know that you and Matt are hurting because of the deaths of your loved ones. We are sympathetic and fully understand your desire for some kind of justice."

Amy nodded, but then added, "But, you see, I am the face of EirePharma. I am the face of the Redmond family now. We're not the majority shareholders anymore, but EirePharma is the family company. It always will be. If we go down this road, then EirePharma is going to get some bad press. If all this goes the distance to real legal action, then you'll be asking me to act against the best interests of the family business. That will be very, very difficult for me. My position makes me culpable, too. One of my worst nightmares is that we would lose the company forever and all go to jail over something we had no control over!"

Deke leaned forward and looked her in the eyes. "Amy, I understand exactly what you're saying. First off, though, if there's any legal action from us, it would be a civil case, not a criminal one. No one would go to jail. Civil cases are usually all about money. I can't ensure that what develops along the way as a criminal issue is something that I can contain, but clearly that will be my goal. I know that you and Matt are concerned about this man Devlin. A civil case can remove him from the company if that is what is warranted and just. That said, if we uncover evidence of real criminal activity, then law enforcement would have to get involved. It's how we work. It's the right thing to do. Matt has expressed doubt as to whether your Uncle Charles really committed suicide. If we find that there's a chance that he didn't, well . . . you see? I'm not asking you to make a commitment now, but before my firm agrees to invest time and money in all this, we'd need to know you're on our side. Or not."

Paul Baker answered for her. "I think it's safe to say that Amy will consider all of her options on a step-by-step basis. She is, after all, president of EirePharma, and you're asking her to be a whistleblower. I mean, that's what this is all about, right?"

"I hadn't used that term," Deke said, "but, yes. I suppose whistleblowing is exactly what this would be. And there are protections in place in our governing agencies that will shield whistleblowers from harm. But a step-by-step evaluation is certainly fine with us, Amy."

Baker looked at Amy, and she nodded. "Okay." She took a breath and then said, "The crux of it all is that my boss, the current CEO of EirePharma, is performing unethical and, I believe, criminal activities in order to make more money than is warranted. At least I *hope* these things aren't criminal."

"You're talking about Connor Devlin," Deke said.

"Yes. I mean, we all want our companies to be successful and make a lot of money. I have a personal investment in EirePharma for it to be successful. But not if it's doing things that are ultimately harmful to consumers of drugs like insulin. My father, Andy Redmond, died because he couldn't afford insulin. Ironic, right? Granted, he had a lot of other issues. His autopsy report revealed that he was hooked on heroin. He drank excessively. He was not in good health by any means. But he chose to skimp on insulin *because* it wasn't as affordable as he would have liked. Andy was disowned from the family fortune so his financial situation was solely centered on his own musical income, which had more or less petered out over the last twenty years. When Matt or I attempted to help him out with money, he refused it. He had a lot of pride. Yeah, one could argue that he shouldn't have been spending what money he had on illegal drugs and alcohol. And he had let his premium payments to Medicare lapse. That's on him, for sure. Medicare is a great deal for seniors, especially in Illinois, but if you get kicked off the program for not paying your premiums, then you're stuck with having to pay outrageous prices for insulin. I'm thinking now not just about my father, but about any average American who doesn't have insurance and who has to buy insulin.

"EirePharma, along with other PBMs in this country, are pushing the price of insulin—and other drugs—outrageously high just for the sake of profit. The price gouging is worse than it's ever been before. And none of this was happening at my company until Connor Devlin took it over. Connor is connected . . ." She paused to think about what she was going to say.

"Go on, Amy," Matt said.

She went for it. "Connor is connected to organized crime. I can't say it's a legacy group like the Mafia or anything like that. It's a cabal of very wealthy Irishmen who have known each other a long time, and their roots go back to their mother country. I met some of them when I went with Connor to Ireland last year. Connor was born and raised in Ireland. He has a lot of secrets. I don't know how he got to be as wealthy as he is, but he seems to be interested only in gaining more money. There was a time when most people got into the medical industry because they cared about people."

Matt interjected. "That was before Wall Street raiders started reshaping the industry. Connor Devlin is far worse than even the typical bloodsucking Wall Street crowd. You see, I really believe there is no line Devlin won't cross. Literally no line! He just cares about himself and his pocketbook."

Amy made a face that indicated that she agreed with that assessment.

"What kinds of things is he doing?" Michael asked.

Amy continued, "Connor is not above using blackmail, intimidation tactics, and physical harm to get what he wants from his competitors and enemies. Worse than that, he uses those same tools to get what he wants from *allies*! To get people to fall in line with his policies. He will use extortion and physical threats to force drug manufacturers, PBM officials, insurance representatives, and even doctors to go along with his schemes. Connor has some mobster-type men working for him personally. They are not EirePharma employees, but they accompany Connor everywhere he goes, even on EirePharma business. They are very scary guys, and Matt and I both think they're watching us."

"They are," Matt added.

"Do you know their names?" Michael asked.

She nodded. "Ronan Barry is Connor's right-hand man. He's a thug. I don't know how else to describe him. Lance Macdonald is another one. There's a new guy named Pat Beckett. There's another one at the house in Kenilworth who acts as a guard at the front gate. I'm afraid I don't know his real name, but he goes by 'Smithy.'"

Michael jotted down those names on a pad of paper.

Amy thought of something else. "In Ireland he mentioned someone named 'Petey-o.' Sounded like he was one of the bigwigs in the Chicago area. Does that name mean anything to you?"

"Nope," Michael said, "but I'm adding that to the list."

"Anyway . . . just the other day," Amy continued, "Connor got a rival PBM headquartered in Los Angeles to go out of business. EirePharma is going to take them over. Connor and his spin doctors anonymously put out false PR about the company. They started losing clients. The Feds came in and busted them for what I believe was planted evidence that they were defrauding consumers. But they weren't, as far as I know. There is a clear correlation between how badly he wants something and how far he is willing to push his criminal conduct to get it."

"Have you ever witnessed Devlin committing an illegal act?" Deke asked.

"I've seen him threaten people with their livelihoods. He can get quietly angry, and it can be unsettling for anyone who is the recipient of that anger."

Michael said, "Being mad at an employee or business associate is not criminal behavior."

"But planting some incriminating material in the home of a business rival certainly is," she countered.

Deke asked, "He's done that?"

Amy looked at her attorney, who raised his eyebrows. *Be careful*, his face expressed.

"I . . . I *think* he did. I don't have proof. But I'm working on getting it. There's an insulin manufacturer here in Chicago that we work with called InsoDrugs. Connor had a hard time convincing their chief operating officer, Doug Frankel, to work with his company to raise the price of insulin. Mr. Frankel committed suicide over the Christmas holidays. I don't believe in coincidences."

"Another suicide," Matt said. "Coincidence? I think not."

"Are you suggesting foul play?" Deke asked.

Matt made an exaggerated shrug. "I don't know. Just thinking out loud."

Michael asked Amy, "Are you saying Devlin planted something in Mr. Frankel's home or office in an attempt to blackmail him?"

"Yes."

"How do you know?"

"I don't. It was something Connor said one night when we were discussing InsoDrugs' reluctance to raise prices. Connor and I had a lunch meeting with Mr. Frankel that did not go well. At the time, I'm afraid I was so caught up in Connor's spell that I went right along with whatever he was saying to Frankel. Then, that night, Connor said, and I'm paraphrasing, 'I've heard Dougie Frankel has prurient desires. It'd be too bad if the police found that out, too.' I remember asking Connor how he knew that. Connor just said, 'Sometimes you have to supply the truth yourself.' I asked him what he meant by that, and he changed the subject."

"Tell them about the judge," Matt said.

"Oh, right," she said. "Several months ago, EirePharma was the target of an early class action lawsuit over marketing misrepresentations and the pricing of insulin. The judge in the case, Roberta Carver, has a temper, and Connor exploited that. He somehow got a PR firm he hired to blast all kinds of negative stuff about the judge on social and traditional media, so much so that she began screaming and even dropping F-bombs at our lawyers in the courtroom. He succeeded in having her recused from the case, and the lawsuit was dismissed by a friendlier judge, someone I know is in Connor's pocket."

Deke turned to Michael. "Ask Gina or Sarah to get the details of that lawsuit." He then leaned forward and said, "Amy, Matt has told me about your Uncle Charles. What makes you think that he didn't commit suicide?"

"Because Uncle Charles would never have done that. It wasn't his nature. He wanted to sell the company, and at first he thought Connor Devlin was the right man to buy it. He was totally charmed by Connor—we all were—everyone, including the board. The deal was set in stone, but right before Uncle Charles died, he told me in confidence that he was getting cold feet and that he had new reasons to distrust Connor—but he wouldn't give me the details. I thought Uncle Charles was being unreasonably cryptic, even ridiculous. We all loved Connor. This was also when my romance with Connor was in full bloom, and I admit I was not thinking straight. My head was in the clouds. So, when Uncle Charles died suddenly, I was in total shock. Since the deal of the sale had already been approved, the board went ahead in April and May last year, and EirePharma was sold to Connor. I was immediately promoted to be president, and Connor became CEO. We became incredibly busy, which helped me combat my grief over Uncle Charles—who as you know was more like my father than an uncle. Within a few months, Connor had saved the company. We were indebted to him. At least that's what I thought at the time. I never got the chance to think carefully about Uncle Charles's suicide. I know that in those days before his death Charles was working on something to discredit Connor. Something that would hurt him. Maybe get him out of our lives. And . . . well, it's just a gut feeling, but I tend to have guts that are usually right on certain issues. My gut feeling *now* is that my Uncle Charles didn't jump from that building—he was pushed."

"You know we will need proof in order to make an accusation like that?" Michael asked.

"I'm working on it. As for what Connor's doing with the company, I've been keeping a diary and a collection of things that I've noted. Things Connor has said or done. Copies of documents that I find suspicious. These are materials that, if you read between the lines and understand how the PBM business works, shows that Connor is orchestrating a Rube Goldberg–style cause-and-effect machine that gets insulin manufacturers, PBMs, insurance companies, and pharmacies to collaborate on raising prices and screwing over consumers."

"That's good that you're documenting everything," Deke said. "How exactly are you uncovering his secrets?"

Amy rolled her eyes and gave him a little smirk. "Because I live with him. We've been engaged to be married since last June! We've been an 'item,' as they say, for a year, but I have to say that things have cooled between us. Drastically. He knows it, too, and he doesn't like it. Connor's the type of guy who needs to be in control. I'm afraid I've become trapped in a complex and challenging situation. I want to break off the engagement, but he's going to make it difficult for me to leave him."

"Why can't you?" Michael asked.

She looked away and said, "If I tried, you might see a news report that *I* jumped off a building."

5

It had been a short, two-day trip to Chicago for Deke and Michael. Now, back in Spanish Trace, Deke assembled the team in the conference room to discuss what they'd learned. The group consisted of Deke, Michael, Gina, Sarah, and the firm's top two investigators, Jake Rutledge and Carol Morris.

Jake was once a lawyer in West Virginia who had worked with Bergman-Deketomis on a high-profile opioid case, but he ended up being disbarred after he released privileged information to the public. He was even once addicted to opioids, which contributed to his poor choices. However, Jake managed to get clean, transition his formidable skills into investigating, and keep in touch with Deke. As Deke always believed in second and sometimes third chances, he hired Jake to work for Bergman-Deketomis. A few years younger than Michael, Jake was lean, mean, and fearless. He had been instrumental in digging up hard-to-get evidence in past cases.

Carol was a few years younger than Deke and served as head of safety, security, and investigative services for the firm. She was an ex-cop and the daughter of an army staff sergeant. Many at Bergman-Deketomis considered Carol to be the toughest, most no-nonsense member of the team. Her role often required her to go out in the field with the lawyers to not only protect them, but also perform some of the more unorthodox tasks that could be considered dangerous. Carol was known for her short fuse and sarcasm, which sometimes got her in trouble on the outside—but she could also frighten the opposition into submission. She was a valuable commodity.

"Okay, ladies and gents, where are we at?" Deke began. "Michael, tell everyone about our trip to Chicago and how you feel about it."

Michael didn't need to glance at his notes. "We had a good preliminary meeting with Matt and Amy Redmond. Amy was slow to commit to any kind of action we might take against her firm and against the man who seems to be causing all the trouble over there."

"That would be Connor Devlin?" Carol asked.

"That's right. She did, however, back up Matt's story, or rather, Matt's suspicions that Devlin is a mobster-style businessman who performs shady and possibly illegal acts to get what he wants. Is there violence involved? We don't know for sure right now other than her word, but, yes, I'm betting on it."

Carol spoke again. "Can I say something?"

"Go ahead," Deke replied.

"I've read over everything you gave us that summarizes your first meeting with Matt Redmond, Deke, and I have to say I'm not sure I trust his veracity. I mean, seeing that he nearly got disbarred and was forced to resign for assaulting a senior partner in his firm, can we believe what he says? As he's not a lawyer with a firm, and appears to have given up that calling . . . and he's, what, just bumming around and living off the Redmond name and his family money? It doesn't give him much credibility. You also put in the report that you thought he was drinking too much when he was here."

Michael raised a finger and said, "Let me just interject. In Chicago, we didn't see Matt have a drink until dinner, and that was only a couple of glasses of wine. Who knows what he might have done when he got home, but, Deke, was his demeanor different in Chicago than what you witnessed when he visited you here?"

Deke nodded his head. "He didn't seem as nervous and paranoid in Chicago. That said, I hear you, Carol. But as Michael said, Amy corroborated his accusations. I think I can vouch for Matt."

"And another thing," Carol continued. "Right now all we've got to go on is what they're saying. She's indicated that she won't testify. What good will that do us? We'd have to get her testimony on the record, or she'd have to supply us with hard evidence that has a solid chain of custody for anything she gives us. I also have to say, gee whiz, why is she still *engaged* to that man, Connor Devlin? If she's the president of her company and has all these suspicions about him and he's a class-A jerk and a possible mobster, why is she still living with him?"

"Wow, you really showed up as the Doubting Thomas today, Carol, but, yes, those are potential problems," Deke said.

"I, for one, believe what she had to say," Michael offered. "Carol, you know how some people can be in a toxic relationship and can't get out of it. Even intelligent, strong women. I could see it with our first meeting. Amy Redmond is under the thumb of a very powerful, charismatic man who has given her success and wealth. The couple is apparently part of the Chicago social scene and society pages. It's my opinion that Amy is being gaslighted by this man. For a year she has been in a whirlwind of an overwhelming romance, and she's just now starting to come up for air and see reality."

"She's also frightened," Deke added. "I could see that. She was terribly fraught. It didn't take a psychiatrist to understand that she is a very conflicted person. She very likely was in love with Connor Devlin, maybe she still is, but she's now seeing a dark side to the relationship."

"Bingo," Michael agreed. "But I agree with Carol; we're going to need a lot more from Amy Redmond. 'I think my uncle was pushed off a building' is not going to get much traction in court. As for what this fellow Devlin is doing with EirePharma and the price of insulin, is that something we can win? There are dozens of lawsuits already out there that are going after the drug manufacturers and PBMs over the escalation of insulin prices. Are we going to join that fray?"

Deke said, "In 2023 Eli Lilly agreed to pay $13.5 million to end a six-year class action lawsuit that alleged the company overpriced its insulin. It can be done, guys. Look, I've known Matt Redmond a long time. I realize he's had some problems lately. But I know his character. Most people retain the character they grew up with, no matter what kinds of negative forces affect their lives. I have a good sense when it comes to judging people, and I still think Matt is a good person. I don't think he's making any of this stuff up. And I agree with Michael. I believe Amy, too."

Carol shrugged. "Okay, Deke, I know you're a lot like me. We both have a freaky superpower of lie detection. I can tell when someone is lying during an interview, and I guess you can, too . . . but doubting and confirming is what you pay me for."

Deke continued. "There's a lot here we need to look at. What happened to Amy and Matt's uncle? Charles Redmond jumped off a high-rise in Chicago just before Devlin acquired EirePharma. We need to know more about that background. And there was another man who committed suicide who was connected to Devlin."

"Doug Frankel," Michael reminded him. "I put him in my report, too."

"Right. Can we find out more about what exactly happened there?"

"I'm on that," Jake said.

Carol spoke up again. "All this is going to keep us busy, for sure, but I also gotta ask . . . Does anyone understand this PBM business?"

There were a few chuckles around the room. Jake murmured, "Thank you, Carol."

Deke looked at the paralegal in the room. "Sarah's been working on something about that very subject. What do you have for us, Sarah?"

"Well," she said. "This stuff *is* complicated. But this is it in a nutshell." She consulted her notes. "A pharmacy benefit manager, or PBM, is a go-between intermediary company that negotiates the prices of prescription drugs. They're in the middle of a web of pharmacies, drug manufacturers, and insurance companies where everyone gets a cut of every pill sold in America. The PBMs decide what drugs are on what is called an insurance formulary list. That's a list that states what drugs you are permitted to buy under insurance coverage. So PBMs make deals with drug manufacturers. The deal is that if the PBM puts a manufacturer's drug on their formulary list, the drug manufacturer has to pay a kickback that they call a 'rebate.' To simplify it, it's the equivalent of legalized payoff to the PBM."

"Excuse me," Carol said. "The industry calls them 'rebates?'"

"The PBM types like to use the word rebate rather than bribe or kickback. That's how the PBM makes its money. And whatever drug the PBM puts on an insurance company's formulary is the drug that consumers must buy because that's the only one their insurance company pays for. PBMs also charge what they call 'administrative fees' for their services. That's just another level of legalized bribe or payoff. The PBMs simply say they are legally being paid for services, as vague as that might be."

Michael piped in. "Isn't the American pharma business great? Basically pigs at the trough."

Sarah continued. "But wait, there's more! In addition to all that legal bribery and kickback money, this thing called the PBM, which our government has blessed, has two or three other ways they gouge money from patients who sometimes are having to buy the only drug that will keep them alive or healthy. I won't go into those details right now because your head will start spinning, but you'll have a white paper from me on all this in the next couple of days. I'll end with the money shot. This pharma industry-created monster is a three-hundred-billion-dollar profit center for the PBM folks every year. Kickbacks and bribes are big money in the pharma business, and it's all *legal*."

Carol said, "Sounds to me like organized crime is moving into this space that was controlled by the traditional Wall Street mob. Hell, it sounds more profitable than illegal drugs, numbers, hijacking, and prostitution all put together."

Deke said, "Interesting you should say that, Carol, because Matt used the words 'Irish mob' when we spoke. We need to look into that more and see if that's really the case."

Sarah nodded. "You got it. Yes, it's been happening in this country for a long time. PBMs were originally contracted by insurance carriers simply to negotiate with pharmaceutical companies, but in recent years, PBMs have hijacked the prescription drug marketplace to the detriment of pharmacies and patients. Corporate media doesn't tell the story because they are making so many billions off the drug industry's advertisements."

"I just feel warm and fuzzy all over knowing this is part of our FUBAR healthcare system," Michael added.

"And there's a complete lack of transparency in how these PBMs do business," Sarah said. "It's virtually impossible to regulate, even if the US government was actually motivated to do it."

Jake raised his hand and spoke. "So is this what's going on when I go into my local pharmacy to pick up a prescription, and the pharmacist says, 'Sorry, this drug isn't covered by your insurance?'"

"That's correct," Sarah answered.

"But the PBM is not my doctor."

"Bingo. The criteria is that the PBM doesn't make as much money off that particular drug as opposed to this other one that may or may not be a similar drug, but it's one the PBM has negotiated to be on your insurance formulary and has received a kickback rebate from that drug's manufacturer."

"How the *hell* is this even legal?" Carol demanded. "I don't see how these PBMs are allowed to dictate how consumers pay for drugs that are prescribed by doctors. Aren't there Hippocratic oaths being trampled here? Sounds like there's a lot of ignoring the 'do no harm' rule!"

"When this kind of money is involved, there are no rules," Deke agreed.

Michael added, "Sarah is right about the lack of transparency in how PBMs operate. They are actually legally protected. They don't have to reveal their methodology. How they negotiate with drugmakers and how they influence insurance companies is all privileged information."

"And so bad guys can easily manipulate the system," Gina suggested. "They can use whatever means necessary to get what they want. And it appears this is what Devlin is doing. This industry is a gold mine for a sophisticated mob operation."

"Gina, have you got your report on Devlin ready?" Deke asked.

"Not quite, Deke. I'm still working on it. The man is a cipher. He has covered his tracks very well."

"That's not a good sign," Carol ventured. "I know a good private investigator in Chicago. Fellow by the name of Lou Doonan. Anyone else know him?"

They all shook their heads.

"I could see if he can help out. I know he has all kinds of resources in the Chicagoland underworld, such as it is."

"Let's hold that thought, Carol," Deke said. "We can go to him later if we need to. I don't want to spend a lot of money on this yet. Okay, people, we have work to do. Let's get to it."

MIKE PAPANTONIO

"Hmpf," Jake muttered. Everyone looked at him. He had his wallet out and was examining his insurance cards. When he noticed that everyone was staring at him, he shook his head and said, "Oh, sorry. I was just reminding myself of what insurance we have here at the firm. I was just starting to wonder something."

"What's that?" Deke asked.

"Are each and every one of us, and everyone out there in the world who has insurance, are we participating in a criminal enterprise just by going to the drugstore and buying our medicine? I mean, all of this PBM bullshit sounds like nothing but a big *scam* to me!"

6

If Amy Redmond didn't have to be at the office for some reason on a Saturday morning—and she often did—it was the only time that she could do tasks such as shopping for groceries or going to her gym. She had long ago made the commitment to herself that she would go swimming whenever possible, but those instances were fewer and farther between since she'd become president of EirePharma ten months earlier.

Nevertheless, on the last Saturday of March, Amy took advantage of Connor being away for the weekend to leave their opulent mansion on Sheridan Drive in Kenilworth, one of the wealthiest suburbs on the North Shore, and drive the short four miles to the Evanston Athletic Club. She had been a member there for ages, and today she was determined to do a few laps.

Living in an old, historic house of twelve thousand square feet that sat on an acre and a half of manicured lawn and gardens, and protected by a guardhouse, gate, and wrought iron fence that surrounded the property, was luxurious even by Redmond standards. Growing up in the household of Charles and Mary Redmond in another lavish old-money manor in Highland Park had made her accustomed to the "good life," but Connor's Kenilworth home was more of a fortress. When they had first started seriously dating a year ago, she only occasionally spent nights in Kenilworth. For the past few months, though, she had essentially been living there. Connor had been pressuring her to let go of the apartment she owned in Northbrook and make their companionship "official" with a permanent move. She had considered selling the apartment, as the utilities, maintenance, and taxes added up to a pretty penny, but now she was glad that she hadn't. The apartment could very well be a life raft for her if she finally made the decision to leave Connor.

That move was inevitable. Life had become untenable with the man, but being with him was the only way she was going to be able to collect information and evidence that could be useful to the attorneys.

On the way to Evanston, Amy stopped at the Lake City Cleaners to drop off two business suits and a winter coat to be dry cleaned. After delivering the clothing and taking the pickup ticket, she went back out into the brisk, 39°F air to climb into her 2021 Lexus RX 350 Premium to continue the few blocks to the athletic club. There was still snow and ice piled up at the edges of the streets from the last snowstorm, but today the sun was shining and there wasn't a cloud in the sky.

Amy got into the car and adjusted the rearview mirror so that she could check out a blemish on her cheek that she had noticed in the bathroom that morning. In doing so, her eyes focused instead on the black Lincoln Town Car parked across the street. Exhaust flowed out the back, indicating that the driver had temporarily parked there and kept the motor running. The tinted windows prevented her from seeing who was behind the wheel.

But she knew.

It was one of Connor's Town Cars, and Lance Macdonald was likely driving it.

Amy cursed to herself.

It had been going on for a couple of months. The prick was still having her followed.

* * *

Down in Spanish Trace, Florida, research into the case was slow going. Deke and Michael were tied up with other court cases and weren't able to devote much time to the project. Carol's schedule was hijacked by having to oversee an upgrade of the firm's security system that was way overdue. The firm was busy, which was a good thing, but everyone had multiple endeavors on their plates. Nevertheless, Gina and Sarah worked together when they could on the mystery regarding EirePharma's sale to Connor Devlin just after Charles Redmond's suicide. They scoured news sources from March and April 2023 and were able to piece together a timeline, but the "why" eluded them. Jake concentrated on the more recent case of Doug Frankel. Thus, it was the end of March before Deke called the team back into the conference room for another meeting to get progress reports.

Jake went first. "All right, this guy Doug Frankel was chief operating officer at InsoDrugs. This is a drug manufacturer based in the Chicago area, and they make insulin. They're one of the companies that raised their price. EirePharma is one of the PBMs that works with them. So, EirePharma was a client of InsoDrugs."

"Or is it the other way around?" Carol asked. "Maybe InsoDrugs is a client of EirePharma! This PBM stuff is all so confusing!"

That got a mild laugh from the group, and then Jake went on. "That distinction of who's working for whom with these folks is almost meaningless. They are all working to gouge out profits. Anyway, in December of last year, police were called to Frankel's residence in Chicago. It was between Christmas and New Year's. He lived alone. He was divorced. Forty-three years old. Police found him on the floor behind his desk in a makeshift home office in one of the bedrooms. He had blown his brains out, sitting at the desk. No one knew why. He didn't leave a note. I'm sure the police have more information, but that's not available to the public. There's a quote in the *Chicago Tribune* from his former wife, Elaine, where she says that he was under a lot of stress at work, but he had *always* been under a lot of stress at work. He didn't talk about work much. His colleagues at InsoDrugs were also shocked and surprised by his death. The interesting thing is that InsoDrugs raised the price of insulin exactly two weeks later, at the beginning of the New Year."

"Well, it's possible that the man's suicide might not be related to EirePharma at all," Deke ventured.

"Deke," Gina said, "Sarah and I have learned that Connor Devlin purchased a controlling interest in EirePharma's shares only a month after Charles Redmond's death. That's another instance of a mysterious suicide followed by something happening that affects EirePharma.

We found some articles in the business sections of various publications and medical journals about how EirePharma was losing money between 2019 and 2023. There's one piece in *Forbes* from January of that year that says there were 'rumors' indicating that Redmond was privately looking for a buyer. Close friends were saying he wanted to retire. EirePharma is a privately held company. At the time, members of the Redmond family owned all the stock shares. It is believed that Charles owned the majority of the shares."

She looked at Sarah, who continued. "According to the Securities and Exchange Commission, Charles Redmond owned 51 percent of EirePharma's stock. It is believed the other 49 percent was distributed among other Redmond family members. We don't know how much Amy Redmond owns. When the news broke that Connor Devlin was purchasing EirePharma, it was assumed in the trade papers that he was buying Charles Redmond's 51 percent. His widow, Mary Redmond, is quoted as saying that Charles had been working on a deal with Devlin to sell the company, so the board went ahead with it because it made financial sense."

"But why did Charles take a nosedive off a building before executing the sale?" Carol asked.

Gina said, "The sale happened shortly after the suicide. Common sense should at least hint at the possibility that the two events are not random. Then InsoDrugs raised the price of insulin after Frankel's suicide."

There was silence in the room as Deke rubbed his chin. Finally, he said, "I'd like to know a little more about the Doug Frankel case since that's the most recent one we're talking about. Jake, how would you like to go to Chicago to sniff around?"

"I go wherever I'm told to go, boss," Jake said with a smile.

"Let me see if I can get you in to talk to a friend of mine in the police force in Chicago. In fact, now he's the Bureau of Detectives chief. His name is James P. McClory. I met him when I was a prosecutor in the Broward County State Attorney's office. We had a case in Chicago. I don't know him well, but we got along and he was helpful. He was a captain then. I could put in a call and see if he'll talk to you and share the file on Frankel."

"That would be good, Deke," Jake said.

"I'll also call Matt and tell him you're coming. He can be your wing-man while you're there. I'm sure Matt will be happy to lend a hand."

"Chicago in April. What to wear, what to wear," Jake muttered, mostly to himself.

"Hint," Gina offered with a smile, "it won't be those Hawaiian shirts and cargo shorts that you kick around here in every day, Jake."

7

April 2024

As the new month began, the temperature in Chicago remained just above freezing. Jake Rutledge knew that this was par for the course in the Midwest, but he didn't have to like it. He had grown up in the mountains of West Virginia, so he was fairly accustomed to cold weather, but it wasn't the same. Jake tended to agree with Chicago natives' adage that there were only two seasons in the Windy City—winter and construction.

After landing at O'Hare, Jake rented a Nissan Altima and drove into the city to the Canopy Hilton on Jackson, paid an exorbitant amount to park the car, checked in, and made a call to Matt Redmond as arranged.

"Mr. Rutledge, I take it that you made it safely into our fair city," Matt said.

"Call me Jake, please. Yes, sir, I'm at my hotel. Deke arranged for us to meet Chief McClory at the police headquarters at three o'clock."

"Then we have time for lunch. Take a cab to the Metropolitan Building at Randolph and LaSalle, and I'll meet you at a fancy place called 312."

It was indeed a rather upscale establishment, and Jake didn't protest when Matt offered to treat him. Jake had an excellent gnocchi dish while Matt went for the seared pork medallions.

"It's pretty impressive that Deke got us a meeting with the chief of detectives," Matt said.

"Do you know him?" Jake asked as he stuffed his face.

THE MIDDLEMAN

Matt shook his head. "I tend to steer clear of cops. Mind you, when I was a lawyer, I had to deal with a lot of them. Mostly, they're good guys, but there are a few bad apples in this city."

"That's true everywhere, I guess."

"Yeah. But Chicago really has an old-school, good ol' boy fraternity that goes way, way back. If you're not in the circle, they're not too receptive to you looking inside of it. The way I understand it, McClory is the chief of detectives. He's in charge of the detective division. Just like the chief of patrol is in charge of all the districts. Both of them are referred to as 'chief,' but they'll also have a deputy chief, and you call him 'chief,' too. Unless the real chief is in the room, then I don't know what you call the deputy."

"Deputy Chief?"

Matt shrugged. "Probably. Bureaucracy, don't you love it?"

* * *

Matt drove them to the City of Chicago Public Safety Headquarters at 3510 S. Michigan Avenue, which was south of the Loop. It was an impressive building, but it would have to be to house the busy command center that policed the sprawling city. Jake and Matt checked in at the reception area, were given guest IDs, walked through metal detectors, and were then greeted by a uniformed woman who introduced herself as Sergeant Zaritsky. She told them that Chief McClory was "extremely busy" due to a rash of gang shootings on the South Side that occurred over the weekend, but that he would give them a few minutes of his time.

"We appreciate it," Jake said.

They were ushered into the Bureau of Detectives wing, which was naturally a beehive of activity. Men and women in plainclothes and uniforms bustled about, their voices booming across the space as they communicated with each other the old-fashioned way. At first Jake was struck by what seemed to be chaos, but as they marched through the maze of desks, cubicles, and personnel, he began to think that in reality the place was a well-oiled machine.

Chief James P. McClory was a large, heavy man with thinning gray-black hair, a drooping walrus mustache, and perspiration on his forehead. He sat behind a desk littered with paperwork. When Sergeant Zaritsky knocked on his open door, he looked up, raised his bushy eyebrows, and stood.

"Chief, I have Jake Rutledge and Matt Redmond here to see you," Zaritsky said.

"Come in, gentlemen," McClory said as he came around the desk to shake hands.

"Thank you so much for agreeing to see us," Jake said.

"Pshaw, I was surprised and happy to hear from my old friend Deke. How is he doing?"

"He's just great, sir. He sends his regards and his thanks."

McClory turned to Matt. "And you're one of the Redmonds. I don't believe we've ever crossed paths, have we?"

"No, sir, I don't believe so," Matt answered.

"I knew Terrence Redmond slightly. He was your . . . father?"

"That's correct."

"I knew your uncle, too. The one that . . ." He bowed his head and paused a few seconds, a gesture that was an attempt to appear sympathetic.

"Charles? Or Andy?"

"I meant Charles. I never met your rock star uncle." McClory then gestured to the sitting area in the office. "Please make yourselves comfortable. Can I get you anything?"

Jake and Matt glanced at each other and read each other's thoughts. "Thank you, but no, we just had a very filling meal, sir," Matt answered.

"No problem." McClory took a seat in front of them and leaned back. He reminded Jake of a sea lion basking on the beach. A plastic, green novelty derby hat sat on the coffee table in front of him. McClory laughed and picked it up. "Sorry, I meant to put this away after Saint Paddy's Day. I wore it in the parade. You ever been to Chicago on St. Patrick's Day, Mr. Rutledge?"

"Call me Jake, and no, I haven't. I'll bet it's a blast."

"Oh, it is. We dye the Chicago River green. It's a fun time. Now, what can I do for you?"

"I'm not sure exactly what Deke has told you—" Jake began.

THE MIDDLEMAN

"He said you want to know more about a couple of suicides," McClory interjected. He nodded at Matt. "Your uncle is one of them. And the other is that fellow in Lincoln Park. It's always a tragedy when someone ends their own life. I'll never understand it. We run across these things all the time, though. You wouldn't believe how many suicides we deal with."

"Could we start with my Uncle Charles?" Matt asked. "My family knows what we've been told by the police, but we've never been able to come to terms with it. We just can't believe Uncle Charles would kill himself. It simply wasn't in his nature."

McClory nodded. "I understand how you feel. Like I said, I knew Charles. And his wife Mary. My wife, Alice, and I would often see them at various charity galas in the city. Charles and I bonded at a golf tournament in Lake Geneva, oh, about four years ago. We got along splendidly there. I was especially distressed to hear what happened to him."

"Did you personally investigate his death, Chief McClory?" Jake asked.

"Me? No, no, that would have been the detectives in the 18th District, where Charles's high-rise is located near Navy Pier. I was interested in the case, though, and I thoroughly reviewed all the reports."

"Can you tell us what you recall about those reports?" Jake asked.

"The incident was at the end of March last year. You know then that even though Charles and Mary lived in Highland Park, they kept an apartment in the Loop right there on Lake Michigan. Beautiful spot, too. Charles apparently used it as his getaway when he wanted to work alone away from his office in Deerfield. You knew that, right?"

"Yes. He and my aunt also used the apartment whenever they wanted to go into Chicago for a weekend. Saved them from having to commute by car." Matt shrugged. "They could afford it."

"Right. Well, as I understand it, sometime after noon on that Wednesday, he went up to the roof of his building and just . . . jumped. He'd left a note on his desk in the apartment saying goodbye to his family and friends. Terrible thing."

Matt blinked. "Wait. What? Did you say he left a note?"

"Yes."

51

"But . . . he didn't leave a note."

"I'm pretty sure he did, Mr. Redmond."

"We were told by the police that they didn't find a note. It's why the suicide was such a mystery to everyone!"

McClory looked confused. "Really?"

"Do you have a copy of this note?"

"Well, sure. I took the liberty of pulling the files you were interested in." He pulled himself up from the chair and waddled over to his desk. He found a folder, opened it up, and produced a piece of paper. He brought it to Matt. Jake looked over to view it as well.

It was a photocopy of a piece of notepad with "Charles Redmond" printed at the top. Scribbled in block letters were the words, "MARY— PLEASE FORGIVE ME. I LOVE YOU. CHARLES."

Matt's jaw was open. "This is it? This is the note?"

"Yes, sir," McClory said as he returned to his chair and sat.

"I . . . I've never seen this before. I don't think my Aunt Mary has seen this either. Where is the original?"

"That would be stored away with evidence. Kept in a plastic evidence bag, you know."

"This is nuts, Chief McClory," Matt said. "How come my family was never shown the note? How come we were told there *wasn't* a note?"

"Are you sure you weren't told about it?"

"Yes!"

"Well, that's very strange."

Matt put his hand to his brow. "Detective . . . Detective . . . Brazos! That was who investigated it."

"That sounds right. Enrico Brazos."

"Can I talk to him? I need to confirm this. I don't think I'm wrong. I remember talking to my aunt and my cousin about it. The lack of a note was what made the whole thing so crazy."

"I'm afraid Detective Brazos is no longer with the Chicago PD," McClory said.

"No?"

"He and his family moved last Christmas. To Oregon, I believe. It had something to do with his wife's family, they had to go be near her mother. I can't recall. I can try to get you his forwarding information though."

"Could you please?"

"Yes. Leave me your number and I'll do that. I can't help but think there's been some kind of miscommunication."

"I'll say!" Matt was visibly upset. Jake wasn't sure how he should handle the situation, so he didn't say anything.

"I will share something with you, Mr. Redmond," McClory said. "My wife and I saw your uncle and aunt at the mayor's Christmas party in 2022. I noticed that he wasn't dancing with his wife. She was mingling with people she knew, but Charles was sitting on a couch staring at the fireplace and drinking bourbon. I asked him if he was all right, and Charles said, 'Oh, I'm just contemplating ending it all, how are you, chief?' I thought he was joking. I asked him what he meant by that, and he said, 'Never mind. Just feeling old.' Those were his exact words. I thought he seemed down, rather depressed. And I told him so. Charles just waved a hand at me as if it were no big deal, and he told me to forget about it. We then had a regular conversation, but then I got up and left him there on the couch. That's the last time I ever saw him."

"You think my Uncle Charles was suffering from depression?" Matt asked.

"It appeared that way to me. Hard to say. I'm no psychiatrist." The man looked at his watch, an indication that they were short on time.

There was a bit of an awkward silence until Jake spoke. "Can we talk about the other case? Doug Frankel?"

McClory nodded. "Right. That happened just a few months ago."

"Between Christmas and New Year this past year," Jake confirmed.

"Uh huh. Another tragedy. Mr. Frankel lived alone in a house in Lincoln Park, the 20th District. Apparently, he was sitting at his desk in his home office, and he shot himself in the temple with a Browning 9mm handgun. Now, *he* did not leave a note. The detectives working the case found no evidence of foul play, and Frankel's financial records did not indicate anything weird. The man was divorced, and he may have been distressed about that, but the divorce was already two years old. His widow claimed she didn't think he was upset about the marriage breaking up. It had been his idea to get divorced! No other stressors came up in the investigation. No, it was an open-and-shut suicide. The 'why' will likely always be a mystery. Suicides often are. They don't always leave a note or hint to anyone that they might do something like that."

"Chief McClory," Jake asked, "did the investigation look into his company, InsoDrugs, and anything that was going on there?"

"Yes, absolutely. The investigators found nothing at his work that might have been a reason for him to shoot himself. His colleagues at InsoDrugs were all shocked and surprised. Several were interviewed. Frankel was in good standing at the company and was well liked."

Jake then asked, "Chief, do you know a man by the name of Connor Devlin?"

McClory cocked his head slightly and answered, "I've met him a couple of times, but I don't *know* him. Why?"

"What do you know about him?"

"He's a successful businessman in this town, one of those wealthy VIP types." He looked at Matt. "Isn't he running your uncle's company now?"

"Yeah," Matt said. "He is."

"There wouldn't be any red flags around Mr. Devlin, would there?" Jake asked.

McClory laughed a little. "Red flags? Not that I know of. From what I've heard about Mr. Devlin, he likes to live big, spend money, and make money. He pops up in society pages a lot." He nodded at Matt. "Often with your cousin, Ms. Redmond!" He shrugged. "I think he's supposed to be a popular guy around town. I suppose to some folks if a fellow is rich and successful, then he must be corrupt or something. There are always rumors and whispers about men like that, aren't there?"

"So there *are* rumors and whispers about him?" Jake asked.

McClory shrugged. "I didn't say that. Just an observation from a working civil servant."

Jake and Matt looked at each other and nodded slightly. Then Jake said, "Well, Chief, unless you have anything else you can tell us, I think that's probably all we need today."

THE MIDDLEMAN

"I've told you all I have, gentlemen." Jake and Matt stood and waited while McClory strained to stand. "I don't know if I gave you what you needed, but I was happy to help. Mr. Redmond, write your name and number on that pad on my desk, and I'll send you Detective's Brazos contact info as soon as I lay my hands on it. Feel free to call my office, too."

"I'd appreciate that," Matt said. He went over to the desk, found the notepad, and scribbled the information. Then the men shook hands.

"Thank you for your time," Jake said.

"Give my best to Deke, and good luck with the work you're doing," McClory said. "And you have my condolences, Mr. Redmond."

Outside on the street, Matt said, "I need to talk to my Aunt Mary, and probably to Amy, too. This thing with the suicide note is bonkers."

"It is indeed odd," Jake admitted.

"What do you want to do now? I think I'm going to go to my aunt. Why don't I drop you at your hotel and we can touch base later?"

"Yes, let's. I'll grab my car and take a drive up to Lincoln Park," Jake said. "I'd like to get a look at Doug Frankel's house."

8

Matt dropped off Jake at his hotel and then headed up I-94 toward Wisconsin to the North Shore suburb of Highland Park. His Uncle Charles and Aunt Mary had lived in an amazing house there for as long as he could remember. He had fond memories of playing in their vast backyard with his sister. There were three huge silver maple trees that provided shade in the summer and gorgeous white canopies in the winter. Although at the time the couple didn't have children of their own, Uncle Charles had installed a swing set and monkey bars in the backyard especially for his nephew and niece. It was as if it was their own private playground. When cousin Amy arrived on the scene, Matt was already too old to pay much attention to her; he was in high school. He got to know Amy only in his later years, and it was more of a "Hi, how are ya?" kind of relationship. Amy's father—Matt's Uncle Andy—eventually came back to Illinois when Matt was in his thirties, and it was then that he and Amy shared a common admiration for the poor old rock star with more drug habits than the list of tracks on the Red Drops' *Greatest Hits* album.

As his speed crept up to seventy miles per hour on first the Kennedy and then the Edens Expressways, his cell phone rang. Coincidentally, it was Amy calling. Matt pushed the button on his steering wheel to place her on speaker.

"Hey, Amy, how are ya?"

"Hi, Matt. Did that investigator from Florida come in?"

"He did. Jake Rutledge. Nice guy." He began a rundown of the conversation with Chief McClory. "Do you know who he is?"

56

The Middleman

"Uh, I think I may have seen him on television news when he's doing a press conference or when his picture's in the paper. Never met him."

Matt continued to tell her about their talk. When he got to the question of the suicide note left by their uncle, Amy was clearly incensed.

"*What*? We weren't told about a note!"

"That's what I said. I saw it, though, Amy. Well, a photocopy of it."

"I distinctly remember the detective telling Aunt Mary and me that they didn't find a note."

"It's very strange. Chief McClory said he would send me Detective Brazos's contact information. That was the guy, right?"

"Yeah, that was him. Do we need to hire a lawyer just for this? This sounds like, I don't know, fraud or something."

Matt replied, "Let's give McClory a few days and see if he sends the info. Like he said, it could be a case of miscommunication or a stupid bureaucratic error."

"Screw that, Matt. I think it's pretty serious when the family is told one thing and the reality is something else."

"I agree, Amy, believe me. Let's just give it a few days and revisit it. In the meantime, how are things going with you and you-know-who?"

He heard Amy sigh heavily. Then she said, "Connor is suspicious about something. He's still having me followed. I spotted one of his henchmen on Saturday when I went to the dry cleaners. Have you spotted anyone?"

"I don't think so, not since I first thought they were after me. But then, it's possible I'm not looking very hard. There was a time I spotted that guy Ronan Barry. There were a couple of times when someone was outside my house, but when I went out to confront them, they drove off. Black Lincoln sedan."

"That's what they drive."

"I guess I'm not as freaked out about it as I was. Now that my friend Deke is listening to us, I feel a little better. I'm not as worried."

"Well, I'm very uncomfortable. I'm not sure what I should do."

"Amy, you need to leave Connor Devlin. Get out of that house. Go back to your old apartment. You still have it, right?"

"I never gave it up. All my mail is being forwarded to Connor's house, though."

"That's easily reversible."

"Leaving is not going to be easy, Matt. Connor is . . . very possessive. If I say I'm leaving, he's going to blow his top. There's no telling what he might do. Frankly, I'm scared of him. Besides, I'm still trying to collect information and evidence that we need."

"It's not worth the risk, Amy. Get out."

"And then there's the situation at EirePharma. He's the CEO of the company, and I'm the president. If we break up, things will be very awkward. It will affect work."

"I don't think he can fire you, though. You're a Redmond. You own stock in the company."

"Makes no difference."

"He can't fire you without cause, Amy. There are laws. You could sue his ass. And with your experience and clout, you could easily find another job."

"I don't want another job. And you saw what happened to Judge Carver. Connor and his followers practically ruined her career. There's no telling what he might do to me. Matt, my job is very important to me. I'm the last Redmond at EirePharma, and I feel an obligation to stay."

"Well, if EirePharma is doing unethical things then you shouldn't be a part of it. Amy, you could end up in jail!"

"The society pages would love that," Amy said with a little laugh. "I can see the headline: 'Love Nest Power Couple Convicted for Ethical Misconduct.' Geez, this is all so messed up. I often feel lost, stuck between a rock and a hard place. What are you doing now?"

"I'm on my way to Aunt Mary's. I want to ask her about the suicide note. In the back of my mind I'm wondering if you and I missed something. Maybe they told her about it and not us. I have no idea. I just want to confirm that she knew nothing about a note."

"Matt, what did the note look like?"

"It was on Uncle Charles's notepad stationery." Matt repeated its exact words.

"Did you recognize his signature?" she asked.

"Uh . . . you know, it wasn't a signature. The entire note was written in block letters. Including his name."

"That doesn't sound right. Uncle Charles always signed his name in cursive. The only time he wrote in block letters was when he'd list items for a grocery list and stick it on the fridge with a magnet. And I don't think he'd write such an impersonal note to Aunt Mary. No way."

"Are you saying the note's a fake?"

"What do you think?"

"I think we need to talk to Detective Brazos. Look, Amy, I'm approaching the exit to Highland Park. Let's talk later."

"All right. I have a meeting to go to, and Connor will be there. I'll need a few minutes to calm down. I don't want to be too flustered, or he'll notice. He's very perceptive. Matt?"

"What?"

"He knows something is up."

9

Jake arrived at Doug Frankel's former house in the Lincoln Park neighborhood. He knew that the area was a classic homestead for longtime residents but also a desired destination for hipsters and young middle-class families. The park itself contained a popular zoo, a lakefront trail, a conservatory, and gorgeous landscaped grounds. Historic row homes were the mainstay of the streets around it, but there was also the occasional detached house on the outskirts of the community. Frankel had lived in one of the latter. Jake had thought the ranch-style structure might contain three bedrooms, but from the outside it appeared too small for that. A little two-bedroom cottage, most likely. Perfect for a divorced single man, especially because the place was a rental. As Jake understood it, that was unusual for the Lincoln Park district.

He parked on the street in front of the house, ignoring the signs that indicated only permit holders were allowed to do so. Jake didn't think he'd be too long and was willing to risk getting a ticket. He got out of the car and approached the front of the house. Yellow police tape still covered the front door, although it was looking a bit ragged after four months.

Jake had done his homework by calling the realty office that rented the property to see when it was going to be available again. The fellow he talked to sounded frustrated and angry. "The police are dragging their knuckles. What else can they do there? I've complained and asked nicely and raised my voice to tell them to release the so-called 'crime scene' back to the owner so we can rent it out again. Of course, we'll now have to lower the rent because, you know, who wants to live in a place where a former tenant blew his brains out? Why don't you give me your name and number, and I'll put you on the growing list of interested parties." Jake replied that he'd "keep looking," and thanked the man for his time. It did indeed strike Jake as odd, however, that the police had not released the house if, as McClory had said, the case was an "open-and-shut suicide." Perhaps in a city the size of Chicago the police were overworked and overwhelmed, and something like removing tape from a house was a low priority.

Jake walked up the driveway to the front door. He wasn't about to force an entry, so he peered through a picture window to the left of the door. He could see furniture in the living room; a space for a flat screen television that had been mounted on the wall was empty. Next, he moved to the left side of the house and found two bedroom windows. Drapes on the inside blocked any view of the rooms. A wooden fence protected the backyard, but a gate that had no locks beckoned Jake to open it. The next thing he knew, he was standing on a rather pitiful deck against a sliding glass rear door. A small, decrepit Weber grill stood in the corner of the deck beside a lawn chair. Jake peered into the glass door and made out shapes of a kitchen counter and a dining area. The door was locked, of course.

He was beginning to think the trip here was a waste of time. Nevertheless, Jake moved to the other side of the house and found yet another window, this time with its inner drapes open. Jake could see a dresser and the edge of a bed. Possibly the master bedroom? On a whim, he tried to open the window . . . and it slid easily.

Jake was still on the back side of the wooden fence, hidden from the street. He eyed the neighboring houses. The rear of row houses was behind him. If someone was looking out their back window, they might see him. But it was the middle of the day. The neighborhood was quiet. No one seemed to be around.

What the hell . . .

He dug into his pockets and pulled out a pair of latex gloves. Once they were on, he placed his hands on the eave, hoisted himself up, and torpedoed his slim, lithe body through the opening. He managed to swing his legs around and drop to the carpeted floor.

He was indeed in the master bedroom. The covers and sheets had been stripped from the mattress. Jake opened the clothes closet and found it to be empty; only a few hangars were left on the rods. He then moved to the dresser. Surprisingly, there were some socks and underwear in the drawers along with folded T-shirts and other items of clothing. Jake supposed that whoever cleaned out the closet just wanted the suits and dress shirts, assuming that's what had been in there. He rummaged around the drawers to see if anything interesting might have remained, but he figured that the police likely did a fairly thorough job of checking out the house.

Jake moved on and took a quick look in the living room, kitchen, and little dining area. There was probably nothing of note there, so he went to the scene of the crime, such as it was. Was suicide still an illegal act? Jake knew it was in some states. But what were they going to do, arrest the victim?

He found the bedroom that was a makeshift home office. Drapes covered the windows, so he opened them to cast some light on the place. The desk and chair were still there, and two units of metal filing cabinets stood against the opposite wall. Bookshelves still contained a number of titles—mostly business and medical texts, but also a few thrillers in both hardcover and paperback.

A dark bloodstain decorated the wall behind the desk.

Jake moved closer and saw that the desk, too, had a few splatters of stain on top.

That's when he noticed the odor of the room. Musty, dank, sour. He figured the house had been closed up for four months, and the residual smell of death had stuck around to greet visitors. More light would help to examine the desk, so he reached over to a lamp on the desk and switched it on . . . but nothing happened. Jake realized then that there was no power at all in the house. Of course, it would have been cut off by the owner until it was rentable again. Why the police hadn't let the guy clear out the place and get it cleaned up was mind boggling. Had the cops simply forgot about it, and the task was lost in a bureaucratic bottomless pit?

Jake got out his phone and turned on the flashlight. Holding it in one hand, he went around to the back of the desk and opened the drawers, one by one. There was nothing of significance, just a stapler, a box of paper clips, pens, pencils, a Scotch tape dispenser, and reams of blank printer paper . . . the usual office junk. Of course, there was no computer. The printer, however, still sat on a small table. Jake wondered if printers kept stuff in their memory, but he ultimately thought looking into that would become a rabbit hole.

He didn't know what he was looking for. What could there possibly be in the house that would have any relevance to the case? Surely the cops had combed the joint. Technically, he was trespassing, so it was probably a good idea to just forget it and get the hell out of there.

On the way down the hall, though, he passed the bathroom. Was anything left in there? Jake decided to check it out. Using his phone flashlight, he went through the medicine cabinet (no meds, just a box of Band-Aids, a little tub of Vaseline, some dental floss, and travel toothpaste tubes). He opened the vanity drawers and found nothing. He'd struck out again.

"Let's go, Jake," he said aloud to himself.

As he started to step out of the bathroom into the hall, the light on his phone caught something pink on the carpet. He squatted to take a look, and he saw that it was a pinch of that cotton-candy-like woven fiberglass that is used as insulation in attics. Jake looked up, and there it was—the hatch to the attic, complete with a pull cord. It was the type of contraption into which stairs were built. Jake pulled the cord, opened the hatch, and the steps to the attic descended and hung there a foot off the floor. He stepped on the first slat, determined it would hold his weight, and then climbed up into the dark space.

The area was the size of the master bedroom and was full of . . . nothing. Just dust and cobwebs. Some of the insulation had indeed fallen or been loosened somehow and littered the wooden attic floor. Jake sighed and turned to descend the stairs. And then he saw it.

A black gym bag sat in the corner behind the opening in the floor. The cops obviously hadn't bothered to search the attic. It was an "open-and-shut suicide case."

He went over to it and saw that a piece of masking tape on the side displayed the legend: "D. Frankel." He picked it up by the handles. The thing wasn't empty.

Jake squatted and unzipped the bag. The only thing in it was an 8x11 brown envelope.

Jake pulled it out and opened it. Inside were a few 8x10 photographs and a note.

"Holy shit," he said. "Oh, my God. No."

He stared at the contents of the envelope for several seconds. Then he laid it all out and photographed everything. He then quickly put it all back in the envelope, stuffed the thing into the gym bag, and got the hell out of there.

Outside in his car, he called Gina at the law firm. When she answered he said, "Gina, it's Jake. I'm going to send you an email with some attachments. Don't look at the attachments. I mean it. I want you to move them into our encrypted digital vault in a folder marked 'Frankel evidence,' and then I'm deleting them from my phone. Got it?"

"Sure," she said. "But what are they? Can you give me a hint?"

"No. You don't want to know. Trust me."

10

Mary Redmond let Matt into the Highland Park house and then gave him a hug.

"How are you doing, Aunt Mary?"

"I'm fine, dear. Come in, come in. To what do I owe this lovely surprise?"

"I just wanted to talk to you. And see how you're doing, of course."

"Well, come in, it's very good to see you."

"And you, too, Aunt Mary."

Matt followed her through the large foyer to a living room space that was right out of a back issue of *Architectural Digest* from the 1990s. The furniture was an attractive mixture of expensive antiques and modern accents that resembled a faux but stylish French farmhouse. Charles Redmond had done very well in his career, and his home reflected it.

"Luisa is out right now doing the grocery shopping for me," Mary said, "but I can get you something. Coffee? Tea? Have you eaten?" Matt knew that Luisa, a longtime maid and cook, was also now Mary's part-time caretaker and helper. Both Matt and Amy thought she was wonderful for their aunt.

"I don't need anything, Aunt Mary, but if you're having coffee I won't say no to that."

"Have a seat, Matt, and I'll whip it up. I have one of those Keurig things, and they're fast. How do you take it?"

"Black, please. I'll follow you, and we can catch up in there while you make it."

65

Matt followed her as the woman passed through a swinging door and into the elegant dining room. A long table that could accommodate sixteen places dominated the space. Matt had enjoyed many meals here, but he had never witnessed a dinner with that many people at the table. When he was kid, there were often Thanksgiving and Christmas dinners at the house. Matt's parents were alive then, and he'd attend with them and his sister. He recalled Andy Redmond having a Thanksgiving dinner with everyone way back in 1970 when he was at the peak of his rock star years. Matt had been four years old. Amy hadn't been born yet. Andy had come dressed in a concert T-shirt, not for a holiday dinner with the family. He had also brought an uninvited guest—some woman with long blonde hair who was wearing too many beaded necklaces. Andy spent the dinner talking loudly and laughing a lot. Matt was too young to understand the dynamics going on, but he could read the room. The rest of the family was not happy with Andy that day. Matt had thought he was funny.

Another swinging door led to the kitchen, which was the size of most studio apartments. It was decked out in what had been modern furnishings twenty years earlier. Everything was spick-and-span. Mary and Luisa ran a tight ship.

Mary was tall, like her deceased husband. She did appear to be much frailer since the last time Matt had seen her. She had been ill for some time, even before her husband's death. It was some kind of neurological disorder. Matt had never thought much about the fact that his aunt was only eleven years older than he was (his Uncle Charles had been only fifteen years older), but she now appeared to have aged more than her sixty-nine years, especially in physical movement. Charles's demise had taken a lot of the vitality out of the woman who'd once been known for being the life of the party and a delightful hostess.

"Have you talked to Amy recently?" she asked as she started the Keurig.

"Yes, we've seen each other a few times in the past couple of months."

"Well, she hasn't seen *me*. I haven't seen her since Andy's funeral."

"Amy has said that she needs to visit you. I know she's very busy at EirePharma. She's taken on a whole lot more responsibility since . . . well, since Uncle Charles left us."

"I understand. But I'm practically her *mother*, you know."

"I do, and she does as well. I'll drop a subtle hint to her the next time I talk to her that she should come see you. I know she wants to, Aunt Mary."

They talked of the garden in the backyard that gave Mary something to do and how the play set that Charles had built so many years ago was simply rotting in the rear of the house. "Without grandchildren, that stuff is useless," she said. "Maybe you could see about getting someone to take it out of here? Donate it somewhere?"

"I can look into that."

Once the coffee was ready, they went into the dining room and sat at one end of the long table.

"So, what is so important that my nephew decided to come talk to me in person about?" she asked.

"Aunt Mary, I want you to know that there's a very good law firm investigating Connor Devlin, EirePharma, and the rise of insulin pricing. They're also looking into Uncle Charles's death, as well as Uncle Andy's."

Mary stirred her coffee for a few seconds and then said, "Did Amy initiate this?"

"We both did. It's a law firm in Florida run by a friend I went to law school with."

She nodded. "I was wondering myself if there were some legal issues involved with everything that's happened in the last year; you know, that insulin lawsuit—I still see and read the news. I have to say that I'm worried about Amy. I think she's lost her way a little bit. What do you think, Matt?"

"I think she's just very busy."

"You know, Amy got closer to her father after he moved back here from California. Charles was a little hurt by that. Oh, we knew that Andy was her real father. We accepted that. But Charles and I raised Amy. Charles was her *father*."

"She knows that, Aunt Mary."

"We didn't object to her getting closer to him, but we disapproved of his lifestyle. We had nothing to do with him, I'm afraid. Sometimes

Charles regretted that, but not often. You know that Charles and I have lived a strict Catholic life, and Amy was brought up that way, too. Andy Redmond's use of drugs and alcohol, his running around with trashy women, the way he squandered what money he made from his so-called fame . . . it was not worthy of the Redmond family name."

"And yet, Aunt Mary, Andy Redmond is more famous than any of us," Matt said with a bit of a chuckle, hoping to bring a little levity to the conversation.

"Hmpf. And what about you, Matt Redmond? You left the law practice. What are you doing with yourself now? Are you going to end up like your Uncle Andy?"

"No, no, that's not going to happen." Matt knew he needed to steer her in a different direction. "Listen, Aunt Mary, let me get back to the law firm and the investigation. I need to talk about Uncle Charles and . . . that day."

Mary sighed. "All right."

"When Uncle Charles . . . died . . . did he leave a note?"

She visibly stiffened. "You know he didn't."

"You were never told by the police that he left a note?"

She looked at him with wide eyes. "What are you saying?"

"One of the investigators from the law firm is in town. We went to talk to the chief of detectives in the city, um, James P. McClory. You've met him, right?"

Mary furrowed her brow. "I don't know. Maybe at some function in the city."

"Anyway, he showed me a photocopy of Uncle Charles's suicide note. Or what was allegedly his note." Matt knew that this would be a sensitive topic, so he did his best to deliver the news as gently as possible. He proceeded to tell her all about it, what the note said, and the questions surrounding it in terms of the block letters and such.

Mary sat silently for a full minute. Matt had to prompt her. "Aunt Mary? Are you okay?"

She inhaled deeply and said, "That was never shared with me. And that doesn't sound like Charles at all. That's how he would say goodbye to me? To *me*?" Tears formed in her eyes. Matt reached out and took her hand.

"Aunt Mary, I didn't mean to upset you. I just had to find out if the police told you something but didn't tell Amy or me. Now I know. I think that note we saw is a fake. It has to be."

"But why would they have a fake note?"

Matt leaned back in his chair. "Aunt Mary, what do you think of Connor Devlin?"

"Does he have something to do with this?"

"I don't know. Maybe. We're looking into it."

"I forget when Charles and I first met him. Well over a year ago. At first I thought he was so charming. Very handsome. He could have been on TV. He was a very smooth talker, too. I liked him a lot. Charles did, too. Charles thought he walked on water. I know that Charles and Mr. Devlin discussed the sale of EirePharma. Charles was enthusiastic about Connor buying the company at first."

"But something happened. Didn't it?"

"Yes, but I don't know what. Charles became obsessively worried about work."

"Would you say he was depressed? Chief McClory mentioned that he saw you both at some kind of holiday party and that Uncle Charles seemed depressed."

"I don't think he was the kind of depressed that would make a person jump off . . ." Her breath caught, but she quickly recovered. ". . . jump off a building. Unfortunately, Charles never discussed business with me."

"You have no clue what Uncle Charles was upset about?"

"No. He started spending more time at our apartment in the city. Sometimes he'd spend days there and not go into the office in Deerfield, and work from 'home,' as he put it. Then he was dead. Shortly after that, the board approved Connor's offer to buy the company. All of Charles's shares in the company were bought out. That includes me; I have no claim whatsoever on EirePharma. I believe Amy made out fairly well in part ownership, but Connor owns the majority of the stock. It's a private company, you know."

"I understand."

"Don't you have some of the stock?"

"Yes. My sister and I have a whopping 19 percent, so nine and a half shares each. I believe Amy has thirty shares. Connor Devlin has fifty-one, the majority."

"At the time I thought this was all a good thing. The company was in trouble, apparently. And Amy seemed to make out well in the deal. And she and Connor . . . well, you know."

"Yes, I do. I think that relationship is cooling down now. Do you approve of Amy and Devlin's engagement?"

"Oh, at first I did. I thought it was wonderful. Now . . . I don't know. I see Amy so very little these days. She is so busy at work. I suppose I have some doubts about it, especially if it's, as you say, 'cooling down.'"

Matt nodded. "You said you found Connor Devlin charming at first. What do you think now?"

"I don't know what to think. Charles's enthusiasm for the man had begun to wane. I really didn't know why, but perhaps that affected my own feelings toward Connor. But whatever reservations about him that I was beginning to have were quelled by the fact that Amy liked him and they were seeing each other."

Matt nodded. "What can you tell me about Uncle Charles's last few days? I'm sorry if this is painful, but I need to know."

Aunt Mary sighed. "Like I said, he was spending more days downtown. He conducted business there and hardly went into the office in Deerfield. Board members and others would have to travel to Chicago to meet with him there. I spoke to Charles on the morning of the day it . . . happened. He didn't seem any different. In fact, he said he'd be coming home over the coming weekend."

"You told that to the police?"

"Of course. They gave me some story about how certain people who commit suicide are very good at hiding their pain and will tell loved ones things they want to hear."

"Do you remember Detective Brazos? He investigated what happened."

"I . . . I think so. There were several policemen who talked to me. I was so flustered and upset that I'm afraid I don't remember a lot about it. Maybe I've tried to forget!"

"That's understandable, Aunt Mary. I won't bother you anymore about this now. I'm going to see if I can find Detective Brazos and ask him about that suicide note. I just have one more thing to ask you. Do you know if Uncle Charles saw Connor Devlin at all in those last few days?"

She paused, turning away to think. "You know, the police never asked me that," she said after a beat. "I never really considered it either. He might have." She suddenly put a hand to her cheek, facing him again. "My God, now I remember. I'd completely forgotten it. Now that you bring it up, I believe . . . I'm almost *positive* that Charles told me he was having lunch with Connor that very same day. I don't know if he did, though."

"You're not sure?" Matt asked.

Mary shook her head. "I never spoke to Charles again."

11

Another day at the office, another weeknight not at home.

Amy Redmond noted that the time was nearly 8:00. She'd had hunger pains two hours earlier, but the task at hand eventually became archaeological, and she wasn't sure if she'd be able to find what she was looking for before she became faint. It could happen if she missed a meal. She could become so engrossed in her work that she'd forget about eating, and then when it came time to stand up, she would feel dizzy and have to sit down again.

But it was the time in the evening when practically no one else was in the EirePharma office building. At least, they weren't in the office of Financial Records. Amy knew there were workaholics on the payroll in various departments elsewhere in the building who might still be at their desks. More power to them. Hard work is what made EirePharma a success.

Amy wasn't really doing EirePharma work, though. Since Connor was in Minneapolis and wouldn't return until the next day, she thought it was a good opportunity to comb through some of the tax files and financial statements stored in the secured room. Kenneth Malloy, EirePharma's chief financial officer, had left for the day. Kenneth ruled his fiefdom in the company with a barbed fist, and even Amy, the president, would have to provide a reason to be allowed into the records room. It was usually locked with a keycard entry device available only to upper echelon employees, including Amy. Technically, she should be able to go into the Financial Records storeroom any time she wanted, but if Kenneth were present, he would invariably ask, "What can I do for you? Is there something specific you're looking for? Maybe I can help." And then he wouldn't leave her alone until she stated exactly what she wanted. He'd always been that way.

In this case, though, she wouldn't have wanted Kenneth Malloy to know what she was after. He'd become very tight with Connor after the changeover in leadership. They were practically bosom buddies. Connor and Kenneth played golf together, and they were always in meetings to strategize the "future of the company." Whatever wrongdoing, if any, that Connor might be involved in, Kenneth was likely an accomplice.

Ever since Amy and Matt had been discussing the suspicious issues surrounding EirePharma, one of the topics that always came up was that of InsoDrugs and the case of Doug Frankel. Amy wanted to study all the files on InsoDrugs and determine exactly what was going on between EirePharma and the drug manufacturer. A lot of the material was digital, of course, and she had already scrutinized Docusign contracts and monthly statements of payments from InsoDrugs to EirePharma for its PBM services. She had also already seen EirePharma's bank statements that laid out the company's income. Unfortunately, the bank statements did not always indicate the payer of an amount that went into EirePharma's coffers. Many times companies with whom the PBM did business paid through a third-party service that handled their accounting. You'd have to manually open the details of an electronic transaction in order to find out exactly where a payment was coming from. That took time, and being online in the digital files left a footprint. Kenneth would know she'd been looking around online.

Stored in the Records room, however, were hard copies of transaction receipts. Ever since an IRS audit back in the early 2010s, it had been a company policy that physical documentation of transactions be created and stored. This had come in handy during the recent class action lawsuit over insulin pricing. Kenneth Malloy had produced some magic evidence that the second judge in the case completely bought, and it had come out of the records room. Amy thought that if only she had been paying more attention to what was going on last year with that case and the treatment of Judge Carver, she might have done something about it.

Or would she have?

Amy knew fully well that she had been blind and oblivious to the company's actions over the previous year. She'd been under Connor's spell. He had placed her in the position of spokesperson and "face" of EirePharma, and at first she'd enjoyed it.

But now it was wearing off.

She sat at a small desk in the records room, going through the several manila folders that contained InsoDrugs material. EirePharma had done business with InsoDrugs for years, but right after the PBM was sold to Connor Devlin, things changed. Connor's big thing was insulin, and he wanted prices to go even higher. Last fall Connor had wined and dined InsoDrugs' COO, Doug Frankel, who had been skittish about raising the price of insulin, to Connor's frustration. This was despite the fact that her uncle, Charles, and Frankel had indeed agreed to raise the price a couple of times in small increments. InsoDrugs' CEO, Steven Scales, hadn't had much to do with any of this—it was more Frankel's bailiwick.

One day before last Thanksgiving, she had come into Connor's office to hear him ending a conversation on the phone. Connor was laughing and acting like whoever was on the other end was his best friend. When he hung up, Amy had asked him who he'd been talking to. Connor, still in the aftermath of a good laugh, said, "Oh, that was Steven Scales. He cracks me up." Amy didn't say anything. But she hadn't known Connor was so friendly with InsoDrugs' CEO. She'd thought he dealt only with Frankel.

She now had in her hands physical statements that displayed very interesting data. Amy took out her phone and took photos of all the relevant documents as she perused them.

Beginning in February 2024, a month after Frankel's apparent suicide, the price of InsoDrugs' insulin tripled. This resulted in major profit for EirePharma in the form of payments for "services." Amy knew that those were actually kickbacks.

Links and references to several insurance companies directed Amy to track down contracts and agreements with them, and sure enough, InsoDrugs' insulin had simultaneously been placed on the Tier 1 approved drug formulary list of insurance firms with which EirePharma did business. InsoDrugs had granted Devlin the price increase he was after. InsoDrugs increased their profits, and EirePharma was entitled to bigger payoffs because of that. This also meant that consumers' carriers would have to pay more of the insulin cost if they bought InsoDrugs' product as opposed to that of the competition. That was simply the cost of doing business for most insurance companies. Consumers would be the real victims as their costs for copays continued to increase. It was pretty clear to Amy that crime had paid big dividends for EirePharma almost overnight.

She wasn't well versed in the law, but Matt had his own ideas. If their suspicions were correct, then Connor considered Frankel to be an obstacle and he had somehow manipulated the man into committing suicide. If Connor had blackmailed Frankel, how was this done? Some kind of extortion? Wouldn't that be a racketeering scheme?

The door to the records room opened, startling the hell out of her.

"Oh, there you are!" Connor exclaimed. He seemed simultaneously happy to see her and confused by her presence in this location.

"Connor!" She quickly closed the folder that was open, swiveled in the task chair, and put the folder away in its space in the filing cabinet drawer. She pretended to thumb through more files, turning her head back and forth to him. "I thought you were in Minneapolis!"

"I was. I just got back."

"You didn't spend the night?"

"Didn't have to. What are you doing in here?"

She turned back to him and presented an exaggerated sigh, as if she'd been working hard. "Oh, I was trying to track down the contract with Anthem in California. It's up for renewal. and I wanted to see what was in the old one. I thought I'd find it in here."

"Isn't it online?"

"No, it wasn't a digital contract then. It's somewhere in here."

Connor stepped over to the filing cabinet, which was still open. "Maybe you're looking in the wrong drawer. That's H through L. Wouldn't Anthem be over there with A?"

Amy laughed. "Probably! I first needed to look up something else over here—oh, never mind. It's not important, it can wait until tomorrow."

She closed the drawer with a flourish. She stood and embraced him. "I'm glad you're back. I'm starving. The time got away from me. You know how I get."

Connor caressed her hair, kissed her, and then said, "Yes, I do know how you get." He studied her face for a moment.

"What?"

"Nothing, just looking at my dream girl. Come on. I'm hungry, too. Let's go home."

Amy let him go first. She paused at the door and thought she would die. She closed her eyes and took a deep breath.

Oh, my God . . . does he suspect anything . . . ?

She shook it off. She had to.

"You coming?" he called from the hallway.

"Yes!" She quickly looked around to make sure she hadn't left out anything incriminating, hit the lights, and closed the door. It automatically locked behind her.

"I just need to get my purse and coat," she said, heading past him down the hall.

"I'll wait for you at the elevators."

"All right."

When she got to her office, she noted that her heart was pounding furiously in her chest.

12

Jake was back in Florida after his short visit to Chicago. Deke called the team together for another quick status discussion in the conference room. The jury was still out on whether it was really something with which the firm should bother. It might be May before Deke could give the thing any serious consideration, but he thought it was beneficial to hear what his colleagues had to say.

"I have here a report from Matt Redmond." Deke said. "I believe copies have been distributed to you all. According to Matt, Charles Redmond's widow, Mary Redmond, claims that Charles told her that he was going to have lunch with Connor Devlin on the day that Charles jumped off the high-rise in Chicago. Does that get your interest at all?"

Michael spoke first. "Okay, that's a start."

Deke said, "I'm more interested in what Matt and Amy Redmond say about the suicide note. The police never told them about it. Was it something that was later found by the cops? How does something as important as that get screwed up in a police investigation?"

"That would never happen by mistake," Carol added, "unless you were dealing with a bunch of morons doing the investigation. That's terrible for the family."

Jake said, "You'll see in my report that Chief McClory mentioned that the lead investigator on that was a Detective Brazos, who moved away from Illinois. Matt said he would try to find him and clarify that."

Carol asked, "Have you spoken to your police chief pal about it, Deke?"

"Not yet. I will, though, because our next order of business might involve him. Jake, please follow up with Matt about Detective Brazos. Now, are there any other thoughts about what Matt had to say?"

Gina answered, "It all sounds so slimy. Something is definitely not right about any of this. That said, Sarah and I have been looking into the sale of EirePharma to Connor Devlin and so far we can't find anything wrong with it. The EirePharma board approved the sale and it went forward without a hiccup after Charles Redmond's death."

"You have some information regarding Mr. Devlin now?"

"Yes, we've also been digging into Mr. Devlin's life. What we know so far is that he came to the United States from Ireland in 1993 and worked for Baxter Labs in the Chicago area for a few years as a sales exec. He was in his early thirties then. Mr. Devlin is fifty-seven now, if his immigration records are correct. He became an American citizen in 2003."

"When did he leave Baxter Labs?" Deke asked.

Sarah replied, "In 1997. He then apparently got involved in the insurance business, and his employment record shows that he jumped around several firms for six or seven years, both in Illinois and in California. In 2004, he suddenly became the head of a start-up PBM in Wisconsin, but he managed to get that sold to a bigger company in Illinois—with him moving with it into a top executive position. In 2010 he was listed in *Chicago* magazine as a 'Chicago businessman to watch' because he had by then struck out on his own as the head of Devlin Clover, Inc. This was a consulting company devoted to telling PBMs, mostly small start-up drug companies and smaller insurance companies, how to maximize their profits. It was essentially a one-man band. In most cases, his advice was to flip the company. He became a millionaire during this period."

Gina added, "He was wealthy to begin with. Family money in Ireland. We're still trying to figure out what those ties are. We're not exactly sure what kind of 'family money' he ended up with. Oh, and the majority holdings of EirePharma shares were sold to Devlin Clover, Inc., and not to Mr. Devlin personally. But Mr. Devlin *is* Devlin Clover, so it doesn't make much difference."

THE MIDDLEMAN

"That's a start, thank you," Deke said. "Michael, do you have anything?"

"Oh, I distributed some of those names of Devlin's associates to everyone to see if we could dig up any information about them. Ronan Barry, Lance Macdonald, Pat Beckett, Smithy something or other, and someone called Petey-o."

"Petey-o?" Carol asked. "Really?"

Michael shrugged. "Amy mentioned him." He looked back at Deke, who then turned to Jake and raised his eyebrows.

"Am I up?" Jake asked. "Okay, then. You all have my report on Doug Frankel. You know me. I couldn't help entering Frankel's house to have a look around."

"It's not the first time you've committed the crime of breaking and entering," Carol said with a smirk.

"Only in the pursuit of justice. Besides, the door was unlocked!" Jake protested.

"Was it a door or a window?" Michael asked.

"All right, so it was a window. Still, it was inviting me to slip inside. The house was just sitting there with police tape on the door that was so old it was falling off."

"But you found something significant," Deke said.

"I did." He had distributed copies of *some* of the photos he had taken on his phone. "Look at the handouts. The first is the hatch to Frankel's attic with the stairs going up. The police obviously didn't search the attic. They figured Frankel committed suicide, so what was the point of climbing up into the attic? Well, I did it. The second is the view of the attic where the gym bag was sitting. The third is the contents of the gym bag open, and you can see the envelope. I purposely did not include the pictures of the photographs that were in the envelope."

"Why not?" Gina asked.

Deke answered, "You don't want to see them. It's child pornography. Terrible stuff. It's beyond disturbing. Jake, I hope you've deleted those photos from your phone."

"Oh, I have, believe me. The only copies are in our digital storage locker marked as evidence. That last picture you all have is of the note that was included in the envelope with the offending photographs. As you can see, it's a printout of an email. It's from Frankel, that's his email address in the 'From' line. The addressee is blackened out, so we don't know who he sent the email to. The subject line is 'Insulin.' There's no salutation, no 'Dear so-and-so.' It's a short-and-sweet missive in which Frankel simply says that he refuses to raise the price of insulin any more than where it's already at, and that it's already gone way beyond what is right. He asks that he not be contacted about it anymore. Now . . . someone took a black marker and wrote on the printout beneath Frankel's message. I believe that whoever received this email did it. He handwrote his reply, and then he sent it back to Frankel with the photographs. The envelope was postmarked December 22, 2023, so Frankel likely received it either right before or right after Christmas. He was dead a few days later."

Deke said, "The guy's message is clear. 'Agree to the terms presented to you by the PBM doing business with you or the police will find these photographs. If you destroy them, more will appear where you least expect them.' It's blackmail, plain and simple. Note that it's worded so that is reads as if a third party wrote it, and not someone at EirePharma."

Sarah slightly raised her hand and looked at Jake. "I have a question."

"Yes?"

"Is Mr. Frankel in the photographs?"

"Thankfully, no. We don't know if these are pictures that Frankel took himself as the photographer, or if he in truth had nothing to do with them. Unfortunately, when it comes to child porn, it's very difficult to prove the evidence doesn't belong to you. Just the accusation would have ruined him."

Michael said, "I wonder if Frankel's widow knew about her husband's special interests, assuming he really did have those kinds of thoughts."

"They did get a divorce," Jake replied, "but it's my understanding they were on speaking terms and that the divorce was his idea. I'm thinking that she didn't know and still doesn't."

Carol asked, "The police never found that gym bag, right?"

"I don't think so, no. It was just sitting up in the attic. I think Frankel himself hid it there."

"Wouldn't he have destroyed the photos if he were planning to kill himself?" Carol reasoned. "Why keep them up there for somebody to eventually find?"

"That's a good question," Jake agreed, but then shrugged. "Unless he really didn't kill himself."

"Geez, the plot thickens," Michael muttered. "Are we making the leap to suspect someone of murdering Frankel? Why?"

"The insulin prices did go up *after* Mr. Frankel's demise," Gina offered. "I've been noting the pricing of the drug during the time periods we're talking about. InsoDrugs did raise the price a couple of times, but only in small increments. Frankel was an impediment to raising the prices a lot."

"A blackmail followed by a suicide I can understand," Jake said. "But you'd think Frankel would get rid of that blackmail material first. Why would he want anyone to find it? And if he was murdered, then what's the point of the blackmail? Unless we're talking about two different things perpetrated by two different entities."

Deke said, "Well, look. We can't do anything about this evidence. It was obtained illegally. It informs us of some unsavory things, but it's nothing we can work with in court. What I think I will do is forward a message to Chief McClory in Chicago and tell him that we have reason to believe that there may or may not be evidence in Frankel's case up in the attic of his house. If he wants to know how we know this, I'm going to say our investigator learned about it from an anonymous source." Deke shrugged and rolled his eyes.

Jake said, "It's the truth, Deke. Whoever left the bag in the attic is anonymous—to me."

Deke nodded. "Hopefully, the Chicago PD will investigate further into why Mr. Frankel shot himself. Or not."

"And more importantly," Michael said, "who was blackmailing him."

Carol cleared her throat and grumbled, "I'm beginning to have some suspicions about who that might be."

13

May 2024

Matt Redmond slammed down the empty tequila shot glass on the bar counter.

"Another?" the bartender asked.

"Why not, George?" Matt said with intentionally exaggerated enthusiasm. He'd lost count of how many he'd already had. Seven? Eight? And these were on top of two glasses of Woodford Reserve Double Oaked bourbon, his favorite. Did tequila and bourbon mix? He was about to find out.

George, a man who appeared to be a hundred years old but with the energy of someone in their twenties, poured another shot glass of premium Teremana Tequila. "You do know whose tequila this is?"

"You mean who made it? Who owns the label?"

"Yeah."

"The Rock, man. Dwayne Johnson!"

"You win the no-prize!"

"It's mighty fine."

"Yes, it is. By the way, this is last call."

Matt looked at his watch. It was *way* past his bedtime. "Damn, it's almost time to get up and have breakfast and coffee." He looked up at George and said, "If it's last call, then pour one more shot glass of the Rock, please."

The bartender was happy to oblige, and then handed Matt the tab.

Two a.m. in Chicago was when bars that played by the rules served the last drink of the night. Matt knew it would be cold outside when he left the Quality Time bar. The weather was finally spring in the Midwest, but nights could still be chilly. Especially near the witching hour.

George swiped Matt's credit card and then handed it and the receipt back to him. "Thank you, Matt. Be careful going home. You want me to call you a cab?"

"I'm fine, George," Matt said.

"Well, you're slurring your words a bit, buddy, and it's my duty to at least offer."

Matt waved a hand at him. "I've got my Uncle Andy in me, you know. He could drive anywhere, anytime, and he'd be much more stoned or drunk that I am. I just feel a buzz. Seriously. I'm okay. And besides . . . you forget that I *walked* here. I live a quarter mile away!"

George smiled. "I did forget. Sorry. You know, speaking of your uncle, the Red Drops was one of the first concerts I ever saw. Back when the Kinetic Playground was in operation. Remember that place?"

"I sure do! Although I was too young then to go. The Red Drops played there when I was, uh, three. Or four. I don't know. It closed when I was about six."

"I remember seeing Led Zeppelin, Jethro Tull, and Savoy Brown there in 1969, all three in one night. Man, to tell you the truth, I'm surprised *I* remember it, ha ha!"

"You old man. Me, I'm a young sprout." Matt held out a hand and George shook it. "See you later, alimony."

"In a while, crocadoodle dandy."

Matt managed to stand, and that's when he considered that perhaps he had indeed imbibed more than he should have. He donned his light jacket and left the near-empty bar. Like most big cities, Chicago was also one that never slept, but traffic was practically nil at 2:10 a.m. The streetlamps illuminated Diversey Street quite well. It would be a short fifteen-minute walk to the townhome on Richmond Street that he'd bought several years ago. It was a chic neighborhood at the northern edge of the Logan Square area, so the prewar home cost a fortune. He loved it, though. It was his Bachelor Pad Royale.

The night air was bracing, as he'd expected, but this helped to sober him up some. He walked from the corner bar to the corner of Richmond, crossed Diversey, and headed south.

Matt thought of his Uncle Andy. Yep, the rock star absolutely would have gotten behind the wheel of his Econoline van full of his gear after downing three times more alcohol than Matt had that evening, chased it with two joints, maybe a little coke, and who knew what else. And Uncle Andy had experienced his fair share of fender benders and smash-ups. He never killed anyone or himself, though, not that this was an excuse to get behind a wheel while intoxicated.

As he walked, these thoughts brought back into his head the situation with insulin and EirePharma. He hadn't heard from his pal Nick Deketomis in Florida in a while. The last message was after that investigator, Jake, was down to look into a few things. Deke had shared with him what they'd learned, including what they'd discussed about Uncle Charles's strange suicide note. However, Deke was busy on another case, so there wasn't much that could be done at the moment. His friend had also warned him that they didn't have a lot to go on, and that it was possible that they couldn't pursue a lawsuit.

That had been a few weeks earlier, back in April. Matt decided that he'd give Deke a call in the next day or so and nudge him a bit. Matt was also tired of waiting for Chief McClory to get back to him about Detective Brazos. He made a mental note to call the chief's office in the morning to rattle that man's cage.

Just another couple of blocks to go and he'd be home. Matt continued to muse about his uncle as he walked, when two men emerged from a black sedan that was parked at the curb up ahead. They wore coats and appeared to be big guys, but Matt was too far away, and the lighting on the side street of Richmond was not the best. As they got closer, though, he knew exactly who they were.

"Matt Redmond!" the tallest one declared. "Fancy meeting you here in the middle of the night like this!"

"Yeah, how you doin', Matt?" the other asked.

"Gentlemen," Matt said, "I'm just on my way home. Have a nice night." He kept walking, but as he passed them, they turned around and accompanied him, one on either side.

"You know, Matt, you've been drinking," the tall one said. "It's not good to walk alone at night in Chicago, especially if you're inebriated."

"Yeah," the other one agreed. "You might not be aware of your surroundings. Chicago can be a rough town."

Matt knew he was in trouble. "Guys, I'm fine, thanks, now just take a hike." He kept going, but he prepared himself mentally for the possibility that he might have to defend himself.

The street came to a T-intersection with an alley. A passageway for city garbage trucks, it was a dark, unlit, narrow, unpaved road the width of one vehicle. Trash dumpsters lined the back of townhomes and other buildings that disappeared into shadow.

Matt attempted to bolt away from the men and run across Richmond, but the tall man was ready for the move. He swung an arm around Matt's chest and threw him back to the second guy. Matt struggled, throwing wild punches anywhere that he could. The fact that he was soused didn't help. Some blows connected, but the two bigger men easily overpowered him and forced him into the alley.

"Hel—!" Matt cried, but a sledgehammer punch to his face cut off his call of distress. It was likely no one could hear him in the alley anyway, and most people living in the houses around them were almost certainly asleep.

A powerhouse fist drove into Matt's abdomen, causing him to completely lose his breath. As he gasped for air, he doubled over, exposing the back of his head for a piledriver slam that sent Matt to the ground.

"We heard you been talking to lawyers, Matt," the tall man said.

"Yeah, this is what you get for talking to lawyers, Matt," the other one echoed.

Then the kicks began. Repetitive, damaging, steel-cap shoe kicks. Delivered to Matt's head, neck, ribs, back, kidneys, legs, and arms. The punishment continued long after Matt lost consciousness.

It persisted long after the two men thought that Matt Redmond was no longer breathing. It had evolved into sport.

The two men finally stopped, caught their own breath, and then nodded to each other with a sense of accomplishment. The shorter one squatted next to the corpse and frisked it. He removed a wallet, took the cash and credit cards, and dropped the empty wallet next to Matt's bloody head. The driver's license was left inside so that the cops could identify him. Next, the thug took Matt's cell phone. Without another word, they left the alley and walked back to the black sedan, still parked at the curb.

Connor Devlin sat in the back seat. Before getting in the car, both men removed their gory shoes and put them in separate burlap bags. Their leather gloves followed. The tall man popped the trunk, and they threw the burlap bags inside. This was a routine that the two henchmen had perfected. The evidence would be properly disposed of later. Then they both got into the car. The tall man settled behind the wheel and put on a second pair of shoes. The other man took the front passenger seat, also donned another set of footwear, and then handed the phone to Devlin.

The phone required a PIN to access it, which Devlin had expected, but he was confident his IT guy could hack into it. In the meantime, he shut it off completely so that cell towers would not be able to track its location.

"All good, Ronan?"

Ronan Barry started up the car and pulled out onto the road. "Cops'll think he was the victim of just another Chicago mugging. Hell, twenty to thirty people get shot every weekend in this shithole city. What's one more old drunk being beaten to death going to mean to anyone?"

Devlin nodded to himself.

The man in the passenger seat added, "Oh, and by the way, there was enough cash in the wallet to treat us all to a dinner at Morton's Steakhouse."

As the car headed for the I-94 expressway, Devlin put the phone in his pocket and settled back for the drive to the suburbs.

"A juicy tenderloin sounds pretty good," he said. "We'll put that on the agenda."

The two men in front laughed.

PART TWO
JANUARY 2023–JANUARY 2024

14

Sixteen Months Earlier: January 2023

Amy Redmond hated sitting in with Nancy Shick, the human resources manager, when there were layoffs. Unfortunately, this unpleasant task was occurring more often. EirePharma simply wasn't raking in enough profits to justify the expense of the huge campus and building the company owned in Deerfield. The payroll alone was enough to sink the ship. Thus, her Uncle Charles had dictated, with the board's approval, to gently begin the layoffs four months earlier. Too many corporations often laid off employees at Christmastime, and Amy had fought hard not to do that. There had been a few axes falling in October and November, but none in December. Now that it was a new year, there had to be a few more.

As vice president of EirePharma, Amy had many responsibilities and, unfortunately, playing wingman to Nancy's HR firings was one of them. The president, Aaron Blinken, certainly wouldn't stoop to perform such a task. It was not appropriate, understandably, for her Uncle Charles, the CEO, to do so. Amy was the most senior ranking executive of the corporation outside of those two men, so she had no choice in the matter.

Nancy finished with the tenth and final terminated employee just before lunch. Amy commiserated with her colleague on the difficulty of that job, but at least no former employee had made a scene. It wasn't unexpected. There had been a pall over EirePharma over the last year that layoffs were coming. Some of the staff had even quietly begun looking for alternative employment. In the long run, the morning turned out to be not as bad as she had feared.

Amy had just sat at her desk in her own office to open a sack lunch she'd brought from her apartment in Northbrook when the phone buzzed. Normally she would have let it go to her voicemail, but it was her uncle's line. She picked it up.

"Hi."

"Amy, how did this morning go?" Charles asked.

"All right. There were no tears. No one cursed. Aloud, anyway."

"Well, sorry you and Nancy had to do that."

"And it's not over."

"No, I'm afraid not. Listen, are you doing anything? Can you come to my office?"

"I was just about to bite into a sandwich. Is it pressing?"

"Finish your lunch and then come down, please." With that, he hung up.

"Okay, Uncle Charles," she said into the dead receiver.

* * *

Charles Redmond, the seventy-one-year-old man who had taken over EirePharma when his brother, Terrence, passed away twelve years earlier, was a tall, thin, and chiseled man with fading red hair. The color was a shared trait among the Redmond family, but the older they got, the once flaming red became lighter in shade. Amy was not one to be biased toward her family's looks, but she had been known to thank Mother Nature for the Redmonds' attractiveness. Everyone in the family could have been models—men and women alike. When her father, the rock star Andy Redmond, had first hit the music scene in the late 1960s, he'd been considered to be a redheaded dreamboat. High school- and college-aged girls had posters of him on their bedroom walls. Charles didn't inherit the star quality looks his half-brother had, but he was still a distinguished, striking man. His pleasant and friendly demeanor also helped him to be well liked among his staff and peers.

When Amy came into his office, Charles was sitting at his desk reading stacks of material. He also seemed to be humming to himself.

Humming to himself?

Now Amy really wondered what was up. Her uncle had been relatively low-key over the holidays, down over the bad fortunes of the company. Now he was . . . chipper?

Charles looked up and said, "Ah, come in, Amy, have a seat."

"What are you working on?" she asked as she plopped into the big comfy chair that faced him.

"Oh, just these insurance company statements. Tedious stuff. Just double-checking the work our team has already done. The buck stops here, you know." He waggled his eyebrows, something Amy hadn't seen him do for ages. She just smiled and waited for him to continue. He set aside the sheet he'd been reviewing and then looked at her. "Are you free at three o'clock today?" he asked.

"I think so. Why?"

"I'd like you to meet a potential buyer of the company. He's coming in to talk about it."

Amy blinked. "What?"

Charles grinned. "I know. It's a shocker. I've been meaning to let you in on what I've been thinking."

"I didn't know the family business was up for sale."

"It isn't. Not really," he said, leaning back in the reclining chair. "But, as you know, we've been losing money and the board isn't happy. Thankfully, the Redmond family controls all the stock, but are *you* happy that your shares are losing value?"

"To tell you the truth, Uncle Charles, I don't even keep track of it. I never look at stock prices. We're a private company. Who cares?"

"Well, *I* do. So should you. We don't want to *lose* the family business, do we? At least, not before we *sell* it for a good price if we have to. Look, I just thought it would be prudent to entertain some offers just to see how far someone will go. There have been some."

"Really?"

Charles nodded. "This PBM business is a competitive field, Amy. I'm afraid I'm not quite the shark that some CEOs are that do this kind of work. It's pretty cutthroat out there. They play dirty, and it's the dirtiest ones that make the big money. We'll never be in that crowd, Amy."

"I know that."

"This thing with insulin is a big headache. All the drug manufacturers are raising the price of insulin, and their PBMs are pushing the increases and, in turn, profiting from it. InsoDrugs, so far, hasn't bowed to the pressure. They still have one of the more affordable products."

"If you have insurance."

"Right. I've had some discussions with Doug Frankel over there, and he's not willing to raise the price too much. Over the last year we both agreed that the price should go up a little, and it did. Very small amounts. But he doesn't think that raising the price a lot is the right thing to do. I tend to agree with him. What kind of CEO does that make me?"

"It means you're honest and ethical, Uncle Charles."

He smiled at that. "Thanks, I appreciate it." Then his demeanor immediately changed. "I think I might have to get rid of Aaron."

Amy wasn't surprised. "You've mentioned that to me before."

"You haven't said anything to anyone, have you?"

"About Aaron Blinken? No."

"He suspects something is up. He'll be at the meeting this afternoon, too, by the way."

Amy said, "He hasn't been pulling his weight. Who would you replace him with? Someone from within EirePharma?"

Charles raised his eyebrow at her. "You want the job?"

"Well . . . sure. I could do it."

Charles cocked his head a bit to indicate that the thought was now safely in the back of his mind. "Amy, come back here at three and meet this character. I think you'll like him. He's quite an interesting fellow."

"What's his name?"

"Connor Devlin."

* * *

Back at her desk, Amy placed a set of worldwide news items compiled by the company's analysts that studied trends and significant items of interest that might affect EirePharma. Before she could begin to read, though, her cell phone rang. The caller ID was "Dad." She answered it.

"Hey, what's up?"

"You busy, darlin'?" Andy Redmond asked. His voice was scratchy as hell. Amy immediately knew he'd been up all night, probably drinking and smoking.

"I'm at work, Dad, of course I'm busy. Anything wrong?"

"No, no, maybe I just wanted to hear my daughter's voice. I had a rough night again."

Amy closed her eyes and silently wished the problem away, but it was no good. "What's wrong now?"

"It's the damn diabetes. It's making me feel like shit. I need more insulin and can't seem to get any."

"Dad, don't you have a prescription from your doctor?"

"Nah, he's a quack. I ain't going back to him."

"Well, gee whiz, Dad, what am I supposed to do about it? You need a prescription for insulin that you will actually use, and you'll just have to go find another doctor, and fast. Go to one of those walk-in clinics. There's an NCH Immediate Care office near you. We've been there together, remember?"

"Yeah, I know. It's just, well, I can't afford it."

"Dad, Medicare pays for it."

She heard him go into a coughing fit. It was a few seconds before he finally got back on the phone, hoarser than before. "Uh, Medicare's not gonna help me."

"Why not?"

"Amy, I'm afraid I let my coverage lapse. I got dropped."

Amy winced and shook her head. "Dad, you can get back on. They give you a two month grace period to pay the premiums you missed. Can you do that?"

"Uh, two months already passed."

"What? Dad! Couldn't you have told me this sooner?"

"I know, I know, I'm a screwup. It's just . . . I couldn't afford the premiums. I just don't make enough money every month."

"Dad, your Social Security is more than enough to cover it, isn't it? They take your Medicare premium out of your Social Security, don't they?"

"Uh, well, my Social Security isn't that high, babe. I had to pay the premium out of pocket."

"You never told me that!"

"Well . . . "

"Well, what?"

"I don't want to talk about this on the phone, Amy."

"Well, when are we going to talk about it?"

"Can you come out to Libertyville?"

"Tonight?"

"Yeah."

"I don't know, Dad. I'm *really* busy."

"Come on. Please? I haven't seen you in a while."

"Geez, Dad."

He went into another coughing fit. Amy switched off the speaker and held it away so she wouldn't have to hear it. She'd grown to admire and, yes, love her father, but most of the time he drove her nuts with frustration. When the hacking finally subsided, she turned the speaker back on.

"Look, Dad, I'll try, okay?"

"Thank you, Amy."

"I'll see you later. I'll stop by Portillo's and get you that Italian beef you like."

"Oh, that'd be swell."

"I'll try to be there around seven. Is that okay?"

"Sure, sure. Oh, and, uh . . . Amy?"

"What?"

"Do you guys *have* any insulin you could bring? Can you get it?"

Amy rolled her eyes. "Dad, we're not a drugmaker We're not a pharmacy. I can't just 'get it.' You need a prescription, and you have to go to a pharmacy to get it."

"You're a medical company!"

"Not that kind of medical company! I've explained it to you before what we do. Dad, have you been taking drugs you aren't supposed to be taking?"

"What? No, no . . . no drugs."

She believed that like she believed her father would once again be a famous rock star.

"I'll see you later. I've got to go, Dad."

Amy ended the call and looked at her watch. Five minutes until three. Time to go meet that prospective "buyer."

* * *

She entered the conference room at precisely three o'clock and saw that Charles and Aaron Blinken were already seated.

"Good afternoon, Amy," Aaron said, nodding at her.

"Aaron." She took a seat at her usual spot next to her uncle at the big oval table. The picture window on one wall looked out at the EirePharma campus, which was covered in snow and ice at this time of year, every year. It was awfully gray outside. It matched Amy's mood, and she gazed at the tableau for a couple of minutes in the silence.

But then the door opened and Kenneth Malloy, the company's chief financial officer, entered with a tall and extremely handsome middle-aged man who might have been the anchor of a major network news show. Amy immediately thought he might be a retired pro football player due to his build. The man simply oozed animal magnetism, and Amy couldn't help but feel her heart rate increase. His presence was indeed that striking.

"Folks," Kenneth said, "may I introduce Mr. Connor Devlin?"

The guest flashed pearly white teeth with a grand smile. "Good afternoon, folks!"

15

Amy did her duty and drove from the office in Deerfield to Libertyville to see her father, which would have normally been a twenty-minute drive. Rush-hour traffic and the cold temperatures seemed to slow everything down, though, and it took her nearly double the time. After adding the stop at Portillo's to order some take-out food, she didn't get to Andy Redmond's little shack until nearly seven.

And a shack was what it was. Her father even referred to it as such ("Come out to the shack, and we'll have dinner!"). Amy found it unfathomable that a man who was once one of the most successful rock stars in the country now lived in a dump. Areas of Libertyville, especially in the north, were working-class neighborhoods. The houses and apartment buildings were decades old. Farmlands surrounded the area amid the urban spots, and these communities, to Amy, were still much the same as they'd probably been in the 1950s. Her father's tiny house was on the upper outskirts of Libertyville and was once a fieldworker's residence on a farm property that was no longer active. His rent was dirt cheap and the accommodations reflected the price. There was only one bedroom, one bathroom, a living room space, and a kitchen, but the place was in disrepair and really no better than what might be called a "shack." Andy wasn't the best housekeeper, either, so the place always smelled, was filthy, and was generally an unpleasant place to be.

Parked in front of the shack, Amy's Lexus looked out of place. Andy still drove a van in case he needed to haul his amplifier and guitar anywhere, and it took up most of the single driveway. Amy wasn't sure how old the vehicle was—at least twenty-five years. It, too, was a dump. She frowned when she saw that her father had not bothered to plow the snow and ice off the drive and front porch. Stomping through it to get to the door was a pain.

Andy opened it before she could knock.

"There's my girl!"

"Hi, Dad." She held up the Portillo's bag. "Italian beef and fries coming up."

"You're the best. Come in, come in."

Amy winced as she stepped inside. The living room reeked of tobacco and pot smoke. Ever since weed had become legal in Illinois, Andy had wasted no time taking full advantage of the new laws. She coughed and waved her hand in front of her face. "Jesus, Dad, do you have *any* oxygen in here?"

"Sorry, honey, I opened a window earlier to air out the place. It's too damn cold outside, though. Can you stand it for as long as it takes us to eat?"

"I guess I'll have to."

She gazed around the living room and noted the empty liquor bottles and beer cans in the trash can, and the ashtray on the coffee table full of ash, cigarette butts, and a couple of marijuana roaches.

Once a rock star, always a rock star . . . she mused.

Andy took the bag and went over to the Formica table in the kitchen that he used for meals. The table was a hygienic nightmare. Amy took the liberty of spreading out the napkins that came with the food to form place mats. Her father made his unsteady way to the fridge and produced two cans of Coors. He set one down for Amy in front of one of the two beat up chairs at the table and had a seat. Amy stared for a moment at the Coors and thought, *I didn't ask for that . . . but what the hell . . . being here* calls *for a beer.*

"So, how's work?" he asked as he bit into the sandwich, dripping grease onto his side of the table.

"Oh, you know. It's a busy place. Even though we're laying off people and trying to keep our heads above water, there's always work to do."

As they ate, Amy noticed that her father looked even worse than he had the last time she'd seen him. He was morbidly overweight, he had that alcoholic red bulbous nose and rosy complexion, and his eyes were bloodshot. The once flaming red hair had faded and was thinning at an alarming rate. In spite of all that, he seemed to be in his usual good spirits.

"And how's my half-brother doing?" he asked.

"Uncle Charles is fine, but he's a little concerned about the money we're losing. He's actually considering selling the company."

Andy did a double take. "What? I don't believe it."

"Yeah. We met with a potential buyer today." Amy reflected on the meeting with Connor Devlin. It had gone extremely well, and he had done an outstanding job of charming the pants off Charles Redmond and Aaron Blinken. With his *GQ* looks and his statesmanlike delivery, Amy had to admit that even she was very impressed with the bright, elegant man. In more ways than one . . .

"Do you think he'll sell? The family business?" Andy asked.

"I don't know. Maybe."

Andy shrugged. "Well. The family business was never my thing, you know."

"I know. It's my thing, though. The Redmond family thing. Is selling a good idea? To tell you the truth, I don't know. EirePharma has been in the dumps lately, so it could give the company a much-needed shot in the arm. I want the *thing* to survive."

Her father just kept eating, as if he hadn't heard her. Talking about EirePharma with him was useless. Instead, she looked around the kitchen and saw two framed gold records on the wall, one of them being the *Greatest Hits* collection that was the band's biggest-selling title. "Didn't you have a lot more of those?" she asked, pointing.

"Yeah. I sold them. You wouldn't believe what collectors will pay for memorabilia." Andy eyed the two on the wall. "I could sell these, too, and who knows? Maybe I will. I might have to. But I've kept these two for sentimental reasons."

"How's your income, Dad?"

"Terrible." He shook his head. "My last royalty check was ninety dollars and five cents. The record label canceled the retrospective box set they were going to put out. That deprived me and the other surviving Red Drops of some much needed income. I'd been counting on that. Damn Spotify is hardly worth it. We make, like, a billionth of a cent when someone streams one of our songs. I don't see any income from Spotify. Apple Music is a little better. So is Amazon. The CD sales have plummeted. None of our albums have been re-pressed in vinyl. Nah, the ol' music career has kind of sailed off into the sunset."

"No live performances?"

"The last one I did was at a bar in Libertyville. And I was the opener for a younger band. That was . . . two years ago."

"I'm sorry, Dad."

He waved a hand at her. "Don't be." He gestured at the space around him. "This is where old rock stars come to die, and I'm perfectly happy with my choices."

"Don't say that."

He shrugged again. "The diabetes is gonna kill me, Amy. Probably sooner rather than later."

"Dad, I can't believe you allowed your Medicare to lapse. What can I do to help you get back on?"

"The grace period came and went. It's going to be difficult getting back on. I'd have to pay a lot of months' worth of premiums that I've missed. Not to mention getting a supplement and drug plan. I simply can't afford it, Amy. Which is why I can't get insulin."

"You're buying cigarettes. Beer. Booze. Marijuana."

"A man has to have his priorities."

"Dad! If you don't have insulin you *will* die. You want me to buy it for you? I'll pay for it."

"With no insurance it's around seven hundred dollars a month, Amy."

"If I have to, I will."

"And I won't let you. And just so you know, if you do try to send me money, I promise you it will only go toward more Jack Daniel's and a higher quality of Mary Jane." He shooed her with another wave. "So please stop with the dutiful daughter thing. I mean it. Like I said on the phone, if you could somehow get it for free or something, then, sure,

I'd take it. But I will not let you spend a dime on insulin for me. Just like I've told everyone who makes offers like that. I will not be a charity case!"

Amy knew enough to drop the subject. He'd just get angry, and then the entire evening would become more unpleasant than it already was. His pride dominated everything. It saddened her, though. Despite the man's obstinance, recklessness, and maddening self-destructive tendencies, she knew he had a good heart and was a kind person. He loved her unconditionally. And she had grown to love him in return. She didn't want him to leave any time soon.

"What if I got you in to see a therapist? Maybe someone who could help you to see more clearly better ways you could take care of yourself?"

"No way, Amy," he snapped. "Come on. No shrinks. I know what I'm doing. I know I'm a disappointment to you. I'm sorry I'm not the father I could be. I'm just glad my brother is."

"Dad . . ."

He held up a finger, indicating that he would speak no more about it. They continued to eat in silence until they were done. She got up and cleared away the trash and threw away the empty beer cans. Amy then made the excuse to leave. It was a longer drive to get to Northbrook and her apartment.

"Thanks for bringing dinner," he said. "I love you, girl."

"I love you, too, Dad. Hey, Dad. I've always wanted to ask you . . . why are there no photos of my mother in your house?"

Andy got up from the table, went over to the grungy divan in the living room, and started to light one of the roaches in the ashtray. Realizing that this likely was not a good thing to do while his daughter was there, he stubbed it in the tray and leaned back. "Amy, your mother didn't want anything to do with me, or you, after your birth. I'm sorry to say that, but it's true. I've told you that before. I've told you everything there is to say about her. You know she was in that car accident a year after you were born. Louise was into more drugs than I was. She was high or drunk, and she was lucky she didn't hurt anyone else. We were together about . . . eleven months total. It was hardly a relationship. I think I gave you the only photo I had of her, and it wasn't a very good one. I'm sorry. Believe me, she fully bought into a lifestyle of sex, drugs, and rock and roll far more than anyone in our band."

Amy sighed. "Okay. I'm surprised I turned out healthy if she was such an addict when I was born."

"You were a bundle of joy and life. A miracle. For a brief moment, I thought that maybe you would be the catalyst that would change Louise. But it didn't happen. She upped and left us both, Amy. And then that wreck happened and she was gone."

Amy just nodded, picked up her purse, and then went to the door. "Dad, promise me you'll do something about getting insulin. I will help you."

"Amy, stop. I'll be okay."

She left the shack depressed and frustrated. Par for the course. As she drove south toward her home, words of inevitability—"This won't end well"—repeated in her head like one of her rock star father's broken records.

16

It was exactly a week later on the cusp of February, one of the cruelest winter months in Chicagoland, when her Uncle Charles invited Amy to dinner at their Highland Park home on a Wednesday night. Snow and ice still covered the ground, and the wind off Lake Michigan was indeed a chiller. Amy often thought that she could usually withstand Chicago winters, but only if the winds were still. But they called Chicago the "Windy City," so . . .

Amy had not wanted to go to her aunt and uncle's house midweek; things were simply too busy at EirePharma to take off from work early. Charles had insisted, though, and he told her it was something of a business dinner with a guest, and he wanted her there.

She arrived at the stately home at 6:30 p.m. on the dot, having driven straight from the Deerfield office. Luckily, the distances between her frequently visited landmarks in the north and northwest suburbs of the city were not too far. She didn't mind the driving as long as it didn't involve motoring in and out of Chicago proper, where traffic was horrendous and expressway movement could be painfully slow.

Hector, a part-time family helper who had been with the Redmonds for as long as Amy could remember, answered the door. He was often hired to act as butler on special occasions in which Charles and Mary entertained.

"Evening, Miss Amy," the man said with a slight bow. He was wearing his tux, reaffirming Amy's suspicion that this evening's guest was someone important.

THE MIDDLEMAN

"Good evening, Hector," she answered. "I hope you are well."

"Thank you, I'm fine, ma'am. You're looking quite well yourself. Cold night, huh?"

He took her heavy coat and scarf and hung them in the foyer cloak closet. "Your aunt and uncle are in the library."

Amy found them in what served not only as a library full of thousands of books, including first editions, but also as a den where Charles could entertain guests or relax alone with the newspaper. Welcome warm flames roared in the fireplace, casting the room with a golden glow. Charles stood by the bar, where he was busy mixing martinis. Mary, already holding a glass of red wine, sat in the comfortable leather chair that was positioned at a right angle to the leather sofa. She faced a man who wore a formal kilt.

Connor Devlin.

"Oh, Amy!" Charles announced as she entered the room. Mary and Devlin's conversation halted and they both looked up. Devlin stood, revealing the entire ensemble of the traditional kilt made of wool fabric. The plaid colors included shades of green, red, blue, brown, and black.

"Ah, Miss Redmond," Devlin beamed. "How nice to see you again."

Amy was astounded, not only by the mere presence of the man, but also by the kilt.

"I didn't know you were Scottish, Mr. Devlin," Amy said, allowing him to take her hand. He didn't just shake it—he kissed it. Amy had the inclination to bob a curtsy for some reason, but she didn't.

"I'm not. This is an Irish kilt. Irishmen wear kilts, too, you know. Invented by the Scottish Celts and borrowed by the Irish Celts. But we are all Celts at the end of the day."

"Oh, I beg your pardon. Of course, I knew that. I'm Irish American! And, yes, I can now hear that bit of Irish brogue in your voice."

Charles walked over with a martini and handed it to Devlin. "I think the only time we see Irishmen in kilts is in Chicago on St. Patrick's Day. It's fine looking, isn't it, Amy?"

"I'll say. What lovely colors in the wool."

"This is the tartan of County Waterford in Ireland. It's where I'm from," Devlin said, taking the drink and adding, "Thank you, Charles."

103

"Amy? Martini?" Charles asked.

"I'm having red wine," Mary held hers up.

"Oh, Aunt Mary, I believe we're going to outnumber you," Amy said. "I'll have a martini, please."

"Coming up," Charles declared, heading back to the bar.

"I must admit I didn't expect you to be here, Mr. Devlin," Amy said.

"Please, call me Connor."

Charles said, "Amy, you know that the board has been discussing Connor's attractive offer this past week."

"Yes, of course." Then it hit her. Connor Devlin's attendance could mean only one thing. "Are we . . . selling EirePharma?" she asked the other three in the room.

Devlin spoke. "Miss Redmond . . . may I call you Amy?"

"Of course."

He held up his martini glass as if toasting. "I have indeed made the offer, but I'll let your uncle explain."

As he mixed her drink, Charles said, "No, Amy, I haven't made any decisions yet, and I would surely discuss them with you first. But the board members and I all agree that Connor could take EirePharma into uncharted and truly profitable areas."

Amy noted that her uncle was beaming. He radiated an enthusiastic acquiescence toward Devlin. Her Aunt Mary, too, seemed to be enthralled by their guest. The man cut a dashing figure in the kilt, and he had the physique and looks that could break hearts. As the conversation progressed, it didn't take Amy long to sense that her uncle seemed to be seduced by Devlin's charm, by his velvet voice, and his refined Irish accent. She, too, couldn't take her eyes off him.

"Amy," her uncle said, "we all know that EirePharma is losing money. Mr. Devlin has nearly convinced me that we need to join the movement that began seven years ago. If drug manufacturers like, say, InsoDrugs, one of our biggest assets, started increasing the cost of certain drugs, we could turn around EirePharma in a very big way." He handed her the martini.

"Are you talking about insulin?" Amy asked.

"Yes, among other drugs."

"Uncle Charles, I'm surprised. You've always been so scrupulous about this. You know there are lawsuits already underway against major insulin manufacturers and PBMs," she said. "InsoDrugs has already raised the price twice, and we're getting a lot of flak about it." She decided not to bring up Andy Redmond's name. Thoughts of her father—his desperation and pride at odds with each other—swam in her head. She couldn't even help him now. What if the price of insulin was raised further?

Devlin laughed. "The lawsuits are frivolous. We . . . *you* . . . have the right to negotiate pricing with drug manufacturers, and with insurance companies. Don't worry, the PBMs will win these lawsuits."

The man seemed awfully confident. As if he knew something that everyone else didn't. Amy looked at Connor Devlin and wondered what power this man had that he could change the minds of people around him. Uncle Charles seemed to be changing his tune in a big way!

Luisa stuck her head in the archway entrance. "Dinner is served, Mrs. Redmond."

Mary stood. "Oh, thank you, Luisa. All right, everyone, please. No business talk at the table. I want to hear more about Ireland, since I've only been there once and that was just to Dublin."

"My dear," Devlin said, taking her free hand in his to lead the way. "I can regale you with tales of the Emerald Isle for hours if you have the tolerance. You might have to stay up past your bedtime."

Mary blushed and laughed. "Oh, Connor, you're incorrigible."

Devlin turned to Amy, grinned, and winked at her. While gazing at Amy, he spoke to Mary in an exaggerated Irish brogue, "Come with me, lass, for I, your lucky leprechaun, am at your service."

Amy watched them leave the library. Yes, the man was irresistible. She understood why her aunt and uncle were under his peculiar spell.

The dinner of marinated lamb chops, roasted asparagus, and mashed potatoes was superb. Amy had always eaten well at her adopted home. She missed Luisa's cooking after she had moved out to go to college. Connor Devlin assumed the role of troubadour and spoke of the Ireland he had known growing up. Some of it had been flavored with an aspect of "tall tales," but Amy figured this was intentional for amusement.

But as much as she would have liked to stay and talk to Devlin more, Amy finally stood and made excuses to leave. "I have a very busy day tomorrow, and I've got to drive to Northbrook."

"Northbrook isn't that far," Devlin said. "But I understand. I'm going to Kenilworth." He made a show of looking at his Rolex. "You're right, tomorrow is a work day. I suppose I should take leave of your gracious company, Charles and Mary. It was a wonderful dinner. I thank you sincerely."

"You're quite welcome," Mary said.

Devlin said to Amy, "Why don't I walk you out? I wouldn't want you to slip on any ice."

Amy smiled. "Sure."

After saying more goodbyes and taking their coats from Hector, Amy and Connor Devlin walked outside together. He accompanied her as she went to her Lexus in the circular drive. "Your aunt and uncle are marvelous," he said.

"Oh, I know. I call them my aunt and uncle, but they're really my parents," she said, still warm and fuzzy from the drinks and meal. "Are you genuinely going to buy the company, Connor, if the board approves?"

"If your Uncle Charles wants to do it and is happy about it, then, yes, Amy, I will. And I promise you, you won't be sorry. Amy, have you ever been to Ireland?"

"No, I haven't!"

"That's probably why you didn't differentiate between a Scottish kilt and an Irish one. Listen . . . I was wondering . . . would you like to have dinner with me sometime? Somewhere . . . special?"

Amy was a bit stunned. He was asking her on a date. A real date.

"Sure. I'd like that," she said. Then with a bit of a laugh she added, "Where is somewhere special . . . Ireland?"

He replied only with, "I'll call you soon." He held out his hand to shake. When she placed hers in his palm, he raised it to his mouth and once again kissed it.

17

Six Weeks Later: March 2023

Amy was now officially dating Connor Devlin. Almost overnight after the dinner at her uncle and aunt's home, she had found herself in a whirlwind romance. For only a moment did she worry if the relationship might not be ethical, considering that Connor was about to buy her family's company. The fact was that it had been way too long since Amy had been in any kind of amorous coupling, and the influx of endorphins in her long-starved system trumped everything else. Given that her marriage of years ago had broken up due to her workaholic personality, this new development in her life was particularly exciting because Connor might be involved with EirePharma!

When she had announced to her uncle and aunt in late February that she and Connor were dating, they seemed pleased to hear it. Now, more than a month into the romance, Amy was spending more time at Connor's exquisite Tudor-style mansion on Sheridan Drive in Kenilworth, surely one of the most upscale communities on the North Shore. She resided like a queen in the twelve-thousand-square-foot fortress, and she often teased Connor about that description. The fact that the house was situated some distance from the road and protected by a wrought iron fence and gate, along with the presence of hired security men who hovered around at all hours of every day, made her feel that she was in the home of an important head of state, movie star, or other type of celebrity.

She often wondered how Connor gained his wealth. He was obviously a millionaire several times over. No one could live in such a palace without being one of the richest people in Chicagoland.

Amy did find it odd that Connor didn't employ a full-time maid or cook. Personnel of that sort seemed to be on call and would appear at a moment's notice, but they didn't stay in the house. It was up to her to make coffee and her own breakfast in the mornings, not that she minded. The security men did the same—they took care of their own meals. Even Connor professed to be a chef, and he often made dinner for the two of them. If not, then she did it. It was not an issue. She was used to fending for herself. After her brief marriage and divorce, she had managed quite well, thank you very much, in her lovely, pricey two-bedroom apartment in Northbrook. Connor had already suggested more than once that she give up the apartment and move in permanently with him. It wasn't a marriage proposal by any means.

He just wants to play house.

Well, it was way too soon in the relationship to consider something like that. In the meantime, she was happy to spend a night or two there, go home, go to work, go about her daily routines, and then maybe see him again on the weekend. So far, their fling—or whatever it was—seemed to be going well. It had just the right amount of commitment with which she was comfortable. And, like any new romances, the passion and physical attraction was a lot of it. Amy had to admit that in bed Connor Devlin lived up to his good looks and charisma.

For now, Amy was just going with the flow. She was enjoying herself. She liked being around the man and his milieu. Amy didn't really know him well enough to think about anything beyond that. One day—and night—at a time.

It was a Sunday morning. Amy had slipped out of bed, put on the pajamas that had come off during the night, adorned a robe, and traipsed down the stairs from the second floor to the massive kitchen space. She was alone. She hadn't heard Connor get up earlier, but obviously he was somewhere else in the mansion.

She made her way to the kitchen and started to make coffee. One of Connor's hired hands, a man dressed in a dark suit but without a tie, appeared.

THE MIDDLEMAN

"Good morning, Amy," he said.

"Oh, hello. Lance, isn't it?"

"Yes, I'm Lance."

"Do you know where Connor is?"

"In his office. This is the time of day when he's on the phone to Ireland and Europe. Time difference, you know."

"On a Sunday?"

Lance shrugged. "He works constantly. Never stops. Is there anything I can get you?"

"No, thanks, I can manage."

"Very good." Lance then disappeared, but in his place came the patter of paws on the hardwood floor.

Deamhan, Connor's beautiful and fit German shepherd, bounded into the kitchen to greet the houseguest. Amy squatted to give him some loving, and the dog was surprisingly affectionate in return. Usually he still regarded her as an intruder and growled.

"Hello, boy, good morning, Deamhan!" she said in that baby talk all humans tended to use when speaking to pets. "Are you a good boy? Are you a good boy?" She went to the jar on the counter where Connor kept Deamhan's dog treats. Deamhan's ears perked up and his long wide tongue panted. He knew exactly what she was doing.

"It's not too early for a T-R-E-A-T?" She fetched one and stood in front of the dog. "Sit!" He did so. "Shake hands!" Deamhan held out a paw. Amy shook it and then gave him the treat, which he devoured in one snap. "Good boy. Don't take my fingers off, though!"

At first Amy had found Deamhan to be quite intimidating. He had growled and bared his teeth at her when she'd first met him. Connor assured her that this was the dog's training kicking in. He'd said, "Deamhan can tear a person limb from limb. He's the best guard dog I've ever had. He can be deadly to a stranger." It had taken two or three sleepovers before Deamhan got somewhat used to Amy being around. Now, the dog still treated her with suspicion. She was growing fonder of him, though. Nevertheless, she could see that the German shepherd was fiercely protective of his master. The dog obeyed any command Connor gave him. Amy had never seen a canine so well trained, except perhaps

109

K-9 police animals. However, she couldn't help but spoil the dog in the hopes that the animal would accept her as a true member of the household. Connor preferred to withhold treats because he was afraid Deamhan would grow "soft." Amy thought that was rather harsh, so she had begun to pamper the animal in secret.

With a full coffee mug in hand, she wandered out of the kitchen, into a lounge area with a broad picture window that faced the expansive grounds in the back of the house, and then to a hallway that led to Connor's study. The corridor was made of wood that appeared to be stone, as if it were a passage in an old castle. It was lined with antiquities from Ireland, for Connor had attempted to re-create the interior of a real Irish castle. Wooden torches sat at angles in steel holders affixed to the walls, but they were actually specially designed electric lighting fixtures. The "flames" were LED bulbs. Two suits of medieval armor—Connor had told her they were authentic specimens from the fourteenth century or thereabouts—stood "guard" on either side of the door to the study. Connor had admitted to being a kind of castle nut. He collected fancy relics from the past that might have been used in everyday castle life. Many of the examples were rare tapestries and drapes that lined the hallway and the inner foyer of the house at the front entrance.

"I love castles," he'd told her on the first night she'd spent with him. "I think I may have been a nobleman who lived in one, now reincarnated. I love the myths and mythology of the knights and all that. I like to lose myself in the echoes of great halls made of stone. They're alive, Amy. They vibrate with personality. I think of castles as having souls."

"But there are so many valuable tapestries and drapes on the windows. The halls are lined with them," she had said. "Aren't you afraid you'll accidentally burn down the house?"

"No more than the castle dwellers of yesteryear worried about it."

"Weren't castles made of stone and brick?"

He had cocked his head at her. "They could still burn, and there was plenty of wood in castles, too. I am confident, though, that my castle here is protected from such a malady. If I'd had my way, I'd live in a stone castle, but when this lovely old Tudor popped up for sale—and you must admit that it does resemble a castle—then I had to live here.

My smoke alarm system is state of the art, and my men who work for me are always around. You know the main reason why I like castles so much?"

"What's that?"

"They're romantic."

Indeed. Amy often felt she was living in medieval times when she was staying with Connor in Kenilworth.

It was just another aspect of the man's mystery that was fascinating.

She found the door to the study ajar. Amy peeked in and saw that Connor wasn't sitting at his desk. He wasn't in the room at all. She figured he'd stepped out for a moment and would return soon.

Deamhan followed her as she stepped inside. Amy felt that she was entering some sort of inner sanctum. She'd been in there only a couple of brief instances and had never really had a chance to look around. She thought that if there were a book in which she could look up the definition of a "noble, old-school European gentleman's study in a mansion," then photos of this room would appear. Interestingly, the study was not located in the house near a perimeter wall, so there were no windows. The place had a rustic, green and brown color scheme, and it contained expensive leather furniture. Bookshelves lined some of the walls, and the rest were covered by tapestries of Celtic design. She knew that they, like those in other parts of the house, were also old and valuable. The green, white, and orange flag of Ireland flowed from an ornate flagpole near the door. Another suit of armor stood erect behind the desk and a large steel broadsword hung horizontally on the wall. The desk was wide and surprisingly neat. Old-fashioned In-Out trays sat on a corner, and there were a couple piles of manila folders and papers, a telephone, and a wooden box.

Deamhan growled a little as she moved closer to the desk.

"What is it, boy?" she asked him. The animal was obviously protecting his master's domain.

The unique container appeared to be made of very old wood. It was some kind of antique. It was the size of a woman's hatbox, big enough to hold papers, photographs, and keepsakes. The top of the box was carved with what she recognized as a round Celtic knot design. Beneath the knot were rows of sliding wooden tiles upon which numbers, letters, and symbols were carved. It reminded her of one of those children's sliding tile puzzles with numbers, the kind in which you had to move one particular tile to another part of the board by sliding other tiles in different directions to create the correct path. Currently, the layout of the tiles made no sense to her. She tried moving a couple of them. They slid easily. The thing was cleverly and intricately designed. The tiles, when maneuvered correctly, could move up, down, and sideways, and one tile trough led from all the others to a single isolated row. Amy intuitively figured that the object of the "game" was to move certain tiles to that isolated row to accomplish . . . what?

She reached out to pick up the wooden box and discovered that it was heavier than she expected. Maybe ten or fifteen pounds.

"Ah, you discovered my Hate Box!"

Deamhan barked and bolted to his master, who stood in the doorway. Both the voice and the dog had startled Amy, and she dropped the box back on the desk.

"Connor! You scared the dickens out of me!" she exclaimed.

He, too, wore silk pajamas and robe. He patted Deamhan and greeted the dog, and then came into the room. "Sorry, dear, I didn't mean to. I see you're up. I didn't want to wake you earlier. I had some calls to Ireland I needed to make. You okay?"

"Sure. I've made coffee; it's very good."

"I have only the best coffee." He put his arms around her and kissed her. "My God, you're beautiful. And you just rolled out of bed!"

"Oh, stop." She playfully slapped his chest. "Hey, what is this box, really?"

"I told you. It's my Hate Box. It's an old puzzle box, a family heirloom. Would you believe it's from the 1600s? Made by some uncanny leprechaun in Ireland."

"Hate Box?"

He laughed. "I keep decades worth of hate mail and other materials that have tried to take me down over the years. Someone like me . . . well, I have a lot of enemies. Can't be helped. I keep all the nasty missives in there. Attempts to blackmail me. Extortion letters. Lawsuits.

Unwanted subpoenas. Even the occasional traffic ticket if I felt the policeman issuing it was simply doing it because he didn't like rich, white men." Connor shrugged. "I suppose it's become a bit heavy as time has gone on."

"Why do you keep it?"

"I keep it because it makes me feel superior to the idiots who have crossed me! One day I'll have a massive bonfire and destroy it all, an exorcism of sorts. But for now it's just my little Pandora's box. Can you open it? I challenge you to. Give it a try."

"Oh, I'd have to think about that a while. What am I supposed to do?"

"There are certain tiles that comprise a particular equation that go in that one row that's isolated from the others. You have to figure out what those tiles are and then move them in the correct sequence into that slot. Once you do that, the box magically opens."

"Show me."

He shook his head. "Nope. Sorry. I'm the only one who knows the combination. Well, me and . . . him." Connor nodded at a portrait on the wall behind the desk. It was a painting of a formally dressed man in clothing from the seventeenth century.

"Who is that?" she asked. "A great-great-grandfather or something?"

"No. That, my dear, is someone you should know, being in the medical profession. That is Robert Boyle, the great Irish chemist who lived between 1627 and 1691. Why, Robert Boyle is the father of modern chemistry. Did you know that?"

"I've heard of him, now that you mention it."

"He's famous for 'Boyle's law,' one of the most important equations in chemistry."

"I must have studied it in school. I think I had to memorize it at one time, but I've forgotten it. Remind me what it is."

"Nuh uh," he shook his head. "You'll just have to figure it out some other time. Right now, I'm starving. How about some breakfast?"

Deamhan knew that word and barked in approval.

18

It was on the last Thursday morning of March when Charles called Amy into his office at the EirePharma headquarters. He had just returned from a trip, having flown into O'Hare that morning. She found him sitting at his desk, staring quietly out the picture window. The snow had melted and spring was flirting with the populace, but there was always the possibility in Chicagoland that April would bring more cold weather and flurries. One could never bet on the weather.

Could this be the day when Charles finally anointed her to be president of the company? Ever since Aaron Blinken was dismissed in February—with a substantial severance package—EirePharma had been without a leader other than the CEO. Amy had expected that her uncle would indeed promote her and that the board would approve. So far, it hadn't happened.

"Hey, Uncle Charles," she said as she entered. "You want to have lunch today?"

He slowly turned and looked at her. Amy could sense that something was off about him.

"I can't today, Amy," he answered. "I have to go into the city in a bit. I'll be at the condo today."

"Where were you for the past couple of days?"

"Delaware."

"Delaware! What were you doing in Delaware?"

"I had some business to attend to. No concern of yours."

This was odd. She took a seat in front of the desk. "Is anything wrong?"

Charles took a deep breath and exhaled. It was a sign that he had something important to say and was weighing how to go about it. Amy let him take his time.

Then: "Amy, I think you need to stop seeing Connor Devlin."

This startled her. "What? Why?"

"I have my reasons, but suffice it to say that I simply don't trust him."

This was practically a 180-degree shift from her uncle. What was the problem? She and Connor had been back twice as a couple to the Highland Park residence for dinner and were welcomed with open arms by Charles and Mary. "Uh, why not?" she asked.

Charles shook his head and turned away so that she couldn't see the pained expression on his face. Amy knew him too well, though.

"Uncle Charles. Speak to me. I thought negotiations to sell the company to Connor were going well."

"I don't think it's a good idea," he said, turning back to face her. "Frankly, I'm getting cold feet."

"But what about everything we've talked about? You're well aware that I wasn't a fan of the idea to raise the pricing of insulin, but you said it's something we needed to seriously consider. EirePharma is losing money; we've been laying off employees. We might need to do another round of layoffs, and if that happens, the company will be in the trash. You know that some of the insurance companies we work with as a PBM have been getting customer service complaints from consumers due to delays in claims processing, and now a handful of regulators are looking at us as if we're doing something wrong. I once told you I don't really care about the worth of our family's stock, but it's way down there right now, Uncle Charles."

He actually snapped at her, which was something he never did. "Just do your own job, Amy, and I'll do mine!"

She jerked as if she'd been slapped. "Uncle Charles!"

Charles rubbed his brow and put his elbows on his desk. "I'm sorry, Amy. I think I'm under a lot of stress lately. Yes, we need to sell the company, but I'm just not sure Mr. Devlin is the right person at this stage. I can't really go into it. Not yet."

Amy steeled herself to make the announcement. "Uncle Charles, I was going to tell you and Aunt Mary over dinner this weekend, but I think I should tell you now. Connor has asked me to marry him."

Charles's jaw visibly dropped. He stared at her.

After a beat of silence, she insisted, "Say something."

Another inhale and exhale. "Amy, I want you to be happy. That's the important thing. Do you love this man?"

"I . . . I think so."

"That's not very convincing."

"To tell you the truth, I'm not sure what I feel. I truly enjoy his company. He treats me very well. You and Aunt Mary know I haven't even been thinking about dating for a decade since I got divorced—much less marriage—and now suddenly there's a proposal on the table."

"But . . . ?"

She thought for a moment. The truth was that Amy had been completely shocked by the proposal, barely two months into their relationship. Those things happened only in the movies. But then again, Connor Devlin was no ordinary man, and she was forty-three. The promise of stability and a shiny new chapter in her life was turning the wheels in her head. And yet, admittedly, she wasn't ready to say yes. "There is . . . well, there is still a lot of mystery about him. Things I don't fully understand. Things he's been unwilling to explain."

"Such as?"

"Mostly his background. What he did in Ireland before coming here."

"Amy, the way he conducts business is also yet to be seen." Charles said.

"He's outlined all that. We have documents and papers and declarations and . . ."

Charles dismissed that with a wave of his hand. "Listen to me, Amy. I have to go now. But I want you to know something. I've been working on something that will change how this company is run. I think you'll be very pleased. I can't reveal what it is just yet. It's why I was in Delaware. I'd like to ask you to please hold off on making a decision about the proposal of marriage for a little while. Can you do that?"

116

THE MIDDLEMAN

"I suppose so. Connor is a rather impatient man, though."

"I understand." He stood and began to gather his things. She watched him, completely puzzled by what was happening. He finally came around the desk and placed both hands on her head. He gently moved her face to his. "I want you to know how much I love you. I love you as my daughter. You *are* my daughter."

"I know that."

He nodded. "I'll talk to you later. I must run."

Back in her office, Amy felt confused and anxious. What had that been all about? Business in Delaware? What could it be? She had never seen her uncle so agitated and cryptic. Sure, he'd gone through times when the job was stressful and he could be stern with everyone in the building. But this was different. Why did her uncle seem to suddenly distrust Connor? It was unreasonable and strange. Connor was her *boyfriend*! Amy couldn't help but feel a little insulted.

She picked up her phone and dialed Connor. His voicemail picked up with the message that was now familiar to her. "This is Connor Devlin, please leave a message." It was somehow endearing that his Irish accent was more pronounced in the voicemail greeting than in live conversation.

Amy hung up without leaving a message. There was still work to do, so she got busy at her desk and didn't think any more about the talk with her uncle.

* * *

She worked until 6:05 p.m., and then left the building to drive to Connor's house in Kenilworth. Amy often put on the radio and listened to NPR along the way, and she did so as she pulled onto Skokie Highway to head south. The news was already in progress.

". . . apparently jumped from the roof of the building. Police say the man, as yet unidentified, fell from the fifty-six floor ParkShore Condominiums building at approximately 4:25 p.m. No one on the ground was injured, but police say . . ."

What?

Amy felt a sudden, constricting vise around her heart, and she experienced a wave of nausea. The ParkShore. Her uncle and aunt's condo was in that building. Where Uncle Charles had said he would be that afternoon. Surely the man who jumped wasn't . . . ?

As if preordained, Amy's cell phone rang. The caller ID indicated it was Connor.

She punched the button on her steering wheel so that she could talk hands free. "Hello?"

His voice sounded solemn and direct. "Amy. Where are you?"

"I'm on my way to the house. Connor, I just heard on the news about someone jumping off the ParkShore building!"

"Listen, Amy . . . I have some bad news."

19

Five Months Later: August 2023

Amy Redmond looked out of the window of their suite in the Westbury Hotel at the magnificent cityscape of Dublin and simply said, "Oh, my." She wrapped the silk robe tightly around her body and practically hugged herself. The garment, along with a set of gorgeous silk pajamas, had been a gift from Connor the previous night before they'd gone to bed.

She couldn't believe she was finally in the country of her family's heritage.

Amy and Connor had arrived after dark, so she hadn't really seen the beauty of the old metropolis until they had awakened that morning.

"Isn't it lovely?" Connor asked as he stood behind her and wrapped her body in his strong arms. "That, my dear, is Ireland. And it's only the beginning."

"I can't wait to get out and see the sights," she exclaimed.

"Savor it, my love. We'll spend three days here and then begin exploring the country. As I promised, we'll end our holiday at Lismore Castle in the county where I'm from. There's a little dinner party being thrown in our honor."

"A party? You didn't tell me that. Who's throwing it? Family members?"

"More accurately, family in a sense. They are people with whom I've done business for many years. But first, we must have a good Irish breakfast. I'm starving!"

Amy turned away from the window and embraced the man to whom she was engaged. It had been a turbulent few months since the tragedy that had occurred at the end of March. Her Uncle Charles's sudden suicide had shocked and surprised everyone in the Redmond family, as well as every employee of EirePharma. During the first two weeks of April, no one seemed to know what would happen with the company. The board had appointed Amy to serve as "acting president" until further notice, but she'd had no confidence that the firm would be around much longer. It seemed that whatever plans her uncle had been working on to take the company in a new direction had died along with him.

Then, as April rolled into May, the EirePharma board approved the sale of the company to Connor Devlin. Apparently, his offer couldn't be beaten. The deal was such that Devlin would acquire all of Charles's stock, and, after some time had passed, deliver a portion of this stock to the board members to split equally. Mary Redmond would not contest the sale and would receive a very generous lifetime annuity. Amy would retain her 30 percent of the stock, and her cousins Matt and Candace kept 9.5 percent each. This, in essence, meant that EirePharma was still the Redmond family business, even though Devlin owned the majority of the company and was now CEO.

The best thing about the deal was that Devlin immediately appointed Amy to be officially president of the company, and the board unanimously approved.

Devlin immediately got to work repairing the company's faults and began renegotiating contracts with drug manufacturers and insurance companies. Amy didn't know how he did it, but Connor managed to secure better terms very quickly. She had heard whispers of "strong-arm tactics" and "bullying" with regard to Connor's arbitrations, but she had not been present. Connor had insisted that she concentrate on running the company, and that he would handle the rest. That's what she planned to do. Connor knew what he was doing! Didn't all businesses have ugly rumors about questionable dealings with allies and competitors? That's all they were—rumors. She was confident that Connor Devlin was a successful and savvy businessman. How else would he have become a multimillionaire living in a mansion in Kenilworth?

THE MIDDLEMAN

These were things Amy told herself as she tackled the immense amount of work that was needed to save the company. She had no time to grieve her uncle's death, nor could she pay much attention to the tiny, nagging circumstances that surrounded it. The suicide was suspicious. Charles had expressed doubt about Connor. And yet—Connor had come through. Amy reluctantly admitted it, but Connor was proving her uncle wrong despite the office gossip. Not only that, Connor was taking care of her every need—professionally and emotionally. She had come to rely on him during a stressful period of busy activity.

The romance between Amy Redmond and Connor Devlin had blossomed. She had accepted his proposal of marriage in June, and now they were officially engaged and on a lovers' vacation in Ireland. He had whisked her away from whatever doubts and concerns she may have had.

Amy thought she was in heaven.

* * *

Amy had learned all the history of that little slice of heaven she occupied.

Lismore Castle in County Waterford was built in 1185 by the lord of Ireland, Prince John of England. Over the centuries the impressive property had been owned and occupied by various noblemen, including several earls of Desmond, Sir Walter Raleigh, the first earl of Cork and colonial adventurer Richard Boyle (and his son Robert Boyle), and many dukes of Devonshire. The Cavendish family, of which the dukes of Devonshire were members, had owned the castle from 1753 to the present. Currently the twelfth duke's son and heir had an apartment in the vast building and managed it. The castle was normally not open to the public except for the expansive gardens that were designed in the 1800s. However, certain spaces within were available to hire for private events and stays for small groups, and the castle had to be rented in its entirety—it was not a hotel. However, the rental included the banqueting hall with meals prepared by the family's head chef.

The cost was around €16,000 a night, not including the food.

The tour of the island had been a whirlwind, and Amy was completely enthralled by the land, the people, and the man with whom she

121

traveled. Now, the culmination of the trip was this remarkable castle where they were staying two nights. Their fellow guests were men and women known to Connor, people in business who were obviously very wealthy. She wasn't sure if Connor was footing the bill for the castle, or if his friends were doing so. It didn't matter. She was having the time of her life, and she was finally relieved to have a chance to learn more about his history and where he had come from.

The black-tie gala dinner was exquisite. The trout had been caught fresh from nearby River Blackwater, the vegetables grown at the castle. It was all decadent, delicious, and delightful. Over the meal the guests discussed world politics, global economics, and the medical industry. Connor and some of the others spoke of Robert Boyle, whose portrait hung in Connor's study back home in Kenilworth.

"Can you believe it, Amy?" he asked her. "Boyle was born right here in this castle in the year 1626. The father of modern chemistry. You owe a debt to him, darling. Everyone in the medical profession does!"

She was also perhaps drinking too much expensive champagne. The bubbly was the only part of the dining experience that didn't originate in Ireland ("My dear," Connor said, "Only France makes the best champagne.") The introductions of the other guests flew by her. There were names she barely caught, and most everyone spoke in thick Irish accents that were somewhat difficult for her to follow. But she caught surnames like Clancy, Griffin, Byrne, Kinahan, and McGovern. Several of these men possessed demeanors with very hard edges. It was as if they'd been in a few wars and had lived to tell about it. They were friendly enough, but Amy sensed that these men, like Connor at times, should never be crossed. She was also never sure what kinds of businesses the men were in and why Connor knew them. Conversations on those subjects had been oddly ambiguous. It was slightly discomfiting. Most all the men Connor introduced as his longtime friends seemed to have little in common with him, at least from first appearances. They all could have been mistaken for barroom brawlers and street fighters way out of place in any top-tier corporate structure. Tattoos, gaudy gold bling, and huge diamond-studded rings on almost every finger were just a few of the oddities that caught Amy's eye.

THE MIDDLEMAN

One thing they all had in common was that the men wore Irish kilts.

One of the women who was the companion of a much older man whispered to Amy, "Do you know what they have on underneath those kilts?"

"I suppose they'd have on underwear," Amy had answered, but she knew what was coming.

"Nuh uh. All of those men are going commando, dearie," she said. "Better watch out!"

At one point, the host of the event, a man called Kinahan, asked Connor, "So what happened to Petey-o?"

Connor replied, "Petey-o couldn't make it."

"Who's Petey-o?" Amy asked him.

"An old, trusted friend in Chicago. I don't believe you've met yet," Connor told her, giving her a squeeze around the waist. "Pardon me, dear, I must speak to my friends in private."

Connor then went off with the other men to smoke cigars and talk presumably about their wealth and business dealings. Amy felt a bit abandoned. When Connor had told her he'd be introducing her to old friends in Ireland, part of her believed she'd be schmoozing with other professionals in the Irish medical and pharmaceutical world and flaunting her new role as president. Apparently, that wasn't the case. To make up for it, she had some more of the exceptional champagne. There was no question that she was becoming intoxicated. The Ireland trip had been overwhelming, and now this—the castle, the rather sinister businessmen—made her suddenly feel as if she didn't know her fiancé at all.

She became unsteady on her feet and caught herself on the corner of a stone wall.

"Are you all right, dear?" one of the women asked her.

Amy turned to see that all the various wives and dinner dates were in the same boat. Their companions had gone off to be "men." Amy felt that the women seemed to be watching her with bemused interest.

"Oh, I'm fine," Amy answered. "Thank you. It's this champagne. It's very good, isn't it?"

"Yes, there's nothing but the best when we come to the castle."

123

"Do you do this often?"

The woman shrugged. "Once every year or two."

"I'm sorry, I must not have caught your name," Amy said.

"Nan McGovern." She shook hands with Amy. "And you are Amy Redmond, engaged to be married to Connor Devlin."

Amy couldn't help but giggle like a schoolgirl. The alcohol had truly gone to her head. "That sounds rather bourgeois, doesn't it? I'm sorry, which of those men is your partner?"

The woman didn't smile. "Pierce McGovern. The tall one with the handlebar mustache."

"Oh, yes. Handsome man."

"Hm." The woman leaned in and spoke quietly. "If I may impart some advice, dearie . . . Marry Connor Devlin for his money, if you wish, but if I were you I would not get too close to the man."

This took her aback. "Why on earth not?"

"He's one of them. And these men corrupt everything they touch."

20

One Month Later: September 2023

"Don't worry!" Andy Redmond told his daughter. "I'm fine. Really. I have it all under control."

"You don't look fine, Dad," Amy told him. "I'm worried about you. I think you need to see a doctor."

It was not a pleasant visit to Andy's home in Libertyville. The place was even more of a mess than it had been the last time Amy had seen it. Dirty laundry lay on the floors of every room, and the kitchen was stacked with filthy dishes. Instead of being able to sit down and have a nice meal of Portillo's Italian beef sandwiches, Amy spent two hours cleaning up the mess in the sink. While she did that, Andy sat on his couch with his red, swollen feet up on the coffee table. Amy could see that the diabetes had clearly progressed and was affecting her father's mobility.

When she was finished, Amy knew she couldn't spend any more time there. She had a big board meeting to attend the next morning and she needed to prepare a presentation. Her work had increased exponentially since Connor had taken over EirePharma, and she was determined to please him as well as herself. The company was rapidly regaining traction, and the stock had risen at a remarkable rate in the past two months. She hadn't believed it was possible back when her Uncle Charles was in charge, but Amy was now fully behind Connor's sledgehammer management style in running the company. Results didn't lie.

Amy knew she needed to hire caretaker help for her father, but he absolutely refused. They argued incessantly about it until she was exhausted from the effort. She was well aware that elderly parents could be fiercely obstinate about losing independence.

Despite his health, Andy still had a happy-go-lucky attitude about it all. Amy suspected that marijuana, alcohol, and illegal opioid street drugs kept him high enough to get through each day. He told her that he'd been taking insulin, but when she went into the disgusting bathroom, she found no evidence of any.

Amy finally had to leave and get back to the office for a late night of work. They said their goodbyes and she promised to see him in a week or so—if her job didn't consume her.

* * *

The board meeting began at nine o'clock sharp. Connor Devlin insisted on promptness and seemed to have no tolerance for tardiness, laziness, or excuses. The nine members were there, six men and three women who had been on the team for years. They were all professionals in various fields—medical, financial, and insurance—although a third of them were retired. Each member was wealthy and had the ability to network as a fundraiser for the company. Unfortunately, the results of their efforts prior to Devlin buying the firm had been poor. Now that EirePharma was back in the black, the mood at these meetings had improved.

Amy expected nothing but good news to be shared. Devlin opened the meeting and immediately called upon the CFO, Kenneth Malloy, to make a report. Amy had noticed that since Connor had become CEO, he and Malloy spent a lot of time in private discussions that didn't involve Amy. Apparently, though, whatever schemes the two men cooked up were working. Malloy reported that earnings were 22 percent higher this month than the previous one. This was better than anyone had anticipated.

"Of course," Malloy said at the end of his presentation, "if InsoDrugs would raise the price of insulin and be competitive with other drug manufacturers, our profits would be even higher."

THE MIDDLEMAN

Connor thanked him and then said, "Amy, you're up next."

Amy gave a rundown on the staffing situation, the current status of how the company's productivity was handling the increased workload, and where there were areas needing improvement. At the end, she said, "And here's some welcome news. We had to lay off employees over the past year, but now it appears that we actually need to hire back some folks. It's gotten that good, people. I'm going to consult the department heads to see which former employees could be candidates to offer restored positions, and I don't see why we can't go ahead with that. I've already spoken to Connor and Kenneth about this, and we all agree."

The board nodded its approval.

Connor thanked her and said, "Before I tell you what I've been able to accomplish in the past month, does anyone have any questions or concerns?"

Board member Vernon Bunker, a seventy-one-year-old retiree who had been a hedge fund manager, stockbroker, and financial advisor, raised his hand.

"Yes, Vernon?"

"Uhm, Connor, I wish to express a couple of concerns. I've been thinking about this a lot. I don't know about the rest of us here, but I'm a little uncomfortable about this insulin business. Raising the price. I'm not sure that's a good thing to do. Sure, it'll make us all more money, but what does that do to the everyday Joe on the street who needs the medicine?"

Connor interrupted him. "Insurance companies pay for it, Vernon. Not Joe."

"But what if Joe doesn't have insurance? Then it's a big problem."

"If Joe doesn't have insurance, that's *his* problem. Not ours."

"Well . . . isn't that a bit callous?"

Connor stiffened. "What did you say?"

The intensity in the CEO's voice gave Vernon pause. "I . . . I was just expressing my opinion that . . ."

"Your *opinion* does not gel with mine," Connor said with ice in his voice. "Your opinion is basically just that—an opinion. The thing is,

Vernon, opinions do not make a company successful. It's actions that do that. I've been performing *actions* ever since I became CEO. I have turned the company around. Maybe some of my actions are controversial to you. But you can't argue with success. You heard Kenneth's report. We're doing better than ever. Now, what was your other concern?"

Vernon Bunker's red face was an indication that he did not appreciate being spoken to that way in front of the rest of the board. After a beat, he spoke softly, "Very well. Connor. When the board voted to sell EirePharma to you, we were promised a certain amount of stock shares out of Charles's holdings—which are now yours. Do you have an idea when that will occur?"

Connor Devlin slowly turned his head toward the picture window. He was quiet for a moment, but Amy could see that the man was attempting to control his anger. The others also shifted a little in their seats. The room had suddenly become very uncomfortable.

The CEO waited a full minute before looking back at the people around the table. "Is anyone else in the room as impatient as Vernon?"

Vernon gasped and then said, "Connor, it's not that I'm *impatient*, it was just a question, it was about a deal that was made—"

"*I know about the goddamned deal!*" Connor shouted. Then he stood. He walked around the table to where Vernon was sitting, took hold of the swivel chair, and forcefully spun it around so that Vernon faced him. Connor leaned in, inches from Vernon's nose, and continued. "I decide when the best time is to dole out stock shares! Maybe I have a plan! Maybe I am waiting for the right time! Maybe I'm waiting for when I fucking feel like giving you my money! I have noticed that you, yes, you, Vernon, have been the one wimpy voice in this room over the past few months that likes to challenge my judgment. If there's one thing I can't stand is a whiny, pathetic, impatient board member who doesn't go along with the vision of the company. And that vision happens to be *my* vision, and it's *working*!"

Vernon shrunk deep into the chair, shriveling until he appeared to be very small. The others in the room watched the scene with their mouths open, unable to move or speak. Amy, too, was shocked by Connor's outburst. She wanted to stand and scream at him to stop. But she couldn't. She was frozen in her chair.

THE MIDDLEMAN

"The next time we have a board meeting, I want you to think long and hard before you cross me, Vernon!"

With that, Connor straightened himself, twisted his head and audibly cracked his neck, and strode back to his seat at the head of the table.

The silence in the room now was torturous.

Vernon Bunker was shaking. He did manage, though, to gather his notepad, stand unsteadily, and walk out of the room.

When he was gone, Connor said, "We need to weed out the weaklings. And I think that's all I have to say today. Do I hear a motion for adjournment?"

No one said anything.

"Do I hear a motion for adjournment?"

Amy spoke. "I . . . I, uh, motion to adjourn."

Someone said, "I second."

Connor nodded sharply. "Meeting adjourned."

Minutes later, Amy was back in her office. Her mouth was dry and she felt as if she had no strength in her legs. The display in the boardroom had been beyond disturbing. She knew that Connor had a temper, but she had never seen *that* before.

She suddenly felt ill. Amy decided to go to the ladies' room and splash some water on her face. When she had completed that task, Amy considered going to Connor's office and gently telling him that perhaps he had been out of line. What could he do to her? She was his fiancée. She was the president of the company. It was her duty to tell him that he couldn't talk that way to board members.

Amy headed for Connor's office, but she halted in her tracks.

Ronan Barry, one of Connor's personal "assistants," was leading Vernon Bunker into the office. The door slammed shut behind them. Amy was tempted to go put her ear to the door, but Connor's executive secretary was right there at the desk nearby. Amy had lately noticed that the men who worked for Connor at the house were often at the EirePharma headquarters during the day when their boss was in the building. Ronan Barry was a bit of a scary guy. What was he doing escorting Vernon around the office?

129

Connor is apologizing, she thought. *That's it. Ronan brought Vernon in so that Connor could say he was sorry.*

Amy turned and went back to her office.

An hour later, a memo was issued to executive personnel saying the Vernon Bunker had resigned from the board.

21

A Few Weeks Later: October 2023

At first, Connor didn't want Amy to accompany him to a lunch meeting with InsoDrugs' COO, Doug Frankel.

"Connor," she said, "I'm president of the company. Yes, I'm also your fiancée. I'm aware that eyebrows have been raised about our relationship mixing business and personal, but you're the one who always says, 'Who cares?' And you're right, I'm sure it's not the first time a CEO and an executive officer of a corporation have engaged in a romantic relationship. That's not what this is about, is it?"

"No, of course not!" Connor spurted.

"Well, I'd like to see you do your thing. InsoDrugs is one of our biggest clients. Perhaps I can help persuade Mr. Frankel that what you have to say is sound. You know I was hesitant about raising the price of insulin, but you won me over on that. I should come to the meeting."

Connor rubbed his chin as he sat behind his desk, eyeing her up and down and appreciating her form. So far, Amy was convinced that he had been keeping her on a short leash. She felt that she hadn't been allowed to exercise her full potential as the managing head of the company, and she told him so.

Finally, Connor agreed. "All right, Amy. But please, let me do the talking. I know how to handle the likes of Doug Frankel. He's a bit intimidated by me. I can play on that."

131

She made sure to smile when she countered, "Who isn't intimidated by you, Connor?"

He gave her a look, unsure if she was kidding or not. "Grab your purse and jacket and meet me at the elevator."

* * *

Since InsoDrugs headquarters was located in Chicago's north side, they met equidistantly in Evanston at a fine-dining restaurant called Oceanique. Amy had met Doug Frankel before and had not been impressed with him. He reminded her of the actor Don Knotts from the old *Andy Griffith Show*, only without the humor. Small in stature, slightly balding and with glasses, he was a rather nervous man. He had obviously gotten along with her Uncle Charles and was apparently a scrupulous person, but she knew that Connor Devlin would eat him alive.

The pricey eatery was not crowded, so Connor requested a table where they could talk in private. He tipped the maître d' a twenty, so the trio ended up at a table on the other side of the dining room, away from the guests already there. This way, whatever Connor said to the man would not be overheard.

The luncheon began smoothly. Everything was pleasant as they ate the seafood meal. Connor and Amy spoke about their trip to Ireland, a place Frankel indicated he'd like to visit someday. He mentioned that his ex-wife had never wanted to travel to foreign countries, and now that he was single again, he could do it. The man chuckled and said, "Of course, I've been single again for two years and still haven't gone anywhere! Work, work, work, you know how it is."

"Yes," Connor said, "and I suppose that's a good segue to talk shop." The dishes were cleared away and coffee was ordered all around. "I'll get right to the point, Doug. InsoDrugs has raised the price of insulin nominally over the past couple of years, but not nearly enough. Your competition is strangling you. As your pharmacy benefit managers, we want you to please do something quickly to rectify this error in management."

Frankel jerked his head. "Error in management?"

"You heard me. It's quite obvious that you're making a huge mistake by not going through with what we've requested. When you get the price up to where we want it, then EirePharma can make sure that your insulin product is on the Tier One formularies of all the insurance companies that we deal with. Your profits will skyrocket. What's wrong with that? Don't you want profits that soar into the stratosphere?"

"Look, Connor, we've talked about this before," Frankel said. "We've already raised prices. Your predecessor got me to do so." He nodded at Amy. "Your uncle, Amy. Charles and I agreed to it." Back to Connor. "The increases were reasonable. Isn't it unethical to raise the price so high when it costs us only four measly dollars to produce a single vial? You want to charge a consumer hundreds of dollars for that? And if not the consumer, then insurance companies will have to pay it. Don't you see how high costs like these are what fuel the problems that exist with healthcare in this country? The media and the public both are constantly on the attack about how greedy drug manufacturers are, when in fact, it's the PBMs that are the greedy ones. And I would love to educate the public about that little fact. You understand the same truth that I understand. PBMs have become a nightmare for healthcare."

Connor raised his eyebrows. "You're calling me greedy?"

"Not you, personally! PBMs in general."

Connor turned to Amy. "I don't know, Amy, I think he called me greedy. Did you hear that?"

Amy blinked but knew she had to play along. "Sounded like it to me."

Connor laughed and shook his head. "Doug, Doug, Doug. You know what's going to happen? You're going to come around and see things our way."

"I am?"

"Yes, you are. By the end of the year, InsoDrugs will join your competitors and raise the price of insulin even higher than the others have."

Frankel shook his head. "I don't think so. You do know a class action lawsuit is underway right here in Illinois? It's going to trial in a couple of weeks! EirePharma is named in the lawsuit. InsoDrugs is named, and this is for the price raises we've already done! Other companies you work

133

with are named. What are you going to do about it? InsoDrugs wants no part of it."

"The class action lawsuit?" Connor rolled his eyes. "Listen, the judge that's handling the case is going to either dismiss the suit or she's going to be removed."

Frankel frowned. "How do you know that?"

"I know things. Trust me. Don't worry about the lawsuit. Just raise the goddamned price of insulin, Doug, and soon."

"I just don't agree it should be done, Connor."

"And what does your CEO say?"

Frankel seemed puzzled at the mention of his boss. "Steven?"

"Yes, Mr. Steven Scales."

"I believe Steven will back me up on this."

"Will he?"

"I hope you're not going behind my back and talking to Steven, Connor."

"Me? Would I do something underhanded and sneaky like that?"

Frankel began to look around for an escape. This had turned into a lunch from hell. He then addressed Amy. "Do you go along with this? Would your uncle have gone along with it?"

Amy took a breath, thought about what she should say, and stated, "Connor is CEO of EirePharma now. He has strong visions for the company, and it's my job to back him up."

Did I just say that?

She felt as if she were running on a hamster wheel and couldn't get off. The ship had sailed, and she was right there on its deck.

"Let's go, Amy." Connor signed the bill and left it on the table. He and Amy stood. "Good to see you, Doug. You will change your mind. I promise you that."

"Is that some kind of threat?" Frankel asked.

Connor walked by Frankel's chair, placed a hand on the man's shoulder, and squeezed it firmly. "Not at all, my friend. We'll be in touch."

* * *

THE MIDDLEMAN

That night, Connor pulled back the covers of the king-size bed in the master bedroom to slip in beside Amy. He was naked. She wore the pajamas that he had given her in Ireland. He nestled next to her and kissed her neck.

"I appreciated that you backed me up today at lunch," he said.

Amy shuddered inside. She had been kicking herself for the rest of the day. She hadn't understood how she could have done it. They had treated Doug Frankel horribly. Her Uncle Charles would not have approved of her actions. It was almost as if she had transformed into a different person at that meeting.

"Amy?"

"Connor, are you sure that what you're doing is legal?"

"What do you mean?"

"How you go about getting . . . getting your way with these people. It seems as if you're . . . not playing nice."

Connor chuckled. "Not playing nice is not necessarily illegal, Amy, darling."

"You belittled the man. We were having a nice lunch. It could have been a reasonable business discussion and you tore him apart. Just like you did to poor Vernon Bunker at the board meeting. That was shocking."

"Amy, that's how I get my way, as you put it."

"Connor, it's not right."

"Well, I've heard that Dougie Frankel has 'prurient desires.' It'd be a shame if the police found that out, too."

Amy winced. "How do you know that?"

Connor simply gave her a sly grin. "Sometimes you have to supply the truth yourself."

"What do you mean by that?"

He shook his head, waved a hand, and said, "Don't worry about it." His palm gently landed on her right thigh and caressed it. "The main thing is that you were there for me. You said the right things. It turns me on when you stand beside me," he whispered. "It's as if you're my queen, and we're ruling our kingdom together."

What the hell? Amy was suddenly ill at ease.

135

The hand moved up to her waist. "I want you, Amy. My queen."

He continued to kiss her as he moved his hand to her breast.

"Connor," she protested.

With his other hand he tugged her hair to move her face toward him so that he could reach her mouth.

Now she began to physically resist.

He held on to her, squeezing her roughly, and then he abruptly rolled on top of her with determination.

"*Connor! No!*"

Amy struggled, pushed, and strained to move out from under him. She eventually slapped him on the forehead three times. Wincing, he finally lifted himself up and off of her. "What's wrong with you?" he growled.

"What's wrong with *you!*"

"What, are you going to grab that little knife with the pink diamond-encrusted handle from your purse and stab me to death?"

Amy's jaw dropped. She simply stared at him.

"That's right, I know you have that thing," he said with a mocking tone.

"I carry it for protection! It's legal! I would think you'd understand carrying a weapon." She slithered out from under the covers, sat up, and threw her legs to the floor.

"Where are you going?"

"Away from you. I'll sleep in one of the other rooms. Hell, I don't even know who you are anymore. You're looking and acting like all those brutes who you introduced as your family over in Ireland. And you know what? I think they're all gangsters!"

"Amy!"

"Good night, Connor." She moved across the room and out the door, slamming it behind her.

22

November—December 2023

In the middle of November, Amy accepted a lunch invitation from her cousin, Matt. She hadn't seen him since Uncle Charles's funeral. She knew he'd had some trouble recently at the law firm where he practiced and was now out of a job. Could he want to enter the family business and hook up at EirePharma? Did they need another attorney? The class action lawsuit over insulin pricing was ramping up and there was a lot of publicity—mostly bad—about the case in the news.

She agreed to meet him on a Saturday in the Glen, a chic shopping and restaurant area in Glenview, just south of Northbrook. Amy still had her apartment in Northbrook, and she was beginning to stay there more often. Her relationship with Connor had cooled somewhat, but they were still engaged. He had an uncanny ability to sweet-talk her and alleviate the unpleasantness. She continued to sleep over at his Kenilworth fortress a few nights a week. Northbrook, though, was actually much closer to the office in Deerfield.

They met at the Yard House, a sports bar–style eatery that was a little more upscale than most places of that kind. The cousins embraced each other warmly and were shown a table. Amy reflected that Matt didn't look too well. He had that "drinking man's" face—puffy and red eyes, reddish nose, and fuller cheeks. In fact, he had put on several pounds since she'd seen him last.

"Good to see you, Amy," he said. "You want a drink?"

"Not at lunchtime, thanks. Good to see you, too, Matt." She told the server that she'd have iced tea. Matt ordered a vodka martini, lunchtime be damned.

They caught up with a few trivial items, and then Amy asked, "I got the feeling from your call that you wanted to talk about something specific. But do you know what you're going to do now?"

"I do. Nothing. I don't really want to go back to law. I've got money to live on. I have a nice little house in Logan Square now, and I just want to enjoy myself. I'm a bachelor again, and, who knows, maybe I'll find some lucky—or unlucky—woman who'll want to date me." He waggled his eyebrows, causing Amy to laugh. "We'll see."

"Well, I *was* going to ask if you might be interested in joining EirePharma as one of our corporate attorneys. I guess that's not in the cards."

"No, no, I don't think so. But thank you for thinking of me. Nah, that's not something I want to do. But that does bring me to what I wanted to talk to you about."

"What's that?" she asked.

"What in the bloody hell is going on at the family business? This class action lawsuit in the news . . . EirePharma is named, InsoDrugs is named, and a bunch of other PBMs and drug manufacturers. Your fiancé is all over the place, and, frankly, he's not coming off well. He reminds me of certain politicians I don't like."

Amy pursed her lips and nodded. "I know. But that's his public persona. I wish you'd get to know Connor a little better. He's not as bad as . . . oh, God, Matt. I don't know what I've gotten myself into." She closed her eyes and fought off a sob.

"Amy?"

She held up a hand. "No, I'm all right. We're still engaged to be married. We have a date planned for July of '24, but I don't know if I want to go through with it. How did I get here, Matt? Wait—I know. After Uncle Charles died, everything happened too fast. It was as if someone pulled the wool over my eyes and put me on autopilot. And that someone was Connor Devlin. I've been on an oxytocin high from a grand Irish romance. I've been blind to what's happening. I can now see that Connor is showing some chinks in his armor."

"Well, he's certainly putting out the PR. The judge in the case sounds like a hellion from the deep," Matt said.

"Oh, Lord." Amy shook her head. "I hadn't planned to share all this, but you brought it up, and I need to unload. Maybe I've been feeling guilty or something, but I've started collecting receipts. I'm taking notes. I'm tired of being Connor's 'queen' president. Anyway, Connor has brought on a new team of lawyers to handle the lawsuit. Have you ever seen *The Godfather*?"

"Sure."

"Well, these guys remind me of Mafia consiglieri, you know, the attorneys who work for mobsters. I mean, they're not Italian, but you know what? I'm pretty sure they're all Irish. They all have the appearance of Irish boxers and rugby players with law degrees."

"Pretty much the opposite of your friend Connor."

"Yes. Nothing refined about this bunch of mouth breathers. So he's got *them* working on the case, and they're very heavy-handed, to put it mildly."

"Wow."

"And Connor has hired this PR firm. They're called Shock PR. That's really their name. I'd never heard of them. Believe me, I tried to vet them and find out more. They're very . . . discreet, for lack of a better word, when it comes to web presence. They're kind of a PR organization slash lobby group, because they're involved in politics, too. So, Connor has them putting out what I feel is really disinformation about the case. They're using social media in a big way, putting out memes and talking head videos to accuse the judicial system and the attorneys representing the lawsuit as, I don't know, *fraudulent*. In other words, the PR firm is using disinformation to make it look like the other side is using disinformation to fool consumers and the courts."

"That doesn't sound good," Matt said.

"No. But it's helping EirePharma. It's helping public opinion on our side."

"And what about this judge? Judge Carver?"

"Roberta Carver."

"She's been quoted as saying some things that sound a bit biased."

"Yeah, but did she really say them? Matt, look, Judge Carver is a black, progressive, liberal judge, there's no question about that. She favors the plaintiffs. I think that's pretty obvious, too. So what? But you've seen some of the—" Amy made quote marks with her fingers. "photos and videos?"

"Uh, yeah."

"They're fake! And they're all attacking the judge and making her look bad. They're allegedly dug up material about past cases over which she presided in order to create a consistent pattern of always siding with the more liberal or progressive party. Our lawyers are arguing that this makes her unacceptable as a biased judge."

"I've noticed that she has ruled against the defendant team's motions a lot. Most of them, anyway."

"You are correct. So Connor and his thug attorneys do have a point, and they're exploiting it way beyond what I think is reasonable. The more crap that is churned out against the judge, the angrier she seems to get. I guess she has a short fuse, too, and unfortunately she's shown it. It's pretty clear what they're doing."

Matt nodded. "I saw the video of her on the street outside of the courthouse. When that newsperson straight out asked her if she was biased, the woman lashed out. It wasn't a good look."

"No, she was provoked. And you know what? That newsperson was someone hired by Shock PR. They have planted about a dozen similar fake reporters to follow this judge around and unleash attack questions. There's a conservative internet news show that's very popular. One of Connor's lawyers, a guy named Rob Flynn, was on last night—and this was set up by Shock PR—and he flat out urged the appellate court to take action against Judge Carver. His argument was that judges like her put the entire justice system at risk."

"It's a well-organized hit job."

"Exactly," Amy said. "It's also dangerously close to being racist and it's certainly full of falsehoods."

"Amy, you guys might win this little class action suit, but this could be damaging to EirePharma in the long run."

"Tell me about it. I've started keeping a journal in Word, documenting everything that's going on. I don't know if I'll ever need it, but I'm putting it all down on the computer. I'm saving receipts. I'm doing my best to keep a record of conversations I'm part of or overhear."

"That's a good idea."

Amy stopped and took a breath. "Matt, I'm engaged to this man. I feel like I can't walk away. He's CEO. I'm president. There could be bad blood. It could hurt the business. All the financial rags love a good management conflict story."

"Amy, if you don't love the guy, you can't marry him. It's as simple as that."

She didn't respond. Instead, they agreed to get together again in a few weeks' time.

* * *

Amy spent Christmas Eve and Christmas Day with her Aunt Mary in Highland Park. It was just the two of them. Connor had flown to Ireland for the holiday. He'd said he had business there but he also wanted to be in his boyhood land for Christmas. He had asked Amy to accompany him, but she refused. It had been too long since she'd spent much time with her aunt. Plus, her father, Andy, was not doing well. She needed to be close to home. Connor had not been happy. They had fought until Amy simply got up and left the house.

Thus, Christmas was a dull and quiet affair. While Aunt Mary was very happy to have Amy for company over the holidays, Amy was miserable. The situation with Connor was becoming worse.

He was expected home three days after Christmas, and he had asked that she be at the house when he arrived. Amy felt as if she had no choice. Part of it was that she couldn't help believing that she owed the man. He had promoted her to be president, he had pulled the company out of the red, and he had bestowed her with lavish gifts and prestige. Their appearances in the Chicago society pages alone were new and exciting experiences for Amy. For months, her head had been in the clouds.

Lately, though, she was coming back down to earth and was viewing the true landscape behind the smoke and mirrors, and it wasn't pretty.

Now, wandering around the huge mansion on the evening of Connor's arrival, occasionally passing the likes of Ronan Barry, Pat Beckett, or Lance Macdonald, she nevertheless felt very alone. The men in the house were cold, humorless, and damn scary at times. They ignored her, always giving the impression of minding their own business. Amy wondered what they would do if she just started smashing things in the house. She had no doubt that one of them would pull out a gun and shoot her.

Only Deamhan kept her company. He might be a ferocious guard dog and would likely tear her to bits if Connor commanded him to do so, but without the master around, Deamhan stayed close to Amy. She could occasionally give the dog commands of her own that he would obey. Amy wasn't sure if Deamhan completely trusted her, yet, but he had grudgingly acknowledged that she was there to stay.

With nothing better to do, Amy went into Connor's study. Sitting on the desk was the strange Celtic Knot wooden box along with several days of the *Chicago Tribune*. One of the men always placed the current paper on the desk, whether Connor was in town or not. Right now there was a small pile of them.

Amy sat in Connor's chair and began to look at the papers. One of them was from right before Christmas. She picked it up and thumbed through it to find what she wanted. She knew what it would say, of course, but there it was in black-and-white. The class action lawsuit had been dismissed. Judge Carver had been removed from the case the second week of December. The new judge had promptly held a hearing, followed by a second one, and then, on December 20, made the pronouncement.

Amy hadn't been surprised.

Connor had used that as one of the reasons to take off for Ireland— to celebrate the firm's good luck.

Luck, indeed.

She stuck that issue in its proper place in the pile and grabbed today's paper. A headline she hadn't noticed screamed at her: DRUG FIRM EXEC FOUND DEAD. Amy began to read and muttered aloud, "Oh, my God . . ."

The short article proclaimed that the chief operating officer of InsoDrugs, Doug Frankel, had been found dead in his home in Lincoln Park, apparently of a self-inflicted gunshot wound.

Amy was by now used to chills running up and down her spine when it came to events related to Connor and EirePharma, but this one was intense.

She recalled the lunch at which Connor had berated Frankel. Amy had heard it with her own ears. Had Connor done something? Had he threatened Doug Frankel with something horrible?

Amy made a mental note to document all this in the journal she was keeping on her computer. Furthermore, it was time to back up her notes and documents onto something that she could hide, like a flash drive. She didn't *think* Connor spied on her computer when she wasn't looking, but just to be on the safe side . . .

She looked at the puzzle box again. For the umpteenth time, Amy attempted to solve it by sliding the tiles around. Unfortunately, she had no idea what the phrase was that she was attempting to isolate. Amy looked up at the painting of Robert Boyle. There was nothing on the portrait that was a clue, was there? It was just a guy from the seventeenth century dressed in seventeenth-century clothes depicted in seventeenth-century paint.

Deamhan, who had been lying on the floor by the desk, suddenly perked up and whined. That could mean only one thing.

Connor was home.

Amy quickly left the study to greet him. Would he be bearing gifts? She hadn't received anything for Christmas yet. For him, she had bought something small and not very expensive. She'd thought the tie tack was pretty, though, and that it would go well with the neckties he favored.

When she heard him call her name, Amy finally made up her mind about the issue that had been bothering her for weeks.

She no longer wanted to be his fiancée.

23

January 2024

After two days of Andy Redmond not answering his phone, Amy knew that she had to get in the car and drive to Libertyville. Had he not paid his phone bill? If he couldn't afford insulin or other essential medical needs, how did he pay a phone bill? Of course! Booze, pot, and who knows what other drugs were more important!

She'd never understand the mind of a former rock star.

Three days after the New Year, Amy bundled up after work and drove to her father's shack. His beat up van was still in the driveway, so he had to be home. She got out of her Lexus, hurried to the front door to escape the biting wind chill, and rang the doorbell. Usually he answered it quickly, but nothing happened. She rang again. Then she knocked loudly.

He had given her a key to his house "in case of emergencies." Amy dug into her purse and couldn't find it. She was so cold that she had to run back and get into her car before she could adequately go through the purse. After some excavating, she discovered it in the bottom, but by then the feelings of apprehension were overwhelming.

Amy had a painful hunch of what she was going to find inside the home. Had she failed her father? She'd been watching a train wreck happen over the years she had built a relationship with him.

She built up her nerve, got out of the car, and rushed to the front door again. The key went into the slot and she flung open the door.

Andy Redmond was lying face down on his living room floor.

The Middleman

* * *

It was only at the end of the month that the medical examiner's test results finally came back. The verdict on cause of death was "diabetes mellitus." The examiner discreetly told Amy that there was also heroin, marijuana, alcohol, and what appeared to be an amateur moonshine oxycontin in his bloodstream. He assured her, though, that while all these drugs certainly contributed to Andy's demise, it was indeed diabetes that killed him.

When the news got out that Andy Redmond had passed away, there were a surprising number of tributes and retrospectives in rock music journals and online about the once very successful leader of the Red Drops. *Rolling Stone* did a complimentary piece on its website with the promise of a feature in a future printed edition. Suddenly, FM radio stations were playing music by the Red Drops again. As next of kin, Amy was contacted by Andy's record label. They told her that plans to rerelease all of Andy's music on vinyl were underway. She wanted to ask them why they hadn't done that while he was alive, but she kept her mouth shut.

Only Amy and Matt attended a simple private service that had occurred two weeks after she found her father. Since Andy had no funds to pay for his funeral, she and Matt went in together for everything. Mary Redmond did not attend, nor did Matt's sister travel from France. Candace hadn't bothered to attend their Uncle Charles's funeral either. Other than Mary, now it was really just the two of them left to hold down the Redmond fort, so to speak.

For their efforts, Amy and Matt each took one of Andy's framed gold records that had been on the man's wall. Amy was happy to have it and would display it proudly.

After the service, she and Matt went to Portillo's in honor of Andy's love for their Italian beef sandwiches. They sat and ate and reminisced about the man and how they wished things could have been a little different for him and his relationship with the family. The conversation then predictably turned to the state of affairs with EirePharma, Amy, and Connor Devlin.

"It should have been easier for Uncle Andy to get insulin," Matt said.

Amy shook her head and discreetly tried to wipe back tears. "Matt, I hope you know I did all I could to try to give him money to live. Time after time he told me that all he would do with that cash is buy liquor and drugs. I'm pretty sure he never even used the insulin samples that I supplied from time to time. It's like he *wanted* diabetes to kill him. I realize now he was very depressed, and maybe that was his chosen way out the door. But what really stirs some anger in me about Andy is that there are so many people out there living in shambles just like him who would have given everything just to have access to affordable insulin."

"Two thoughts about that, Amy. First, your dad lived the life he chose to live almost from the day he was born, and nothing you could have done would have ever changed that. Secondly, that's a timely thought because just yesterday InsoDrugs has raised the price of insulin to $350 a vial."

"*What?*"

Matt pulled out his cell phone, manipulated the screen, and then showed her the news item. Amy read it with wide eyes and mouth open.

"Steven Scales. The CEO says blah blah blah . . . Of course it was Scales. How come I didn't know about this? I'm the frikkin' president of their PBM!" She cursed some more. "I have to call Connor. I'll bet *he* knew about it."

Matt put his hand on hers. "Don't. Leave it, Amy."

"You know what I think?"

"What?"

"Connor kept this news from me until it was a done deal. That bastard."

"I take it you and he . . . ?"

"Oh, we're still together. I haven't left him. Yet."

"Are you still engaged?"

"Just before New Year's I told him I didn't know if I wanted to get married."

"How did he take it?"

"Not well. He thought I was just 'confused' and that I'd still come around. He knew very well that we'd been bickering more often and that I was keeping my distance. I told him I needed some 'space.' But we spent New Year's Eve together anyway. I don't know, Matt, he has a hold on me that I can't seem to break. I know I need to get away from him, but I'm just so tied to him—not only physically but through the company. But you know how I told you last month that I've been keeping records of stuff on my computer?"

"Yeah?"

"I couldn't do that if I weren't around him. By being close to him, by being in his house, by being in his damned *bed*, I hear things that are oh so incriminating. I'm then able to write them down. Have you ever heard the term, 'sleeping with the enemy?'"

"Yes. That's what you're doing, Amy. I'm sorry that you're in this situation. I know how difficult it must be. I hate to say it, but the man has been gaslighting you. You've been betrayed by someone you thought cared for you. I'm glad you're becoming aware of the truth."

"Thanks, but . . . I know this sounds crazy, but I do think Connor really does care for me! In his own egotistical mind I'm one of his treasures! Matt, I think he's doing incredibly illegal things. I believe . . . oh, Matt, I think he had the man at InsoDrugs, Doug Frankel, killed. I don't believe Doug committed suicide."

"And I sure don't believe Uncle Charles jumped off that roof."

She looked at her cousin. "Nor do I." She exhaled loudly. "There. I said it. I don't think I've ever allowed myself to go there before now. I can't explain what happened with Uncle Charles, but it simply doesn't seem right. I've been so caught up with—"

"It's not your fault, Amy. Look, we have to do something. This man is turning the family business into some kind of racketeering enterprise. You've told me about the men around him. They act like hoods, plain and simple."

"You're right, Matt."

"Listen," he said. "I know this attorney down in Florida. We went to law school together. He's a pretty big lawyer; he's handled some major high-profile cases. This sounds like the kind of case he would jump on. If drug manufacturers and PBMs and insurance companies are all conspiring to illegally raise drug prices through some kind of organized scheme, that is racketeering, plain and simple. The real bonus to that, though, would be exposing who Devlin really is and what caliber of crimes he's been involved with."

"That's going to be difficult. I have seen firsthand how he charms everyone into accepting—even supporting—whatever he does. The man can threaten someone in broad daylight, and he'll have witnesses clamoring behind him," Amy said.

"Why don't I go down to Florida and talk to my friend? Just lay it out for him. See what he says?"

"I don't know, Matt. I'm scared. If Connor finds out we're talking to attorneys, he could . . . it might be very dangerous for us. You, especially. Look what happened to Uncle Charles."

Matt was quiet for a moment.

"Matt?"

He lowered his voice. "Amy, have you noticed that we're being watched?"

"What?"

"Don't look right away. But sitting several tables at eight o'clock from ours behind you is one of Connor's men who stays at the house. I think it's Pat Beckett."

Amy inhaled sharply. "Well. That's interesting." She knocked a plastic fork off the table, giving her an excuse to bend down to retrieve it. She glanced that way and rose back up. "Yeah, that's him."

"So, Connor Devlin is having us watched."

"Likely it's just me."

"Amy, I've made up my mind. I'm going to Florida. We can't waste any time."

"I'm nervous about it, Matt."

"Don't you agree something needs to be done? Someone needs to interpret the evidence you've been collecting."

Amy thought about it. Finally, she nodded.

"Okay," he said. "Done."

"Who is this lawyer?" she asked.

"His name is Nick Deketomis. Everyone calls him 'Deke.' As lawyers go, he is the top of the food chain."

PART THREE
MAY–JUNE 2024

24

Four Months Later: May 2024

Deke got out of the rental car, locked it, and checked his necktie in his warped reflection on the driver's side window. The flight to Chicago had been rushed and inconvenient, but he felt he needed to offer his condolences and respect for his old friend.

Matt Redmond's wake and funeral mass was being held at Kelley & Spalding Funeral Home in Highland Park. As Deke walked into the large multipurpose room being utilized for the occasion, he could see a small gathering of mourners milling around a table that was covered with refreshments. Twenty to thirty people, tops. The size of a small parish. The usual accoutrements of a sanctuary were present—an altar, candles, and a reredos figure. Flower arrangements surrounded the closed casket that sat just to the left of the sanctuary in front of the first rows of chairs.

The service would begin in roughly a half hour, so Deke put on his best face to greet Amy and meet some of her family and friends. Deke spotted her speaking to her attorney, Paul Baker, near the refreshments table, so he moved closer to them. Amy looked up, recognized Deke, and smiled.

"Mr. Deketomis! How good of you to come!"

"Hello, Amy. My deepest condolences for your loss."

"Thank you. You remember Paul Baker?"

"Yes, I do." The two men shook hands.

Amy asked, "How long are you in town for?"

"It's just a whistle stop, Amy. I have to fly back tonight. We're very busy at the firm right now. That's a good thing, of course, but it tends to make one covet every minute of the day. But I'm glad I came. I felt that I should pay my respects."

"I'm sure Matt would have appreciated it." She lowered her voice. "He was not a religious person, which is why we're not at my aunt's church. I made the argument that he wouldn't have wanted that. Having the wake and service here was a compromise. At least there will be a priest and a real funeral mass. Matt probably wanted to be cremated, but Aunt Mary wouldn't hear of it. The Redmonds have a family plot in Lake Forest Cemetery, so that's where he's going. I will, too, someday, come to think of it."

"Hopefully that won't be any time soon," Baker said.

"Knock on wood!" Amy wryly whispered.

Deke also kept his voice down. "Amy, I was hoping we could get a chance to talk privately. I know this is a bad time, and we're all here for the wake. If you can't, maybe we can arrange a Zoom meeting or something."

"Let's talk now. The service doesn't start for a little while, and everyone here is visiting and talking about everything except Matt." She jerked her head toward the front of the room where the casket sat. "There's no one over there. Come on."

"You two go ahead," Baker said. "I'm going to get some more punch."

Amy led Deke to the casket where they could speak quietly and give off the appearance that they were paying respects to the deceased.

"Do we know any more about what happened to Matt?" Deke asked.

She sighed. "The police ruled that Matt was killed in a street robbery, and there are no suspects. It was very near his home. Frankly, I'm still in shock. The funeral home did a spectacular job covering up Matt's facial wounds, but he still wasn't very presentable. The killers delivered as much damage as possible to his entire body. The autopsy report is very difficult to even read."

"No suspects. No street cameras or anything?"

"It was in an alley, so no. But if you ask me, there are some pretty big suspects." Deke raised his eyebrows and she continued. "I believe

Connor Devlin killed Matt. Or had him killed. Whatever. Connor knew Matt had been talking to you, I'm sure of it. I'm sorry I haven't been in touch with you, but the truth is that I've been afraid. I hope you've kept my name out of anything you've been doing."

"Is Mr. Devlin here?"

"No. Well, not yet. He could walk in, I don't know."

"Amy, we did some preliminary investigation but the case has not progressed very far. The results of that last class action lawsuit regarding the price of insulin were not encouraging. However, we're thinking that the best way to go about this is with an antitrust suit against Mr. Devlin and EirePharma itself. I'm afraid that puts you in a precarious position, though, seeing that you're president of the company."

"What does an antitrust suit mean, exactly?"

"Antitrust lawsuits are used to stop practices that restrict trade and the free market and to compensate all the folks who are harmed by those practices. In this case, plaintiffs could be diabetes sufferers who have trouble buying insulin."

"About my position at EirePharma, I have a couple of things to tell you. First off, Connor and I . . . Well, I broke off our engagement two days after Matt's murder. I told him it was all too much, and I needed some time to grieve. But the truth is Matt's death was the final straw. I finally see clearly who Connor is—now I just need to prove it. I've moved back to my apartment in Northbrook."

"How did he take it?"

"Not well. We still have to work together, though. God, I picked a great time, too. Next month EirePharma has this huge marketing event we're hosting at the Drake Hotel, and Connor and I have to plan it. It's awkward. So, truthfully, I don't know if he'll show up. He might, and I don't think you and I should be seen together."

"I understand. We'll make this short. What's the other thing you wanted to say?"

"Mr. Deketomis, I haven't told anyone about this yet, and I need to talk to my lawyer, Paul, about my contract. But I'm thinking of resigning altogether."

"That's a big step, Amy."

"I know. I'm struggling with it, but it might be the best thing for me to do. Especially if I become, well, a whistleblower."

"That would of course be your decision, but please keep me informed about that, Amy. Are any of your other family here?"

She nodded at an older woman sitting at one of the few tables where attendees could enjoy the refreshments. Next to her were a young man and woman who appeared to be in their twenties. "That's my Aunt Mary, the woman I think of as my mother. And with her are Ricky and Sharon, Matt's children by his first wife, Sally. Matt stayed in touch with them but they didn't grow up with him. I'm not sure how they feel about losing their real father. Sally and her second husband are over there." She indicated a couple talking with a small group of people of similar age. "Those are some of Matt's college friends." She looked around. "I don't see Matt's second wife, Erin. That marriage didn't end too well, so I guess it's not surprising she's not here. Neither of the two exes helped me arrange the funeral. Oh, and that's Candace, Matt's sister." Amy nodded toward a middle-aged woman with blonde-gray hair joining Mary Redmond and her two grandchildren at the table. "Candace flew in from France. She's probably not going to stay long."

"Any reason why Candace isn't close to the family?"

"No reason. Just temperament, I suppose. She's a nice person, don't get me wrong. We were never close, not like Matt and me. Candace went away after she graduated from high school and basically left behind her Illinois roots. She had the wanderlust."

"I see."

"And that's what's left of the Redmond family. Listen, I've been collecting information about Connor and everything I've witnessed at the company and at his home. I think you'll find it very useful, and I also believe you can build a case with it. Matt thought it was good evidence against Connor. I've got it all on a flash drive. I need to get that to you at some point."

Deke said, "I suggest giving it to me as soon as possible, and then simply start another flash drive with any subsequent material. You don't have it here, do you?"

"No, I'm sorry. It's with my laptop."

THE MIDDLEMAN

"You should maybe hide it somewhere more secure."

"Believe it or not, it's sitting in my laptop case with other flash drives used for work. Only I know which one it is. But you're right, I think I'll . . . Oh, crap, there he is."

Deke looked up and recognized the tall, white-haired man who just entered the room. He was followed by a younger man who might have been a secret service agent protecting the US president, except he looked more like a gangster than a government employee.

"Go," Deke whispered. "Call me."

Amy gave him a nod and moved away quickly to a flower arrangement and acted as if she was inspecting it. She then walked back to the refreshment area where all the other mourners were gathered in groups.

Deke stood for a few moments at the casket as if he were in silent prayer, and then he, too, went back to get a cup of punch. He figured that Devlin likely knew who he was. If the man didn't see him with Amy, then perhaps he'd be invisible amid the crowd. Deke watched as Devlin went over to the table where Mary Redmond sat. The man graciously took the woman's hand and spoke softly to her, obviously giving her his condolences. Mary introduced him to the grandkids and to Candace.

Devlin then went to Amy and held out his arms to embrace her. Deke could see that she hesitated, but then, so as not to cause a scene, she allowed him to do so. They spoke for a few seconds, Amy shook her head, and Devlin gave a little shrug. He then moved away from his former fiancée. That's when he spied Deke. Devlin blinked a couple of times and then stepped forward.

"Are you Nick Deketomis?" Devlin asked, holding out his hand.

"I am," Deke shook it. Devlin used a little extra strength to squeeze Deke's palm.

"I'm Connor Devlin."

"Pleased to meet you."

Their hands came apart. Deke set down his drink on a table next to him.

Devlin then asked, "And why in hell is a two-bit lawyer from Florida at this wake?"

Deke did his best not to show that he was taken aback by the question. "Matt and I went to law school together. We were friends. It's a tragedy what happened to him."

"Yes, it was a tragedy. A tragedy indeed." Devlin almost smiled. He then leaned in to speak quietly in Deke's ear. "After this is over, I don't want to see your face around here again."

Deke immediately moved in closer to Devlin. With his best wicked smile, he said, "In the words of Mick and Keith, 'you can't always get what you want.' So save the threats, my friend."

Devlin answered, "We will see." He then walked away, dismissing Deke as if the lawyer were invisible, approached the other guests, and immediately switched his demeanor to his trademark charm and the guise of appropriate sympathy for the occasion.

25

In the early afternoon on the Tuesday after Memorial Day, Amy met with Paul Baker at his office in Evanston. Ever since she had broken off the engagement with Connor, she had not returned to Connor's Kenilworth mansion, even though she had left a few items of clothing and toiletries there. As she had told Deke, her relationship with Connor at EirePharma was now awkward and uncomfortable. Given all that she knew about the man—or at least what she suspected of him—Amy had come to an important decision and wanted to discuss it with Baker.

The older man greeted her warmly and offered coffee, which she accepted. She had wolfed down a sandwich for lunch and needed to get back to the office fairly soon. The caffeine would help her stamina.

"What can I do for the president of EirePharma?" Baker asked.

"Paul, it's almost June, and you know we have a huge marketing event at the Drake Hotel in a week. I'm sure you received an invitation," she said.

"I did."

"Will you come? I'd like you to be there."

"I plan to. I'm not sure I understand what it's all about, though."

"Well, I guess it's intended to be a surprise. Connor wants to go back to the old days when EirePharma owned and operated retail pharmacies. He's courting investors to finance a spinoff company. It will be a chain of medical clinics all over the country that will provide walk-in service and pharmaceutical products. It's really a push to sell insulin. EirePharma is teaming up with InsoDrugs to do it. They'll of course manufacture the drug, and EirePharma will build the infrastructure to distribute it."

"What do you think about it?"

"It's a big gamble. The company was built on retail pharmacies, you know, back when my grandfather and Uncle Terence ran it. Ultimately, Uncle Charles sold them off because they were a money loser. Connor thinks he can make it work again, but I have my doubts. Nevertheless, I've helped come up with a business plan. We started it months ago, so I'm pretty involved in it. The thing is . . ." She hesitated and looked away.

"What?"

"I think it's really going to be a scheme to charge insurance companies a lot more money than is warranted. The markup on the drugs will be even more outrageous in any store he controls. We will end up doing our part to make the health care industry in our corner of the world even more dysfunctional than it is now."

Baker raised his eyebrows. "The Feds have a lot of power when it comes to this kind of thing. They could be a valuable watchdog on it all."

She rolled her eyes. "The idea of federal government watchdogs is almost laughable. Those people are always looking for a cushy job in the industry they are supposed to be regulating." Amy heard herself and blinked, realizing that she was beginning to sound like Connor himself. She then added, "You can bet that Connor understands how to take advantage of that."

"Is this what you wanted to talk to me about?"

Amy shook her head. "Not really. I wanted to tell you that I'm thinking of resigning."

"Really?"

"Yes. I'm going to tell Connor I'll do the marketing event, and then I'm out. EirePharma used to be the Redmond family business. Now it's Connor Devlin's business. Devlin Clover, Inc., Connor's company, owns EirePharma, you know, and he's refashioning it to suit his purposes. Paul, I think the man's a criminal. I . . . I suspect he had something to do with Uncle Charles's death, I suspect he had something to do with

THE MIDDLEMAN

Matt's death, I suspect he had something to do with InsoDrugs' COO's death. . . . Paul, the man is a mobster. The last thing this industry needs is another mobster in its ranks. I can't be a part of it anymore. I have to get away. As president, I thought I could help retain some element of the Redmond family in EirePharma. But I didn't realize that when Uncle Charles died and the sale went through, Connor Devlin had already won. EirePharma no longer belongs to the Redmonds. So I need you to go over my contract and see if there's anything that could prevent me from doing what I want to do."

Baker nodded slowly. "I can do that this afternoon and get back to you." He sighed. "It is indeed a sad state of affairs. End of an era."

"I'd like to tell Connor tomorrow. Can we talk again this evening?"

"You have my home number."

"Thank you."

Baker shuffled uncomfortably in his chair. "Amy, I advised Charles not to do business with Connor Devlin. At first he was very gung ho about it. Toward the end, he started to listen to me. When you and Devlin got involved romantically, I felt it was not my business to interfere with that. I should have. I should have warned you, too. Amy, I agree with your decision on resigning. I think you'll likely land elsewhere with at least an equivalent job and maybe better. And, frankly, I'll be glad to get away from EirePharma business, too."

Amy detected a subtext to that statement. "Paul? Do you know something you're not telling me?"

The man just shrugged and shook his head a little, which Amy interpreted as an affirmative answer to her question.

"Are you being threatened?" she asked.

Paul sighed. "Devlin thinks I know something about Charles's finances that weren't disclosed prior to the sale of the company. He and his . . . goons . . . came to see me. I don't know what he's talking about. However . . ."

"What?"

"I know that Charles *did* consult another attorney about the sale. Not me. I mean, we were talking about it for weeks, months . . . and then he stopped talking to me and consulted someone else."

159

"Who?"

"Someone in Delaware."

Amy leaned forward in her chair. "I remember . . . Uncle Charles had come back from Delaware on the day he died. I had no idea why he'd have gone to Delaware. He wouldn't tell me, either. But then he told me later that he was working on plans to turn the company around in another direction."

"I believe this attorney he talked to is someone who is just as shady as Devlin. Charles kept everything from me, which was unusual."

"What's this attorney's name?"

"Markus DeStefano." Paul lowered his voice. "He's an attorney who represents a lot of white-collar criminals. Even men who are the fronts for drug cartels in this country. You might try googling him. His name pops up in trials of organized crime figures, but everything DeStefano does is all legally aboveboard. He's never been arrested or charged with any crimes. I think he advises people on how to manipulate money."

"What do you mean?"

Paul shrugs again. "Overseas banking. Offshore accounts. Hiding assets. Even washing money. That kind of thing."

"I see. What would Uncle Charles be doing talking to a guy like him?"

"I don't know."

Amy slumped in her chair. She knew she needed to talk to Nick Deketomis again, and fast.

* * *

Diana buzzed Deke and said, "Amy Redmond on line one."

Deke picked up the call. "Hello, Amy?"

"Hi, Mr. Deketomis."

"Please, call me Deke. It's good to hear from you. Is everything all right up there?"

"I wanted to thank you again for coming to Matt's wake and funeral."

"No need to thank me, Amy, it was something I was glad to do. It also gave me a firsthand look at Mr. Connor Devlin, and I appreciated that, too. I now have a good idea of who this man is."

"Well, I wanted to advise you that I plan on telling him that I'm resigning from EirePharma." Amy then explained her reasoning in the same speech she had given her attorney. She planned to give Devlin the news tomorrow, with the request that she could leave as soon as the marketing event at the Drake Hotel was over.

Deke responded, "I know that must be a difficult decision to make, Amy, but I have to say, in my opinion, it's probably a good idea. My encounter with Mr. Devlin at the wake inspired me to dive into the EirePharma case again. My team and I are gearing up to pull everything together. It will take some time, but I'd like to get Devlin where it hurts—in his wallet. An antitrust case is the way to go. But I'm going to need your full cooperation."

"I'd be testifying against my own company?" Amy asked.

"Your resignation would put you in a position of strength. It makes total sense for the Redmond family itself to be one of the plaintiffs and go after Devlin for turning their company into a criminal enterprise. More importantly, Amy, it puts you in the position of being a legitimate, well-informed whistleblower, which is extremely helpful in a case like this."

"There's no one left, really. Matt's gone, and I don't think his kids or ex-wives would be interested."

"Would your Uncle Charles's widow be willing to help?"

"Aunt Mary? You know what? I think she would. I'll talk to her. Mr. Deketo—Deke, right now you might be the only one that gives me hope. You've got my full cooperation. I told you I've been gathering a bucketload of what I feel is good evidence, but I want to organize it better and maybe get some final pieces from the office. I can get it to you after the marketing event next week. It's all on a flash drive. I can make a copy on another drive and FedEx it to you."

"Sounds good, Amy. Good luck tomorrow. Let me know how it goes."

"I will. Hey, I wanted to ask you something. Have you ever heard of an attorney in Delaware named Markus DeStefano?"

Deke searched his brain. "No, I'm afraid not. Why?"

"My Uncle Charles was talking to him right before he died. Paul Baker thinks this DeStefano guy is a shady character."

MIKE PAPANTONIO

"I'll ask my team what they know," Deke said, "but rest assured we will know everything about him by the end of the day."

"Thanks. I have to go now."

"Amy, I don't want to upset you any more than you already are, but I need to say this. We have handled many cases against the Devlin types over the years. Most people never recognize the fact that criminals run some of the biggest corporations on the globe. Some of those criminals are true sociopaths, too. So here is the problem. Just like Devlin, they don't look like criminals to the average person. They are cloaked in expensive suits. Just like Devlin, they have an impressive education and tons of polish and sophistication. But beneath all that, at their heart they are still criminals. Some are more dangerous than others. I believe you are involved with one of the truly dangerous ones. That has got to be top of mind for you in everything you do with him. Keep yourself safe and check in with me regularly. Can you do that for me?"

Deke ended the call and then buzzed Sarah with a question: who the heck is Markus DeStefano?

26

June 2024

Amy chose the Drake Hotel's Camellia Room, which overlooked the Magnificent Mile and lakefront, for EirePharma's marketing gala at which Connor Devlin planned to unveil his plans to reestablish the company's chain of retail pharmacies. With its crystal beaded chandeliers and its warm and appealing color palette of deep blues and golds, it was an ideal banquet space. They didn't expect a large crowd, so the Camellia, which could hold up to two hundred guests at dining tables, was perfect. With only sixty-two targeted invitees (with plus-ones) scheduled to be in attendance, there was enough room for the dinner on one side, and a separate area with chairs for the multimedia presentation portion of the evening. Amy felt it was one of the more gorgeous venues in the historic hotel.

She had arrived at the Drake in the afternoon, checked into her hotel room, and gone down to the Camellia to see how everything looked. As president, she was not responsible for the setup or actual running of the event, but she had done most of the planning with the help of the director of marketing. The team had done a marvelous job. She spoke to the IT folks, and they assured her that the audiovisual components for the presentation had been tested and were working beautifully. Connor Devlin had no patience for technical screwups.

Back in her room, Amy set up her laptop so that she could do a little work prior to the evening's event. While the presentation was stored on the marketing team's laptop that was already downstairs in the Camellia, Amy had brought her own computer just in case. She had learned long ago that one should always have a backup. Besides, she had to go over some of Paul Baker's documents regarding her resignation from the company. Now was as good a time as any. After tonight's event, Amy would no longer be an employee of the family business.

She thought back to the morning when she announced to Connor that she was leaving. She'd had no idea what to expect and was fearful that he might do something . . . bad. Indeed, at first he was furious, but he attempted to hide it. The man switched on the charm button and endeavored to sweet-talk her into changing her mind. He promised an amazing raise in salary and a huge bonus, but Amy stood firm and gave two weeks' notice after the marketing event. Devlin then turned nasty. He told her to "feel free to leave the day after the presentation." If she wasn't going to stay, then he'd rather that she exit her position as soon as possible. They both knew, however, that her presence at the marketing soiree was important to establish continuation of the brand and to represent the Redmond family.

So, this evening was her last night on the job, and Amy wasn't sure how she felt about it. It was indeed bittersweet. She had dreaded informing her Aunt Mary of the decision, but the woman who had raised Amy as her own child was surprisingly supportive. "I'm so glad you're getting away from that man," Mary had said. Amy had then asked her about the Deketomis law firm's possible antitrust suit against Devlin and EirePharma—would she be willing to help? A smile played on her aunt's face for a moment, and she had answered, "I'll think about it."

Once it was a done deal, Amy had called Deke and told him that she would be leaving EirePharma, but the public announcement wouldn't be made until after the event. The lawyer had invited her down to Spanish Trace, Florida, so that they could go over all the evidence she had collected on her flash drive. They would spend a few days with her processing the information and building the case. Deke also gave her a URL so that she could securely upload the files to the law firm's website. She had agreed to do so. After a day of rest following tonight's occasion, Amy would hop on a plane on Monday and go.

Earlier that morning, she had spoken to Deke once again to confirm the plans. He recommended that she make a copy of the flash drive to keep for herself and not leave the files on her laptop after she uploaded them. The day had been crazy-busy, and she didn't have a blank drive. Before arriving at the hotel, she had stopped at Best Buy and bought the extra device. Now, she sat at the desk in her hotel room and foraged through her laptop case until she found the original drive with all the information already on it. Amy felt confident that it had been safe in the case among several other work-related flash drives. She stuck the original and the blank drives into her laptop's USB ports and began the copying process. It wouldn't take long. She wished she could have done it sooner, but the stress of preparing for the evening's event and her upcoming actions had occupied every moment of her time. While the files copied, she typed the URL that Deke had given her into her browser.

An error message appeared on the screen. No connection.

She tried again, but then realized she couldn't access any other websites. The Wi-Fi wasn't connected. Amy went through the motions of signing on to the network with the room password, but it still didn't work. Something was wrong.

Picking up the room telephone, she called the front desk. When a man answered, Amy reported, "Oh, hi, I'm trying to connect to your Wi-Fi, and it doesn't seem to be working."

"Oh, yes, I'm so sorry," the man said. "The Internet just went down a few minutes ago. We have IT working on it as we speak. It should be up soon. I apologize for the inconvenience."

Damn it!

Well, she'd just have to try later. She hung up and went back to her computer. At least she didn't need the Wi-Fi to copy the files.

In the meantime, Connor had insisted that she stop by his suite on the penthouse floor to give him confirmation that everything was ready to go. She dreaded doing that. He would once again likely try to talk her out of resigning. The man had become a bit pathetic. Connor claimed that he loved her and still wanted to marry her. That, of course, was only half true and certainly no longer in the cards. It had taken Amy months to figure out the real reason. If she stayed as Connor's president, she would remain under his thumb. He needed her close so he could continue manipulating her to control his narrative. The worst thing for him would be if she were to slip away.

Might as well get it over with, she thought. Then she could relax for the rest of the afternoon. Maybe get a massage from the hotel masseuse. She would take her time getting dressed and putting on her "happy face" for all the investors and business press that Connor would woo that night. Despite how she felt about Connor, Amy was still a professional, and she would do her job.

The computer finished the copying process. Amy tried the Wi-Fi again, but it was still out. Cursing under her breath, she removed both flash drives and buried the original deep into her purse. She held the second one in her hand, thought about where she could hide it, and finally set the purse on the desk, went to the bathroom and stuck the drive in her toiletry bag. Amy then made sure she had her key card in a pocket and left. She had been able to book a nice room that was at the end of the hallway, somewhat more isolated from the rest of the units on the floor. Less noise. No slamming doors in the corridor late at night.

She took the elevator to the penthouse and stepped out. Connor's suite was also at the far end of the hallway, so she turned the corner and . . . halted in her tracks.

Ronan Barry was ahead of her. He also appeared to be on his way to Connor's room. The man's back was to her. He didn't know she was thirty feet behind him. Amy walked slower so that he would get there first. Barry knocked on the door, but he didn't glance her way. She waited until the door opened and he went inside. Amy then continued walking until she reached the suite.

She heard men arguing inside. The voices were muffled, but she recognized Connor and Barry speaking angrily to each other. Another man was also present, but she didn't know who it could be.

What was going on? Should she knock and interrupt them? Perhaps she should simply go back to her room and call Connor on the phone to give him the confirmation he wanted. Why did she need to do it in person? To hell with that.

However, Amy was still in evidence-gathering node. Perhaps it wouldn't hurt to remain a moment to eavesdrop. She distinctly heard Ronan Barry say the name, "Doug Frankel" within a sentence. Amy faced the door again. She leaned forward and placed her ear against it. She couldn't make out all of the conversation, but the snippets she heard were enough.

The unknown voice said, ". . . police found your envelope in Frankel's attic. He hid it up there."

Connor replied, "Ronan . . . why the hell . . . you didn't search the whole . . . screwup!"

Ronan retorted, "How was I to know . . . looked everywhere for the damned photos . . . the attic was just not on the radar! I mean, come on . . . didn't know that pull cord went to an attic!"

"Tell Petey-o exactly what happened when . . ." Connor's voice dropped in volume.

Petey-o. Amy remembered that name from when she and Connor were in Ireland. Was the third man in the room this Petey-o person?

Ronan's voice was clearer again. ". . . envelope was delivered to Frankel by courier . . . I showed up two hours later . . . Frankel and I . . . in his office . . . said he destroyed the photos . . . I didn't believe him . . . threatened me with a pistol . . . struggled . . . his own gun . . . got the better of him . . . went off and his head exploded . . . big mess . . ."

The unknown voice—could it be Petey-o?—said, "Yeah, yeah, we know how . . . you staged it to look like . . . was half ass . . . and then . . . searched the place?"

"I did! I looked everywhere!" Ronan insisted.

Connor growled, "Keep your voice down. You idiot . . . obviously didn't . . . attic."

"I'm sorry! I had to get out of there after that gunshot! I . . . a hurry. What difference does it make?"

"Tell him, Petey-o."

The unknown voice *was* Petey-o! He spoke so softly she could barely pick up the words. ". . . police were told . . . location of the envelope in the attic by . . ."

"What?" Ronan asked, distressed.

MIKE PAPANTONIO

"That's right, Ronan," Connor replied. "That lawyer in Florida! He knew where Frankel hid the envelope!"

Oh, my God, they're talking about Deke! Amy strained to hear more, but she heard movement close to the other side of the door.

"I have to go," Petey-o said. "I'll let you two . . . it out. And keep an eye on . . . you saw what she did . . . the video feed. As for me . . . my job!"

She had to get out of there fast. Amy bolted and ran toward the elevators. She made it there just as she heard the suite door open at the end of the hall. No time to wait for the car! She eyed the stairwell entrance. Just as she caught a glimpse of "Petey-o" at the end of the corridor, she made a split second change of plan. She scurried down the stairs to her own floor.

Petey-o, an older man with gray hair, looked very familiar to her, but she couldn't place him. Had she seen him on the news? In a newspaper? And what had she overheard? From what she could put together from the fragmented conversation, it sounded as if Connor and Ronan Barry had sent some kind of blackmail material to Doug Frankel. Frankel had hidden it in his attic. Barry had shown up to threaten Frankel, and Frankel told him he'd destroyed the material and refused to capitulate to their demands. Frankel must have pulled a gun. The two men fought, and somehow the gun was used on Frankel himself. Barry had staged the crime to look like a suicide. Afterward, Barry had searched for the blackmail material but couldn't find it. He missed looking in the attic, didn't have time to look, or didn't know it was there. Somehow, Deke had learned about it. How, she didn't know, but he had alerted the Chicago police that an "envelope" was in Frankel's attic. And Connor was not happy about it.

She needed to add this new information to her flash drive contents. If this wasn't a smoking gun, she didn't know what was.

When she got to her floor, she was out of breath and her heart was pounding. She exited the stairwell and turned to walk down the hall toward her room.

Connor's man, Pat Beckett, was walking toward her. Was he staying on her floor?

The Middleman

They passed each other. Beckett nodded at her and said, "Good afternoon, Amy. Ready for tonight?"

"Yes, Pat, thank you," she managed to say. She continued on to her room. At the door, she looked back and saw Beckett turn the far corner to the elevator banks. Amy used the key card and went into her room. She then sat at her desk and saw that her purse appeared to be in a different position than how she'd left it.

A grip of terror seized her.

Amy grabbed the purse and rummaged through it. She then dumped the entire contents onto the desk. The flash drive wasn't there. She frantically sorted through everything again, but amid the usual contents, which included the knife with a four-inch blade and pink handle that she carried for protection in the mean streets of Chicago, there was no drive. It was gone.

Her heart was pounding. She got up and scurried to the bathroom and emptied her toiletry bag.

No flash drive there, either.

Oh, my God, oh, my God . . . ! Had Pat Beckett been in her room? *I'm such a fool!*

She stared at her pale face in the mirror. The fright was unbearable.

How could she have been so damned stupid? She was the head of a major corporation and she had let this . . . *monster* . . . seduce her and trick her and target her pride . . . "I'll make you president of the company," he had said, sweet-talking her.

And she had fallen for it.

Why had she agreed to "spy" on him? She was not a private investigator! Why had she tried to gather all that evidence? Was her hubris out of control?

Now it was all an ugly and dangerous mess, and her blind stupidity would be her disgrace. For the first time since all the trouble with Connor Devlin began, Amy Redmond began to sob with remorse.

27

The event was off to a good start. The total count of attendees, including plus-ones, was 114. The no-shows were insignificant. The guests included some of the biggest names in the financial and medical worlds in Chicago and New York.

Amy had done her best to get cleaned up and dressed in a formal gown. The makeup she applied suitably covered her swollen eyes. She was thankful that she had no responsibilities at the event other than to meet and greet the guests, thank them for coming, and pretend that she was the happiest PBM president in the country.

Easier said than done.

Cocktails were served first as everyone mingled in the beautiful setting. Amy needed a strong drink, so she asked the bartender for a vodka on the rocks. She then stood on a side of the room and surveyed all the well-dressed, wealthy people who were among the 1 percent. She spied Connor Devlin, who was easily in his element. He was glad-handing with everyone, kissing wives' hands, and displaying his trademark charm.

"There you are."

She turned to see Paul Baker. "Oh, Paul, thank God you're here."

He detected the anxiety. "Is something wrong?"

She kept her voice down. "I'm in trouble, Paul. Big trouble."

"What's going on?"

"All of the evidence against Connor, all the information on the company's dealings over the past year, everything I've been collecting . . . it's gone. They've stolen it. The jig is up; I'm a dead person."

170

THE MIDDLEMAN

"What? Wait, slow down. Start from the beginning."

"Paul, I was keeping all that stuff on a flash drive. I had it and a copy of it with me here in the hotel. In two days I was going to fly down to Florida, meet with Mr. Deketomis, and give all of it to him. I stepped out of the room for a minute—and I overheard something serious, I have to tell you about it—but anyway, when I got back to my room, both flash drives were gone. I saw one of Connor's so-called assistants in the hallway. Pat Beckett. Paul, I think he somehow got into my room."

"How did he know what to look for?" Paul asked.

"I don't know, but Connor has eyes and ears everywhere." She then told the attorney what she'd overheard regarding Doug Frankel.

"That does sound bad," Paul said. "Who is this Petey-o fellow?"

"I don't know. Someone Connor works with. Likely a bigwig in the Irish crime syndicate that Connor must be a part of. I first heard that name when we were in Ireland last year. I got a quick look at him in the hallway and he seemed *very* familiar to me. I just can't place him, though."

"Well, try to calm down. Get through the evening and then get the hell out of Dodge."

"I plan to. I should probably leave now. In fact, I think I will. Paul, I need to call Mr. Deketomis. It's a Saturday night, so I'm sure he's not in his office, but I can leave a message. Maybe I can get on a plane tonight or at the earliest tomorrow morning. I—"

A server approached them with a tray holding two full champagne flutes. "For the toast," he declared. Amy and Paul took them and thanked the young man. They looked around and saw that all the guests were also holding flutes of bubbly. The servers were just finishing doling them out when Connor picked up a fork from a table and dinged his own flute several times.

"May I have your attention, please? Folks, may I have your attention?"

The guests halted their conversations and gazed at their host.

Connor, exhibiting his million-dollar smile, spoke eloquently. "Ladies and gentlemen, I want to thank you from the bottom of my heart for being here tonight. In ten minutes we'll sit down for an exquisite meal prepared by the excellent chefs of the Drake Hotel. Afterward, we have a short presentation for you to view over on the other side of the room where the chairs are set up. I promise you—we have some exciting news to share. It's been an incredible fourteen months since I became CEO of EirePharma, and in that short time we have turned the company around from near bankruptcy to being one of the strongest pharmacy benefit managers in the USA. But I couldn't have done it alone. I owe so much to the Redmond family, my predecessor Charles Redmond, and especially, to our current president, Amy Redmond. Amy, where are you?"

Oh, God . . . no . . .

He spotted her quickly, indicating that he had already known where she was standing. "There you are! Come here, please. Come!" He beckoned her with a hand. Suddenly she was on autopilot, once again under his spell. Amy left Paul's side and moved through the crowd to stand beside Connor.

He took her free hand with his and squeezed hard. Very hard. Amy tried not to wince.

"Amy has been the face of EirePharma, and she has performed in her position as president with exemplary flying colors. I look forward to *many more years* of her being my colleague. Please, give her a round of applause!"

The room erupted with cheers.

What did he say? I'll be his colleague for many more years? What??

She put on her happy face, smiled, and curtseyed to the applause. She then managed to pull her hand away from his.

"A toast!" Connor announced. "To the Redmonds, to EirePharma, to all of you here and your successful businesses . . . may the future be very bright!"

"Hear, hear!" someone shouted.

Everyone drank, including Amy.

* * *

Amy was not happy that the place setting assignment positioned her next to Connor at the head table. At first she thought about attempting to switch, but the others at the table were some of *the* top investment bankers in attendance. She had to do it. Luckily, Paul Baker was placed on her opposite side.

The usual beef, chicken, or vegetarian selections were offered, and Amy chose chicken. The meal was surprisingly good for hotel banquet food, a testament to the Drake's reputation. At one point, a waiter came by with a bottle of champagne and refilled her glass. He then did the same for Paul. One of the other guests held up an empty glass, and the waiter said, "I'm empty, sir, I'll be right back with a full bottle."

The earlier vodka drink and first glass of champagne were doing a number on Amy. While it helped take the edge off her anxiety, she was still frightened. She was determined to leave as soon as possible following the presentation. She downed the second glass of champagne and continued to eat, making ridiculous small talk with the other people at the table.

At one point, Paul rose and whispered to her, "Men's room." He wavered a little, and she asked him if he was all right. "Yeah, I think the drinks were a little strong, heh heh." He left the room.

Amy turned to see that Connor was watching her, practically studying her face.

"What?" she asked.

"Nothing, my dear. You look radiant tonight. The fields of Ireland are in your eyes. I would so much like to take you back there. We had such a good time, didn't we?"

She wanted to spit in his face, but Amy replied, "It was lovely."

And then . . . her stomach lurched. She closed and opened her eyes. Connor's features were slightly blurred.

Have I really had that much to drink?

She took a sip of water, and then another bite of food.

The plate in front of her seemed to be slowly pulling away as if her eyes were a camera and the lens was zooming out.

Part of the conversation she'd overheard outside Connor's hotel suite door came back to her. What was it that "Petey-o" had said at the end? "Keeping an eye on" something. He referred to a "she." Had he been talking about her? He mentioned a "video feed."

My God!

Mike Papantonio

That's how they knew where she'd placed the flash drives. Some kind of video feed. Was her room bugged?

She immediately felt dizzy and on the verge of being sick.

"Excuse me," she said, pushing her chair back. She stood, grabbed her purse, and held on to the edge of the table as she felt the room tilt.

"Hurry back, dear," Connor said. "You don't want to miss the presentation."

She nodded and awkwardly made her way out of the Camellia and into the hallway where the restrooms were located.

Ronan Barry stood in the corridor as if he were some kind of sentinel. "Evening, Amy," he said.

"Evening, Ronan . . ." she managed to acknowledge. She attempted to focus on the entrance to the ladies' room and headed that way, but suddenly the distance increased. The alcove was now far, far away.

What's happening to me . . . ?

She was determined to reach a toilet stall within the sanctuary of privacy and safety.

Closer . . . closer . . . almost there . . .

And then the hallway abruptly rotated sideways. She felt a hard slam against her body, and the last thing she knew before the darkness befell her was that she had fallen onto the carpet.

* * *

When her eyes opened, the blurriness sluggishly sharpened to reveal a room that was askew. It appeared to be a hotel room. A nightstand was directly in front of her face. The lamp there was on and a bit bright. She squeezed her lids shut and opened them several times.

She felt woozy.

Amy moved her arms and legs and realized she was in bed, her head on a pillow. She tested the feeling in her fingers and toes and attempted to decipher her surroundings beyond the nightstand. As her senses returned, she understood that she was in her own hotel room at the Drake.

What the hell happened to me? How did I get here?

THE MIDDLEMAN

She twisted her body and became aware of the soft sheets against her bare skin. All over. She was naked.

What the . . . ?

Amy slowly raised herself up. Something . . . smelled. It was a familiar stench; one she knew from when she had been in college. She'd had a job as an assistant to the administrator at a hospital.

The smell was that of something common in an emergency room. Blood.

It was then that she felt the presence of weight in the bed beside her. She jerked around and her eyes focused on the horror.

The color of crimson was everywhere. A horrible, sickly mess.

She screamed, but her throat spasmed tightly, producing nothing but a hoarse croak.

A man, covered in blood, lay on his back on the other side of the bed. A knife protruded from his chest. It had a pink handle and was encrusted with white stones—just like the one she carried in her purse. Was it *her* knife?

Who IS this?

She forced herself to focus on the dead man's face, and his features eventually became clearer to her.

The nightmare had just become worse than it already was.

She recognized the naked corpse to be Paul Baker, her attorney.

28

Now

After being sick in the bathroom, sitting beside the dresser, Amy continued to stare at the horror on the bed.

"Amy! Open the door!"

More pounding.

Connor was in the hallway.

She wanted nothing to do with the man. Unfortunately, she realized that he was perhaps the only person who could help her now. Whatever had happened here, it would destroy her.

The continued knocking at the door blew away the fog that was clouding her brain. Amy got up and staggered to it. The feeling of being on a rocking boat was finally dissipating. She unlatched the chain and opened the door.

Connor Devlin was still in his tuxedo, and he held a bottle of champagne.

"Amy, I thought we should celebrate with more champ—my God, what's the matter?"

"Connor . . . I . . . uh . . ."

She almost collapsed again but caught herself on the edge of the open doorframe. Connor strode in, followed by his two shadows, Ronan Barry and Pat Beckett. Of course they'd be accompanying Connor.

Connor's eyes swept the suite and took in the ghastly sight. He handed the bottle to Beckett, and then he took hold of Amy's waist, helping her to stand.

"Let's sit down, Amy."

"Connor, I don't know . . . I don't know what happened . . ."

"Sit down. *Please.*"

He led her back to the seat at the dresser. The two other men stood gaping at the bloody bed.

"Did you call the police?" he asked.

"I . . . no . . . What . . . what time is it?"

"Just after midnight, Amy. You're obviously quite intoxicated." Connor turned and went closer to the bed, gazing at the dead man. "He's your attorney."

"Yes."

"Were you and he . . . ?"

"No! Of course not! Connor, I don't remember anything! I was . . . Like you said, I was drugged! I had to have been."

"I'm not sure I believe you, Amy. What's been going on with you and Mr. Baker?"

"Nothing! This is some kind of . . . setup! I didn't do this!"

Connor squinted at her. "Okay, if you were drugged, what's the last thing you remember?"

"I was at the event! I . . ." She rubbed her brow as images began to come back to her. "I went to the ladies' room. That's the last thing I remember. I was in the hallway . . . or . . . maybe I was in the ladies' room . . . and I must have blacked out."

"And then what?"

"I woke up *here*! In bed with . . . *him*!"

Connor quietly spoke to Barry and Beckett, and they leapt into action. They began to comb the suite, looking closely at pieces of furniture, the television, and the drapes over the window.

He then came back to Amy. "All right, I believe you. Don't worry, I'll take care of this." He gently stroked the tears on her cheek with the back of his hand. The sensation of his fingers on her face ignited a wave of emotions. She should have recoiled from his touch, but in this moment, she found it eerily comforting. Only because Connor Devlin could perhaps make this nightmare go away.

"I didn't do this," she said, starting to sob uncontrollably.

177

"Amy . . . Amy. Take it easy." He squatted so that his head was level to hers. "We don't know what happened here. But it doesn't look good. I recognize that knife. It's yours, isn't it?"

She nodded.

"Amy, the man's throat was cut, and then he was stabbed in the chest."

Amy turned away and wailed.

"Amy, keep quiet!" he snapped. "We don't want to wake up everyone on the floor." He placed his hands on her shoulders. "Please. Try to pull yourself together. We're going to get you out of here."

"Look at this, boss," Barry said as he fiddled with something on the flat screen television. Connor went to him. Barry pulled on a wire and let it dangle in his hand.

"Over here, too, boss," Beckett said. He stood by the drapes, pulling on a string or something in the hem.

Amy looked up. She saw the men huddled in the middle of the suite, examining the objects they had found. Connor told them to check the bathroom, too, and then he walked back to her.

"Amy, Ronan and Pat have found bugs in the room. Cameras. Someone spied on you and your attorney. It's safe to assume that they have photos or video of the whole scene."

She gasped. "Wait . . ." Amy shook her head in an attempt to make the cobwebs disappear. "If there are cameras, that means they recorded . . . the whole thing. Wouldn't it show . . . that I didn't really kill Paul?"

Connor grimly replied, "Whoever set you up likely means to blackmail you. They'd just use video stills of you with him and dispose of any recording that happened before."

Her mouth dropped open, and she felt as if she might throw up again. "Who . . . who would do that?"

"I don't know. Enemies of EirePharma, most likely. I'll bet your fingerprints are all over that knife, too. Someone wanted you framed, and I think I know exactly who it is."

"*Who?*"

And then she remembered. A conversation upon which she had eavesdropped prior to the event. Something about a "video feed." And her flash drives that contained incriminating evidence against Connor Devlin.

Oh my God . . . It was him, it was Connor, it's always been him! I've been such an idiot, a damned fool!

Devlin shook his head and answered, "Don't you worry about who or what or how. I'll take care of it. You know I always do."

Right. She did know. Connor Devlin had ways of "taking care" of problems.

Very unorthodox ways.

"It's a good thing you didn't call the police, or you'd be in a jail cell," he said. "You'd easily be charged with murdering this man. Whoever is behind this is counting on the fact that your reputation would be ruined, our company would take a big fat negative PR hit, and you'd probably go to prison for life."

"Oh, God . . ." Amy started crying again. *Liar, liar, liar . . .*

"I can help you, Amy. You know it's what I do. Go take a shower and get dressed. You're not going to fall apart. You're a strong, tough woman. I need you to be that experienced dynamo of a corporate executive. Try to remember what that Amy looks like. We will make this go away."

He placed a hand on her upper arm and squeezed.

"The loyalty between you and me matters more than ever right now," he added.

They were words that sent shivers of ice down her back.

PART FOUR
JUNE 2024

29

Now

It was a busy Monday morning at the Deketomis-Bergman law firm. The team was preparing for another conference room meeting while Deke caught up on messages and phone calls after a not-very-relaxing weekend. He'd expected word from Amy Redmond regarding her visit to Florida and was a little surprised that he hadn't heard from her. Had she resigned as she'd told him she would? Had the event that was held on Saturday gone well for her? Deke hit the intercom button.

"Diana, could you try to get Amy Redmond on the phone? We have her cell number, don't we?"

"We do, Deke. I'll try it." Deke went on to some of the paperwork on his desk, and a few minutes later Diana buzzed him back. "She doesn't answer, Deke. I left a message for her to give you a call."

"Thanks, Diana. Oh, you know what? Try calling her attorney, Paul Baker. You have that number, right?"

"Yes." And, once again, his assistant came back with the news. "Deke, Mr. Baker's office says he hasn't come in yet today. His secretary said it's unusual, and she's been trying to reach him at home. I left a message for him to call you, too."

"Okay, nothing else we can do for now."

Before hanging up, Diana added, "Oh, Deke? Have you heard the weather forecast?"

"No, what's going on?"

"A big tropical storm is headed our way. It'll be here in a couple of days."

"Oh, great. That's all we need. Does it look bad?"

"Might be."

"Well, keep me informed. Sometimes these things peter out and never become hurricanes by the time they reach landfall."

"Will do."

It was midmorning when Diana buzzed him again. "I have Chief McClory in Chicago on the line for you."

"Thanks, put him through!" Deke had phoned the chief of detectives after Matt's funeral and was hoping for a return call.

After Deke greeted him, McClory said, "I'm sorry, I just got the message that you had called. I've been on vacation. Just got back in the office."

"I hope you went somewhere fun."

"Not really. The wife and I stayed in town. Visited with the grand-kids. We did go up to the Wisconsin Dells for a weekend, though. The kids love that money pit. What can I do for you?"

Deke pulled out his notes on Matt's case. "I wanted to ask you some questions about Matt Redmond's murder, if you don't mind."

"Well, that's an ongoing investigation, but I can share some things with you, I suppose," the man said.

"So you haven't closed the case?"

"Hell, no. The suspects haven't been caught. We're still looking for them. I'm afraid we don't have a lot to go on, though. Between you and me, unless someone comes forward and says they saw the whole thing go down and can at least give us descriptions of the muggers, then we're not going to solve it."

Deke figured that would be the answer. "What about Matt's phone? Was that recovered?"

"Nah, the muggers must have taken it."

"Did the police have the phone company ping it?"

"Hold on, let me pull up the file on the computer," McClory said. In a moment, he came back and said, "I don't see anything in the report about it. I see a copy of the request to the phone carrier, but no response.

Huh. You know, if they pinged it and there was no signal, that means the phone is either turned off or it's been destroyed. Captain Bianchi was in charge of the investigation, and he's a good man. I know he dots all the Is and crosses all the Ts. I'll see if I can ask him about the ping situation. But you know, Deke, these street criminals in Chicago are enterprising bastards. They can reconfigure a cell phone in no time and sell it before the phone company even has time to ping it. I'm sorry, Deke. I know Matt was a friend of yours, and I liked him when I met him. It's a shame."

"It is. Okay, my friend, I'm sure you've got a lot on your desk that you need to deal with since it's your first day back from vacation. Thanks for your time."

* * *

The team assembled after lunch, and Deke asked for progress reports. Michael Carey raised his hand, and Deke nodded at him.

"I've managed to find two women who were regional managers for Walgreens; they had bad experiences with EirePharma reps over the price of insulin," he said. "Roberta Short and Carlene Webster are in the Chicago area. They've since resigned because their lives were threatened."

"Their *lives*?" Carol spurted. "Over insulin prices?"

"It's what they say. I think they might be good to interview. I had a brief conversation with Ms. Short, and she said that she and Ms. Webster are willing to talk to us."

"That's good," Deke said. "Anything else?"

"Yes," Gina said. "There was a voice message on the main line that came through this morning. It was from a man named Vernon Bunker, who was on the EirePharma board of directors until last year when he was forced to resign. He hinted that Connor Devlin used intimidation and threats to get him to do so. He said he wants to talk."

"Did he leave a phone number?" Deke asked.

"Yes."

"You sure it's not a crank message? And how did he know to call me?"

She shrugged. "Sarah looked him up in EirePharma records and confirmed that Mr. Bunker was indeed on the board for many years until September of last year, but who knows?"

"If it's real, then it sounds promising. Carol, would you call him back and find out if there's anything there?"

"Sure thing," she answered.

"Anyone else? Jake?"

Jake shook his head. "I've gotten nowhere on the Doug Frankel business. I mean, we have that evidence of blackmail, but even that is sketchy. Did you ever hear back from your police guy in Chicago about it?"

Deke nodded. "I told Chief McClory about the envelope in the attic after you'd found it, and he said he'd have a team of investigators go back to Frankel's house. He hasn't said anything else about it, but I did talk to him this morning about Matt Redmond's case, though." He relayed the gist of the conversation to the team.

"Sounds like a big fat dead end," Carol said.

"Unfortunately, I think you're right," Deke replied. "It's a shame. Matt deserves better. I wonder if the Chicago police whose boots were on the ground investigating the murder did a very good job. They can't even find Matt's phone."

"It's probably at the bottom of the Chicago River or Lake Michigan," Jake mused. "Oh, hey, I just remembered. Did Matt ever track down that Detective Brazos about Charles Redmond's suicide note?"

Deke slapped his forehead. "I completely forgot to ask McClory about that! No, if Matt didn't get back to you about it, then that fell through the cracks. Jake, can you try to find Mr. Brazos?"

"Will do."

"Anyone else?"

Michael spoke up again. "Oh, you had wanted to find out more about this Markus DeStefano? The attorney in Delaware?"

"Right."

"He's legit. It's like you said. DeStefano handles a lot of trusts, estates, and financial planning. He's had some interesting clients, though." Michael named some well-known New York organized crime families from yesteryear, men who had committed high-profile white-collar crimes, and other miscreants. "And regular folks, too," Michael added.

"Why in the world would Charles Redmond want to consult him?" Deke asked, mostly to himself.

"DeStefano is also a securities lawyer," Michael answered. "He specializes in what we all know are the complex and changing laws and regulations that apply to financial investments. Someone like him, if he's good at his job, can provide significant benefits both in planning investments as well as recovering losses from wrongdoing. And he can broker the transfer of stock from one person to another."

Deke rubbed his chin. "Charles Redmond consulted him before the sale of EirePharma to Connor Devlin. I'm guessing he handled, or was going to handle, the transfer of Redmond's stock to Devlin."

"Right."

"We might need to talk to DeStefano."

"I've already done it. He expressed no interest in speaking to me. Mr. DeStefano said that the discussions he had with Charles Redmond were protected by client-attorney privilege, and he hung up on me."

Deke rolled his eyes. "It figures. I guess we won't know what went on. Thanks, Michael. Anyone else?"

Sarah raised her finger. "Perhaps I've saved the best for last."

"You hinted before the weekend that you may have a breakthrough," Deke said. "What do you have?"

Sarah cleared her throat. "As you know, Gina and I have been researching Connor Devlin. When Gina got busy with her recent court case, I took over the job myself, and I've learned some interesting things. I've managed to track down some of Mr. Devlin's background using Ancestry.com and, from that, leads to online newspaper articles in Ireland. Some of this stuff was archived, and I had to subscribe to some papers for access, but I think it's worth it."

"I'm all ears," Michael said.

"Connor Devlin was born in Tramore in County Waterford. His father was Ciaran Devlin, a man who was heavily involved with the IRA in the middle of the twentieth century. He was married to Maeve Kinahan, who was also a part of the organization. When Connor was born, Ciaran Devlin's occupation was supposedly that of a waste and refuse worker, and his mother worked in a textile mill. That said, Ciaran was in and out of jail for a number of petty crimes. It turns out Maeve Kinahan was part of the Kinahan family in Ireland that has a reputation of, well, organized crime."

"I've heard of the Kinahan Crime Group," Michael said. "They're still active. They're a serious outfit."

"Yes. These days the Kinahans are on several most wanted lists. They run drugs and do a lot of business in the Middle East. Anyway, Connor apparently was a troubled youth. I found a record of an arrest in Dublin when he was sixteen. He was involved in a bank robbery. The charges were dropped due to lack of evidence, though. He did serve time in Ireland for financial fraud when he was in his twenties. He served five years in Cork Prison. When he got out, he somehow made it over to America. How he got past immigration with his record, I don't know. I have a theory, though."

"Let's hear it," Deke said.

"I believe Mr. Devlin was a member of the Kinahan Group then, and I believe he still is." Sarah removed several pieces of paper from a manila folder and distributed them around the table. "This is a photocopy I made of a photograph I found in the *Irish Times* when I was doing searches for Devlin and the name Kinahan."

Everyone examined the picture, which displayed a group of men in a pub. The quality of the photo was poor, and it was difficult to discern clearly who any of the men might be. All but one sat at a table with beer steins in hand. The man standing was dressed in an Irish kilt, so it could be presumed that the tabletop obscured other kilts worn by the men sitting.

"This picture was taken in 2014," Sarah continued. "The article is about the Kinahan Group and how the upper 'management' get together in secret locations every couple of years. No one here is identified by name. As you can see, the caption reads, 'Kinahan Group leaders in a Lismore pub, taken surreptitiously by a barmaid.' The name Kinahan popped up in the search and that's how I found it. Do any of these men look familiar?"

THE MIDDLEMAN

Deke raised his copy and pointed at a man sitting at the table. "That's Devlin. I know it. I was standing right next to him. The photo is blurry, and I doubt the picture could be used in a court of law for identification purposes, but I recognize the guy. That white hair. The shape of his head. The broad shoulders. That's our man."

Jake made a slow whistle and said, "So you're saying Connor Devlin is a member of a major organized crime organization? What's he doing in Chicago then?"

Michael gave it a stab. "Maybe these criminals have decided that legitimate drugs like insulin can be a moneymaker if exploited the way mobsters do it. The American pharmaceutical business is a perfect opportunity for mobsters. They fit right in. Devlin is working as a 'medical business professional' as cover, representing what could be a global scheme by the crime group to move in on the US medical insurance and pharma industry . . . What better way to do that than through PBMs?"

"Exactly," Sarah said.

"Man," Deke said after a moment's silence by everyone in the room. "I may be taking this a little too personally after my encounter with him at Matt's funeral, but I really want to ruin this guy's day."

* * *

Only a half hour had passed since the team meeting had ended when Diana buzzed him again in his office.

"Deke, I have Mary Redmond on the line for you."

"Really?" This was a surprise. "By all means, put her through!"

The woman's voice was a bit raspy, but she sounded strong and vibrant. "Mr. Deketomis?"

"Speaking. This is Mary Redmond?"

"It is. I was given your name and number by my niece, Amy Redmond. For all intents and purposes, though, she is my daughter."

"I am aware of your relationship to Amy and its significance, Mrs. Redmond," Deke said. "Amy herself and your late nephew Matt have fully educated me about your family. I am very happy to hear from you. How are you doing these days?"

"Oh, I'm hanging in there. I have a rare neurological disease called myasthenia gravis that makes my muscles weak, and I appear as if I'm aging faster than normal. But that's all very boring and not why I called you."

"What can I do for you, Mrs. Redmond?"

"Amy has told me about the work you're doing to go after Mr. Connor Devlin and the ways in which he's turning my late husband's company into a stinking heap of sewage."

That made Deke almost laugh. "We are indeed revving up a case. Amy has been very helpful."

"Well, I want you to know that I'd like to participate. If you need my name on your list of people who can help, you've got it."

"That's fantastic, Mrs. Redmond."

"What do I need to do? I suppose I need my own lawyer?"

"I understand Paul Baker, whom I've met, is your family attorney?"

"He is."

"You can involve him if you like, Mrs. Redmond, but we would be your attorneys in the case. So it's really not necessary for Mr. Baker to be a part of it unless you want that. We'll need to interview you and take a sworn statement in the very near future. Are you up to that, Mrs. Redmond? We can come to Chicago and do it all close to your home in an office setting. Or, if we need to, we can come to your house with a court reporter and set up a sworn statement there."

"Oh, I can get in a car and be driven wherever you need me to be. I have a helper who drives me places."

"That's wonderful. Let me get some information from you." He asked her for a good phone number and email address, which she provided.

"Terrific," Deke said. "One of my team will be contacting you very soon. By the way, have you heard from Amy recently? I've been trying to reach her today."

"No, I haven't," Mary said. "She had a big event with the company on Saturday. I believe Paul attended as well. Those things can be exhausting. Perhaps she took the day off. Actually, she had told me she was going to resign. I'm not sure when that was supposed to be."

THE MIDDLEMAN

"Yes, she told me about that, too. Well, it's just Monday. Maybe she is simply busy with other matters. If you do talk to her, could you please ask her to call my office?"

"I will do that. And thank you for what you're doing."

"It is my pleasure. Thank *you* for reaching out. We appreciate your willingness to help. We'll be in touch very soon."

The call ended, and he immediately sent out an email to the team informing them of the good news.

* * *

Carol dialed the number that Vernon Bunker had left on the company's voicemail.

"Hello? Who's calling?" a man answered, sounding a bit frantic. His voice betrayed his age, which Carol knew was in the seventies.

"Is this Mr. Bunker?" she asked.

"Who's calling? Who's calling?"

"Mr. Bunker, this is Carol Morris at the Deketomis-Bergman law firm in Spanish Trace, Florida. You left a message on our company voicemail?"

"Oh! Yes, yes, I did. Yes, this is Vernon Bunker. What did you say your name was?"

"Carol Morris. I'm the head of Safety, Security, and Investigative Services at the firm. Mr. Deketomis asked me to give you a call."

"Right, yes, I asked that he call me."

"How can we help you, Mr. Bunker?"

"Well, I understand you're suing Connor Devlin and EirePharma."

"Not yet we aren't. I'm afraid I can't reveal any information about current or future cases that the law firm may or may not take on. Where did you hear this?"

"I actually thought the case was already underway. I've had my ear to the grapevine. There are whispers going around. Something happened to me with regard to EirePharma, and afterward I had a conversation with the company's attorney, Paul Baker. He was very sympathetic to

191

my story and confirmed to me in confidence that legal issues were afoot. Your firm's name came up."

"Hm. All right. What happened to you? How can we help you?"

"I was on the board of directors of EirePharma for twenty-seven years. I'm retired now, but I was a hedge fund manager, stockbroker, and financial advisor in Chicago since 1975. I was threatened with violence by Connor Devlin if I didn't resign from the board last year, simply because I questioned some policies he was enacting. If I had attempted any legal recourse, I have no doubt that I wouldn't be speaking to you now."

"That's quite an accusation, Mr. Bunker."

"It's the truth!"

Carol was getting excited. This was good stuff. "If it is, then we will want to properly interview you and take a sworn statement. If one of our attorneys comes to Chicago, are you willing to speak to us formally?"

"Yes, but I have some conditions."

"What are they?"

"First of all, I'm in hiding. I fear for my life. Devlin and his henchmen have been watching me ever since I walked out of the building."

Carol thought he might be exaggerating. "All the time? You know they're watching you daily?"

"Well, no, not daily. Every once in a while. I would see one of their black sedans on my street. One day there was a fellow at my house. He worked for Devlin. He said he'd come by to 'see how I was getting on' and if there was anything Devlin could do for me. I knew that was just bullshit. They were checking up on me. They wanted me to know that I was being watched. I finally decided to get out of my house, rent a place that was secluded and out of the way, and get in touch with you people. I'm hoping you can put me into some kind of witness protection thing."

Carol winced. "Mr. Bunker, we'd have to see about that, depending on what you have to say. Why don't you tell me—"

"And another thing . . ."

"What's that?"

"I'll talk only to Mr. Deketomis. He's the one who has to come down and meet with me."

"Why is that?"

"I . . . I have my reasons. I don't trust anyone. I'm scared. He'll have to meet me first in a public place, like a bar or something. If I feel comfortable after a preliminary conversation, then we can make plans to go forward. Is that a problem?"

"That shouldn't be an issue. Can I call you back in a few minutes? I need to speak with Mr. Deketomis about this."

"Okay, but hurry. I'm going a little nuts hiding like a fugitive."

Carol hung up and marched to Deke's office and knocked on the open door. He looked up, and she asked, "How would you like to go back to Chicago?"

* * *

A few hours later, Deke and Michael boarded a private jet bound for O'Hare.

"Diana's a miracle worker," Michael said. "How'd she line up these meeting details so quickly?"

"Because she's Diana," Deke replied.

It had been a frantic rush to gather materials at the office, drive to their respective homes, pack overnight bags, and ride separate car services to the airport in the nick of time. Deke had thought it best to get out of town that very day. The tropical storm was moving across the Gulf much faster than was originally projected, and it would likely be causing chaos with air travel within twenty-four hours.

Deke himself had returned the call to Vernon Bunker, and they agreed to meet Tuesday somewhere near where Bunker was temporarily staying. Deke promised to call the man in the morning, and Bunker would provide a place and time.

In the meantime, Michael had reached out to one of the two Walgreens women, Roberta Short. He asked if they were available Tuesday to meet with him for a preliminary conversation. Roberta quickly checked with Carlene Webster and returned Michael's call. The former pharmacy employees were able, willing, and enthusiastic about telling their stories. Diana was also tasked to set up a meeting with Mary Redmond and promised to let them know if that was possible.

Thus, Deke and Michael had separate missions in Chicago. If the interviews went as well as they hoped, then the trip would be productive and pertinent to the case.

"Think we can do what we have to do and make it back before the storm hits?" Michael asked Deke.

"Doesn't sound like it. I just hope the storm's not too bad and that it's over before we have to fly back home. But if we have to spend an extra day in Chicago, I don't mind. Do you?"

Michael shrugged. "I know a guy who can maybe get us Cubs tickets."

Deke turned to look at him with one eyebrow raised. "Oh? Really?"

30

Amy felt as if she'd been hit in the head with a hammer. The only comfort she felt was that she was no longer lying in bed next to her murdered friend.

Peering at her reflection in the bathroom mirror, though, she saw no injuries. Her face was indeed haggard from being asleep for nearly forty-eight hours. The remnants of the makeup she had applied on Saturday evening were still on her face and needed to come off. Soap and water helped, but she needed some serious micellar water. The shower was calling her name, too, and she would get there eventually.

A bottle of generic acetaminophen sat on the counter, probably meant for her. She opened it, popped out two tablets, filled up one of the provided paper cups with water from the sink, and swallowed them. Perhaps they would alleviate the pain in her head.

She was still unsteady on her feet, and she was nauseated. There was no question that she had been drugged.

Amy staggered back to the bed, fell into it, and closed her eyes. The images of Paul Baker with blood all over him and her knife sticking out of his chest would not go away. This was a recurring nightmare. She had already shed tears and would likely produce more in the hours and days to come.

Damn Connor, she thought. *Damn him straight to hell.*

She was a prisoner in one of the upstairs bedrooms of his Kenilworth mansion. In all of the months she had spent there, Amy had never seen this room. It was a suite, of sorts, with a queen-size four-poster bed, nightstands, and dressers, and there was a sitting area with a couch, a coffee table, and two chairs. All of the furnishings appeared to be antique, items from another era. Very European. The only piece of modernity was a flat screen television that was mounted on the wall of the sitting area. It actually worked. Thank goodness a private bathroom with a door lock connected to the bedroom. It could have been a unit at an old Dublin hotel.

The door out of the room, though, was locked from the outside. One of the men—Lance, Pat, Ronan, or one of the other thugs who worked for Connor—would rattle keys, unlock the door, and roll in a cart containing her meals on a tray. She hadn't eaten much since she'd regained consciousness and become aware of the reality of her situation. When she asked if she could leave, Lance had told her, "Sorry, Amy, I can't let you. If there's anything you want, I can see that you get it, but I cannot allow you to leave the room." He explained that someone was sitting outside the room in the hallway twenty-four/seven. "It's usually me, but when I sleep someone else will be here. We're, uh, keeping watch on you for your own safety."

Yeah, right. Once when she had managed to stand and walk to the bathroom door as Lance was rolling in the cart, she was able to see into the hallway. There was indeed a makeshift station there consisting of a chair and small card table. She had studied what was on the table. A deck of cards. A book. A handgun. *And her phone.* Were they attempting to hack into it?

Yes, she was a prisoner. Could she attempt an escape? Someone would stop her, and she was in no physical shape to attempt anything dramatic. The only window, in the bedroom half, faced the back of the house and its expansive lawn sprinkled with tall trees. There was no way anyone might be alerted to the flashing of lights. Opening the window and calling for help would be futile. And the room was too high to attempt a jump.

At least she could lock herself in the bathroom for privacy, but that was no getaway. The men could likely easily break in to get her if she refused to come out.

Thanks to the television, which she had briefly turned on, she knew that it was now Monday night. Otherwise she would have lost all track of time.

The Middleman

The events since Saturday night were hazy in her mind. Yet the scene in the Drake Hotel room was all too vivid. Connor and the two men coming to her "rescue." Finding cameras and recording equipment hidden in the space. She'd obviously been drugged and framed for Paul's murder. The video equipment in the suite—and the bathroom, too!—caught her hiding the flash drives. Connor's claim that someone wanted to blackmail her was nonsense.

She had showered that night in the hotel room while Connor's men started tidying up the place. He had made a call and more men had arrived. A "clean-up crew," he called it. Men whose job it was to cover up the scene of a crime. After she had dressed, Connor ushered her out of the hotel and into one of his black sedans. She had passed out again in the back seat of the car.

It might have been Sunday evening when she had come out of her troubled slumber. Connor was sitting there with her in the bedroom. Patiently and calmly, he had informed her of where she was.

Amy had been groggy and confused, but she had managed to force herself to be cognizant enough to address her situation.

"Connor . . . what is this room?"

"It's just one of the bedrooms in the house," he had answered. "A place where I keep furnishings from my past in Ireland. Antiquities. You are privileged to be resting here." He had then stood and began to slowly walk around the room, gently touching the bedposts and dresser. "It all belonged to the woman who . . . raised me."

"Your . . . your mother?"

Connor shot a glance at her, stared for a moment, and then gave her a tight grin. "In a way." He had moved past the bed and faced the sitting area. "Have you seen my family there on the back wall?"

"I . . . did." A huge portrait painting hung on the wall in the farthest corner of that half of the suite, and next to it the line of smaller oil portraits. Each portrait depicted men who appeared to be between the ages of thirty and fifty. The black bow ties that most of the subjects wore failed to hide the collective vibe of being a rough, hardened, all-male lot. More like rugby players than an assembly of family members. And she knew why three or four of them looked

197

familiar. "The large portrait is my father. Quinn. I owe everything I am to that great man."

"And your . . . mother?"

"My mother, Claire, refused to have a portrait painted. One of the most striking redheads you would have ever laid eyes upon, and not an ounce of vanity attached to all that beauty." He sighed. "Both my dear mother and my father are finally back together, hopefully looking down on this room and feeling thankful that I have met a woman like you, Amy. You would have adored both of them."

She had somehow known that his words were false, but she didn't challenge him. With each breath of air, her head had cleared just a little more. "And the other portraits?"

"Ah. All of those men are alive and well. You met some of them! Don't you remember? I was an only child, but they were cousins who helped to create fabulous memories for me. They are all as close as brothers to me. Everyone on that wall in some way helped me to improve my life. What I remember the most about all of them is that when I was at an important crossroads, wondering what to do with my life after my postprimary education, they were there for me. My mother and father were in terrible health. I could choose to stay home with them the last years of their life, or I could keep pushing ahead and attend Trinity College in Dublin. Not only did they take care of my mother and father, but they helped me make ends meet when I was short on money."

Connor had sighed again, turned, and returned to the seat beside the bed. He had then leaned forward, his demeanor hardening.

"Amy, I have saved your ass, so to speak," he'd said. "My crew completely wiped that hotel room clean, sanitized it, and got rid of any trace of you and your attorney. You were checked out of the hotel, and the bill was paid. The police will never know that anything occurred because we removed the camera and video equipment that was planted in the room. I'm sorry about your friend and attorney. If we had allowed his body to be discovered, then you would have been implicated. That would have been a terrible thing for you. So, well, we had to dispose of the body, and it will never be found. Mr. Baker will simply be a missing person. When the police investigate his disappearance, they'll learn from the hotel staff that Mr. Baker never slept in his own bed that night after our event. No one will know what happened to him after he got up from the dining table and went to the men's room."

"Why?" she'd whispered weakly. Although she knew the answer, Amy wanted to hear what he had to say about it. "Why did this happen? Who . . . who did this?"

Connor didn't speak for several minutes. He just stared at her. Those cold, blue eyes pierced through hers. At that moment it was more than apparent that what she'd suspected from the instant she had rolled over next to Paul's bloody body was true.

Connor had done it. It was so obvious.

"Amy," he'd finally said, "you have disappointed me a great deal." It was then that he'd held up two flash drives. "You were working with the enemy, Amy. Talking to lawyers. You and your cousin Matt. Plotting and conspiring against me." He shouted, *"Against ME!"* Amy recoiled and assumed a fetal position on the bed. She started to sob.

He'd pocketed the drives and said more quietly, "I will hold on to this evidence of your betrayal. This will go into the Hate Box. You owe me now, Amy. I've covered up the murder for which you could be blamed if those photos ever got out."

"You know . . . I . . . I had nothing to do with . . . what happened in that hotel room," she had managed to say.

Connor had shrugged. "It doesn't matter. No one will know about it . . . unless I choose that they do."

Amy may have had drugs in her system, and she was likely not thinking straight, but she knew with every fiber of her being that Connor Devlin was lying. The cameras and recording equipment were there to keep tabs on her in the room. What could Connor possibly gain from releasing "evidence" of her committing a murder? All his staged murder would accomplish would be an investigation that would ultimately turn over all the rotted logs he had successfully been able to cover up.

Connor was bluffing. He wanted to confuse her. Disorient her. And, yes, blackmail her. Get her to do something. But what?

"What do you want, Connor? What do you want from me?"

Connor had stood then. "We'll talk about it when you feel better. Maybe in a day or two we'll have a serious talk. For now, you rest up and enjoy your little respite here in the comfort of this lovely suite and *think about what you've done to me.* We'll make sure you have plenty of food and drink. Maybe if you're good, I'll allow Deamhan to come in and visit you."

"Can I . . . can I have my phone?"

Connor had laughed at that. "Your phone? Are you joking? Amy, Lance has your phone. He's right outside the door at this very moment. We're monitoring your calls. Yes, I knew your PIN to get into it a long time ago. Don't worry. We'll make sure the world knows you're all right."

"What do you mean?" she'd asked.

"Everyone will know that you've come down with COVID and are isolated in my home. We'll take care of getting the word out on your social media. Why, we've already posted a photo of you in bed here, telling your followers that you're taking a break from Instagram and Facebook while you recover. And that you don't feel like talking on the phone. Your posts will say, 'Don't worry, folks! I'm in *good hands.* Connor has a doctor on call in case I need one.'"

Amy began to writhe and roll about on the bed. The nausea was getting worse. "No . . . no . . ."

He made his way to the door. "Get some more sleep, darling. If you need to throw up, the bathroom is right there."

The door closed, and she had heard the key turn in the lock.

Now, twenty-four hours later, she had not seen hide nor hair of Connor. Only the procession of sycophants bringing her food that she had no desire to eat.

It was all so clear now. Amy had been in denial that she was a victim of a form of domestic abuse. She had been a blind pawn to serve his ambitions. She was supposed to be smarter than that, but she had gone along with all of it.

And now . . . what was the endgame here? What did he want from her? Was Connor going to kill her?

If so, what was he waiting for?

31

On Tuesday morning, Deke and Michael met in the Andiamo Restaurant of the Hilton at O'Hare International Airport to have breakfast before heading out on their separate errands in Chicagoland. When they sat at a table with their respective cups of coffee, plates of eggs, bacon, and fruit, Deke asked, "Did Diana give you a copy of the Devlin photo?"

Michael nodded. "She did. I have it here in my briefcase. Mr. Devlin and two of his unidentified goons in front of the Lake County Courthouse in Waukegan. That was reproduced from . . . ?"

"The *Chicago Tribune*."

"I can show it to the ladies I'm interviewing and see if there's anyone they recognize."

"I'll do that with Mr. Bunker, too. We're meeting at a dive bar in Schiller Park, right next to the airport."

"What time?"

"Eleven-thirty."

"Deke, I think I should go with you. You may need backup."

Deke shook his head. "Not necessary. I talked to the guy this morning. He sounds very nervous and paranoid. He wanted to meet alone at this bar that he says is hidden in a corner of nowhere, and that he'd feel safe there. Mr. Bunker seems more afraid of Devlin and his henchmen than anyone. I'll be fine. It's just a preliminary fact-finding conversation."

As they were finishing up, Michael looked at his phone and said, "Looks like a tropical fury is working its way around north Florida right now. We got out last night just in time, Deke."

MIKE PAPANTONIO

Deke stood after writing his room number and signing the check that the waitress had slapped on the table. "I saw the weather this morning on TV. They didn't think Spanish Trace and Pensacola would get hit very hard, but Diana will close the office if there's any risk. I spoke to her. It's raining heavily there, the wind's blowing, but she said it wasn't terrible. Yet. Everyone's been through these things before; it's not their first birthday party."

Michael squinted at Deke. "Don't you mean it's not their first rodeo?"

Deke looked at him with a straight face and shook his head. "No."

"Oh my God, Deke! I totally forgot. Happy birthday, man. Geez!"

Deke chuckled and shrugged. "Thanks."

* * *

Michael drove into the city to a Starbucks on Addison in Wrigleyville, right across the street from the famous ballpark. He got lucky and found a metered parking spot a block away. He paid the fee at the pay box and began walking back to the coffee shop. Michael gazed at Wrigley Field and remembered to call his buddy about getting tickets to a game. It would be the perfect birthday present for Deke. Michael had already checked to see if the Cubs would be in town that night, and the news was what he wanted to hear. The team would be facing off against the Baltimore Orioles. Michael made the call on his mobile to his attorney pal in Chicago, got his voicemail, and left a message, trying not to sound too needy.

He entered the Starbucks and looked around but didn't find two women matching Roberta Short's or Carlene Webster's descriptions. He ordered a Grande coffee and then sat at one of the tables in the back away from the customers who typically decide to camp out at coffee shops all day with their laptops on the free Wi-Fi.

They were ten minutes late, but eventually the women, a brunette and a blonde who appeared to be in their thirties or early forties, entered the cafe. Michael stood and gave a little wave. They spotted him, waved back, and headed toward him.

"You must be Mr. Carey," the brunette said. "I'm Roberta Short."

"And I'm Carlene Webster," the blonde added.

THE MIDDLEMAN

"Please, call me Michael. Thanks for coming in. What can I get you?"

They allowed him to buy coffees for them, and then they sat and got down to business.

"This is just an informal, preliminary talk," Michael said. "I want to get a better idea of what you both have to say. If it's appropriate, I would then make a recommendation that we get sworn statements from you at an office with all the bells and whistles on a future date."

"Do we need lawyers?" Carlene asked.

"We would be your lawyers, but you're welcome to include your own attorney if you already have one. Now, do I understand correctly that you were district managers?"

"No, we were both pharmacy managers," Roberta explained. "I had a store in Lake County, up in Gurnee. Carlene handled one in Cook County, right on the north side of Chicago. Our jobs were to oversee and manage, as well as monitor and evaluate, prescription drug orders, dispensing drugs, educating patients, providing immunizations, completing drug regimen reviews, and filling prescriptions."

"So, you're really pharmacists," Michael said.

"Yeah," Carlene answered. "But our job title was pharmacy manager."

"Okay. So, Roberta, you told me on the phone that you were getting complaints from customers about the price of insulin going up."

"You bet we did. It was nationwide. It was over the last year that the prices went up twice, and they went up a *lot*. Most people have insurance that covers the drug, but some don't. And the insurance companies didn't like it, either. Some insurance companies put a cap on what they'd pay, and it started getting nasty when customers were again and again watching their copay obligations continue to skyrocket."

"Roberta and I have been friends a long time, and we just happened to get the same job with the same company," Carlene continued. "We agreed that we'd have a word with EirePharma sales reps when they came in the next time."

"And I guess that's what happened?" Michael asked.

"Yes," Roberta said. "We pushed back hard at these reps, who were slick male-model types. We told them about the time when we had to call the police because a customer at my store became out of control, and we thought

203

he'd be violent. Mainly because he couldn't afford to pay the endless escalating prices for insulin that, in fairness, he literally needed to survive."

"We had rehearsed what we both would say, so the reps got the same speeches at both stores."

"What did the reps say?" Michael asked.

"Not much," Roberta answered. She chuckled a little. "We ended it by basically telling them we wouldn't fill their drugs anymore unless the prices went back to what they'd been. Not sure we really could *do* that, but it's what we said. We just wanted to rattle them."

"Uh oh. Then what happened?"

"They left, and a day later, we got a visit from two other men," Roberta continued. "It happened to me first, and then to Carlene. These two men in dark suits came. Scary-looking men. They asked to see me in private and said they were attorneys representing InsoDrugs, the maker of the insulin. I took them into the little room where we give patients immunizations. One of the men spoke while the other guy blocked the door. They made me very nervous. The fella who spoke said that I had better shut up and comply regarding the prices of insulin or he would have me fired. He then named my home address and said one of those things that gangsters say in movies, you know, that sort of disguised threat. 'We'd hate for anything unforeseen to happen to your house and kids.' And I do have two kids."

"The same thing happened to me," Carlene said, "word for word. And I have kids, too."

"When they left, I was shaking. I went home and talked to my husband . . ."

"I'm divorced," Carlene interjected.

". . . and we both agreed I should just quit. Things would be a little unstable for a while, but I was scared of those guys. And both Carlene and I decided that we couldn't stay on and capitulate to their demands. I could get another job with another company. So far, though, I haven't."

"And I feel the same way."

Michael opened his briefcase and pulled out the photo of Devlin and his sycophants. He showed it to the women, asking, "Do you recognize any of these men?"

Roberta immediately pointed to the two who stood slightly behind Devlin. "That's them."

"Yep, same guys that came to see me. Who are they?"

"We're investigating that," Michael said, "but you can be sure they don't work for InsoDrugs. The fellow in front is a man named Connor Devlin. He runs EirePharma now. Those two men work for him. At least that's what we believe to be true. They're his bodyguards and assistants. We believe they do Mr. Devlin's dirty work. We have a witness who has given us names of some of Mr. Devlin's men, but we haven't been able to show her this photo yet, and we couldn't put names to faces. Is there anything else you have to tell me?"

"I got a phone call at home," Roberta said.

"Me, too," Carlene whispered.

"A man just said he was 'reminding' me to keep my mouth shut and 'do my job.' That was a couple of days after I'd already quit, so he might not have known I had."

"Same here."

"I'm pretty sure the voice was the same as the guy who talked to us at the store."

Michael nodded. "All right. I think we can use your testimony, both of you. The next step is we'll get together again at a later date and draw up affidavits that tell your stories. You'll have full approval and you'll sign them. At some point we may need to take your deposition. All the information you give us will be evidence we will use in court if we get that far."

"Will we have to testify in court?" Roberta asked.

"Maybe. You don't have any problems with that, do you?"

"Nope," Carlene said after looking at her friend, and they shook their heads simultaneously.

"Excellent," Michael said. "I think we're done here for now. I will be in touch soon. Thank you very much for agreeing to meet me."

"Mr. Carey?" Carlene asked.

"Michael, please. Yes?"

"Are we in any danger?"

"I don't think that you are, especially now that you're no longer employed at the pharmacies. But if you get any more threatening calls,

MIKE PAPANTONIO

or if you see those men again, anywhere, then you phone me immediately. Okay?"

The two women, wide-eyed, nodded furiously.

32

When Deke had spoken to Vernon Bunker that morning, the man had suggested they meet at a bar called Ken's Viaduct Lounge at noon. It was in the village of Schiller Park, not far from O'Hare. It was a tiny place that looked as if it had once been a house. It was on a busy street, and there were a few parking spaces in the back. Deke pulled his rental car into the driveway beside the joint, drove to the rear, and left it in a spot. –

The bar was darkly lit, even at this time of day. Oldies music piped from a sound system. A semicircular bar dominated the room, and there were already a few patrons on stools being served. A few tables and chairs sat against the walls amid the various electronic gaming machines such as a mini-bowl apparatus and an area for darts. It was indeed the epitome of a dive bar.

A man who matched Bunker's description—in his seventies, thin, wearing glasses—sat at a table near the dartboard. Deke met eyes with him, and the man responded by raising his brows. Deke mouthed, "Mr. Bunker?" and pointed. Bunker nodded and beckoned him to the table with a wave of his hand.

"I'm Nick Deketomis."

"Vernon Bunker."

The men shook hands, and Deke took a seat across from him. Bunker was already nursing a draft beer. "What can I get you?" the man asked.

"Nothing, thanks." Deke winced as he looked around the room. "That music's a little loud; I'm not sure we can have a decent conversation here, Mr. Bunker."

"Oh, I just wanted to meet in a public place first. Maybe just get to know each other a bit. I apologize for being paranoid, but I gotta tell ya—I fear for my life."

"Mr. Bunker—"

"Call me Vernon, please, Mr. Deketomis."

"Well, you can call me Deke. Vernon, have there been any recent threats?"

"Uh, not since what I've already told you. But I do think I'm being watched if I go back home. Right now I'm renting a little house about five minutes away from here on Wagner Avenue. I don't think they know where I am now, but I can't be too careful. I'm not exaggerating when I tell you I think they want to kill me."

Deke observed that Bunker was way beyond simply nervous. His hand shook as he picked up the glass of beer and took a sip.

"And you know for certain that Connor Devlin and his men are the ones targeting you?"

"Absolutely. And I have evidence. I have a lot of stuff I can give you. Valuable evidence against the guy. Emails that he wrote to me. Veiled threats. The so-called resignation from the board letter I was forced to write. I was keeping notes of everything I found fishy at EirePharma ever since Devlin became CEO. It's all a pile of paperwork about an inch high."

"Do you have that with you?"

Bunker shook his head. "I've got it at the house I've been renting for a couple of months. Locked in one of those portable safes. Bought it at Home Depot. I was hoping you'd just take it off my hands. I'm afraid to be carrying it around!"

"We can certainly hold it for you if we make an agreement for us to represent you and you allow us to use your material."

"How much does that cost me?"

"Nothing."

"Well, that's an attention-getter. What do we do?"

"Vernon, I'd like to record our conversation about all this," Deke said, "but it's too noisy in here."

Bunker rubbed his chin. "I guess I trust you enough. You want to come over to my little house? I can show you the evidence I have, and you can record our conversation. What, is this like a deposition or something?"

"No, no, it's just a preliminary talk to see what you've got. I'll record you and we'll get it typed up, and this would be your sworn statement. We don't do what you call a deposition until there's a real trial going on."

"All right, but I have to tell you—I'm leaving town soon. I can't stay here. I don't know what I'll do about my house, that is, my *real* house, my *home*. That's in Vernon Hills." He laughed. "Just like my name! That was just a coincidence, but it did influence me buying a house there many years ago when I was still married. Louise is gone now." He shrugged.

"We can come to wherever you are, Vernon, as long as you don't disappear on us."

Bunker looked around the bar to make sure no one suspicious had come in. He downed the rest of his beer and said, "Okay, I've already paid for the drink. You want to follow me to my secret abode?"

"I tell you what, Vernon," Deke said. "I need to call my office down in Florida first. Give me the address, and I'll be there in ten minutes."

Bunker told him, and Deke made a note of it on his phone. They shook hands, and they walked out of the bar together. Deke got into his rental car and watched as Bunker slipped into a shiny tan Cadillac. The man waved at him as he backed out of the space and left the lot.

Deke dialed Carol.

"Deke?"

"Hi, Carol. How is it down there?"

"Getting hairy. But by our standards this really is more of a bad tropical storm than the kind of hurricanes we're used to. We've briefly lost power twice. They're saying we should see the worst of the storm within a couple of hours. Cell phone coverage is spotty. To tell you the truth, it is still drivable around here, but it might be a good idea if we all stay put right here at the office."

"I'm sorry to hear that. Is everyone staying calm?"

"We're okay. It's a little nerve-racking, but I'm sure we'll be fine."

"I sure hope it passes over you quickly. Stay away from the windows!"

"We know what to do, Deke, thanks. What's up, did you want something?"

"Yes, a couple of things. I've called home a couple of times and, needless to say, my wife is scrambling around making sure everything is secure at the house. If it is still safe to drive around there, have one of our investigators go by and see if they can offer any help. She will say no but check anyway. Also, I have an address here." He told her where Bunker was residing. "Check it out, will you, if you're able? I'm about to go over there and see what he's got. We just met at a bar and he seems okay, but, man, he's scared to death. Doesn't trust anyone."

"Where's Michael? Isn't he going with you?" Carol asked.

"Nah, it's not necessary. Michael went to interview the two women from Walgreens. I can see what Mr. Bunker has and make a determination whether or not his stuff is actually valuable evidence. I don't think he's a crackpot. After all, he was once on the EirePharma board."

"Okay, but be caref—"

The line went dead.

"Carol? Carol? Hello?" Deke hung up and redialed her. He got the recorded message indicating that his call couldn't be completed as dialed. He quickly checked out the weather app on his phone and looked up Spanish Trace. The outside edge of the storm that the breathless talking heads on all the weather channels were going off about looked like it had a slim chance of developing into a hurricane.

"Damn," he muttered. He tried dialing Diana's line and got the same result. Next he tried the firm's landline, and nothing happened at all. He figured that only time would correct these issues and he prayed that his team would be safe. He realized he should have been proactive yesterday and told everyone not to come in today, but at the time the storm didn't appear to be much of a threat. More importantly, he never seriously anticipated that he would have to worry about leaving his family to fend for themselves in even a potential minor hurricane like the one edging near his home.

At that moment there was nothing he could do except rely on Diana and Carol to solve his personal problems while he scrambled around nine hundred miles away to solve someone else's problems. It was a life that Teri, the love of his life, had accepted and supported for his entire

THE MIDDLEMAN

career. It was when everything was going sideways that he most recognized that he had married a remarkably strong woman. Right now was one of those times.

Deke had to live in the moment and focus. He was hoping that Carol could give him some information about the house that Bunker had rented, but he figured it probably didn't matter. The old guy didn't exhibit having any screws loose. He was just frightened out of his wits.

Deke plugged in the address to his phone's GPS and headed out.

* * *

The place was a little ranch house at the corner of the street. Bunker's Cadillac sat in the drive. Deke parked at the curb and noted the time on his watch—12:40. He got out and went to the front door. Bunker answered it quickly and held it open for Deke to enter.

The living room, such as it was, was practically empty. A table, a couple of chairs, and three cardboard boxes sat on the bare wooden floor.

"I'd give you the grand tour, but there's nothing to see," Bunker said. He pointed to an archway that led to a hallway. "There's a bed in the master bedroom, and that came with the rental. There's another small bedroom that has nothing in it." He then indicated a swinging door on the other side of the living room. "Through there is the kitchen. There's a stove and fridge, but I don't have any dishes or pots and pans, silverware, or glasses. I eat out. I brought two suitcases of clothes with me and my computer, and that's it. I don't have Wi-Fi here. I go to a coffee shop when I want to check email. To tell you the truth, I can't wait to get out of here. I may leave tomorrow. Have a seat, Deke. I'd offer you something, but I don't have anything."

"That's all right, Vernon." Deke took one of the chairs and placed his phone on the table. Bunker sat in the other chair. He looked toward the archway that led to other parts of the house. He acted more nervous than before. "You okay, Vernon?"

"Huh? Oh, sure. Let's do this."

"Try to relax. I honestly don't think they know where you are. This place is pretty remote."

"Yeah, you're right." Bunker glanced toward the hallway again.

"No one else is here, Vernon?"

"No, no, we're all alone."

"Okay. Do I have your permission to record our conversation?"

"Sure, sure."

"Like I told you, this is just a preliminary conversation in preparation for what could be a sworn statement. Just tell me the truth, tell me your story in your own words, and just be yourself." Deke pressed a button on the phone. "Okay." He identified himself, the date and time, and then said, "Please state your name."

"Vern—uh, I think maybe I should get a glass of water. Sorry. I'll be right back."

The man stood, looked at the hallway, and then went the opposite direction through the swinging door.

Puzzled, Deke stopped the recording and sat back in the chair. The guy was so agitated that he was a wreck.

Wait . . . didn't he say he didn't have any dishes or glasses?

A shiver ran down Deke's spine. His internal radar suddenly went off, sending red flag alerts to his brain in rapid succession.

Vernon Bunker had set him up! He'd probably been coerced to do so.

He immediately stood, grabbed his phone, and headed for the front door just as two men emerged from the hallway. Deke recognized them as the same two bulky thugs that were in the photo with Connor Devlin.

Before he could reach the door, one man pulled a handgun and spat, "Freeze, asshole."

Deke held up his hands.

"Turn around."

He did.

The other man had quietly crept up behind Deke and was ready for him. A fist slammed into Deke's face with tremendous force. Deke fell backward, crashing against the closed door. He instinctively put up his fists in a feeble attempt to defend himself, but his head was spinning. Another blow hit his abdomen, causing him to double over and fall to the floor.

Unfortunately, that was only the beginning.

33

The Bergman-Deketomis employees in Spanish Trace had gathered in various inner rooms of the office—any place without windows. Carol, Jake, Gina, Sarah, Diana, and five other staff members hunkered down in the conference room. The power was out again, and the building was dark. Earlier, Diana had found a box of candles in the supply room and had distributed them to the staff. Unfortunately, there were no holders for them, so she ransacked the kitchen for a few porcelain plates. Diana struck a match to light a candle, dripped wax onto the plate, and then fixed a candle into the wax and let it harden. Voilà—instant candleholder. Two of them were burning in the conference room and provided enough illumination to make everyone feel as if they were teenagers back at summer camp.

It was 12:50 p.m. and the tropical storm was making its presence known outside. The cacophony of howling wind and rain hammering against the structure was frighteningly noisy, even from deep within the offices. Luckily, the place was built of steel and concrete. The team knew they were safe in a hurricane, must less a bad tropical storm.

"Hey, I have some bars on my phone!" Sarah exclaimed as she stared at its screen. "No, wait. Scratch that. False alarm. It was just a blink."

"Don't tease us," Gina said.

"You think DoorDash is working today?" Jake asked. "I'm getting hungry."

"Did you bring lunch?" Carol asked him.

"No. I usually like to go out."

"There might be some frozen pizzas in the kitchen fridge," Diana said. "I don't know how you'll heat them up, though, with the power out."

"Cold pizza ain't bad," Jake said with a shrug. "I think I'll take one out and at least let it thaw." He got up and left the room.

"Did you talk to Deke this morning?" Gina asked Diana.

"Yeah, it was just a quick check for messages and such. And you know what? I forgot something really important. I'm kicking myself for it, too. And I'm surprised no one else here reminded me or said anything about it. You *all* forgot!"

"What's that?" Sarah asked.

"Today is Deke's birthday."

"Oh, crap!" Gina said. "You're right!"

"How did we forget something like that?" Diana shook her head. "It's birthday cake and balloons when he gets back from Chicago."

"I talked to him briefly," Carol said. "Just before we lost power. We were on the phone and got cut off. He was about to go meet that guy, Vernon Bunker, at a house near O'Hare. Some place Bunker was renting and hiding in to get away from Devlin and his goon squad. He asked me to look it up, and I didn't get a chance to."

Jake came back in the room, overhearing her. "I don't think that Bunker fellow could be of any danger to Deke. He's, what, ninety years old?"

"Seventy-one," Carol answered, "and you're right. Deke wasn't concerned."

The lights in the conference room flickered and then snapped all the way on.

"Wow!" Diana shrieked, startled by the brightness. "We have power!"

"How long will it last, though?" Gina asked.

Carol stood. "I'm going back to my desk to check my computer. Maybe we have internet access."

Sarah held her phone out. "I have bars! I have bars!"

Carol hurried to her office, found the piece of paper on which she'd jotted Bunker's new address, and fired up her Mac. Google directed the address search query to a real estate firm in the Chicago area. The house was indeed a rental and was marked as currently unavailable. The firm appeared to be respectable. She then quickly checked LinkedIn, the only social media Vernon Bunker was on. Nothing had changed since the team had last looked at it. As far as she could tell, there were no red flags popping up.

She dialed Deke's number on her mobile and reached his voicemail. "Deke, Carol here. We just got power back again, and it's about one o'clock. Not sure how long it will stay, but I wanted to let you know the house that Bunker is renting is legit. You're probably already there now, though. Try me back when you're free. I'm sure the cell towers will still be standing. It's not so bad out there, and we're all safe and sound. The report on Teri is that she had all those huge storm shutters lowered around your house. Our guy said it looked like a massive war bunker as he drove away. So no worries there! Talk to you later."

Carol hung up and then dialed Michael. He picked up.

"Carol! Are you dry?"

"Barely." She repeated the state of the union regarding the storm and their sporadic episodes of power loss. "But we're fine. I can't speak for your Grand Cherokee you left in the parking garage. It might be upside down and acting as an aquarium for live seafood."

"Don't even say that!"

She laughed. "I'm sure everything's good. I hope. Anyway, have you heard from Deke?"

"Not since this morning. We had breakfast at the hotel and then I headed out to interview the two women from Walgreens. It went very well. There's plenty of stuff we can use."

"Good to know. Listen, I talked to Deke, oh, about twenty-five minutes ago before we lost power. Our call was cut off. He was going to a house rented by Vernon Bunker, and he gave me the address." She read it out to him. "I just tried Deke but got his voicemail. He's probably in the middle of interviewing Bunker, but, I don't know, maybe you want to check it out if you're free?"

"I am. I'm trying to get Cubs tickets for tonight for Deke's birthday, but I can go over there. I'm on the expressway right now driving back toward our hotel. I think I'm ten or fifteen minutes out."

MIKE PAPANTONIO

"Oh, man, *you* remembered his birthday! Can you believe none of us here did? We just now realized it. We're all ashamed and embarrassed."

"Haha, if I get the tickets, I'll tell him they're from all of us."

"I'll plan a belated party for . . ." Carol heard a click and then dead air on her phone. The call dropped . . . and then the lights went out again. "Oh, hell," she grumbled.

* * *

Michael plugged Bunker's address into his GPS, followed the directions off the Kennedy Expressway onto I-294 heading south, and then took the Irving Park exit. From there he made his way to Wagner Avenue and easily found the house in question. Deke's rental car was parked at the curb.

Deke had told Michael that he'd handle the interview alone because Bunker didn't want anyone else there. Michael pulled up behind Deke's car and sat there for a few minutes, wondering what he should do. He texted his boss and told him that he was outside.

Michael removed a switchblade from his jacket pocket and felt the weight in his hand. He often carried the weapon, which had a six-inch blade, when he took noncommercial flights. Why did he feel the need to have it handy at this particular moment?

When no text response from Deke came after a couple of minutes, Michael threw caution to the wind, dropped the knife back into his pocket, and got out of his car.

What the hell . . . he thought. *Bunker has to get used to a full team of lawyers working with him.*

He made his way to the front door and rang the doorbell. Nothing happened. There was no sound of voices or movement. He knocked loudly. Silence.

Michael turned back and looked at Deke's car. *Where is he?*

He knocked again. "Deke?" he called. *Way, way not right.*

Michael tried the doorknob. It was locked, of course.

He took a couple of steps back, raised his muscular leg, and kicked at the door. The wood splintered at the knob and lock, and the door swung open. Michael rushed inside to a tableau of horror.

216

THE MIDDLEMAN

The first thing he saw was Vernon Bunker, sitting in a chair at a table in a bare room. He was slumped to the right. Blood covered the left side of his head and upper body. He had obviously been shot in the temple.

Then Michael saw Deke. His boss was lying face down on the floor near an archway that led to other parts of the house. He, too, was covered in blood.

"No!"

Not caring if the perpetrators might still be in the house, Michael rushed to his friend and colleague, squatted, and gently placed a hand on the man's arm. "Deke?"

Nick Deketomis had been terribly beaten. Was he . . . dead?

Afraid to move him, Michael pulled the phone out of his jacket pocket and dialed 911. He was placed on hold. "Oh, for chrissakes!" he shouted. "Come on!" After several seconds, though, an operator came on the line, and Michael reported what he'd found: two deceased men, likely murdered.

And then Michael heard a soft, almost imperceptible groan.

"Deke? It's Michael! Can you hear me?"

Another faint groan. It definitely came from Deke.

"Operator!" Michael yelled into the phone. "He's alive! Deke's alive! He needs an ambulance! Hurry! Hurry, please!"

34

On Wednesday morning, the storm had abated, power in Spanish Trace was restored, and flights were departing from Pensacola. Carol grabbed a seat on the first plane out to Chicago to assist Michael. The previous day and evening she had been constantly on the phone with him as Deke was delivered by ambulance to Gottlieb Memorial Hospital in Melrose Park. All Michael knew at that time was that Deke had suffered some serious damage. Apparently he had been kicked and punched all over his body—the same thing that had happened to Matt Redmond in a Chicago alley. Michael speculated that the perpetrators had left Deke for dead and likely thought that he was, but there was still some life left in his friend's ravaged body.

Alas, Deke was now in a medically induced coma to prevent brain swelling.

Michael picked up Carol at O'Hare in his rental car at noon and began to drive south on River Road toward the hospital. "Do you know when Teri's supposed to arrive?" he asked her.

"Diana helped her get a flight because they were all sold out today," Carol answered. "She'll be landing late this afternoon. We can pick her up?"

"Sure. Is she staying somewhere near the hospital?"

"I think Diana got her a room at one of the hotels nearby, so, yeah. She didn't want a rental car. She said she'd use Uber or Lyft because all she'd be doing is going back and forth from her hotel to the hospital. She plans to stay as long as she's needed."

Michael nodded. "Deke married well with that one."

"Have you found out anything since yesterday?"

He nodded as he drove. "I've pulled some strings. One of the police officers who arrived at the scene after I called 911 will be at the hospital to talk to us. They normally don't do that, but this fellow, Officer Bud Sanders, was also a pararescueman in the Iraq War. I didn't know him then; he was in a completely different unit. But we were talking after they'd loaded Deke into the ambulance, and somehow that came up. Anyway, I've got his cell number and he has mine, and Bud said he'd meet us this afternoon at the hospital to talk to us."

"That's nice of him."

"It's his day off, apparently. Anyway, let me give you the full update since we last talked. When I found him, he was barely alive. Bunker was dead. While I waited for the ambulance and police to arrive, I quickly ran through the house to make sure those psycho freaks weren't hiding someplace, then I hurried back to Deke and continued to talk to him. He was drifting in and out of consciousness. I wished I'd had all my gear from when I *was* a pararescueman. I could have given him some morphine. I was afraid to move him, though. I didn't know if they'd broken his spine. He was in bad shape, Carol."

"I'll kill the bastards that did this," she said, rubbing a sleeve across her eyes.

"I don't think I've ever seen you cry. To tell you the truth, I cried a little last night."

"I'm not crying! It's just, oh, it's just some tears welling up. That's not crying." She sniffed. "Go on, tell me everything."

"So, I learned all this late last night. He has a few broken bones. Right hand. They must have stomped on it. It's smashed in several places. Three ribs on the left side and two on the right are broken. They dislocated his jaw, so the docs put it back in place. It's going to be sore when he wakes up. Thank God those bastards didn't break it, or he'd be wired up and wouldn't be able to talk for two months. Surprisingly, there were no cracks in his skull. He was hit all over his head, so I'm sure he's got a concussion on top of being in a coma."

"Deke is hardheaded, and I mean that in a good way. This kind of beating would have killed most people."

"On the inside, there's some internal bleeding from being punched or kicked in the abdomen. There's trauma to his stomach and intestines and kidneys, but his pancreas seems to be okay. Looks like his spleen held together. There's no telling about his brain. Last night after the surgery, the doctor told me they wanted to put him in the induced coma. He'll be out for at least twenty-four hours, maybe forty-eight. He's in the ICU, so he's got twenty-four/seven care."

Carol shook her head. She couldn't fathom why this had to happen. She had always thought of Deke as bigger than life and bulletproof since she had seen him work cases much more dicey than this one.

She also felt somewhat responsible, as head of security for the firm, that she didn't fully grasp the red flags of the contact from Vernon Bunker. Carol was reminded of a catchphrase that was often used when she worked in law enforcement—mistakes can be fatal.

* * *

The staff on Gottlieb Hospital's ICU floor were friendly and helpful, but they were reluctant to let Michael and Carol into the room to see Deke. Only family members were allowed. Carol explained that they were his colleagues and were his attorneys, too.

"And we are *like* family," she insisted.

Finally, the nurse said they could peek into the room but they weren't to speak to the patient. Besides, he was in a coma and wouldn't hear them.

The shades were closed and the overhead bulbs in the room were dark, but the indicator lights and LED screens of the various machines around the bed cast blinking, colored illumination on the walls and ceiling. The sounds of beeps and whirring dominated the otherwise quiet sanctuary where Deke lay on his back. An oxygen face mask covered his nose and mouth, and all sorts of intravenous tubes were attached to his body. His head was covered in a thick white bandage, and his right hand was enclosed in a cast that went up to nearly his elbow.

A minute was all Michael and Carol needed. They squeezed each other's hands in silence, and then left the room.

The Middleman

They found Officer Bud Sanders, wearing plain clothes, in the ICU waiting area. Michael introduced him to Carol and the trio sat.

"I'm afraid I don't have much to tell you," Sanders said. "We found Mr. Deketomis's phone on the floor way over in a corner where it likely slid across the room. It had been stomped on, smashed to smithereens, so it's unusable. It was placed in an evidence bag. Fingerprints were all over the house. It's a rental, as you know, and apparently it doesn't get cleaned as well as it should between rentals. Fingerprints aren't going to tell us a thing. There are dozens of different sets, all unique. We had officers questioning neighbors to see if they saw anything, but no one was home yesterday. Everyone was working in the middle of the day. Ballistics will be examining the round extracted from Mr. Bunker's head but getting the results might take a while. Nothing ever happens overnight. It appears that Bunker rented the property a week and a half ago. He stayed at two hotels closer to his home in Vernon Hills prior to that. He must have decided to get out of that neck of the woods and come down near O'Hare to hide out."

"Had Bunker made any official complaints to the cops?" Carol asked.

"About being harassed?"

"Yes. Or threatened."

"No, not that I'm aware of. We've been communicating with the Vernon Hills police, and they had nothing. I'm sorry, folks, but finding the guys who did this is going to be a challenge."

At that moment, a large older man wearing a suit walked into the waiting room. Sanders did a double take, stood, and said, "Well, look who's here . . . It's Chief McClory from Chicago!"

The man looked Sanders up and down. "Do I know you?"

"No, sir. I'm Officer Bud Sanders of the Schiller Park Police. I'm off duty today."

"Officer Sanders, how do you do?" McClory said, shaking his hand. He eyed Carol and Michael. "Are you two with Mr. Deketomis?"

"Yes," Michael said. "We're colleagues—"

"—and friends," Carol added.

Michael introduced himself and Carol. "You're the Chicago chief of detectives, do I have that right?"

221

"That's correct. One of your people came to see me a while back . . . a John Rutledge?"

"*Jake* Rutledge. Yes, he visited you with Matt Redmond."

McClory nodded. "Well, I thought I'd come out and see how Deke is doing. He's an old friend."

"So, you're not here on any official business?" Carol asked.

McClory shook his head. "It's out of my jurisdiction. This is the western suburbs. I'm here because I was concerned. I heard about what happened this morning. Normally, what happens in the suburbs stays in the suburbs, and I don't even hear about it. Why should I? But some news travels fast in the police department. When a high-profile attorney who is something of a celebrity gets assaulted in Chicagoland, that kind of thing crosses my desk. I'm sorry to hear that he's hurt. How is he?"

Michael gave him the rundown on Deke's condition and then said, "Officer Sanders here was just telling us that there wasn't a lot to go on at the crime scene. Catching the men who did this isn't going to be easy."

McClory said, "Well, I know the chief in Schiller Park. I vow to lend him any help he might need to find these culprits and bring them to justice. I can guarantee that they'll serve serious time."

"Not if I find them first," Carol said.

The chief looked at her sideways. When he realized that she wasn't kidding, he said, "I understand your position, but I don't have to remind you that you're not law enforcement personnel, do I?"

"No, sir," she grudgingly answered, although she suppressed a comment that she was, after all, an ex-cop.

"But I appreciate your loyalty to your colleague."

Michael then remembered something and addressed both the chief and Sanders. "Oh, let me show you something. It's a photograph." He opened his briefcase and pulled out the picture of Devlin and the two men. He showed it to the law enforcement men, pointing and saying, "You may know this man as Connor Devlin."

"Yes, I've met Connor Devlin," McClory said. "Can't say I really know the man."

"Do you know the other two men in the photo?" Michael asked.

McClory studied them with a furrowed brow. "No, can't say that I do. Why?"

"We have reason to believe that these two men act as Devlin's bodyguards, but they're also his personal thugs. They take care of, um, *problems* for Devlin."

"You make it sound like Devlin's some kind of mob boss," McClory said.

"If it looks like a duck and walks like a duck . . . ! I mean, come on," Carol added with a little too much sarcasm.

McClory grinned a little. "Well, I don't know about that. He's a well-respected businessman in town. Gets his picture in the society pages all the time. Isn't he engaged to the Redmond woman? What's her name?"

"Amy," Carol said. "I think that engagement is off, though. And by the way, no one has heard from *her* since Saturday night, even though her social media indicates that she has COVID. It smells, sir. Something is way off about it, don't you think?"

McClory seemed flustered by all the information coming at him. He held out his hands and spoke more forcefully. "Look, why would I know anything about her? Does Amy Redmond live in Chicago? No! That would be up to the local police where she lives." The man looked around him and then said, "Well, I was hoping to get a chance to talk to Deke myself, but since he's in a damn coma . . ." The man shrugged.

"Sorry you made the trip for nothing," Michael said.

"Ah, well, it got me out of that stifling building on Michigan Avenue for a couple of hours. Say, do you two have business cards?"

They respectively dug them out and handed them to the chief. He read their names aloud again and then put the cards in his pocket. "I may be in touch," he said. "When it comes to crime in this town, if I put *my* ear to the ground I hear things that others don't. I'll even whisper into some other ears to ask about Amy Redmond, too. Allow me to make some inquiries, if you don't mind. And feel free to call me if there's anything else."

"We'll accept all the help we can get," Michael said.

McClory nodded to Sanders. "I'll speak to your boss."

"Thank you, sir."

The man shook hands with them all, said his goodbyes, and left. A few minutes later, Sanders made his excuses to leave as well, promising to get in touch with Michael if he heard anything new. Now alone in the waiting room, Michael and Carol sat quietly for several minutes.

"He didn't know much," Michael finally said.

"Who, Sanders or McClory?"

"McClory."

Carol sighed. "He's got a big job in a big city. I know from my own experience in law enforcement that the ones in charge at the top don't always know the nitty-gritty details of each and every one of the thousands of cases that cross desks."

Michael nodded. "True. And it was big of him coming to see Deke. I'll give him that."

After another beat of silence, she asked, "What are we doing?"

"I don't know," Michael answered.

"Well, we can't just sit here on our butts. Deke can't talk to us. Why stay here?"

"I have to pick up Teri in four hours."

"I wish I'd thought to ask Chief McClory about Charles Redmond's suicide note. The one that mysteriously appeared when officers at the Redmond's apartment told the family that there was no suicide note."

"I'm not sure that here would have been an appropriate venue to interrogate one of Chicago's highest-ranking policemen."

"Did we ever track down that officer who left the force? What was his name? Brazos?"

Michael nodded. "Enrico Brazos. Matt Redmond was going to try and find him. Jake is supposedly working on it now, right?"

"Yeah, I forgot. This has all been so upsetting I'm not thinking straight." She got her phone out of her purse and dialed Jake back in Florida. "Jake, hey, Michael and I are here at the hospital. Huh? Oh, well, he's unconscious, but it's a good unconscious, if there is such a thing. Medically induced coma, you know. He'll be out for a couple of days, I think. Listen, Michael and I wanted to know if you ever found that officer from Charles Redmond's suicide case . . . Enrico Brazos."

She listened. "Uh huh." She looked at Michael and shook her head. "I see. All right. Well, keep trying. Right. Okay, talk to you later." She ended the call and told Michael, "He said that McClory was going to send that information to Matt. Whether he did or not, Matt never shared it with Jake, so Jake assumes Matt never got it before he was killed. Jake's been searching, and he had one lead that didn't pan out, but he'll keep trying."

"So what do we do before Teri arrives?"

"You remember me telling everyone that I know a spectacular private detective in Chicago? Lou Doonan?"

"Yeah?"

"I think it's time we enlist his help. Lou has done private eye work for the mob in Chicago. He has no scruples. I'm going to give him a call."

Michael nodded, stood, walked to the window, and looked out over the hospital parking lot while Carol dialed the number.

"Lou? Hey, it's Carol Morris!" She laughed and went into a "long time no see" preliminary conversation, then she caught him up on why she was in town. She explained what she wanted to do—mainly pick his brain—and offered to buy him dinner. "Uh huh. Sure! Sounds great. We'll see you there. Thanks, Lou!" She hung up, and Michael turned to face her. "We have a dinner date with Lou at Italian Village in Chicago at 7:30 this evening."

"I've heard of that place. You think he'll really know something that can help us?"

"If not, we'll enjoy some lasagna and a good bottle of wine. I need it."

35

Teri Deketomis's plane was on time and both Michael and Carol picked her up. The woman, who had been married to Deke for nearly forty years and was the mother of their two grown children, exhibited a strong and determined demeanor, ready to face what had happened to her husband. They drove straight to the hospital, where Teri insisted that she stay through the evening, even though Deke was still unconscious. She would get dinner at the hospital cafeteria and told Michael and Carol to go on and do "whatever they needed to do" to find who was responsible for the near death of her husband. They had each other's phone numbers, and the attorneys promised to take her to lunch or dinner on Thursday.

Michael then drove Carol into Chicago. Italian Village Restaurant was in the Loop and consisted of three levels, each a different eatery under the Italian Village banner. Doonan had told them to find him in La Cantina, the basement-level restaurant, which he said would feel like a little slice of Italy.

After parking the car on the street for an exorbitant fee, the duo entered the building on Monroe and were shown downstairs. Indeed, the place immediately evoked romance and old-world Italian mystique, as it was designed to look like the interior of a wine cellar with cozy, intimate spacing of booths and tables. Carol spotted Lou Doonan, a lean and very fit man in his sixties, already sitting in a booth. He waved to her, and they joined him.

Carol made introductions, and the waiter immediately appeared to take drink orders. Doonan ordered a bottle of cabernet, which both Michael and Carol approved, and they eyed the menu.

"This place is the oldest Italian restaurant in Chicago," Doonan said. "The top floor opened in 1927. This one in the basement opened in the mid-1950s, and the ground-floor joint opened in the sixties. Folks mistakenly think that La Cantina is the oldest section because they designed it to look older." He pointed to an alcove in the back of the room. "Legend has it that Al Capone used to eat at that table, but it's not true. As I said, La Cantina didn't open until the fifties. But he did eat upstairs in the original Village. The same family has run the restaurant since the beginning. I could have shown you where they think Capone usually sat, but I happen to like it better down here."

Carol, admiring the fresco-like artwork of Italian buildings and landscapes, said, "This is just fine, Lou, thank you."

After ordering their meals and making a toast with the wine, Lou asked, "So how can I help you, Carol?"

She spent a few minutes giving him the outline of their case against EirePharma and Connor Devlin, the situation with Deke in the hospital, Matt Redmond's murder, and the suspicion that Charles Redmond was also killed. By the time she was finished with the tale, the food had arrived, and the trio dug in.

"I can't get lasagna like this in Spanish Trace, Florida!" Michael declared after tasting it.

"So, back to the business at hand," Michael said, "do you know Connor Devlin?"

"I know who he is. Look, there's something you need to understand. Chicago has always been a hotbed for organized crime, even today. It may not be Al Capone's style of organized crime, but it's still run secretly by a complex web of wealthy men. I'm not talking about the gangs on the South Side that gun each other down at a rate of twenty to thirty every week. All the shootings and crime in the working-class and poorer sections of the city . . . That's not what I'm talking about. What I mean is white-collar organized crime that's all about networking and money changing hands. Most of them these days are walking around in designer suits with college degrees hanging on their walls. Everyone does it. Politicians, public utilities, unions, law enforcement, even *lawyers*. No offense."

Carol laughed. "None taken, and, yeah, you'd be surprised what we've encountered in our careers. What about Devlin?"

"There's no question that he's a man who has his pockets full of politicians, lawyers, and cops. If it were the 1920s, Connor Devlin would be dealing bootleg booze. But he's a 'respectable' businessman. He knows how to charm people into doing what he wants. And if that doesn't work, he knows how to intimidate and then threaten them into complying."

"You know that how?" Michael asked.

"It's my job," Doonan said. "I've been a private investigator in this city for thirty-five years. I've dealt with the Outfit, which is like the old-school Mafia, I've dealt with crooked cops, I've dealt with politicians taking bribes; you name it. I've made a lot of enemies over the years, but I've also made a lot of friends. I know people in the underworld, and yes, it still exists. I hear things. And I trust my sources."

"Could Devlin have been responsible for attacking Deke?" Michael asked.

"Like, who else?" Carol murmured, but loud enough for them to catch.

"It's indeed possible, and I hear you," Doonan said, raising his eyebrows to acknowledge Carol's bubbling anger. "Devlin has some former tough cops and mercenary types on his payroll. It's sort of an Irish brotherhood of really bad apples. Mind you, I'm not saying anyone Irish is bad. *I'm* Irish, and I consider myself one of the good guys."

Michael opened his briefcase and produced the photo again. "Do you recognize the two men with Devlin?"

Doonan nodded and smiled a little. "Sure do. They're the 'BBs.' Pat Beckett and Ronan Barry. They're two disgraced former cops. Beckett is from Detroit, and Barry is from New York. They've kept their identities under wraps here in Chicago. Beckett was caught beating suspects almost to death. Barry participated in robberies and maybe killed a jeweler, but it wasn't proven. Yeah, they act as Connor Devlin's enforcers. I know them personally."

"You do?" Carol asked.

"Yep. Through the Irish *thing* in this town. A lot of cops and private eyes and lawyers and businessmen meet at various Irish pubs and participate in the St. Patrick's Day activities in the city. We've met. Can't say they're *friends* of mine or anything like that. But I know their names, and they know mine."

"Do they reside at Devlin's home?" Michael asked.

"They do. All of his bodyguards do. There aren't many. Four or five, tops. I think. Unless Devlin's gone on a hiring spree lately."

"Does the name 'Petey-o' mean anything to you?" Carol asked.

Doonan rubbed his chin and shook his head. "No, haven't heard that one."

Carol leaned in and spoke quietly. "Look, Lou. We'd like to find these guys. Do they go anywhere when they're off duty? Surely they get some days off? Do they work twenty-four/seven? What's the deal? Help us out here."

"They're rough customers, Carol. I wouldn't put it past them that they are indeed responsible for beating up Matt Redmond and trying to kill your boss. Not sure how you'd prove it in a court of law."

"That's not what we're interested in," Michael said softly.

Doonan raised his eyebrows. "I see. Well. Okay, then. There are some Irish pubs in Chicago that the 'network' frequents. One in particular on the north side in the Avondale neighborhood is called Chief O'Neill's. Pat Beckett has been known to show up there most nights after eleven o'clock. Ronan Barry sometimes joins him, but they're rarely there together."

"Chief O'Neill's."

"That's right. It's actually a very respectable place. Opened in the late nineties, I believe, but it's a very authentic Irish pub. They have live music with fiddles and such, and there's a beer garden. Good food, too."

Carol and Michael looked at each other.

"I don't have plans after eleven," Michael said.

"Me neither," Carol added. She turned back to Doonan. "Thanks, Lou. Do we owe you anything for what you've told us?"

"Nah, dinner will cover it."

MIKE PAPANTONIO

"Thank you. Listen, we may hire you for some more work. Are you interested?"

"Carol Morris, a private dick is always interested in work. And if you need info from police case files that they keep close to the vest, I can get that kind of thing."

"Yeah? Okay, then, we'll be in touch."

"You've got my number."

36

They had expected to go back to their O'Hare hotel after dinner but seeing that they had to turn around and go back to O'Neill's after eleven o'clock, it didn't make sense. Michael had instead driven around the Loop to kill time. Traffic in Chicago was bustling, so it turned out to be an infuriating exercise. For what was ahead, though, Michael welcomed that greater sense of fury. Eventually they headed to the north side, headed east on Addison Street, and found Chief O'Neill's located at the point of a wedge-shaped building. From the lack of parking spots by or near the structure, it appeared that the Irish pub was a very popular place. Michael ended up parking a half block away.

As the pair stepped inside, they were enveloped by lively Celtic music that was a little too loud and the additional noise of perhaps fifty patrons occupying the booths, tables, and barstools in the relatively small space. The music came from a quartet sitting in a corner near an unused piano; the musicians were expertly playing a fiddle, an accordion, a guitar, and traditional Celtic percussion of a bodhrán and "bones."

Carol and Michael looked around and could see another dining room past the bar, but it appeared to be full, too.

"I think we're going to have to stand," Michael said.

"Wait!" Carol indicated a couple who were just getting up from a small round table near the door. She moved quickly to it and hovered while a busboy swooped in and cleared it of dirty dishes and beer mugs. Michael joined her, and they sat.

MIKE PAPANTONIO

"That was lucky," he said. "Can I get you something? Looks like beer is the going thing here."

"Get me something Irish."

Michael laughed, stood, and went to the archway that opened to the other room. He gazed at the customers, took stock of the layout, and then he stepped up to the bar back in the pub section. In a few minutes he returned with two pints—a Black and Tan for himself and a Guinness for Carol.

"I didn't see our man in the other room," he reported. "This is a much bigger establishment than it looked from the front. That's a good-size dining room in there, and beyond that is a lawn with tables and chairs—a beer garden—and it's crowded, too, because it's such a nice night." Fortunately, they were in a position to see everyone in their part of the pub.

"I'll bet he's not the type to socialize with the drinking crowd. If he shows up, he'll go straight to the bar and either stand or sit if he can get a stool, and he'll stay there." She took a sip of the beer, made a bitter face, and then smiled. "That's good and hoppy, all right."

They sat for several minutes drinking their pints, eyeing the clientele but not recognizing anyone. Then, at 11:26, Michael, who was facing the door, said, "Carol," and made a quick nod. She didn't turn around. She waited until a man walked past the table and, sure enough, stepped up to the bar.

Pat Beckett.

He wasn't wearing the trademark suit normally sported by Devlin's men. He had on a Cubs T-shirt and blue jeans. Off duty, he was just a regular, albeit very muscular, guy. It was obvious that he was a body-builder. He was a formidable specimen of a man.

They watched him as he bought what appeared to be a very dark beer. From the rapport he had with the bartender, they apparently knew each other. Beckett then stood alone until eventually someone near him vacated a stool. He took the seat and placed his beer on the bar, his back to the rest of the pub.

"So what's the plan?" Carol asked.

"I guess we should have thought of that before, huh?"

THE MIDDLEMAN

"Wait for him to leave and approach him outside?"

Michael shook his head. "The men's room. I'll have a little talk with him in there."

"How do you know he'll go to the men's room?"

"We have to see that he does."

"But you'll get all the fun. I won't get to play."

"Yeah, you will. What do you think of this?" He leaned closer and outlined what he wanted her to do.

Carol laughed a little and then said, "You know we could get in big trouble for this? If I'm reading the room right, I think this is a popular joint for cops. All the imagery around the place is paying tribute to an old-time Chicago policeman."

"How do you feel about what he did to Deke?" Michael asked.

"I'd like to see him in the hospital, too."

"I'd also like to get a confession. They play dirty with us; I'm going to play dirty with them."

"You *are* an attorney, Michael. Me, I'm just the security officer of the firm. You have more to lose here."

"Really? Are you kidding? Like I've never done this kind of thing before? Besides, this is no longer business. It's personal. Are we going to do this or not?"

She got up from the table and sauntered over to the bar, wavering a bit as if she weren't too steady on her feet. She leaned in right next to Beckett's stool and slurred her words rather loudly at the bartender. "Another Guinness, pleash!" She then awkwardly swayed and bumped Beckett's shoulder. "Oh, pardon me, shir, I'm shorry."

Beckett gave her a sour glare but didn't say anything.

Carol gawked at his upper arms. "My gosh, friend," she said to him, "how much do you bench pressh?"

"Lady, you're drunk," Beckett told her.

"No, I'm not!" she answered belligerently. The bartender set the drink in front of her, and she slapped down a twenty. "Keep the change." She then picked up the pint, turned as if to go back to the table, and spilled the entire beer on Beckett's shirt and lap.

"What the fuck, lady!" Beckett yelled, jumping up.

233

MIKE PAPANTONIO

"Oh, my God, I'm sho shorry! I'm sho shorry, mishter!" Carol whined with believable regret and horror at what she'd "done" and turned back to the bartender. "Help! Do you have a towel? I made a messh, I'm sho shorry!"

The bartender gathered a couple of towels from the back counter and handed them to Carol and her victim, but Beckett continued to curse loudly and point at her. "You damn bitch, you drunken cow, look what you did!"

"I shaid I was shorry, asshhole! Let me help you, damn it!" She started to dab his shirt with one of the towels.

"Get away from me, you stupid bitch!" He raised a fist, and Carol braced herself, ready to fight back if necessary.

"Whoa, Pat, whoa!" the bartender shouted. "Take it easy! Stop right there."

Beckett managed to restrain himself and lowered his arm. "Look what she did, Colm! Look!"

Colm, the bartender, sternly told Carol, "You go on back to your table, ma'am. I'm cutting you off."

"Fine," she said, turned, and went back to the table where Michael was sitting.

The bartender told Beckett to stay put, went over to a cabinet and grabbed a fresh Chief O'Neill's T-shirt and gave it to the man. "Here, Pat, on the house. Go to the men's and put it on. Can't do anything about the pants, though. Sorry."

Beckett jerked the shirt away from Colm and stormed toward the alcove leading to the restrooms.

"That was an Oscar-winning performance!" Michael said, trying not to laugh. He did note that many patrons were staring at Carol and talking among themselves. "I'm afraid you got yourself some attention, though."

"I don't give a crap," she said, holding back her own laughter. "He's going in the men's room now. Better go!"

Michael got up and headed that way. Thankfully, nobody was looking at him. Anyone who still had an interest in the scuffle was goggling at Carol. Michael was invisible as he moved into the short hallway that led to the restrooms, walked past a glass lite door that adjoined the other dining room, and then pushed on the appropriate swinging door.

Beckett stood in front of the sink and mirror, cursing to himself. The wet shirt was off, revealing abs that most men would envy. Michael wasn't concerned, though. His own were just as impressive—once a PJ, forever a PJ, and they were truly among the toughest soldiers on the planet.

Michael went to a urinal and, with his back to Beckett, pretended to do his business. Beckett slipped on the dry T-shirt but scowled at the dark circle of dampness below the waist of his jeans. "Damn it to hell. Did you see that? Crazy drunk-ass bitch."

Michael "finished," made a sound with his zipper, and then went to stand beside Beckett to wash his hands. As he did so, he said, jokingly, "Did you let a woman get the better of you, man?"

Beckett did a double take. "*What* did you say?"

Michael pulled paper towels out of the dispenser and dried his hands, turning to face Beckett. Inwardly, he was preparing for what he was about to do.

"You heard me. I also noticed that you damn near hit that woman. I understand you also like to beat up lawyers who are just doing their jobs. Here, let me help you put yourself back together."

With that, Michael head-butted Beckett in the nose. The man jerked back, completely surprised and off guard. He instinctively raised his fists, but Michael leaned back and delivered a sidekick into Beckett's tight stomach, followed by a kick to the groin that would have ended most fights. Beckett fell back against the door, stunned. Blood streamed over his face. He quickly recovered, though, focused on his prey, and came at Michael like a bull seeing red.

It was an extremely small space in which to fight. Nevertheless, the two men went at it as if they were in the ring, and the cacophony they created was masked by the music in the pub.

Beckett got in a lucky punch that burst Michael's lower lip, so now they were both bleeding. He attempted to repeat the maneuver, but Michael grabbed the man's arm and pulled him forward, simultaneously tripping him at the ankles. Beckett landed face down on the floor, smearing red over the white tiles. Michael immediately plummeted on

Beckett's back and straddled him. He then reached his arm around the man's neck and locked him in a game-over type of choke hold. At the same time, Michael pinned Beckett's arms to the floor with his knees, forcing them down with his weight.

Beckett couldn't speak; he just grunted in agony as Michael applied pressure on the hold.

"It was you who beat up the attorney, right?" Michael spat through his teeth. "Deketomis? Tell me!"

More grunts and groans.

"That's about a five on a scale from one to ten! Shall I go higher?" He did so. Michael knew, however, that if he went too far then Beckett's neck could be snapped. He didn't want that.

"Grunt twice if that's a yes! Did you do it?"

Beckett couldn't take any more. He made two successive throaty gurgles.

"And was Ronan Barry there, too? Tell me!"

Two more distressed grunts.

Michael released the near-unconscious man, stood, and then kicked Beckett in the side of the head hard enough to knock him out. The man stopped moving, sprawled over the tile, his arms out and palms down. Michael thought, *what the hell*, and then stomped hard on Beckett's right hand and elbow, smashing the bones within to bits. *Eye for an eye? Arm for an arm?*

Catching his breath, Michael turned to the mirror and was shocked to see the damage. He splashed water from the sink on his face and was relieved that it wasn't as bad as it had first appeared. His mouth was bleeding, and there was blood on his shirt, but he'd been through worse. He grabbed a bunch of paper towels, held them to his face, and left the bathroom.

Out in the pub, Michael made his way back to the table. Carol's eyes went wide.

"My God, Michael, are you okay? There's blood on your shirt."

"I had to use my special law license. Let's get out of here."

She stood and grabbed her purse. Thanks to the colorful but low lighting, the pair hustled out of Chief O'Neill's without anyone noticing something was off kilter.

37

On Thursday around one o'clock, Diana sent out an email to everyone in the law firm with the subject line: GOOD NEWS! DEKE IS OUT OF HIS COMA!

She continued in the body of the message with the update Teri had relayed to her an hour earlier. Deke would remain hospitalized for a while. The doctor hoped he could be moved out of the ICU on Friday and into a regular private room. He had a long road of physical therapy to accomplish, first in Illinois, and then continuing when he would finally get to go home to Florida. They thought Deke would be able to travel within a week, but with the concussion it wasn't a good idea for him to fly. Teri thought she would rent a car and drive him all the way back from Chicago. This would likely be more comfortable, too, rather than him having to deal with airports and plane seats.

Meanwhile, the team continued working on the case, with Gina and Jake holding down the fort in Spanish Trace. Jake adopted the task of verifying Amy Redmond's social media posts saying that she was sick with COVID. No one had yet to hear from her personally since the Drake Hotel event on Saturday. He thought the first stop might be to call EirePharma and inquire about her. Deke had informed them all of Amy's decision to resign from the company, but officially that hadn't occurred yet. Jake phoned EirePharma, and the automated phone system wanted him to punch in the desired party's extension. It was in the case file, so he entered it. All he got was her voicemail. He tried again and this time selected "0" for the operator.

237

MIKE PAPANTONIO

"EirePharma, may I help you?"

"Yes, I'm looking for Amy Redmond. Is she in?"

"Ms. Redmond is out this week; shall I transfer you to her voicemail?"

"No, I've already been there. Have you actually heard from her?" Jake asked.

"I'm sorry, I can transfer you if you like. Ms. Redmond is out of the office this week."

"Yeah, you said that. You don't know anything else? Is she okay?"

"I'm sorry, sir. That's all I know."

"What about an assistant, does she have an assistant?"

"Hold the line."

Jake waited until he was transferred, and then got the assistant's voicemail.

"Argh!" He hung up.

What next? What about calling Mary Redmond to see if Amy's adopted mother knew anything? The woman's number was also in the case file, so Jake dialed it.

"Hello?"

"Is this Mary Redmond speaking?"

"This is Luisa. Who's calling?"

Jake explained who he was and that he needed to speak with Mary if she was available. Luisa asked him to wait a minute. It was more like three before Mary Redmond answered. The woman sounded frail and weary.

"Hello, Mrs. Redmond, this is Jake Rutledge of Bergman-Deketomis, the law firm that you've agreed to work with regarding Connor Devlin and EirePharma?"

"Yes, hello."

"Have you heard from Amy Redmond since Saturday?"

Mary sighed. "No, I haven't. I did get a call from Connor, though, on, what was it? Tuesday? Yes, Tuesday. He said that Amy has COVID and is recuperating at his home. She is apparently very ill, but not bad enough to go to the hospital. He assured me, though, that his own private doctor is available to see her and that he will monitor her situation. Connor *promised* to take good care of her."

Jake rubbed his chin. That didn't sound legit. "May I ask what you thought about that, Mrs. Redmond?"

"Call me Mary, please. I don't know what to think about it. Connor sounded sincere enough. Apparently he also let her office know, too. I asked him when I could speak to her, and he said that he hoped it would be very soon. Right now, he said, she just needs to rest."

"I see. Well, I'm sure all of us here will be happy to hear that someone is accounting for her, even though it happens to be Mr. Devlin. You have our telephone number at the office, don't you, Mary?"

"Yes, I do. Should I be worried about my daughter?"

"Please don't worry, Mary," Jake said. "If you hear any more, or if you actually talk to Amy, could you please let me know? Again, my name is Jake Rutledge. Just call the office, and the receptionist will transfer you to me."

"What about Mr. Deketomis? Can I talk to him?"

"Mr. Deketomis has . . . He's had a bit of a mishap in Chicago and is currently under medical care. But we expect him back in Florida in a week or so."

"Oh, dear, I hope it's not serious."

"We don't think it is now. We had some good news about his progress today. Thank you for your concern, though."

Jake ended the call and then dialed Carol.

"Speak to me, Jake," she answered.

He relayed to her what Mary Redmond and the EirePharma operator had told him.

"Well, do we believe any of that?" she asked.

"Hell, I don't know. Can we trust anything Devlin says at this point?"

"After last night, I'm sure he'll be gunning for us with all barrels loaded."

"Uh, what do you mean? What happened last night?" he asked.

Carol simply said, "Not over the phone. Let's just say we fired a torpedo, and it was a direct hit. It may have been a really stupid thing to do, too, but I have to tell you . . . *it felt really good.*"

Jake's imagination was running wild. "Knowing you and Michael, I'll bet it did."

"The drawback is that Devlin now knows that we're perfectly willing to play in the mud, too. We've put him on notice. His knees may not be shaking, but one of his employees is on extended leave."

"Well, that's something."

* * *

In another office in the building, Sarah Mercer made a different call to the Chicago area. It had been decided that Amy's attorney, who'd apparently attended the Saturday night event she was at, might have pertinent information about her well-being. So far, repeated attempts to reach him had failed.

"Baker and Cunningham," the receptionist answered.

"Paul Baker, please."

"Who's calling?"

Sarah explained who she was and why she was calling. The receptionist said that she was transferring her to someone who could help. After a moment, a man picked up the line.

"This is Frank Cunningham, Paul Baker's partner at the firm."

Sarah once again went through her preface and then added, "We've been trying to reach Mr. Baker for days. Is he away?"

"We have received all your messages for Mr. Baker, and I'm sorry we haven't returned them. We were going to in due course. I have to tell you that Paul is missing."

"Missing?"

"We don't know where he is. Nobody does. As you're familiar with what's been going on with the Redmond family, then I believe I can tell you this. When Paul didn't show up for work on Monday, we weren't too concerned. We did think he might have phoned in to say he was ill or taking the day off or whatever. But we shrugged it off. On Tuesday he didn't come in either. Our office manager phoned him on his cell and left a voicemail. Paul doesn't have a landline in his home. Paul's companion is a man by the name of Horace Jenkins. We tried him, and Horace was concerned that he hadn't heard from Paul since Saturday. Horace had been home every day since the weekend. Yesterday, that is, Wednesday, Horace and I reported him missing to the police in Glenview, where Paul lives."

"Oh, dear," Sarah said. "I take it the police don't know anything yet?"

"No. They've talked to all of us here at the office and of course to Horace, and they've spoken to people at the Drake Hotel, where he was last seen Saturday night. The staff is saying Paul never slept in his room that night. He was at the event, we believe, but then he just . . . vanished."

"And this event that he attended . . . it would be the one thrown by—"

"EirePharma. Yeah."

Given what had happened to Deke, as well as the mystery behind Amy's abrupt isolation and its matching timeline to Baker's disappearance, Sarah had a bad feeling about this news. "Do the police think, well, do they think foul play is involved?"

"I don't know. They haven't said. Apparently with missing person cases that are not obvious kidnappings, the police give the benefit of the doubt to the missing person for two days! We were told there are all kinds of reasons a person goes missing, and most of them are not 'bad.' We're like, *right*. Paul Baker was the kind of person who would *never* just go off someplace without telling anyone, especially Horace."

"The FBI will investigate missing person cases in which foul play is suspected."

"I know. But the police won't escalate it there yet. They've only been on it for twenty-four hours. I tried to tell them that Paul's been missing since Saturday night. That's four days, not two!"

"You might call the FBI yourself," Sarah suggested.

"I think Horace said he was going to do that today anyway."

Sarah asked Cunningham to please keep her informed and gave him her cell and office numbers. When she hung up, she sent a message to the team informing them of this disconcerting development.

* * *

Jake threw caution to the wind and dialed the office of Chief McClory in Chicago. When the call was answered by the front line desk, Jake explained who he was, that he had met with McClory in Chicago a while back, and that he had been given the okay by the chief to call anytime if he had further questions. Jake was told to hold, and he did so for seven full minutes while new age piano pieces played in his ear. Somehow he hadn't expected that to be the on-hold musical genre of the Chicago Police Department.

Finally, the gruff voice answered. "McClory."

Jake went through the story to remind the man how they'd met in his office with Matt Redmond. McClory remembered.

"I'm happy to speak to you again, Mr. Rutledge, but I happen to be very busy. We had more shootings on the South Side last night, and we've got our hands full. What can I do for you?"

"Sorry to hear that. I'll make it quick. The last time we spoke, you had said you would follow up in getting Detective Enrico Brazos's contact information to Matt Redmond, who is now deceased. I'd like to find him, sir. Can you help?"

"Ah, right, I'm sorry about that. The mess of work, Mr. Redmond's death, and everything else going on in this damned city . . . That contact was at the bottom of the to-do list. I'll try to find it and get it to you as soon as I can."

Jake rolled his eyes and almost told him that he was making better progress by himself. He already had a couple of leads he was pursuing. "Thank you, I'd appreciate that. Okay, next, you said that you knew Connor Devlin personally, is that right?"

"We've *met*, can't say I *know* him. As a matter of fact, I just met two of your people at Gottlieb Memorial in Melrose Park yesterday, and they asked me the same thing. I was sorry to hear what happened to your boss. Deke's a friend of mine, too."

"Thanks, we're very concerned about him."

"Anyway, what's this about?"

"Well, sir, we would like someone of your stature in law enforcement to give this man Devlin a call. Maybe go by Devlin's mansion and talk to him. He knows who you are." He explained the situation with Amy Redmond. "We'd just like to get confirmation that she's really convalescing at Devlin's house and that she's okay."

McClory was silent a moment. He then said, "You know that Kenilworth is not my jurisdiction at all. It's out of Chicago City Limits. Why didn't you call the Kenilworth Police?"

"Because you are my only contact in Illinois, sir," Jake said. "And since you're the chief of detectives, you have a long reach. You're a powerful man, and I'll bet you can make a request like this go places." Jake figured that flattery would help.

The man grumbled a bit and then said, "I'll see what I can do. Give me your number again." Jake did. "Okay, I'll try to see that someone looks into this if we can get our heads above water."

It wasn't until the end of the day that McClory returned Jake's phone call.

"Mr. Rutledge? I spoke to Connor Devlin myself."

"You did?"

"Yes. We do have the means here at the Chicago PD to get someone's phone number. I just called the man, out of the blue. I must say he was a little surprised to hear from me, heh, heh. But of course he knew me since we've met and all, and because I'm in the news a lot."

Jake perked up. "What did he say?"

"He says that Miss Redmond has COVID and is very sick. She's breathing fine, so she doesn't have to go to the hospital. But she has to remain isolated in his house. Luckily, Devlin has a big place. Anyway, he assured me that she is definitely in his home."

"Okay, sir, thanks very much. May we contact you again if we need to?"

"Sure thing, but if that's all for now, I'm going to get back to more important stuff, like murders and shootings and robberies and such." With that, McClory hung up.

Jake transmitted everything he'd learned to the rest of the team. Amy was sick but safe—according to Connor Devlin. Still, something didn't smell right.

38

It was seven o'clock on Thursday evening in the Devlin mansion.

Amy Redmond did not have COVID. She was, however, still in bed. She felt terrible. She figured that Connor was still drugging her, but how? It couldn't be from anything other than her food and drinks. The coffee they gave her tasted just fine. The food didn't have any peculiar tastes. Regardless, she didn't have much of an appetite. Her digestive system was completely out of whack. Any time she got up to go to the bathroom or sit in the other space to watch television, she felt dizzy.

That morning she had refused her breakfast and coffee. She had told Lance, who had delivered it, that she couldn't eat. The truth was that she was going to see how long she could go without food. Perhaps the drugs would wear off.

Amy hadn't seen Connor since Monday night. That was when she'd learned that he was keeping her a prisoner. She still didn't know what he wanted to gain by doing so. When would he tell her?

Once again, she went over in her mind everything that had happened. It was an obsession. She kept replaying every moment of Saturday. First there was her time in the suite that afternoon, doing a little work on her computer and trying to relax. Copying the flash drive. Then going up to Connor's suite. Ronan Barry walking down the hallway in front of her. Listening at the door. The men arguing. Running back to the elevator and deciding to take the stairs instead. The man known as Petey-o almost seeing her. Hurrying down to her floor and encountering Pat Beckett.

Wait a second . . .

244

THE MIDDLEMAN

Petey-o. She had seen his face. It had been a brief glimpse, and he was way down the corridor . . . but she knew he had looked familiar.

It suddenly came to her. Even through the fog of the drugs, Amy knew who the man really was. She was *positive* she'd seen him before . . . mostly in newspapers and on the news.

My God . . . my God . . . Is there any hope for me?

She had to get a message to Mr. Deketomis. He was the only possibility for rescue.

Think! Damn it, use your brain, Amy!

Lance would likely be bringing dinner soon. He had her phone. She had seen it on his card table.

Through the haze, a plan formed. She had no idea if it could possibly work, but it was worth a try.

* * *

The knock came at seven-thirty. This was followed by the jingling of the keys and the sound of unlocking the door.

"Chow time!" Lance announced cheerily. Once again, he rolled the tray inside. The smell of hot food was enticing, but she was determined not to touch it. "I hope you feel good enough to eat this time."

"Maybe," she answered.

He stopped the cart at the side of the bed and lifted the TV tray of food, ready to place it over Amy's torso, dinner-in-bed style. "Wait," she said, "don't give that to me yet. I'll eat it later, okay?"

He gave her the stink eye and set the tray back on the cart. "You need to eat, Amy."

"I will. Lance, can you please do me a favor? There's something wrong with the TV."

"What's wrong with it?"

"Use the remote, turn it on, and look."

He went to the sitting area, picked up the remote, aimed it at the TV, and pressed the appropriate button. Nothing happened.

"Huh. That's weird." He set the remote on the coffee table and walked to the television to check the cables and electrical plug.

MIKE PAPANTONIO

Earlier, Amy had simply removed the batteries from the remote. She had no idea how long it would take him to figure that out, but now was her chance. She got out of bed, did an innocent stretch, and slowly moved to the open door. Lance was preoccupied with the television, wondering what the hell was the matter with it.

Amy eyed the card table in the hall. It was seven feet away from her. Easy. She quickly moved to it, albeit a bit unsteadily. She picked up her phone and was back in the suite just as Lance found the on/off button on the actual television. It came on.

"Well it works if you turn it on manually," he said. "There must be something wrong with the remote."

Amy went into the bathroom and shut the door. Luckily, the bathroom itself had a lock on it. She turned on the phone and waited while it booted up.

"Hey, Amy!" Lance shouted. "There are no batteries in the remote! What did you do with them?"

She moved into the shower stall as the phone's home screen appeared. She quickly opened the phone app, found Nick Deketomis's contact, and hit DIAL.

"Amy!" Lance pounded on the door.

"I'm in the bathroom, you idiot!" she called.

"You better not be pulling something funny!"

The line was ringing . . . and ringing. And then she heard Deke's voice.

"This is Deke. Please leave a message, and I'll get back to you when I'm able."

"Deke, this is Amy! I'm in an upstairs bedroom in Connor's home in Kenilworth. I feel drugged! Oh, and do *not* call the—"

Lance kicked the door open, causing a deafening *CRASH* that echoed in the bathroom. He rushed in, found Amy in the shower stall, and roughly yanked her out. She fell onto the tiled floor, and the phone went flying from her hand.

"You *bitch*!" he shouted. He quickly picked up the phone and pointed at the broken lock and knob on the bathroom door. "Look what you made me do! Connor's not going to like *this*! No, siree, he's not going to like this *at all*!"

With that, he exited the suite and left Amy stunned on the floor.

THE MIDDLEMAN

* * *

It was nearly nine o'clock when Connor Devlin, dressed in a suit with the tie loosened, came to visit. Deamhan was at his side. The dog immediately went to greet Amy, who lay in bed under the covers. But Connor snapped, "Deamhan! Heel!" The dog, visibly disappointed, turned and sat by his master. Connor then stood at the entrance to the bathroom, studied the damage to the door, shook his head, and made a "tsk, tsk" sound. Next he moved to the edge of the bed and sat on the end. Deamhan followed him, but Connor ordered the dog to lie down on the floor and stay.

Connor eyed the food cart and frowned when he saw that she still hadn't touched her dinner.

"Amy, you have to eat to get your strength up," he said. When she said nothing, he went on. "Lance told me what happened. Did you make a phone call?"

She knew that he'd be able to see the call record on her phone, but it had been a very short duration. "I tried, Connor. All I got was voice-mail, and I didn't have the time to leave a message before Lance burst through the door."

"That was a bad thing to do, Amy. It will have to be repaired. The boys will do that in the morning."

Even though she still felt intoxicated from whatever drugs he'd given her, not eating for twelve hours had somewhat helped her lucidity. She had proven to herself that the drugs were indeed in the food. "What have you been giving me, Connor?" she asked.

"What do you mean?"

"In the food. You've been keeping me drugged. I feel awful. What is it?"

"I don't know what you're talking about, Amy. It's just food. You're very ill, Amy. You've had a nervous breakdown."

"Oh, Connor, cut the bullshit. Are you going to kill me the same way you had Matt murdered? The same way you killed Paul Baker? You had something to do with Uncle Charles's death, too, didn't you? Admit it, Connor. I've had a lot of time to think about all of this in here. I'm drugged, and I feel like I'm in a dream most of the time, but I can now clearly see through you and everything you've been doing. You can't keep me here forever. People will wonder. My family will raise hell. So tell me—what is it you want from me?"

Connor stared at her for a long time, making her increasingly uncomfortable. She had to look away and squeeze her eyes shut before he finally spoke. "You have disappointed me, Amy. You broke my heart."

She sighed, opened her eyes, and looked at him. "Gee, poor you, Connor."

"As far as your family and friends are concerned, no one believes you're missing. I told you the other night that we'd be using your social media to post photos and messages from you, and we have. You can't have visitors, of course, you have COVID!"

"What do you *want* from me?"

He shrugged. "Right now I enjoy your presence in the house. I missed you when you moved back to your apartment. But when I get tired of having you here . . . who knows?" He opened his jacket and pulled out an envelope. "I have a little story to tell you, Amy. It's about your Uncle Charles."

She narrowed her eyes. "What about him?"

"Prior to his suicide, Charles *did* see another attorney. Markus DeStefano. Have you heard of him?"

She didn't answer, prompting him to continue.

"Mr. DeStefano resides in Delaware. Certain securities laws are a bit different in that state. This man is a very unscrupulous business attorney who has managed to fly under the law's radar and do questionable things. Help wealthy criminals launder money and such. He handles stock transfer deals between big companies, and he also handles stock transfer deals between criminals. He's good at what he does because he's crafty, smart, and can fool the governing authorities. Do you want to know why Charles hired Mr. DeStefano?"

Amy's eyes shot to his but she still said nothing.

"I'll tell you. It was so Charles could defraud me when it came to selling me his stock in EirePharma. With DeStefano's fingers in the pockets of federal auditors and judges and money men, and his influence in that world, he was able to create counterfeit stock certificates. They were so brilliantly done that everybody, including these expert auditors who have to approve a sale of a large corporation, was fooled by the documents and all the massive paperwork that had to be produced to sell EirePharma to me. And it was these fake stock certificates—21 percent of Charles's total 51 percent of EirePharma's stock—that was made available in Charles's estate as part of the amount that was sold to me in the deal that occurred a month after his untimely and unfortunate leap from the top of his condo in Chicago. Such a tragedy."

Finally Amy spoke. "I don't understand what you're saying."

"Really? What is it that you can't figure out? In order for me to own EirePharma, I had to obtain at least 51 percent of the stock, correct? Charles owned 51 percent. You owned 30 percent. Others in your family owned 19 percent. In the deal, he had arranged to sell that 51 percent of stock to me. The board of directors and the company's attorneys handled it all after his death, but it was his plan. His orders. The problem was that 21 percent of the stock that was sold to me was fake. I got only 30 percent of the real stock. And that, of course, makes me *not* the owner of EirePharma. I have to hand it to your clever uncle. But there is a cost for that dishonesty, as you might expect."

Amy felt her heart begin to pound. She felt woozy again. What was he saying? What did this mean? "What happened to the real 21 percent?" she asked.

"That attorney DeStefano helped Charles place it into a blind receivership in a shell company managed in, you guessed it—Delaware! Because that's the state that can do that. And you probably know that the true owner of a blind receivership is a secret. We now know the extent of the fraudulent transaction that was arranged by your uncle before his death. Your Uncle Charles committed a serious financial crime. Securities fraud. He fooled the board of directors, he fooled the company's lawyers, and he fooled *me*. And now it will take dozens of attorneys, a lot of money, and the federal government to unravel the damage. *And I can't have the federal government involved!*"

"So who owns EirePharma? No one?"

Connor emitted a little laugh. "You really are a little slow today, sweetheart. No, Amy. *You* own it. Charles put the real 21 percent into a blind receivership—and he made *you* the owner of it. Your 30 percent plus that 21 percent gives you 51 percent."

The news made her head spin even more. She felt as if she might be sick.

"Why . . . why didn't he tell . . . me this?" she whispered.

"Oh, that. Well, he was going to. Charles had arranged this deception as an insurance policy, so to speak, in case something happened to him before the sale. He was a prescient man, your uncle. I got wind of what he might be doing in Delaware, so I went to see him that day in Chicago when he was at that beautiful high-rise apartment. I asked him to show me the view from the roof. In fact, I *insisted* that he show me the view. Probably a little more physical persuasion than he expected. So when we got there, he refused to tell me what I wanted to know. Can you imagine?" Connor shook his head. "Poor man. He, um, slipped and fell."

"You *did* kill him! Damn you, Connor! Damn you to hell! You *are* a thug! A *criminal* that everybody tried to warn me about! God, I should have listened!"

He ignored her words and held up the envelope. "DeStefano sent this to you not long after the sale of the company. Per your uncle's instructions, it was to be sent upon the sale. It's a letter from Charles, explaining everything to you. It also contains documents from DeStefano that are all the documents and directives you need to access your stock in the shell company. It's all in your name, darling. Not mine. Yours. Luckily, he made the mistake of sending the letter to your office at EirePharma. I was lucky enough to intercept it. That's how I learned the full details of your uncle's clever criminal-quality treachery. I was immediately impressed, for what it's worth."

"Wait. *How* long have you known this?"

"About a year. Amy, obviously this is why I proposed to you. It's not like I needed a wife. But with you as my wife, we would have owned the company together. It was only after you called off the engagement and everything went south between us that I was forced to do . . ." He waved his hands around the suite. ". . . this."

THE MIDDLEMAN

Amy grasped at straws. "It's . . . it's just a matter of time before this Mr. DeStefano tries to contact me. What then, genius?"

Connor shrugged. "Ha! For all he knows, you got the envelope and decided to let me keep the company. We were getting married. We looked like a happy couple in the Chicago society pages. It's more likely that he couldn't care less, I imagine. He's a busy man. And there are plenty of tall buildings where that chiseler lives, just like there are right here in Chicago." He held up the envelope. "This has been residing in the Hate Box along with all the other weapons that have been used against me over the years, including your little flash drive and its copy. Maybe the time has finally come to burn it all. A nice bonfire in the backyard might be fun for a summer activity."

It was all too much information to fathom. *She* was the true owner of the company? Amy struggled to hold back tears. She needed strength now more than ever, and she was determined not to let him see her cry.

Her voice was hoarse as she tried to speak. "You still . . . Connor . . . you still haven't told me . . . what you want from me."

"Ah. I was getting to that. Amy, the world still believes I own EirePharma. I am giving you a choice. You can marry me as we had planned, in which case we'll be co-owners of EirePharma. I'd still be in control as CEO, but you would remain president. And we'd live a pretty damned good life here. Happily ever after."

"I'll never do that."

He held up a finger. "*Or* . . . you sign over all of your stock—all 30 percent that you had previously owned plus the receivership 21 percent—to me. I would then be the true owner of EirePharma."

Amy turned away from him. "Get out of here, you psychopath! *Get out!*"

Connor laughed a little. "Oh, that's rich. No, Amy, I'm not mad. I am a product of my background, just as you are." He gestured to the portraits on the back wall of the sitting area. "Those paintings . . . I may not have told you everything about those people. My father . . . and my mother . . . they died much sooner than I let on. I was an orphan, and I was raised by Ireland's most stone cold, ruthless collection of businessmen who—"

251

"You mean *criminals!*" she spat.

He glared at her. "Some might call us that. Quinn Gilligan was the patriarch of our group. The man who raised me as a son. The mother I told you about—"

"Claire?"

"*Yes, Claire!*" Connor's cheeks were flushing. His anger began to bubble up, and Amy was happy to push it. "She never existed!" He laid a finger on his right temple. "Only in here did she reside. And the rest of them . . . my cousins! A clan that generated profits in everything from prostitution and drug smuggling to numbers and strong-arm protection rackets . . . *They* raised me to be who I am today! They encouraged me to attend college and help them by using my education to move into legitimate businesses. Now look at me, Amy! I am in control of one of the largest American pharmaceutical companies, and *you* will be at my side. From where I'm standing, the US pharma industry was already being run by a Wall Street band of thugs. I'm simply intent on giving them some competition."

He breathed heavily, gained hold of his emotions, and stood. Deamhan, taking this as a cue that it was all right to get up, did so and stood next to Connor. "Amy, if you refuse to do either of the things I outlined, then I will be forced to reveal to the world your Uncle Charles's fraud and release video stills of you and Mr. Baker at the Drake Hotel. This would ruin you forever, Amy. But that would just be a beginning of what I am capable of doing. It would ruin the Redmond family forever. Oh, and before I do that, the world might be mourning you. It would be such a catastrophe if Amy Redmond should have an accident here at the house due to your delirium from COVID symptoms. COVID is nasty and unpredictable, isn't it? Such a shame. And then that awful news about your uncle would come out, you'd be blamed for Baker's murder, and no one would feel sorry for you anymore. I'd be vindicated as the man who was deceived and betrayed. Terrible stuff. Almost a Greek tragedy, don't you agree? Come, Deamhan, let's let the poor dear have some time to heal."

Connor moved to the door and opened it. The dog looked back at Amy, confused as to why he couldn't greet her. "You know, Amy, you

THE MIDDLEMAN

may think Deamhan is your friend. But if I give the command, he'll tear out your throat and eat it for me. Now that's true friendship."

With that, dog and master left the room.

After holding them back for so long, she now let the tears flow.

39

By Friday afternoon, Deke was lying comfortably in a new bed in a private room. He was awake and alert, but he was still on painkillers. Nevertheless, to Michael and Carol, he didn't seem too out of it. Teri, who was in the room with them, insisted that Deke still had a long way to go to recover, but admitted that he was doing much better than anyone had predicted after only three days since the assault. He mostly complained of a headache and sore jaw, but Michael knew Deke was being stalwart. The areas of broken bones—the ribs and hand—had to hurt, and he knew from experience that injury to the internal organs was always extremely painful. There was still blood in Deke's urine, so his care team was keeping an eye on that.

"Michael, Carol, I want you to bring me up to date," he said with a hoarse voice.

"Deke," Michael said, "you need to rest. We don't want to stress you out. Trust us, we can handle it. We just want you to mend yourself quickly."

"Michael, I'd prefer to continue working. It will take my mind off the pain. You forget I experienced Connor Devlin's evil firsthand. Now, please do as I ask and bring me up to date."

"All right, boss," Carol replied.

An exhausted-looking Teri stood and said, "I'm going to get some coffee and let you guys talk shop. Anybody want anything?"

The three others declined and thanked her. She quickly left the room, something she was used to doing whenever Deke was about to discuss a case with colleagues. There were some things in those conversations that were often too scary to think about.

"First," Deke asked, "do any of you know where my phone is?"

"The cops didn't tell you?" Michael asked.

"No. If they did, I was too out of it to hear it, and I haven't thought about it until today."

"Your phone was smashed to pieces at the scene. The remains of it are with the police, but it's unusable. We'll need to get you a new phone, Deke. I can go get you one today if you tell me what you want."

"Hm. Thanks. You know I'm an Android guy, so get me the latest Galaxy. So what's been happening since I've been in outer space?"

Carol started by telling him that she took the liberty to enlist the help of private investigator Lou Doonan. "Michael and I met with him the other night and, uh, we'll tell you about that in a minute. But he told me he's got a guy who can access Chicago police case files online. Last night I called Lou and asked if he could get the skinny on Matt Redmond's case as well as yours. He said he'd call me this afternoon, so that could be any minute now."

"Okay."

Michael then told Deke about his talk with the two women from Walgreens. All good. Then Carol informed him that Paul Baker was missing, and that they thought Amy Redmond was, too, until Jake learned that Amy had COVID and was recuperating at Devlin's home.

"She's at his house?" Deke asked. "That's a switch. She didn't want anything to do with Devlin anymore. Are we sure about that?"

"That's according to Devlin, of course, but also Chief McClory in Chicago. Jake contacted him and asked that he personally get verification," Carol answered. "Of course, we haven't seen her with our own eyes."

Deke furrowed his brow and rubbed his eyes. "This makes my head hurt. McClory? His jurisdiction is in Chicago, not the suburb where Devlin lives. Why would he do that?"

Carol held out her hands. "You got me, boss. I don't know. Jake asked him to do it, and he did it. I think he thought he was doing you a favor."

"Okay, what else? What about Vernon Bunker? I understand he's dead."

"Yes," Michael answered. "Police are still investigating."

"Have they made any progress in finding out who did this to me?"

Michael glanced at Carol, who gave him a slight nod. "No, but we have. Deke, you saw the men. Did you recognize them?"

He shook his head. "You know, I can't picture them. It's a blur. The last thing I remember was Bunker saying he was going to get something to drink before we started the interview."

Michael went to his briefcase that was sitting on the floor. He opened it and removed the photo of Devlin and the two men. He showed it to Deke. "You remember this picture?"

"Yes. I have one, too."

"Right. Do you recognize the two men?"

Deke squinted at it for a long time. Finally, he said, "Maybe. But at this moment in time, I wouldn't be able to truthfully say that I could do so in a court of law."

"They're Pat Beckett and Ronan Barry, two of Devlin's top enforcers. They killed Bunker, and they left you for dead. I believe they thought you were dead. It doesn't make sense that they would have intentionally left you there alive."

"How do you know they did it?"

"Beckett admitted it to me," Michael said.

Deke blinked twice. "What? How? When?"

Carol said, "Oh boy. Deke, you're not going to like this. But sometimes it's important to create energy and conflict in an investigation to find facts that would never surface any other way."

Together, they told him the story of contacting Lou Doonan and then stalking Beckett at the Irish pub. When Michael outlined what had occurred in the men's room, Deke shut his eyes and slowly shook his head.

"Guys, guys . . ."

"Sorry, Deke," Carol said.

"This could blow our case. Michael, you could be disbarred."

Michael countered, "But Deke, if Devlin is really involved in the kind of crap we think he is, and if Barry and Beckett really murdered

THE MIDDLEMAN

Bunker and attempted to kill *you*, you think Devlin is going to go to the cops to have us arrested? Will Beckett? You really think anyone in that bunch of criminals is going to say a word about this, much less report it to the Florida bar? We did what needed to be done, Deke. We did leave him alive, you know. They won't say a word, trust me! Besides, we think these guys killed Matt Redmond, too."

Carol's phone rang, and she checked the caller ID. "Oh, it's Lou Doonan, let me take this." She walked away from the bed and faced the window looking out at the parking lot. "Hi, Lou. Oh, yeah? Wait a second. Yeah, let me put you on speaker so Michael and our boss can hear you. Yes, he's doing much better." She walked back to Deke and Michael. "Lou, can you hear us?"

"Yes. Can you all hear me?"

"Hi, Lou, it's Michael. And we're with Nick Deketomis at the hospital."

"Hello, Lou, you can call me Deke."

"Hi, Deke, I hope you're feeling all right."

"I've had better days, but please tell us what you have to say. I hope you can make this day better with a little helpful information."

Doonan spoke. "Okay, I have a guy who can hack into the Chicago PD case files online. Everything is online these days. I looked up the Matt Redmond case." The man began reading off what little evidence the police had, which was basically a timeline of the facts.

"I'm afraid that's not anything we didn't already know, Lou," Michael said.

"Is there anything about Matt's phone?" Deke asked.

Doonan replied, "According to the file, the phone company got the request from the cops to ping it. Looks like there was some kind of screwup, and there was a delay in getting the results. They just came in four days ago, apparently."

Deke said, "Hmpf. That explains why Chief McClory didn't have them in the file when I spoke to him at the end of May. What did the ping tell us?"

"The location of the phone was Deerfield, Illinois, on the day after Matt was killed, but then nothing after that."

MIKE PAPANTONIO

"Whoa!" Michael blurted. "Deerfield? That's where EirePharma headquarters is located!"

"If you're right," Carol responded, "what was Matt's phone doing *there*?"

Michael ventured, "Devlin may have ordered that it be turned on so they could see what intel they could get from it. Matt had been talking to Amy and Deke. Maybe they thought there could be emails or something that revealed what Matt was doing?"

"Could be," Deke said.

"Anything else, Lou?" Carol asked.

"That's it. No suspects, of course. And I think you know everything that was in Deke's case. I've got Bunker's autopsy report and the hospital report on your injuries, Deke, but again, the cops in Schiller Park listed no suspects in the file."

"Okay, thanks, Lou," Carol said. "Forward all that to me, will you?"

After the call ended, Deke said, "It's hard to ignore the possibility that Devlin ordered the hit on Matt."

"And Vernon Bunker," Carol said. "And you."

"Guys," Deke said, "this case is edging further into criminal territory. We're going to need help from the district attorney. Maybe the FBI. It's gone beyond a civil case involving the price of insulin and the bad-faith takeover of a family business by a mobster. We're talking assault and murder now." He rubbed his eyes again with his free hand. "I'm worried about Amy. I wonder if she's tried to call me."

"Deke," Carol said, handing him her phone. "You can access your voicemail from another phone as long as it's on the same carrier. We both use AT&T, right?"

"Yes."

"Call yourself. When you hear your own voicemail greeting, press the star key."

Deke followed her instructions and listened. His eyes widened in alarm. "Son of a bitch . . ." he said.

"What?"

He punched another key to replay the message and then put the phone on speaker.

258

THE MIDDLEMAN

They all heard Amy's voice. "Deke, this is Amy! I'm in an upstairs bedroom in Connor's home in Kenilworth. I feel drugged! Oh, and do *not* call the—"

"That's it?" Michael asked. "It got cut off. 'Do not call . . .' what? Or who? What was she saying?"

Deke played the message again and said, "I have no idea what she was about to say."

"Clearly she's in some kind of trouble, Deke," Carol said. "And that's drugs I'm hearing in that message, not COVID."

"I wish we could have heard more, Carol, but we've got to get in there and make sure she's all right."

PART FIVE
JUNE 2024

40

Now

Saturday was a flurry of activity in Deke's hospital room. He began physical therapy in the morning, and that left him exhausted. However, Amy's message gave him the extra boost of energy and focus that he needed.

Jake flew in from Florida and arrived just after lunchtime, just when Deke was ready to start work. It was decided that Gina and Sarah, who came in to the Spanish Trace office on the weekend, would handle tons of paperwork should new pleadings need to be filed in the immediate future. The thrust of the lawsuits would accuse EirePharma and InsoDrugs of racketeering, price gouging, and fraudulent business practices that harm consumers of insulin. A second complaint would be filed against Connor Devlin for mismanagement and fraud, basically a shareholder derivative action, with the plaintiffs being Mary and Amy Redmond. It was Gina's task to get more of EirePharma's board of directors to sign on to the suit.

Then there was the other component of the case—the criminal charges. Deke knew a federal prosecutor who was the acting United States attorney for the Northern District of Illinois. Deke had gone to law school with Dale Butler, but they had not communicated since those heady, youthful days. Gina was able to get hold of Butler's home phone number, and Deke gave him a call. Butler was surprised but happy to hear from Deke, and the two men spent nearly an hour on the phone as Deke laid out everything that was going on. Butler was shocked by the story. Nevertheless, Deke was pleased to hear the attorney say, "You

263

know, Deke, I've met Mr. Devlin on quite a few occasions. I found his defense in that recent insulin class action suit to be greasy as hell. I guess my instincts were correct when I immediately hated that damn hustler. I'm not surprised at all to learn he's probably a bona fide criminal."

They also discussed Amy's situation. The Kenilworth police department was very small and, in fact, Glenview handled 911 calls. Butler drove the point home that Devlin was a powerful and respected man in Chicago, and that Amy, the president of EirePharma, was a high-profile individual, too. They had no proof that she was in real danger. They couldn't conduct what amounted to a raid. A "wellness check," also known as a "welfare check," could be appropriate. A warrant is not needed for that kind of visit. It might be a very good idea to keep the wellness check quiet and not attract the press. They didn't want Devlin claiming that the law firm, or law enforcement, was harassing him at home. Bungling the visit could damage the case Deke wanted to bring against the man.

"Knowing Devlin," Butler said, "I don't think he's going to hurt her, especially since he's already told people that she's at his house. I'm looking at her Facebook page now. There's a picture of her in bed with a tray of food on her lap. She looks like someone who's definitely sick in bed, but she doesn't appear to be in any danger."

"Devlin could refuse to let us enter, even if we're just doing a wellness check."

"True. In that case you *would* need a warrant. I tell you what I'll do, Deke. I'll contact a friendly Cook County judge on Monday morning. She may be willing to issue a very limited search warrant to have in your pocket just in case you need it."

The men agreed that they would speak further on Monday when Butler was at the office.

Deke wondered if Chief McClory might be willing to help them out for a wellness check. The chief had spoken to Devlin previously, so there was precedent. Kenilworth was indeed out of the Chicago PD's jurisdiction, but perhaps he would do it yet again as a favor to Deke. Quiet and simple. Perhaps McClory could talk to Devlin and request that he allow an informal visit from the team to speak with Amy.

THE MIDDLEMAN

With the group assembled in the hospital room, Deke addressed Michael, Carol, and Jake. He told them of his conversation with Butler and then said, "It's vital that we handle this very carefully. We need Amy's evidence that she said is collected on a flash drive. The questions I have are does she still have it? Is it hidden? We need to talk to her. We need to make sure she's okay. If not, then we need to get her away from Devlin. I don't believe this can be handled the same way the police might deal with a kidnapping. What are your thoughts?"

"Is this a domestic crime?" Carol asked. "Amy was engaged to Devlin, but apparently she's not anymore. Is he keeping her against her will in his house? If so, that sounds like kidnapping to me."

"It wasn't clear from that brief phone message," Michael admitted.

"Does she really have COVID?" Jake asked.

"Again, she didn't indicate that," Michael answered. "Look, based on what we already know about this bottom feeder, do we really have to guess about whether or not she's in trouble? I might be inclined to go commando and get her out of there."

"Michael, I don't think you can parachute onto the roof of Devlin's mansion and do a PJ operation like you did in Las Vegas a few years ago to save that young woman from a psychopath," Deke said with a slight laugh that visibly caused him pain. "This is a very different scenario. We need to play it by the book. Let me call McClory. If he's willing to help us out, then I want all of you to coordinate with him. Agreed?"

Reluctantly, they nodded.

* * *

It took the team all of Sunday and Monday to prepare for the "operation," as Michael liked to call it.

Deke had tried to reach Chief McClory on Saturday and Sunday but was unable to do so. It was only on Monday morning that they finally spoke about the situation. Deke informed McClory that he wanted his team to do a wellness check on Amy and talk to her. All would go smoothly if Devlin allowed it; otherwise a search warrant would be executed. Deke was prepared to go to the Kenilworth police and possibly the FBI for assistance; however, he felt that the visit should be discreet and quiet, for Amy's sake. It would be a PR nightmare if a suburban police force or the FBI were involved. He wanted to spare Amy from that, especially if it was all a misunderstanding. Once again, McClory hemmed and hawed about Kenilworth not being in his jurisdiction and that he had already reported to Jake Rutledge a few days earlier that Amy Redmond was recuperating from COVID. Deke explained that he didn't believe that was entirely true and that they needed to get into the house and see Amy with their own eyes and speak to her—infectious or not. Deke also told McClory that at least one of Devlin's bodyguards may have been responsible for the assault that placed Deke in the hospital, but that was a different matter.

McClory grumbled about it quite a bit, but then he said he would phone Devlin again and "put the screws on him" to tell him exactly what was going on inside his house, as well as inform Devlin about the wellness check. Deke accepted that.

An hour later, McClory phoned Deke and relayed what Devlin had to say.

"The man told me, 'Amy is feeling a little better but the doctor said she must have peace and quiet and not be disturbed.' That's a direct quote. I have to say that I believe him. That said, I told Mr. Devlin that you were obtaining a search warrant and that he would have to let you in the house should they arrive with any law enforcement officers. This upset him a great deal, but he finally agreed to let two of your team members in the house tonight. He asked that *I* be the one to accompany your people instead of you involving the local police or FBI at this time. He requested that I accompany, let's see, he gave me the names . . . uh, Michael Carey and, uh, Carol Morris. Mr. Devlin said he would allow those two in, and only those two. And me. Deke, I don't want to do this. It's out of my jurisdiction, and I'm a busy man. However, Mr. Devlin told me that he would donate a sizable amount of money to the Chicago Police Department Memorial Foundation if I oversaw the visit to his house. That's something the foundation could use, so I agreed to it. It

THE MIDDLEMAN

has to be after nine o'clock tonight, as he will be away on business until then. Now, is this agreeable to you, Deke? I think this might be a quiet solution to what you need."

Deke said that was fine and thanked his friend for helping out.

41

Jake sat behind the wheel of a rented Nissan Sentra, parked in the lot of the Kenilworth 7-Eleven convenience store at Winnetka Avenue and Green Bay Road, which was roughly a two minute drive to Sheridan Road and Devlin's property. Michael and Carol sat in Michael's rental in the same lot, away from Jake.

At 9:30 p.m., Chief McClory arrived. He was driving a black 2022 Ford Explorer XLT. Jake watched as Michael and Carol got out of their car and went over to McClory's. McClory got out, shook hands, and the trio spoke for a minute. The man was dressed casually but wore a sidearm at his waist. Michael produced the newly obtained search warrant, and McClory took it and read it through. After a few moments, he handed it back, and then Michael and Carol got into McClory's Ford. The chief backed out and headed east on Winnetka toward Sheridan Road.

Jake pulled out and discreetly followed the Explorer.

Eventually, McClory turned onto Sheridan Road and drove a ways south until he came to the large iron gate and fence that surrounded Devlin's lavish home. Jake watched from a distance as McClory spoke to the guard at the gate. The man let the Explorer through, and it went on toward the house. Jake drove a little closer and parked at the curb across the road but close enough that he could keep an eye on the gate and guard. As it was now pitch dark, his car wasn't noticed.

* * *

THE MIDDLEMAN

McClory, Michael, and Carol got out of the Explorer and went to the imposing front door.

"You ready?" the chief asked them.

Michael held up the search warrant. "As ever."

McClory rang the doorbell. They could all hear a dog barking inside.

"Sounds like a big-un'," the chief said.

The door opened and revealed Ronan Barry. Carol and Michael recognized him and shared a glance. Barry, too, gave them a squinty eye. He was well aware of what they'd done to Pat Beckett.

"Come in, Mr. Devlin is expecting you," Barry said with controlled menace. He gestured for them to enter the spacious two-story foyer.

They were immediately struck by the castle-like ambiance of the wood and plaster decor and the ceiling, high above, also made of plaster that resembled stone but with thick wooden beams at intervals running lengthwise. A large sixteen-wick candelabra stood against the side of the curving staircase. A beautiful tapestry that Michael thought might be a true antique treasure covered the wall behind the candelabra, and more of them lined the foyer perimeter walls going up to the second floor. As all the candles were lit, his immediate opinion was that it was a risky spot for the relics. Other areas of the home led off in two directions on either side of the staircase, and it was from the right that Connor Devlin appeared. He was wearing an exquisite red velvet smoking jacket over green designer slacks and a light yellow dress shirt. The man exuded a confidence and charisma that even the normally cynical Carol noted as palpable.

A very large, very alert German shepherd was at his side, attached to a leash that Devlin held. The dog immediately began to growl at Michael and Carol. The animal then barked ferociously.

"Deamhan! Hush! Sit!" The dog stopped the noise, sat, but continued to stare at the guests with menace. "Hello, sorry, Deamhan takes his job very seriously. I'm Connor Devlin."

"Mr. Devlin, I'm Michael Carey and this is Carol Morris, and—"

"I know who you are. This is my associate Ronan Barry, and over there is Lance Macdonald."

The other man had appeared behind them, likely quietly coming in through the front door.

Michael silently thought to himself, *That's two men plus Devlin and the dog and one man at the gate . . . are there any more? Pat Beckett's still in the hospital.*

"I must say this is ridiculously inconvenient and completely unnecessary," Devlin said. "You are disturbing my work and the sanctity of my home."

"We're here on a wellness check to see Amy Redmond," Carol announced.

Devlin nodded. "I understand. However, if I refuse, you have to present a warrant, is that not correct?"

Michael held up the folded document. "Yeah, well, I have it right here. Why don't you take a peek?"

Devlin snatched the warrant out of Michael's hand and glanced at it. "You want to see Amy Redmond. Fine. I'll take you up. However, I'm not sure you'll be able to talk to her. I believe she is sleeping. She has not been well. Did you bring face masks? She has COVID."

"We're willing to risk seeing her without the masks," Carol said.

"Fine. Let's go." He stuck the warrant in the pocket of his smoking jacket, and then he led the dog to the stone stairs. They ascended together. Michael and Carol went next behind him, followed by McClory and Barry. The man called Lance remained on the ground floor.

At the top of the staircase, Devlin took a left and went down a corridor, passing a few other doors that presumably led to bedrooms or sitting rooms. The light fixtures were electric, but they were designed to look like old-school torches that once lit medieval castles. They eventually came to a closed door. A bare card table and chair stood nearby. Carol immediately wondered why there was a need for someone to sit outside Amy's door.

"This is Amy's room," Devlin said. He noted Carol eyeing the desk. "Sometimes I've sat outside her room, or one of my assistants does, to attend to her if she needs something. She's been very ill."

Barry stepped up to the door, removed a set of keys from his pocket, and unlocked it.

"Why is the door locked?" Carol asked.

"For her protection," Devlin answered.

THE MIDDLEMAN

"Protection from what?"

"From Deamhan, of course. The dog can be quite vicious."

Carol and Michael shared another glance.

All this is sketchy as hell, she thought. *Wouldn't the dog be used to Amy being around by now?*

She looked back at the animal. It was still growling, focused entirely on Carol and Michael. Oddly, Chief McClory stood beside Deamhan, and the dog was paying no attention to him.

The dog knows McClory!

Michael's eyes indicated that he had figured out the same thing. He said to Carol, "We're going to see Amy," with the subtext being that they shouldn't do anything until they'd accomplished what they came to do.

Barry, who had heard him, said, "And here she is." He held the door open. The duo from Florida stepped over the threshold and saw that the large suite was darkly lit but tastefully furnished and decorated in an "old Ireland" style. Several bouquets of fresh flowers were set around the room and the suite was pungent with the smell of them.

Amy lay in bed with her eyes closed.

"See, she's asleep," Devlin quietly said. "We mustn't disturb her."

"To hell with that," Carol said. She pushed past Devlin to go to her.

Devlin reached out to block her. "Stop, you can't—"

Carol brushed him off and kept going.

Michael said, "Mr. Devlin, the warrant plainly states that we are entitled to speak to Ms. Redmond. So how about you and Cujo there take a couple of steps back from my partner."

He did so, but the dog growled again.

"Amy," Carol said, leaning over her. "Amy, wake up. Can you hear me?" She gently placed a hand on the woman's shoulder. "Amy?"

There was movement. Amy's eyes fluttered, and she groaned a little.

"Amy? It's Carol Morris from Deke's office. Deke sent me."

Amy moaned a little louder, and her body shifted. Her eyes gazed at Carol uncomprehendingly, but then she could barely keep them open. Carol carefully used her fingers to open one eye and examine it. She then turned back to Devlin.

"This woman has been drugged. We're taking her out of here."

271

Devlin snapped, "No, you're not!"

The dog growled loudly.

Michael said, "So here's your reality right now, Mr. Devlin. We have presented you with a search warrant and—"

Chief McClory stepped forward and interrupted him. "Not so fast, Mr. Carey. I read your limited warrant. All it says is that you're allowed to see Ms. Redmond and speak to her. It doesn't say you're allowed to remove her from the premises." He moved around them to block the pair from getting near the bed.

Michael and Carol came to the realization at the same time. Chief McClory was on Devlin's side.

"Look here, Chief McClory," Michael said, "as her attorney I *insist* that we be allowed to take this woman to the hospital. Or we could call an ambulance." He eyed Devlin. "That would draw the attention of your neighbors, wouldn't it, my friend? I'm thinking that's not something you want, is it?"

McClory drew a Sig Sauer pistol from the holster at his belt. As soon as he did that, Ronan Barry also drew a Browning handgun from a shoulder holster beneath his jacket. Deamhan began barking with rage. Devlin had to use all his strength to keep the dog from attacking Michael and Carol, who stood in shock at the turn of events.

McClory then said, "It's a shame that you resisted arrest and got yourselves in trouble. 'Judge, these crazy lawyers simply went berserk! They became violent and tried to overreach the terms of the search warrant, and they attacked an officer of the law! I had no choice but to discharge my weapon.'" The man grinned. "Who do you think the judge will believe? You Florida corn pones or the chief of detectives with the Chicago Police Department? You know, sometimes tragedies occur when suspects resist arrest."

Devlin stepped forward, still struggling with the dog. "Words of the wise, Petey-o! Let's get out of Amy's bedroom and let her rest. Downstairs, folks. Now!"

Carol audibly gasped. *Amy's voice message to Deke was that they shouldn't call . . . the police! No wonder she didn't call 911 when she'd had the chance. She'd known about McClory and tried to warn them but was cut off. Why hadn't they put it together? Deke had first told them that the chief's name was...*

"James P. McClory," she said.

McClory raised an eyebrow. "At your service."

"The P stands for Peter."

"It does indeed," he said with a slight smile.

Petey-o, the mystery nickname about which they'd all wondered.

With the two guns pointed at them, Michael and Carol had no choice but to raise their hands, turn, walk down the corridor, and begin descending the stairs with McClory and Barry directly behind them, followed by Devlin and the dog.

42

Michael and Carol exchanged glances. They had both noticed that Ronan Barry had forgotten to lock Amy's bedroom door. He had stuck the keys back in his pocket.

Prior to the operation, they had discussed with Jake and Deke several possible outcomes of their visit to Devlin's home. By outlining *if-then* scenarios, they would at the very least have a plan of action should there be any surprises. *IF this happens, THEN we do that.* They had created an *if-then* strategy for four conceivable developments. Of course, anything they might do had the potential of not going the way they hoped. But it was the risk they had to take. The ability to improvise was everything, and the fact that Barry had slipped up with the keys was just the catalyst they needed.

Carol gave him a perceptible nod.

While they were still at the top of the curving staircase, Michael pretended to trip and involuntarily grab McClory to seemingly break his own fall, but really his intention was to shove the man down the steps. With a forceful push, Michael slammed into the corrupt cop, and McClory went tumbling.

Simultaneously, Carol turned and rushed past Devlin and the dog to the landing and headed for Amy's room.

Devlin, flustered by the sudden turn of events, wasn't sure whether to sic the dog on Michael or send him after Carol. He watched as she ran down the hall toward the closed door and finally pointed at her. "Deamhan! *Kill*!" The dog barked and bolted after her. But Devlin had

274

hesitated too long—Carol made it to the bedroom door, rushed inside, and slammed it shut just as Deamhan reached the threshold.

On the stairs, Michael twisted, grabbed Barry's gun arm and corkscrewed the wrist *hard*, causing the bodyguard to drop the weapon. It flew away, landing somewhere down below. He then body-blocked Barry in an attempt to propel him down the staircase, too, but Barry was too well-trained to allow that to happen. The man swung at Michael and landed a blow to his face, temporarily stunning him.

Inside the bedroom, Carol held the door fast as the dog barked feverishly on the other side and scraped his claws on the door trying to break it down. Carol knew that Devlin would likely hurry back and force it open so that the dog could enter and rip her to shreds.

Michael and Barry continued their melee, knees and foot kicks flying. Michael bent his body and tackled his opponent, causing an unpreventable cascade down the stairs as Michael and Barry rolled down together to the ground floor.

Devlin leaned over the rail and called for Lance to help. When he did so, he saw that McClory lay at the bottom of the stairs, unconscious.

To Carol, it sounded as if the dog was performing body blows against the door. The animal was terribly strong. Could it break down the door?

"Bathroom . . ."

The voice was Amy's. Carol looked back at her. The woman was sitting up, her hand out stretched. "Help me. Bathroom has a new lock . . ."

Carol understood. She scurried to the woman, got an arm under her legs, and cradled her neck and shoulders against the other arm. Carol lifted Amy, carried her to the bathroom, and gently laid her on the tile floor. Carol then slammed the door shut and locked it. The shiny knob and locking mechanism appeared to be jury-rigged, a temporary replacement over damage that had been done to the door. She knew that this was only a short-term barricade. What now? Call Jake? As Amy was groaning, Carol thought the best course of action was to try and revive the woman enough to get her on her feet and out of the house.

Michael and Barry were dazed by the tumble down the stairs. Michael attempted to shake away the stars in his eyes. Only then did he spot a handgun on the floor a few feet in front of his face. Was it Barry's? McClory's? He didn't know and didn't care. He willed himself to snake toward it . . . but Barry beat him to it. The bodyguard grabbed the pistol and got to his feet. Instead of shooting Michael, though, he started kicking him. "This is for Pat!" he shouted. "This is for Pat!" Michael had to curl into a fetal position to ward off the attack, and it was only then that Barry aimed the pistol at Michael, ready to pull the trigger.

Michael's years of PJ training switched on. He had been in a situation like this before, but right now he needed a boatload of stupid luck. Barry had made a critical mistake by putting his legs and feet so close to Michael. Michael retrieved his switchblade, flicked it open, and plunged it into the big man's knee. He then reached to grab the weapon as Barry fired what he meant to be a fatal head shot. Michael felt the heat of the barrel as he redirected the gunfire only micro-measurements from his right ear. The blast was deafening but another minute of survival was all Michael was focused on. Holding onto the barrel for just another chance to regroup and inflict more pain into the body of his would-be killer was his laser concentration as he plunged the knife twice into Barry's neck before he got enough clearance to deal with the other brute in the room.

Barry's gun dropped to the floor just as Lance Macdonald entered the fray, and Michael felt his presence charging in. He propelled his weight and rammed Macdonald into Barry's staggering, bleeding body. Michael then switched from stabbing motions with his blade to a slicing windmill action as he severed the tendons and arteries on Macdonald's right arm just below the elbow. Michael immediately moved to cut the connecting tissues between Macdonald's knees and ankles. The shock from the shower of blood alone that both men saw leaving their bodies in those few seconds was immobilizing. All of it was due to the textbook training that came together with that stupid luck he'd needed. He knew from experience that the bright red froth pulsating onto the floor meant that either one or both men, struggling to move, had less than five minutes to bleed out on the stone floor.

With an expression of shock and pain on their faces, the two henchmen stumbled backward. In what resembled a lovers' embrace, they crashed into the candelabra as they fell to the floor. The flames of the candles instantaneously ignited the priceless tapestries on the staircase wall.

Michael threw his body mass on top of the men, committed to pinning them on the floor with his own weight. Barry and Macdonald struggled to remain conscious, but all Michael had to do was wait.

Upstairs, Deamhan was barking like a rabid dog outside Amy's bedroom, banging its front paws against the door. Devlin, still looking down from the railing, panicked when he saw the flames on the tapestry. He rushed halfway down the stairs and then saw that the fire was spreading to other tapestries that hung higher from the second floor.

"My treasures!" he cried, barely noticing the pile of bleeding bodies sprawled on the floor below.

In the bathroom, Carol was gently slapping Amy's face. "Wake up, Amy. Wake up!"

"They drugged me . . ." the woman murmured.

"Come on, we're going to get you out of here. Can you stand? Please try and sit up!"

Then they heard the bedroom door break. The frenzied dog had done it. Deamhan was now outside the bathroom, barking like crazy.

"Deamhan!" Amy managed to cry out.

The dog continued to howl and slam at the wooden door between them.

"Help me sit up by the door," Amy said.

Against her better judgment and because she could think of nothing better to do, Carol assisted Amy.

"Deamhan!" Amy spoke in her baby talk voice. "Deamhan! Good boy! It's me! Deamhan, heel! Sit, Deamhan!"

Amazingly, the barking ceased. The confused dog whined, still scraping the door.

"Deamhan, good boy. Sit! Sit! It's okay! It's okay! I'm fine! Good boy!"

The dog wailed again, this time plaintively, but the scratching on the door ceased.

"That's a good boy!" Amy reached for the doorknob.

"Oh my God, is that a good idea?" Carol whispered.

"Trust me." She turned the knob and opened the door just enough that she could see Deamhan sitting and panting, his eyes a bit wild and his tongue hanging out. Blood flowed from his snout and paws from the efforts to crash into the bedroom. He whined again and pushed at the door, trying to get in.

"Calm, Deamhan. That's a good boy. Calm!"

These were trigger words that the animal knew. The animal sat.

"Good boy! Come!" She then allowed the dog inside the bathroom, his tail wagging like no tomorrow. Deamhan licked Amy's face as if she'd been gone a long time and was finally returning home to see him.

"Good boy, good boy!" Amy laughed.

Carol stood back in astonishment.

Amy gestured to her and said to the dog, "Look! Deamhan, this is my friend! My friend!" Amy reached out to Carol and gestured for her to pet the animal. Carol hesitantly did so, scratching behind the dog's ears, and received a huge lick in return. Now *they* were friends, too. Feeding all those treats to Deamhan behind Connor's back had paid off.

"I think I can stand now," Amy said. "Help me up."

Smoke alarms began to bellow throughout the house.

On the staircase, Devlin watched in horror as the flames spread to curtains that covered windows.

Damn her, he thought to himself. *No one walks away from this!*

He had to get a weapon of his own, and he knew where to get it . . . at the guard station just outside Amy's door.

Devlin dashed back to the second-floor landing, where thick smoke was now billowing with heavy weight. Coughing, he made his way to Lance's desk, opened the drawer, and found the handgun. He turned to see that the dog had burst through the bedroom door. Had Deamhan killed the women already? He heard no more barking.

He stepped into the empty bedroom and then looked toward the bathroom. The door was open, and Amy stood there with Deamhan at her side.

Devlin pointed the handgun at Amy. "I'll kill you for this!"

Amy said, "No, you won't, Connor." Then she spoke to the dog and pointed. "Deamhan! *Kill*!"

THE MIDDLEMAN

The animal, whose true loyalties now lay with the woman who had shown him love, leapt at Devlin. The man screamed, dropped his weapon, and caught the heavy German shepherd full on. The animal's huge teeth tore at Devlin's arms, torso, and the side of his face. The animal bit him on the arm, the shoulder, and the side of his torso. Devlin shouted, "Deamhan, no! No! Deamhan! No!"

Finally, Amy called out, "Deamhan! No! Heel!"

The animal pulled back, allowing Devlin to crawl away from him. After taking a moment to catch his breath, Devlin marshalled the strength to get up and run from the room. He was terribly unsteady as he limped toward the stairs.

The smoke and fire was now out of control.

Standing at the rail, Devlin looked down and saw the guard from the front gate, a man named Smithy, enter the foyer. The guard stood there, looking like an idiot, unsure what he should do, but then smoke almost completely obscured visibility in the huge room.

Devlin coughed hard and examined the horrible damage the dog had done. He was bleeding profusely from multiple wounds. Deamhan had turned on him! And *she* was responsible! It was yet another way Amy Redmond had betrayed him! He cursed to himself in anger as he stumbled to the top of the stairs and gingerly began a descent. When he got halfway down, shock overcame him and he fainted. Devlin crumpled and then rolled to the bottom, ultimately coming to a rest near McClory's motionless body.

43

Just a few minutes earlier, Jake was sitting about fifty feet down and across the street in his rental car. Time was slowly ticking by as he watched the guard at the gate. After McClory had driven Michael and Carol onto the property, the guard hadn't bothered to close the heavy wrought iron barrier. He must have figured that it would be a short visit. Jake hoped so, too, and that Michael and Carol were able to see Amy Redmond with no problems.

His phone rang. The caller ID indicated it was Sarah, down in Florida. Why was she calling so late? Jake picked up.

"Sarah? We're a little busy right now."

"I know, I just talked to Deke at the hospital, and he said to call you immediately," she said.

"What's up?"

"I found Enrico Brazos."

"You did? Where was he?"

"He was not in Oregon, like Chief McClory told you. He was on the other side of the country, in *Florida*!"

"How did you find him?"

"I located his mother. She lives on the South Side of Chicago. She knew where he was."

"Gosh, that's great work. Well, what did he say?"

Then Jake heard the mansion's fire alarms go off.

The guard at the gate perked up, left his post, and headed for the house. The gate was still wide open.

"Sarah! I have to go!" he blurted. He hung up, got out of the car, ran for the entry, and hurried down the long path to the front door. He found that it, too, was open and that smoke was welling out of it. Jake regretted that he wasn't armed, especially since he was about to enter an unknown situation. Nevertheless, he crept into the foyer—because only fools rushed in.

Jake looked up at the high ceiling through the thick smoke and noted that tapestries and curtains were aflame and the wooden beams were on fire, too. Everyone needed to get the hell out of this place, and *now*.

Before Jake could act, the gate guard—who stood a few feet in front him—turned around and attacked him. Already a formidable street brawler, Jake met the man head-on. The guard hit the floor like a sack of potatoes as the butt of an expensive vase Michael had taken from a table near the fallen candelabra connected with the back of the man's head. Fight over.

Upstairs, Amy experienced a coughing fit and couldn't stand anymore. Carol said to her, "Amy, we've got to get out of here! Can you walk?"

The woman seemed to be losing consciousness. Carol cursed to herself and then looked at the dog, who was whining and lightly pawing at her. "We have to carry her, buddy. Don't growl at me, okay? I'm trying to help her." With that, Carol once again cradled Amy in her arms and picked her up. Deamhan watched with interest, instinctively aware that the strange lady was not harming his friend.

Carol's eyes burned as she made her way to the stairs and began the descent, Deamhan at her side. Amy wasn't terribly heavy, but the smoke and heat made the effort much more of a challenge. Carol was fit but this effort was stretching the limits of her strength. The descent to the ground floor was over in a few seconds, but she almost tripped over McClory's body. As she stepped over him, Carol noticed that Devlin was beginning to stir. She ignored him, intent on getting Amy outside.

"Come!" Carol commanded the dog. She carried Amy outside to the front yard. When she reached a spot some distance from the house, Carol laid Amy in the grass. The woman was already coming to, the fresh air doing wonders.

MIKE PAPANTONIO

Sirens in the distance grew louder.

"I'm going back inside," Carol said to Amy. "Stay here."

Amy grabbed her arm. "The flash drive."

"What?"

"The evidence against Devlin. It's on a flash drive," Amy managed to say. She coughed and drew deep breaths.

"Where is it?"

"In Connor's study. It's in a big wooden box on his desk. It has a Celtic design on it." Amy held out her arms to indicate the object's size.

"Okay." Carol stood and ran back toward the house.

"Stay, Deamhan!" Amy commanded. The dog sat beside her. He wasn't going to let any more harm come to her. "Good boy," she told him, giving the animal much-needed affection.

Michael and Jake grabbed Carol as she reentered the burning house. "Time to make our exit, Carol!" Michael shouted. "This place is a tinderbox!"

Carol grabbed his arms. "Amy says her flash drive evidence is in Devlin's study. It's on his desk in a wooden box with a Celtic design." She mimed the dimensions as Amy had.

"Where's the study?"

"I don't know!"

Michael spotted Jake covering the gate guard, who was now sitting on the floor with his hands on his head. Michael went to the man and shouted, "Which way to the study?"

The guard simply pointed toward a dark, smoke-heavy hallway on the left side of the staircase.

Michael barked orders. "Jake, drag that guard outside and see if McClory is still breathing!" He pointed to the police chief's body at the foot of the stairs. "Carol, I really need you to be out there with Amy when the damn police force and fire department get here. We got some 'splaining to do!"

"Michael, you can't go looking for the study! Let the firemen do it!" Carol gasped.

"I've been through worse!" He took off.

Carol heard McClory scream. "I can't move my leg! Someone help!"

THE MIDDLEMAN

"Damn it, he's alive," she shouted to Jake, "but let's drag his worthless body out of here."

Carol and Jake came to the conclusion that Devlin's two goons were soundly dead. "Let's leave well enough alone. Let this fire take over from here."

She turned her attention to McClory, who had again lost consciousness. "Grab an arm on this useless prick. Let's drag him out of here along with the guard. We can't take much more of this smoke or we're gonna be statistics, too." Jake went to help her, but she stopped and frantically looked around the room. "Hey! Where's Devlin? He's gone!"

44

Michael reached the study and was surprised to find that the smoke was thinner in the space. There were no windows, but he figured that ventilation might be clearing the room. In fact, he could feel the cool central air blowing in from a ceiling grate.

Even though he was in a mad race against flames and smoke, he was struck by the beauty of the room. He had noted the two suits of armor in the corridor that "guarded" the entrance to the study, and there was another one standing behind the desk. An empty plaque rack for displaying what Michael assumed might be a sword was on the wall next to it. A fine study, indeed.

Too bad it belonged to a psychopathic monster, he thought.

An eighteen-by-eighteen-inch wooden box sat in plain sight. It sat on top of the desk, as Carol had said. Michael recognized a round Celtic knot design carved on the wooden lid. The thing exuded "antiquity," and Michael thought it likely belonged in a museum. He picked it up to find that it was heavier than he expected, maybe twenty pounds.

No need to linger. Michael turned and headed for the door . . . but Connor Devlin stood in the way. He had stepped out from behind the flowing flag of Ireland that was displayed on a flagpole by the door, and he held a broadsword that was likely the one missing from its resting place on the wall. Michael guessed that the wide blade was nearly thirty inches long from the decorative hilt.

"I can't let you leave with that," Devlin hoarsely said, indicating the box. His clothing was drenched in blood. The man looked like he'd been the victim of a wild animal attack. It appeared that half of his face was missing.

Without giving Michael a chance to respond, the man struggled to raise the sword and lumbered toward him. Definitely impaired by his injuries, he was limping and staggering from side to side. Michael moved back but butted against the front of the desk. Devlin quickly stepped within four feet of him and swung the sword downward. It missed Michael by less than an inch as he dove for the floor, allowing the huge wooden desk to be the blade's landing place. The weapon was heavy, unwieldy at best, and would take a few seconds and no small amount of strength to lift the thing again for another hit, so Michael only had time to scramble backward over the desk to the other side.

The sword crashed into the top of the beautiful mahogany desk again, splintering it.

Smoke was now beginning to rapidly seep into the room. It wouldn't be long before the two men were unable to breathe.

Michael zipped laterally behind the desk toward the wall and moved around the perimeter of the room to the bookshelves with a tight grasp on the box. Time was running out for both men, but only Michael seemed to be aware of that as he gasped for clean air.

"Damn you!" Devlin shouted. He again raised the broadsword and rushed at Michael. The blade swung crosswise at Michael, who ducked in time. The sword crashed into the bookshelf. Now Michael had an opening. He stayed low and body-blocked Devlin at the waist; but the man didn't go down, despite his injuries. Devlin was built like bricks, sturdy and solid. He remained a formidable adversary. Michael held on, attempting to push Devlin back to the center of the room and perhaps trip him—but Devlin slammed the hilt of the broadsword down on Michael's back. The lead "button" of the hilt sent a shockwave through Michael's nervous system, and he tumbled to the carpet.

Devlin raised the sword one last time as Michael made his last effort to avoid dying. He threw himself squarely into Devlin's knees. As the full targeted force of Michael's body weight hyperextended both of Devlin's knees, he could actually hear the tendons and joints snapping right before Devlin fell to the ground in instant agony. There was no more threat from the sword as it flew out of Devlin's hands. The real threat now was fire and smoke inhalation.

Michael straddled Devlin's chest and punched him repeatedly in the face, trying desperately to land a knockout blow. It was apparent to Michael that the only emotion that allowed Devlin to hold onto consciousness was hatred and a desire for revenge.

For a moment he lost track of where he was and didn't know how many times he had slugged Devlin. The man's face was bloody. The one good eye that Devlin had left opened and stared at Michael, and then Devlin coughed. Blood spat over Michael's chest.

Then Michael coughed, too. Breathable air had left the room.

"Damn it." He knew what he had to do. "Okay, asshole, time for me to go."

He stood, went to the puzzle box, and picked it up. He placed it on the desk so he could take it easily after he hoisted the other thing he had to carry out of the room—Connor Devlin's broken body. Once again, the PJ training kicked in and Michael expertly heaved the large, heavy man into an awkward version of a fireman's carry over his right shoulder. Michael managed to tuck the big wooden box under his left arm and then make his way to the corridor. He recognized that his chances of reaching the outside with all that weight weren't good, but he was intent on pushing through. With the concentration of a PJ, he forced himself forward into the smoky hallway, pumping his legs hard toward the light at the end of the tunnel. As he approached the foyer with both the box and Devlin's dead weight, his chances of living another day improved.

Jake had bravely waited for him. "Michael! Our only way out is straight through these flames to the front door. There's a path, but it's closing fast!" Michael knew that there was no possible endgame where Jake would ever abandon any of his team.

They made it to the door just as the inferno engulfed all of Devlin's ill-gotten treasures, collected for decades in trade for other people's suffering.

45

On Thursday morning, approximately sixty hours since the events at Connor Devlin's Kenilworth mansion, Deke walked with a cane into Amy's hospital room at NorthShore Evanston Hospital. Carol Morris was by his side, carrying a large shopping bag.

Amy was sitting up in bed, having finished her breakfast. "Deke! Carol!" she gushed.

"Good morning, Amy," Deke said. "How are you feeling?"

"Much better! It's so good to see you both, but especially you, Deke! How are *you*? They let you out of the hospital?"

"I insisted. It was past time to be discharged. I'm fine now," Deke said. "Well, fine enough. I have a lot of rehab to do. My wife, Teri, is going to drive me back to Florida tomorrow, and I'll continue the therapy there." He raised the cane. "This thing is only temporary." He then displayed his right hand, still in a cast. "And this darned thing is a nuisance to the extreme. It'll be a few weeks before it comes off. I'm still a little sore in several places, but I feel good enough to get out of that hospital bed and get back to work."

"That's good to hear."

Carol said, "I hope the DA didn't tire you out yesterday. I know he and the other DOJ folks were here taking your statement for some time. Just to let you know, Jake and I were hot boxed in an interrogation room for two days. We were threatened with everything from first-degree murder to arson."

Amy rolled her eyes. "Yeah, they threatened me, too. But I'm pretty sure that lawyer you gave me terrorized them far more than they terrorized me. After five hours of being pushed around by my new best friend, Gina Romano, it was pretty clear they won't seriously consider charges against me or your team. Where in the world did you find that ball of fury, Deke?"

Deke laughed and answered, "Gina is regarded as one of the best trial lawyers in the business. Fortunately, she's been on our team for twenty years. Last year, *Trial Lawyer* magazine had her on their cover with the headline 'Bad to the Bone.' I'm optimistic that you and everyone that helped save your life that night are going to be just fine when it comes to possible criminal indictments."

Carol jumped in to further ease Amy's concerns. "In fact, you need to know that Dale Butler, the chief prosecutor in this town, told an investigator friend of mine that there was no way his office was going to do anything except focus on the dirty cops who were part of Devlin's machine and Devlin himself. Right now, Amy, you just need to pay attention to getting your health back to a 100 percent."

"Thanks, Carol. I'm feeling much better, and I think the doctors are going to release me later today."

"Smoke inhalation is nothing to take lightly," Carol said. "I had a little of it, but not too bad. Michael Carey is here in another room with serious smoke inhalation issues. He got the worst of it from our team. That, plus some wounds from fighting. Jake Rutledge had some physical issues but you couldn't tell it in his two days of a really scary interrogation. You'll be interested to know that 'Petey-o' McClory and the gate guard known as Smithy are in the hospital and under arrest, too. Smoke inhalation and other injuries. Most importantly, Connor Devlin is here, too, under arrest and being treated for smoke inhalation, dog mauling, fractured knees, several other physical injuries, and for being a grade A asshole. I'm not sure he's going to find any plastic surgeon on the planet to reconstruct the damage that your canine hero did to his face."

"It sounds like my former future husband has used up the last bit of his Irish luck!"

Carol set the shopping bag on the floor and then retrieved a small box out of it. Something larger was also inside but she was apparently saving that for later. Carol handed the small box to Amy. "Here you go."

Amy saw the logo on it and immediately realized what it was. "Oh, wow, a new phone! Thank you so much!"

"You'll need to activate it with your carrier and get all your data that's in the cloud. Sorry about your old one. The fire gobbled that one up."

"How bad is Connor's house?"

"It burned to the ground. Literally nothing standing. The fire department turned their attention to protecting the properties around the house more than trying to save a lost cause."

"That's a shame," Amy said. "For Chicago, that mansion had a remarkable history behind it." She then made a little gasp. "Deamhan! Where's Deamhan?"

Carol held up a hand. "Not to worry. Deamhan is in good hands. He's staying temporarily with my friend, a private investigator named Lou Doonan. They're getting along like gangbusters. Deamhan can join you when you get out of the hospital, if you want him."

"Oh, I do."

"Amy," Deke said, "with your statement and subsequent testimony, the DA will likely bring serious charges against Mr. Devlin and his accomplices. Kidnapping, for one, and also assault for drugging you. Did the doctors tell you what Devlin was drugging you with?"

She nodded. "Ambien. Apparently Devlin's men crushed pills and put the stuff in my food and drink. One of the doctors told me that it was in small amounts, just enough to make me sleepy and out of it."

"Thank goodness it wasn't fentanyl or something like that," Carol said.

"And that's not all," Deke added. "Smithy the guard is talking. And so is McClory. Devlin will likely be charged with the murders of Paul Baker, Vernon Bunker, Doug Frankel, and your cousin Matt. Maybe even your Uncle Charles. We finally reached the lead investigator of your uncle's case, a man named Brazos. You were right—there was no suicide note. It appears that either Devlin or McClory—or both of them

MIKE PAPANTONIO

in cahoots—faked the note in the evidence file after the fact to throw off any suspicion of foul play. We'll see if McClory confesses. If not, Brazos's testimony may be enough to reopen your uncle's case. At any rate, Chief McClory will be charged with corruption and aiding and abetting Devlin in the kidnapping charge because he knew all about it. It remains to be seen whether or not he'll be implicated in the murders. He certainly did his best to cover up evidence, and it looks like he's a part of that Irish Mafia to which Devlin belongs."

Amy shook her head and quietly murmured, "Wow."

"And that brings us to this." Deke looked at Carol and nodded.

Carol removed the larger item from the shopping bag—the big wooden puzzle box retrieved from Devlin's study. "This is an item we kept after it was clear that the criminal investigation was taking the correct path, the box you expressly told Carol to rescue from the burning mansion. We have no idea how to open this thing. Do you?"

Amy winced. "Oh, no. I tried a couple of times, but I couldn't figure it out. I'd really have to think harder about it. The combination is something personal to Connor."

"You think your flash drive is inside?" Deke asked.

"I do."

"Then we need it to proceed with our own civil case against Devlin. We're hoping that what you've told us is contained on that drive, and that it meets our criteria as evidence. I suppose we could just have the thing broken into, but it's a sturdy piece of craftsmanship. We're afraid we might destroy some of the materials inside. It'd be best it if it were opened properly."

"Place the box in my lap, please."

Carol did so, and Amy studied the tiles on the lid, all numbers, letters, and symbols that could be slid in the troughs and up to a single tray for the solution. There appeared to be space for only four tiles in the target area.

"What were Connor's passions?" Carol asked. "What are things he was obsessed about? Maybe start there."

"His biggest passion was money," Amy answered with a little laugh. "And Ireland."

THE MIDDLEMAN

"He was obviously interested in the medical industry," Deke offered. "Something to do with that?"

Amy rubbed her brow. "My head, it's still so clouded . . . give me a minute . . ."

"Take all the time you need. We can come back later if you want."

"You know . . . Connor loved that guy Robert Boyle."

"Who?" Carol asked.

"He was an Irish chemist from the 1600s, considered to be the 'father of modern chemistry.' There's a painting of Boyle in Connor's study."

"Why is he the father of modern chemistry?" Carol asked.

"Because of Boyle's law."

"What's that?"

"Uh, if I remember correctly . . . I actually had to memorize it when I was in college . . . something about pressure and the temperature of gas . . . hold on . . ."

Carol produced her mobile. "I can google it . . ."

Amy held up her palm. "No, don't tell me! It's . . . uh . . . it's coming back to me . . . 'The absolute pressure exerted by a given mass of an ideal gas is,' uh . . ."

Deke said, "Maybe we should leave you alone?"

"No, no, I can do this, just wait a second . . . oh! I think I know! 'The absolute pressure exerted by a given mass of an ideal gas is *inversely proportional* to the . . . uh, to the volume it occupies if the temperature and amount of gas remain unchanged within a closed system!' Whew! That's it!"

"Impressive!" Carol said. "What the hell does it mean?"

Amy laughed. "It basically says that the pressure and volume of a gas are inversely proportional, that is, one value decreases and the other one increases with exactly the same proportions, as long as the temperature of the gas remains fixed." She looked at the box again. "I wonder . . . could the mathematical formula of the law be . . . ?"

Amy began to move the tiles. Deke and Carol watched in fascination as she quickly slid the squares across, up, and down, trying to get to specific tiles and move them up to the solution trough. After five minutes of working, Carol muttered, "Should we go get lunch and come back?"

"Just a second . . ." Amy said, still working. The puzzle had to be solved with the two tiles on both ends of the line set in place first, finishing with the two middle tiles. Soon, she had the end tiles, a "P" and a "k," where they were supposed to be. A "V" soon joined them.

"One more to go," she said and kept at it. Two minutes later, the fourth tile was in the trough. There was the sound of a *click*, and the lid opened.

"Wow!" Carol squealed. "Amazing!"

"Good job, Amy!"

"What was the solution?"

Amy beamed and pointed to the tiles in the trough: PV=k. "Pressure multiplied by Volume equals a constant k!"

The trio peered into the box and saw documents, journals, printouts of emails, and handwritten notes . . . and more than one flash drive. Amy easily picked out hers.

"Here you go," she said, handing it to Deke.

EPILOGUE

One Year Later

The press conference was held in the cafeteria of EirePharma headquarters in Deerfield at 1:00 p.m. Many members of the media were present, representing not only major mainstream newspapers and broadcast stations, but also medical industry and finance journalists. Wall Street was watching. The federal government was watching. It was a big deal.

Deke got the ball rolling, supported by his two top attorneys, Michael and Gina. Carol and Jake were present in the background. Deke approached the podium and spoke into the microphone.

"Ladies and gentlemen, thank you for coming today. For those of you in the press, we will not be taking questions at this time. It would not be appropriate, given that trials are yet to occur. My name is Nicholas Deketomis. I'm going to be brief and let Amy Redmond speak for herself. It's been a long, tough year for her and her family's company. Approximately a year ago this week, Amy was the victim of serious crimes and underwent extreme trauma. As you all know by now, District Attorney Dale Butler here in Chicago has already indicted James P. McClory, former chief of detectives of the Chicago Police Department, of corruption, racketeering, and accessory to murder. It is not clear whether or not that investigation will look further into police corruption. The DA has also indicted Connor Devlin, formerly of EirePharma, of kidnapping, assault, corruption, racketeering, and multiple murders. Although their trials are yet to occur, I have confidence in our criminal justice system, and I believe that justice will indeed be served in these cases.

"That brings me to the civil lawsuits that my firm is pursuing against Connor Devlin and, regrettably, EirePharma. After much legal wrangling with the Justice Department and the Federal Trade Commission, the mess of ownership of EirePharma was finally sorted. Connor Devlin was never the true CEO of EirePharma. Amy Redmond was. That said, we are suing Mr. Devlin and EirePharma, and a half dozen manufacturers, PBMs, and distributors for price gouging and fraudulent business practices that harm consumers of insulin.

"My firm, along with Amy Redmond's criminal defense attorneys, have been working for months to clear her name. She is clearly innocent of the wrongdoing that was done by Mr. Devlin while he was acting as CEO of EirePharma. Thanks to evidence and the cooperation supplied by Amy Redmond to the DA and to us, all the prosecuting parties— both criminal and civil—can proceed. I'm going to let Amy speak now. Please give her your attention. Thank you."

Deke nodded to her as she stood from one of the seats off to the side.

Amy, dressed in a fashionable plaid business suit, composed herself at the podium as the cameras clicked and flashed.

"Thank you, Deke. Hello, everyone, I'm Amy Redmond. As you probably know, EirePharma is my family's business, begun by my grandfather Reginald Redmond in 1947. The company has gone through many changes over the years, and it ultimately became a successful pharmacy benefit manager. My uncle, Charles Redmond, was CEO from 2011 until 2023. I was president of EirePharma during Mr. Devlin's reign. Mr. Devlin's criminal business practices regarding the pricing of drugs like insulin were occurring under my watch, and I should have done something about it. I accept the responsibility. I have agreed to pay the fines set out by the Justice Department. We will honor all the other private lawsuits that have been filed against us over the pricing of insulin. In other words, I am liquidating EirePharma and using its assets to pay off these debts in an effort to make it up to the consumers who were wronged by Mr. Devlin's and EirePharma's actions. Our employees will all receive generous severance packages. EirePharma, the Redmond family business, will be no more.

THE MIDDLEMAN

"That said, after negotiations with the Justice Department, I am announcing that I will be building a new company from these ashes. This will be a not-for-profit organization that will act as a watchdog on pharmaceutical industry practices and provide legal support to consumers who have problems with their insurance companies, their pharmacies, or even their physicians. The name of this new company will be Redmond-Phoenix.

"I deeply regret the harm caused by EirePharma. I pledge to work very hard in running Redmond-Phoenix so that it is a force of good and an advocate for consumers, which is so desperately needed for a pharma industry that has financially and physically done so much to victimize American consumers for more than three decades now. Thank you."

The press and the audience applauded as she turned away from the podium and approached Deke.

"Thank you for everything," she said.

"You're more than welcome, Amy," he answered. "I know it was difficult for you to give up EirePharma."

She shook her head. "What I'm about to do is more meaningful. And I think Matt would approve, too, as well as my Uncle Charles. And, you know, it was my father, Andy, who was my inspiration to go the nonprofit route."

Deke could only agree. He held out his right hand for her to shake. It was completely healed now, except when it rained—only then could he feel arthritic creaks and groans in the joints and bones. But that was a small price to pay for the satisfaction he felt. He and his dynamic team had righted a few wrongs, negotiated a positive outcome for his client, and seen the wheels of justice operate in a favorable manner.

Furthermore, a diabetic who had no insurance could now have at least the hope of walking into a pharmacy and purchasing insulin at an affordable and reasonable price. Deke was certain that this was a case that would never make it to trial and end up being a huge settlement in their favor. He knew that there were far too many ugly creatures hiding under rotting logs that the industry had to keep hidden away from an American jury.

Amy went to join her Aunt Mary, and he watched them warmly embrace.

"Hey."

Deke turned to see Michael, holding out a small white envelope.

"What's this?"

"Open it."

Deke did so and found two items.

"What? Cubs tickets!"

"Happy birthday, Deke. Those are for this year, and hopefully it makes up for us not going last year. The game is tonight. I figured we could do that before heading back to Florida tomorrow. What do you think?"

The wide grin on Deke's face said it all.

THE END